AVA & CAROL DETECTIVE AGENCY SERIES

BOOKS 1 - 3

The Mystery of the Pharaoh's Diamonds

The Mystery of Solomon's Ring

The Haunted Mansion

TWISTED KEY
p u b l i s h i n g

2018

First Printing: 2018

ISBN 978-1-94774-419-6

Twisted Key Publishing, LLC
www.twistedkeypublishing.com

Ordering Information:
Special discounts are available on quantity purchases by corporations, associations, educators, and others. For details, contact the publisher at the above listed address.

U.S. trade bookstores and wholesalers: Please contact Twisted Key Publishing, LLC by email twistedkeypublishing@gmail.com.

CONTENTS

Book 1
The Mystery of the Pharaoh's Diamonds

Book 2
The Mystery of Solomon's Ring

Book 3
The Haunted Mansion

AVA & CAROL DETECTIVE AGENCY

BOOK 1
THE MYSTERY OF THE PHARAOH'S DIAMONDS

THOMAS LOCKHAVEN
WITH EMILY CHASE

1
THE SCIENTIFIC BURRITO

Ava woke up annoyed at the world. She blew a wet strand of hair from the corner of her mouth.

"Gross," Ava cringed as she peeled her vibrating phone off her cheek. It made a wet suctioning sound like sweaty legs on a leather sofa.

"Ava," a voice chirped. "Time for breakfast."

Ava took in a deep breath, held it for a moment, then sighed dramatically. *How could anyone be so chipper this early?* She rolled out of bed, landing with a heavy thud, taking her blankets with her.

"You alright up there?" her mother called up the stairs.

"Fine!" Ava shouted.

She rolled across the room, successfully wrapping herself into a blanket burrito. Exhausted from the effort, Ava lay motionless on the floor for a moment, staring at her ceiling. She was compelled into motion by the seductive smell of bacon. Still swaddled, she scooched out her bedroom, across the hall to the top of the stairs. She was about to descend à la bobsled when her mother rounded the corner.

Clearly, she had some type of disaster prevention sixth sense… or an anti-fun gene. Maybe both. "What on earth are you doing? Have you lost your mind?"

"I'm rehearsing for a school play. The 'Cocoon That Could,' a poignant story of a butterfly—"

"Ava," her mother's face tightened.

"Fine. It's for a science project. You don't want to impede scientific progress, do you?"

"How about you choose a project that doesn't end up with you in the hospital in a body cast."

"Mom, be reasonable," chuckled Ava. "We don't get to choose science—it chooses us. You married a scientist. Surely, of all people, you should understand."

"Ava Clarke." Her mother's voice took on a much crisper tone. It was followed by the look that only a mother can give.

"Alright," Ava sighed. She shrugged her way out of her blankets, knotted them up in a ball and threw them onto her bed. Science would have to wait—at least until her parents went to work.

Ava crossed the kitchen, turned on the faucet and washed her hands.

"Here," said her mom, handing her a mixing bowl. "Make yourself useful."

Ava ran her finger along the inside of the bowl and licked the pancake batter off her finger. "Tasty."

As she scrubbed the bowl, she leaned forward and gazed out the window. The tiny town of Livingston was alive with activity. People were fetching their newspapers, walking their dogs, breathing in the fresh September air. Ava decided that she would give the morning another chance, and perhaps, even smile.

"Good morning," Ava's dad said through a yawn as he shuffled into the kitchen. He ran his hand through his thick curly brown hair and plopped into a chair at the kitchen table.

"Good morning, Father," Ava said brightly, drying her hands on a dishtowel.

"Morning Aves," he said, stifling another yawn.

"Late night? Doing sciency things?"

"Yep. The CDC sent me a fascinating report last night that they wanted me to review—amazing reading."

Ava's father was a highly sought-after biologist. She was pretty sure the Center of Disease Control had him on speed dial. "I too tried to venture into the world of science this morning. A little *Physics* experiment, but it was quashed by the department of safety and boredom," Ava gestured to her mother.

"Your daughter was attempting to slalom down the stairs wrapped in blankets," explained Mrs. Clarke.

Charles coughed into his hand. Ava could see a tiny smile forming at the edges of his mouth. "You gotta be careful, Aves. Who else is going to look after your mom and I when we're old and senile?"

A *tap, tap* at the door rescued Ava from answering. "We'll have to continue this discussion later. Friendship knocketh, and I simply can't allow it to wait."

Carol Miller, Ava's best friend stood on the porch, looking as if she were about to burst with excitement. Her eyes sparkled like crystal blue marbles in the sunlight.

"Did you hear? Tell me you heard," said Carol, shaking Ava by the shoulders.

"That you are insane? Yes, come in. My parents have already scheduled an intervention. My mother is burning sage and chanting as we speak."

"Do you ever check your phone? The Hancock Museum was robbed last night!"

Ava hesitated a beat. "Are you serious? What's there to steal?"

Carol let out an exasperated puff of air. "Hello? Ramesses exhibit on loan to our museum from Egypt ring a bell?" asked Carol, following Ava to the kitchen.

"Big brain just said the Hancock Museum was robbed." Carol nodded in agreement.

"I knew something like this was going to happen," said Mrs. Clarke. Ava shot her mom a quizzical look. "The security at the museum…," she shook her head. "Don't even get me started."

"My dad said they updated the entire security system and even built a *safe room* that was approved by an Egyptian dignitary," explained Carol.

"You never told me about that," said Ava.

"My dad's an architect. He's done work for just about everyone in town. The museum was just another job."

"The only reason the Hancock Museum was even allowed to host the exhibit was because Eugene McDunnel—the philanthropist that bankrolled the original Egyptian expedition—his grandson lives here in Livingston," added Mrs. Clarke.

"That's amazing," said Carol. "History makes me swoon."

"'Destined to Be Alone,' the title of a book I'm writing about Carol's life, in case anyone's interested."

"I interviewed Mr. McDunnel for the New Yorker. After it's run here, the exhibit was to go to the Metropolitan Museum of Art in November."

"They just announce where an exhibit is going?" asked Ava. "Seems counterintuitive as far as keeping priceless artifacts safe."

"Look at you, throwing around the five syllable words."

"Thank you, Carol. Contrary to popular belief, I happen to have a massive vocabulary. I simply don't know the meaning of half the words."

"They *have* to announce it to the public, Ava. Museums get a lot of publicity and money by offering exhibitions like this," Charles blew across the rim of his coffee and took a sip. "I would have thought that Hancock Museum would have learned a lesson after what happened to the Isabella Stewart Gardner Museum in 1990."

"Okay, that's oddly specific," said Ava.

"It's the biggest art heist in history," explained Mrs. Clarke. "Thieves dressed up as police officers. They told the security guards that someone had reported a disturbance. The guards let them in, and the crooks stole thirteen paintings worth over 500 million dollars."

"Were they ever caught?" Carol inquired.

"No, the FBI never caught them," said Mrs. Clarke. "I've actually written quite a bit about art heists. The unfortunate thing is eighty percent of them go unsolved."

"Eighty percent?" Ava stroked her chin thoughtfully. "If I ever decide to go into a life of crime, it's going to be robbery." Her parents stared at her mortified. "What?" Ava asked innocently. "Look at the benefits—there's only a twenty-percent chance that you'd have to bail me out."

"I'm sure they'll catch whoever robbed the museum. There are literally cameras everywhere. It's not like they can just walk into an airport with—wait, what did they steal?"

"A sarcophagus," teased Ava.

Ava's mom made several swipes on her phone. "It says that five diamonds were stolen, valued at twenty-million dollars. Carol's right though—they can't just hop on a plane with millions of dollars' worth of diamonds."

"So, what's the use of stealing them? Who are they going to sell them to?"

"My guess is they'll either try to sneak them out of the country somehow and sell them to a private collector, or they'll begin negotiations with the insurance company that is insuring them."

"Why would they talk to the insurance company? 'We've got your diamonds. We promise we won't hurt them. Let's make a deal.'"

"You're not too far off," laughed Mrs. Clarke. "They'll negotiate with the insurance company for a few million. The insurance company will agree to an amount, and they'll anonymously make the trade."

"Sounds like a rip off. But…," Ava conceded, "it's better to pay a few million for something worth twenty million than to not have it at all."

"I'm sorry to interrupt," said Carol. "This is fascinating. Really it is. But the bus is going to be here in about two minutes."

Ava shoveled several forkfuls of pancakes in her mouth and hurried over to the refrigerator. She grabbed a Juicebox for herself and one for Carol, then hurried across the kitchen and slung on her backpack.

"See you guys this afternoon!" yelled Ava over her shoulder as she rushed for the door. Carol smiled and waved to Ava's parents as she followed close on her friend's heels.

2
RAMESSES'S CURSE

The final bell rang, turning the school hallway into a miniature version of the running of the bulls. In full stampede, children hooted and hollered as they pushed their way out of the six bright red doorways leading to freedom. A semicircle of buses arced around Nobel Park Middle School like a bright orange smiley face.

Carol and Ava blinked as their eyes adapted to the brilliant sun, which instantly warmed them. Carol closed her eyes and turned her face upward. "Ah, this is the life," she sighed.

Ava looked at the buses, their diesel exhaust puffing like cigars. "What do you say we walk home today?"

Carol sighed pleasantly. "Please! I just want to fling my arms out and run through a wheat field or grove of wildflowers."

"What about a field of corn instead… could you imagine? Thud, thud, thud as you plow down an entire crop of corn. You'd have serious welts all over your arm."

"Why do you do that? Do you have something against pleasant thoughts? You just destroyed a perfect moment of heavenly bliss," moaned Carol. She paused and stretched out her arms once again, trying to regain the blissful moment. "Nope, you ruined it. It's gone," she let her arms drop to her sides.

"Speaking of bliss," said Ava, stopping at a crosswalk, "how did you do on the geography test?"

Carol frowned as they crossed Elm Street and continued down the sidewalk, heading toward Mall Street. "Sadly, there was no test today. Mr. Downey decided the museum heist was more important than the globe."

"Tragic."

"I agree. He wanted to share his theory on how the robbery was committed and how the thieves got away."

"I'm afraid to ask... but somehow, I feel compelled."

"He thinks that it was Ramesses himself that stole the diamonds. He believes that Ramesses couldn't go onward to the afterlife because he had unfinished business," Carol wiggled her fingers mysteriously.

"In Livingston...," added Ava.

"Of course," snorted Carol. "He's also the same teacher who said that we never landed on the moon, that everything was filmed on a soundstage in Hollywood."

"I unfortunately stumbled onto his YouTube channel where he shot a video to debunk the moon landing. I must say, he takes his videography very seriously. For authenticity, he shot his video in his daughter's sandbox."

"Geez," muttered Carol under her breath. "I hope he doesn't have a cat. That's one lunar landing I wouldn't want to see."

"We're educationally doomed," laughed Ava. "You have to admit, the robbery is the biggest thing that's happened in Livingston."

"Do I? You're forgetting the alien baby in the Charles River."

"Oh yeah, the one that turned out to be an octopus that got its tentacles oddly twisted in a plastic six-pack ring thingy."

"We made the front page of the *National Enquirer* with that one," Carol said matter-of-factly. "Our one fleeting moment of fame and then back into dismal obscurity."

"That was funny," said Ava. "Remember people swore they saw a saucer-shaped spaceship crash into the river just hours before the *octo-alien* appeared?"

"What can I say?" Carol said. "Peeps are gullible and clueless."

Ava nodded, agreeing with her friend. "Speaking of clueless, without looking, what am I wearing?"

"Oh Ava, Ava, you must think you're dealing with a neophyte."

"I'm going to let that one pass because I have no idea what that is. I can only assume that it means possessing godlike qualities."

"Exactly, I promise you that it doesn't mean inexperienced or beginner."

"You're a horrible liar. So…," Ava prompted.

"A large yellow hat with a wide brim, a yellow poncho and galoshes. You may or may not have a mustache."

"Great, you're amazing. You just described the guy that does the fish-sticks commercial."

"Fine. You no longer have red highlights, you have purple. You're wearing your black hoodie that has the word 'ironic' stenciled on it, but no one can see the word ironic because it is stenciled in black."

"It's classic," interjected Ava.

"Let's see, you're wearing jeans and your black converse with the purple shoelaces to accentuate your new highlights. You have purple nail polish on every finger except your ring finger."

The girls came to a stop at the corner and waited as a black SUV with a reinforced grill, tinted windows and multiple antennas sped past.

"Not a part of the Livingston police department," said Carol, eyeing the government license plate.

"Mom said that they brought in the FBI on the art heist in Boston—it makes sense they would be here for this one."

The girls jogged across the intersection to the sidewalk that ran along Mall Street.

"I was thinking about something my mom said."

Carol stopped and leaned against Mr. Gupter's mailbox. "Alright, I see the wheels churning."

"The thief—"

"Or thieves," added Carol.

Ava nodded and continued, "They have *two* options to get rid of the diamonds. One is to sell them to the insurance company and the second was to smuggle them out of the country."

"They don't necessarily have to smuggle them out of the country, especially if they sell them to a private dealer who wants them as an ego purchase."

"Which would you choose? Would you risk working with an insurance company? I mean, there's gonna be some kind of digital footprint, right? You're gonna leave tracks."

"Most likely. It depends on how computer savvy the person is. Remember, our computer club hacked into a bunch of local businesses as a part of *operation safety net* to show how unsecure they were."

"Exactly. You may be a great thief, but that doesn't mean you have the computer skills to communicate with an insurance company and not leave a trace. Plus, you also have to have knowledge of overseas banking. It's not like they're going to mail you a check."

Carol snorted, "'Yes, uhm… if you would please make the check out to Ima. Ima Robber.'"

"I feel so conflicted. Robbers have to be trustworthy. Think about it. If you have accomplices…."

"Cohorts."

"Yeah, that's a better word… you have to trust that they're not going to double-cross you, or that they have the necessary skills to do all the stuff that needs to get done."

"Takes a lot of planning," agreed Carol.

"And how do you find these people? Is there like a website with a drop-down menu where you can select the type of criminal you need?"

"Sort of… it's called the dark web." Ava gave Carol a look. "I don't have all the answers," she shrugged, "just enough to make it look like I know what I'm talking about."

"Honestly, I'm betting the diamonds are probably halfway across the globe by now. Even with all the cameras and technology, it would be simple to hop on a train or boat with them. Plus, the thieves had months to plan. Right now, everyone's playing catch-up."

"I agree."

"I also noticed we walked by my house about five minutes ago," said Ava.

"Eh, you're right," Carol smiled, reversing directions. "I believe I got confused by all the smoke coming from your ears."

"So clever. Maybe next time, try a joke from this century," Ava laughed, bumping shoulders with Carol.

"This robbery reminds me of the great clock heist we solved."

"Oh yeah!" exclaimed Ava. "When Connor and Talon stole all the clocks from the classrooms and sold them on that website where schools request items at a discount in bulk."

"Catching them was our one true moment to shine."

"I loved your article about it in the *Cherrywood Chatter*. 'It's Time for Justice to Prevail.' So how did that story remind you of the robbery?"

"It didn't really. I just felt like reliving the moment. The adulation from our peers, the pats on the back, the reward money."

"I did enjoy the adulation, and the free tacos," said Ava as they walked up her driveway. "Carol, when was the last time you visited the Hancock Museum?"

Carol smiled, her blue eyes sparkling. "Why Mrs. Clarke, are you inviting me on a mission?"

"I believe I am Big Brain. I believe I am."

3
THE BLOODY BRAIN

"Carol and I have decided to solve the museum robbery."

Ava's mom pushed her glasses on top of her head and massaged her temples. "I think the FBI and local police have that covered. However, if you feel like using your deductive reasoning, you could solve the mystery of who keeps leaving their dirty clothes all over your floor."

"Pfft," Ava waved her comment aside. "As an intrepid journalist, I thought that you would be more supportive. We have solved numerous crimes."

Carol held up two fingers.

"Ava, I know that it's your thing to try and fix everything, but sometimes it takes a certain... skillset that comes with practice and time. You wouldn't want to go in for surgery from a mechanic, would you?"

"Depends, some refer to the human body as nature's engine."

"No one refers to the human body as nature's engine," Carol grimaced. "That sounds just *awful*."

"What if it's a surgeon that moonlights as a mechanic?"

"Ava, you don't know the first thing about carrying on an investigation. You have to build up your investigative chops, and that takes a while. Most people find mentors to help guide them."

"That's where you're wrong, Mom. I've been immersed in detective work for over a decade."

"Really? You were *immersed* in detective work since you were two?" Mrs. Clarke folded her arms.

"You told me that you and Dad used to watch *Law & Order* when you were pregnant with me. Suffice to say, I learned quite a bit at a young impressionable age."

Ava's mom sighed. "Why do I even bother? I think the FBI has everything under control. Plus, they've learned a lot since the Isabella robbery."

"I guess you're right, Mom. I don't know what I was thinking."

"Ava," said her mom softly. She stood and wrapped her arms around her daughter. "It's wonderful to have a curious mind and that you want to help. I'm proud of you."

"Thanks. I get it, Carol and I need more practice. Start small but aim high." Ava's mom squeezed her hard, then returned to her desk where there were dozens of papers scattered around her laptop.

"Well, we'll leave you to your work." Ava motioned for Carol to follow her into the kitchen. She grabbed two bowls from the cabinet and grabbed a carton of Ninja Chip Ice cream. *Ice cream, so sneaky, you'll never see the calories coming.*

"I'm guessing, you are going to ignore everything your Mom said."

"Yep," said Ava, licking her spoon. "How are you supposed to *get* experience if you're not allowed to practice?"

Carol eyed the kitchen door. "I think we should continue our conversation in a less public venue."

~~o~o~o~~

Carol draped herself over Ava's bed, letting her head hang over the edge.

"What are you doing?" laughed Ava.

"Filling my brain with blood—it helps me think better."

"It's certainly attractive." Ava grabbed her laptop from her desk and hopped onto her bed. She flipped her computer open and opened a word document. "This is officially our third case."

"Wonderful. Good things come in threes." Carol pushed herself up and scooched over beside Ava.

"Feel smarter?"

"Indubitably."

"Perfect. We need an official name for this investigation. Our last one, 'Find the Clocks,' was quite uninspired. We need something with pizazz."

"The Missing Diamonds?"

"Do you even hear yourself? That's too generic. Something like 'The Case of the Pharaoh's Diamonds,' or—"

"'The Ramesses Heist,'" suggested Carol.

"'The Ramesses Heist.' I have to say, it rolls off the tongue. 'The Ramesses Heist,'" Ava mouthed as she typed. "So, what do we know so far?"

"Honestly not much," Carol screwed up her face. "We know that five diamonds were stolen. That the robbery occurred while the museum was closed."

"That the museum had a new security system," Ava added. "Oh, that it was a traveling exhibition."

"That the show had an Egyptian security specialist that traveled with the show."

"Good one," said Ava as she typed. "Anything else?"

"Not really. The police and the news haven't been very forthcoming with details."

"What's our hypothesis? By the way, Mrs. Wright would be so proud of us right now. Formulating a hypothesis."

"Hmm," Carol chewed on her bottom lip. "That the thieves knew about the exhibit ahead of time. That they most likely cased the museum and had already established what to do with the diamonds once they stole them, and that at this very moment, they are trying to sneak them out of the country."

"That means time is of the essence," mused Ava. "Especially if the thieves are trying to move the diamonds out of the country." Ava typed the details into the case file.

"If they're trying to smuggle them out of the country, they would have to deal with customs."

"Customs is no joke. Last time we went to Mexico, we had to go through an x-ray machine, and they searched our luggage. I'm pretty sure it's going to be that way no matter where you travel."

"I think we should start at the museum and see if we can find any clues there. We have a half-day at school tomorrow, so we can go right after we get out."

"Perfect! I'll look online tonight and see if I can find out anything else about the heist."

"Me too," said Carol, fishing her phone from her pocket. She swiped a finger across the screen and fired off a text. "I gotta run. Dinner's ready."

"Okay." Ava hopped up off the bed and slipped her shoes on. "Let me know if you find anything."

"Will do," said Carol, scrambling down the stairs.

"Oh, one other thought," Ava lowered her voice. "See if your dad can tell you a little bit about the safe room the museum added. You never know what's going to be a clue."

"Good idea."

Ava waited until Carol reached the bottom step before she switched the sprinklers on. She watched as her friend jumped from side to side trying not to get wet. *You always gotta be on your toes*, smiled Ava, closing the front door.

4
THE CRIME SCENE

It was a cloud-free day. The sun was shining brightly, casting a harsh glare off the asphalt as the girls rode their bikes down Main Street. They made a quick stop at Baker's Café, then continued through the center of town toward the museum.

Ava wiped her brow with her forearm, squinting into the oncoming traffic. They hopped off the bikes, and walked them across the crosswalk, coming to a stop at the midnight blue bike racks located in front of the main entrance of the museum.

Ava removed an incredibly small notebook and stub of a pencil from her pocket.

"What, did you rob a Muppet? What's with the tiny pad? Wait, let me guess, you accidentally put it in the dryer."

"You might laugh, but detectives around the world use pads just like this."

"I'm sorry," Carol had the face of someone that had just one more question. "I'm just curious… is there a website that sells tiny things?"

"Yes, I believe it's where your parents got your brain."

"Lashing out. That's how it's going to be."

"You mess with the tools of the trade, and you get knocked down a notch or two." Ava ran her fingers through her helmet hair. "Plus, I know that you're just acting out of jealousy. I pity you."

"Alright. Alright." Carol threw up her hands in surrender. "You caught me. I'm obsessed with your tiny notepad. I wonder if they used a bonsai to make it. You know… because they're so small."

Ava pursed her lips. "You know what? I have half a mind not to give this to you." Ava reached in her back pocket and removed an equally small notepad and pencil for Carol.

Carol's jaw dropped. "You got me a mini pad too?" She let out a low whistle as she examined it. "I take back everything I said."

"That's what I thought," said Ava. "I've jotted down a couple notes for us."

"Did you write them in shorthand? I'm sorry, I can't stop myself."

"May I continue?" Carol nodded and drew her fingers across her lips as if she was zipping them shut. Ava glanced around to make sure no one was within earshot. "Currently, I've only written three directives. One, investigate the museum. Two, question suspects. Three, froyo."

"Impressive. Clandestine stuff right there. Glad no one overheard you."

"Jealousy will consume you until there's nothing left." Ava put her hand on Carol's shoulder. "You'll be an empty husk. Ask yourself, do you want to be an empty husk?"

"I'm going to go in there," said Carol, pointing to the museum, "to start the investigation. If you want, we can stop by the library on the way home, and I'll get you a book on Socrates."

~~o~o~o~~

The Hancock Museum was one of Livingston's oldest landmarks, built over two hundred years ago. The museum had gone through numerous expansions and renovations. The walls were like a patchwork of Livingston history, made of a collage of different colored stones and bricks from the past and present.

Carol placed her hand over her eyes, shading her face from the afternoon sun as they climbed the steps to the entrance. "Do your three directives have to be done in any specific order?"

"Yes, they need to be followed, step by step. Why?"

"I'm so thirsty, and Fro-to-Go is pulling on my soul like a tractor beam."

"Froyo comes last because it will be our reward for a job well done."

"Fine," muttered Carol as she pushed open the glass door that led into the museum. The girls paused in the doorway as a wave of A/C kissed their red faces.

"I've just died and gone to arctic heaven," moaned Ava. She delighted in the chill running from the nape of her neck to the soles of her feet.

"You go ahead," said Carol. "I'll guard the entrance to make sure no one escapes."

"Ahem. May I help you?"

If Mother Nature had a voice, thought Carol, *this is it!* Ava and Carol looked up to see an elderly lady with the kindest blue-gray eyes they had ever seen. She stood behind a gray circular workstation, staring at them.

"Good morning," smiled Carol. "How are you?"

"I'm wonderful. How may I help you?" The older woman had a delightful singsong voice.

"We would like two tickets, please." Carol pulled out a twenty-dollar bill.

"That will be sixteen dollars," smiled the old woman.

Ava noticed a small glass box labeled "Donations." "Can you please put the change in the donation box?" asked Ava, smiling sweetly.

"Thank you," said the woman. "That is very kind of you."

"You're welcome," beamed Ava.

"Do you need a map? We have several new exhibits. Unfortunately, our Egyptian exhibit is currently closed due to… uhm… extenuating circumstances."

"No, ma'am," smiled Ava. "We heard about the robbery. We're here to show our support." Ava looked around the lobby and smiled. "It's been a while. Grandpa Clarke used to bring me here all the time. He had a fascination with trains."

"Oh, wait a moment, are you William Clarke's granddaughter?"

"Yes, ma'am," said Ava, a little unsure. "Grandpa didn't annoy you, did he? I've been told that us Clarkes can be quite annoying. I'm attempting to start a new generation of non-annoying Clarkes."

"Oh my, no! William was a great man," said the woman, beaming. "Yes, your grandfather was very interested in trains. He actually helped build the railroad exhibit on the second floor."

"Wow! He never told me that," said Ava, amazed. "I knew he always loved to spend time in that section, but he never told me he helped build it."

"He was a very sweet and humble man." She smiled and paused for a moment, thinking. "We all miss him *very* much," she said as she patted Ava's hand. Ava blushed, not really sure what to say. "Well," she cleared her throat, "enough of an old woman's ramblings. You're actually just in time—the elementary school will be here soon. You should get some quality viewing time before they arrive."

"Thank you for the heads-up," winked Ava.

"Enjoy your visit."

"Thank you so much…," Carol hesitated as she glanced down at the woman's name tag, "Gladys. I'm Carol and—"

"I'm Ava," Ava piped in.

"Well, it's a pleasure to meet both of you! If you have any questions, please let me know."

"We will," the girls said in unison.

As soon as the girls were out of earshot, Carol turned to Ava. "Did you see the way she looked when she talked about your grandfather?"

Ava nodded, "I'm beginning to think grandpa had more on his mind than trains, if you know what I mean," Ava giggled.

They passed by an office that read "Administration" and then another marked "Security". The door swung open just as the girls reached the stairwell. A tall guard slipped out the door and jogged up the stairs ahead of them. Ava and Carol had just enough time to peek in the door and see another guard leaning back in a chair, staring at a bank of monitors.

"Security," Carol made a face. "That's one job I would not want to have right now."

"No kidding," Ava whispered. "I wonder why they keep that sign up," she pointed to a sprawling, bright red banner that hung twenty feet above their heads—it read "King Ramesses's Secrets—Egyptian Exhibit. August 21– 31."

"It's like a constant reminder of what you've lost."

"Mom said the Isabella museum keeps the empty frames of the stolen paintings hanging, as a placeholder for when they return home."

"That's both hopeful and sad," said Carol.

"Agreed," nodded Ava.

The girls followed the stairs to the second floor where a small sign with an arrow said: "Ramesses Exhibit—Bowyer Hall".

"I don't see anyone up here," whispered Carol, her head swiveling back and forth.

"Bummer. I was kind of hoping we could blend in with the crowd," said Ava.

The brightly lit hallway was split up into four different sections: Early American Indian Artifacts, Livingston Railway System, History of Livingston, and the Ramesses Exhibit. The room for the Ramesses exhibit was dark, and several strips of yellow and black police tape crisscrossed over the entrance to the room.

Security cameras scrutinized everyone who walked down the hallway, every second of every day—which presented a problem for the girls. How were they supposed to get into the Egyptian exhibit and search for clues if it was blocked off and monitored?

"Do you think those cameras are on?" asked Ava, who raised her eyes upward without moving her head. "I don't see a little red light like in the movies."

"I'm sure they are," said Carol, "especially after the robbery."

"That's true," agreed Ava.

"I have a feeling if we so much as walk down the hallway toward the exhibit, the guards are going to be all over us."

"Can you disable the cameras with your phone? You know like hack into their system?"

"Dude, I'm in the computer club, not the Avengers."

"I see," Ava sighed a heavy sigh filled with disappointment. "We need to get the guards away from the monitors." She gestured to a room named the "History of Livingston." "I have a plan! Follow me."

Carol followed Ava into the exhibit. The walls were filled with grainy black-and-white pictures of Livingston. A huge picture hung in the back of the room, showing a panoramic view of the entire town. Beneath the city streets, the picture showed a complex tunnel system that reminded Carol of an ant farm. The tunnels had been sealed in the 1890s after a series of cave-ins.

"So, what's the plan?" whispered Carol.

Ava didn't respond. She noticed a reflection on the picture's metallic frame. Someone was watching them from the doorway.

"Carol," Ava whispered out of the corner of her mouth, "we're being watched. Pretend to be gaga over these pictures."

"Woah," said Carol as she pointed at the huge black-and-white photography. "Is that Bennett's Groceries? Look, it used to be just a small stand selling vegetables."

"That's incredible!" exclaimed Ava.

"Now it's like a megastore."

"Look at this," said Ava enthusiastically as she pointed to a grainy picture. "The Livingston Savings and Loan is over 160 years old! How the heck did they get an aerial picture of the bank? They didn't have airplanes back then."

"A tethered hot air balloon," said a friendly, deep male voice.

Ava and Carol whirled around. A short, robust security guard stood in the doorway. He had a scruffy patch of reddish-brown hair and equally red cheeks. He looked like he had just finished running a race. He walked from his belly as if being pulled by a rope. Heave-ho.

"This picture is from the year 1860," he said. "They raised a hot air balloon to nearly a hundred feet." He raised his hand in the air as if it were a hot air balloon. "And then they tied it to a large oak tree, right here in the front of the museum. Here's a photograph of the hot air balloon," the guard pointed at another picture.

"Aerial photography was cutting-edge technology back then. The big photograph of the city is actually a series of eight photographs all stitched together to make one big picture."

"That's incredible," said Carol as she looked back toward the picture. "I never realized that so many of the businesses in the picture are actually still around."

"Many of the businesses in Livingston are still run by the same family."

"They used hot air balloons in battle?" asked Ava, reading the placard beneath the photograph. "Seems a little risky."

"They sure did. They used them during the Civil War to spy on enemy troops."

"Kind of like we use drones now," said Carol.

"Exactly! The soldiers were incredibly resourceful. Did you know they ran telegraph wires from the balloons, so they could get real-time information to the commanding officers on the battlefield? History is fascinating!" the guard beamed.

"Thank you," said Ava, "you're like a walking computer." She smiled at the guard.

"Thank you," he smiled back. "I'll take that as a compliment."

Carol and Ava moved slowly around the room. They were running out of things to talk about, and they were worried that the guard was going to be a permanent shadow. They were just about to run out of *oohs* and *ahhs* when a voice began jabbering from the security guard's earpiece.

"Please, please, please," whispered Carol.

The guard stepped out of the doorway and spoke quietly. Ava glanced at Carol—her fingers crossed. Good fortune must like crossed fingers because the guard's next words were "I'm on my way." They looked at each other and let out a joint sigh of relief—*finally*!

They pretended not to notice that the guard had left the room in case he checked back in on them—and only when they heard his footsteps descending the stairs did they relax.

"OK, quickly, before he comes back," said Ava. "I've got to get into the Egyptian room."

"How? In case you forgot, there are two cameras. There is no way into that room without them seeing you."

"Well, actually there is. You just have to think outside the box," smiled Ava.

"If your plan involves me being grounded for the rest of my life, I swear to you I will shave your eyebrows and knit the world's smallest sweater," Carol warned.

Ava, despite herself and the seriousness of the situation, snorted. "I promise you that you won't be grounded for the rest of your life. My plan is infallible—there is no way we'll get caught."

Carol tapped her wrist as if pointing to an imaginary watch. "Alright, give me the info before the human shadow returns."

"Here's my plan. When we came upstairs, there was a room marked 'Security.' You saw it, right?"

"Of course...," said Carol, already scrunching up her face.

"I need you to bang on that door, and when the guard comes to the door, I need you to tell him that you ate a day-old egg salad sandwich from a gas station and that you have to find a restroom, pronto. Trust me, people will move mountains to get you to a restroom. No one messes with old egg salad."

"*Trust* is the last thought that is coming to my mind right now...," said Carol warily.

"Listen, I just need the guard to be away from the video monitors for ten seconds," Ava said. "That'll give me enough time to get into the room without being seen."

"You've lost your mind," said Carol. "How are you going to get out of the room when you're done? You want me to run back to the security room five minutes later and tell him there's no TP too?"

"Hmmm," said Ava, stroking her chin with her index finger and thumb. "That's not a bad idea."

"There's one small problem with your plan—how are you going to know when the guard comes to the door?" asked Carol.

"Problem? There's no problem—that is actually the easiest part."

Carol met Ava's eyes with a look of unquestionable doubt, or a look of impending doom—Ava couldn't really tell.

"You have your phone, right?" inquired Ava.

"Yes," said Carol cautiously.

"Well, call me now, and then put your phone in your pocket. I'll be able to hear what's going on. Easy peasy."

"I'm going to look like an absolute idiot banging on the security door," moaned Carol.

"Really? Is this the voice of a seasoned journalist? I thought the *Cherrywood Chatter* was a paper that stood for—"

"All right, all right, I'll do it!"

"Okay," said Ava, holding her friend's shoulders, looking deep into her eyes. "Let me see that look."

"Um, what look?" asked Carol, confused and annoyed.

"Come on, the *I gotta go* look!"

"If we live through this, I'm taking you to counseling—you truly need help." Carol pulled her phone out of her pocket and hit Ava's name. Ava felt her phone vibrate. "I'm changing your name to traitor," Carol hissed.

"You don't mean that," said Ava, putting her hands on Carol's shoulders who shrugged away. "Oh, tuna works too. Old tuna—there's nothing worse."

Carol turned and walked away. Ava could hear the muffled *swoosh, swoosh* of her jeans as she walked down the stairs. Ava stood just inside the doorway of the exhibit so the security cameras couldn't see her, her heart pounding in her chest.

Just a short distance away, as Carol descended the stairs, she pondered her life choices.

The swooshing stopped. Suddenly, Ava heard *bang, bang, bang* as Carol pounded on the security door.

Seconds later, she heard a buzz, and then a very angry male voice.

Hmm, I didn't need the phone after all. Ava didn't hang around to hear what they said. She snuck a peek out the doorway, bolted down the hall, and dove under the police tape into the Ramesses Exhibit. She slid across the room, coming to a stop at the base of a sarcophagus. Her softball coach would have been proud.

Ava stood up, brushed her leggings off, and peeled a long strip of police tape from her forehead. A huge smile spread across her face. She'd made it!

The Egyptian exhibit room was richly decorated. Strips of sunlight painted thin, vertical lines across the room. *Yeesh, this room is creepy,* thought Ava as she slowly turned in a circle.

At the far side of the room stood a huge wooden sarcophagus, encased in glass. The placard beneath it read "Ramesses II—Ruler of Egypt 1279 BC–1213 BC." The walls were covered with pictures of all shapes and sizes of pyramids, burial sites, and Egyptian gods. A replica of the Rosetta stone, sat against the side wall. *Wow, those language CDs have been around forever!*

A decorative gold stand stood in the middle of the room. The top spread out like fingers to support an incredibly thick glass housing that was supposed to protect the pharaoh's diamonds.

A circle, about the size of a grapefruit, had been cut into the top of the glass enclosure. Ava could see some kind of brownish, yellow oil around the edges of the circle. She pulled out her phone and started taking pictures. The glass enclosure was over an inch thick, and a series of massive bolts had been drilled through the glass into the stand. It was securely anchored to the floor by eight more bolts.

Okay, so they used a glass cutter to steal the diamonds. But how did they get in? Would they be brazen enough to just sneak past the guards? Did they come in through the loading zone?

Ava looked up at the corner of the room. A motion detector flashed. Her heart jumped, *why didn't it go off?* She cautiously moved toward it. There appeared to be something over the sensor. It looked like a thick piece of glass, the size of a matchbook.

Ava then eyed the window. Both locks were secured. An alarm with a digital readout sat atop the window frame. It sent millions of invisible pulses to a receiver—if the connection was broken, the alarm would go off. *I don't see any scratches on the locks or any sign of forced entry.* But, Ava noticed, the center of the windowsill was clean, whereas the outer edges had dust on them, as if the center had been wiped down.

Ava took a picture of the window, the locks, and the alarm system. She peered down—it was at least a twenty-five-foot drop from the window to the ground. She spun around and took pictures of the motion detector. *Mental note, the thieves had to have visited the exhibit earlier—there has to be video of them. Figure out how to see the video.*

Just as she was about to take a panoramic video of the room, an angry voice shouted, "What are you doing in there?!"

Ava nearly jumped out of her skin. A very vexed and very muscular security guard stood in the doorway, holding Carol by the top of her arm. Ava recognized him from the security room. He had jet-black hair and barely visible beady little eyes that at the moment, Ava knew, were boring holes into her soul. His walrus-sized mustache would've been funny, but under the circumstances, even his mustache looked frightening.

"You're not supposed to be in there!" he yelled, his face contorted and turned an unhealthy crimson color. "You are trespassing and breaking the law." He jabbed his finger at the police tape.

Ava gulped, her mind was spinning, how was she going to get them out of this one? Carol just stood with her head hanging low, looking like a broken puppet.

"Get out of there right now!" he demanded, pointing an accusatory finger at Ava.

"I'm going, I'm going." Ava considered her options. She could either try running and jumping over the tape, limbo beneath it, or—she decided on the least confrontational method. Ava dropped to her hands and knees and crawled under the police tape. As she stood, all she saw was leg and more leg. *Geez, he's tall.*

The man looked from Ava to Carol and then back to Ava. "What were you doing in that room?" he looked at Ava suspiciously. "And don't try to play games with me! I'm a human lie detector."

"I apologize, I was taking a selfie. Carol and I are into true crime shows, and I accidentally dropped my phone. It slid into the room."

The man stuck out his lower lip and scowled. "I told you, don't *lie* to me." He squeezed Carol's arm, making her wince.

Ava went from being frightened to infuriated. "Let go of her right now. You do realize she's the mayor's daughter, you jerk!" bluffed Ava.

The guard looked taken aback for a moment, and then regained his composure. He lowered his snarling face toward Ava.

She took a step back. He definitely wasn't a fan of mouthwash.

"The mayor is in her eighties. I highly doubt this is her daughter."

"Did I say daughter? I meant granddaughter. You're going to be in so much trouble."

"Her granddaughter cut the ribbon for our new exhibit. She's forty years old."

"Really, then my friend here has been lying to me this whole time. I'm not judging you Carol but pretending to be the mayor's granddaughter." Ava shook her head. "If you are finished accosting my friend, I'll make sure she gets the help that she needs."

Carol shook her head. *I'm so going to kill her*.

"Matter of fact, I should capture this moment." Ava held up her phone and snapped a picture. "You couldn't capture the culprit behind the theft, but you managed to grab a teenage girl."

"That does it. Give me your phone." He grabbed Ava by the hand and proceeded to try to rip it from her. Ava clamped her other hand on top of the phone, squeezing it like an anaconda. The guard grabbed her index finger and pried it backward.

"Ouch!" yelled Ava. Without a thought, she whirled toward the guard and slammed her foot into his shin.

The guard's throat made a weird squeaky noise and his eyes nearly bulged out of his skull. "Yee ouch!" he screamed, even more enraged than before.

Ava's mouth also flew open as stars danced in front of her eyes. She'd seen dozens of kids kick bad guys in the shins, but no one had warned her that it was a toe-crushing experience. She had been led to believe that it was the ultimate bad guy escape trick. Sadly, she had been deceived by Hollywood.

"Ow! Just ow!" she breathed out, walking in circles. Her toes began sending the word ouch over and over to her brain, followed by the heartfelt question of "Why? What did we do to deserve this?"

The guard's face had turned from crimson to a lovely shade of purple. It was as if he had the ability to channel all the colors of the rainbow, or a bag of skittles. He lunged at Ava just as a heavenly voice, like a ray of sunlight, broke through the chaos.

"George Marcel! What on earth are you doing?!" The security guard whipped his head around. He immediately released Ava's hand and let go of Carol's arm.

"What is going on here? Have you lost your mind?!" Gladys's voice rang out powerfully.

Ava and Carol couldn't believe it—Gladys had come to their rescue. They looked at each other and then at George.

"Gladys, I caught this young lady snooping around the Egyptian exhibit. The police said *no one* was to go into that room under *any* circumstances." He looked darkly at the girls. "I think they should be in jail!"

"George, they are children. I hardly think the police are going to arrest them and haul them off to jail. I know that you are under a lot of stress, but really…," she shook her head in disapproval. "I'll take over from here. I know Ava's parents."

She turned to Ava and Carol, her face filled with anger. "Girls," she said sternly, "we are going to go downstairs to have a little chat, and then you're calling your parents to tell them what you've done."

George reluctantly agreed. Under the pretense of reattaching a piece of police tape, he kneeled and whispered, "Next time I catch you girls in this museum, I'm going to lock you in the basement." He smiled an evil, villainous smile, then spat out the word "forever."

Ava and Carol shivered as a chill raced down their spines. Carol looked up at Gladys. She could see the disappointment in her eyes, and the tight tug of frustration at the corner of her mouth.

"I'm sorry, Gladys," she whispered.

"We'll talk downstairs," said Gladys as she grasped Carol's hand. "Now help me down these steps."

When they reached Gladys's desk, Ava looked her in the eyes. "I'm so sorry that I went into the exhibit. We heard about the robbery, and we thought maybe we could help."

"I know it seems silly," offered Carol, "but we have solved a couple of cases. Well, not cases, we're not detectives or anything."

Gladys crossed her arms and shook her head. "Girls, I expected more of you. I am incredibly disappointed in your careless, reckless behavior today. This isn't how you go about things."

Ava nearly choked on her words. She had never truly disappointed anyone before and never been called careless or reckless. Okay, not this week. Still, it hurt to see Gladys so disappointed, she'd rather her be angry or furious.

"I'm so sorry," Ava stammered, "Getting into the room, was my idea, not Carol's. My mom's a journalist and she told us about the Isabella robbery, and how eighty percent of art heists go unsolved—I just thought with odds like that, maybe we could help."

"I guess we should have thought things through a little more," whispered Carol, trying to support Ava.

"Yes, you should have," said Gladys with a nod. "If I hadn't been here, George would have certainly called the police and you two would be talking to them right now, not me. However...," she said with a mischievous smile, "I'm always here, and since I *did* rescue you from George, you've gotta tell me if you figured out anything."

"What?" asked Carol, confused. "Aren't you going to call our parents and tell them they've raised a pair of hardened criminals?"

"No," chuckled Gladys, "but I am going to say this: As detectives, you have to take risks, however, you need to figure out if the outcome is going to outweigh the consequences."

"I get it," said Carol. "We're still pretty new at this."

"So," said Gladys. She laced her fingers together and placed them on the counter in front of her, "Tell me everything you know."

"I haven't had enough time to write everything down, so I'll give you a summary of what I found."

"I'm all ears," smiled Gladys. "Seriously, your ears never stop growing, I figure by time I'm ninety I'll be able to fly to work. Like Dumbo."

Ava and Carol snickered. "You're officially the coolest ever," laughed Carol.

"Alright, before Gladys steals my thunder, here's what I found at the crime scene. Actually, you probably know most of this, so let me know if I bore you with the details."

"Well, *I* don't know anything about the exhibit, so you'll be catching me up," said Carol.

"Oh yeah. So, the diamonds were secured in a big glass box that was bolted to the floor. The thieves used a glass cutter to steal the diamonds. There was an oily residue on the glass too." Gladys nodded for her to continue. "I checked to see how the thieves could have gotten in. I know that the museum upgraded the security system. There was a motion detector in the back corner of the room, and the window had a digital alarm as well."

"Did the alarms go off?" asked Carol.

"No," answered Gladys. "The motion detectors are set to alert the alarm company if triggered."

"But they don't go off all the time, so someone has access to whether the alarm is armed or not, right?"

"That is all controlled by the alarm company. Part of the agreement with the Egyptian government was that we would not have the ability to set or reset the motion detectors. They actually hired the company that monitored them."

Ava pulled her phone out of her pocket. "I noticed this attached to the front of the motion detector. It looks like a thick piece of glass, maybe somehow it stopped the sensor from working."

"I'm not sure. Neither the police nor FBI would really give us any details about how the robbery took place."

Carol nodded, "It makes sense—if they suspect someone on the inside, they don't want to give them any information."

"You said the alarm on the window didn't go off, right?"

"Correct," Gladys nodded her head. "The window was locked, and the alarm didn't trigger."

"Oh, because look at this." Ava swiped her finger across the phone. "See how the center of the windowsill is dust-free, and the outer edges are dusty? Like if someone had slid in through the window."

"It's certainly suspicious, but when the police arrived, the window was locked."

"Are there any other entrances into the room?"

"No," Gladys turned from the girls to the front door. A Livingston Elementary School bus had just pulled up in front of the museum. "Sorry, girls. We've only got a minute or two."

"What about video from the cameras? I'm sure the police went through that, right?"

"Oh yes," nodded Gladys. "The police looked at the security video, but on the night of the robbery, there were three hours of video missing. George said that the new online software they use to record the video lost connection and they didn't realize it until hours later."

"How convenient," said Ava.

"Has that ever happened before?" asked Carol curiously.

"Who knows?" said Gladys. "We've never had to test the system. This is our first robbery."

Carol suddenly stiffened. She shouldered Ava. "We're being watched," she whispered. Ava carefully glanced upward, just in time to see someone dart into the shadows.

Gladys shot to her feet and shook an accusatory finger at the girls. "I'm calling each of your parents. You have no business skulking around this museum. Now, instead of calling the police, I want you here twice a week for the next month to clean the lobby and stairs. Is that understood?"

The girls stood, shocked, their mouths hanging open.

"Do you understand?" she demanded.

"Yes… ma'am," they stammered together.

"Good," said Gladys, winking at them, a tiny smile on her face. "Now go home and think about what you've done."

The girls made it through the doors and down the stairs, just as a crowd of children charged the museum.

5
A WINDOW OF OPPORTUNITY

Ava spun on the sidewalk toward Carol. "My heart is still pounding from Gladys's acting. If anyone was watching, it would have definitely fooled them."

"Thank goodness she stepped in when she did," said Carol.

"Yeah, I was about to unleash a world of hurt on him." Carol gave Ava a look, and they cracked up.

"So," Carol grabbed Ava's hand and they dashed across the crosswalk. "You told Gladys that the windowsill was dust-free in the center."

"Yeah."

"Even though she said the window was locked and the alarm was still set… you think they might have come through the window, don't you?"

"I mean it's a guess. There were only two ways into that room: the main entrance and the window."

Carol nodded in agreement. "I think I know a way we can most likely find out for sure." She gestured toward a small red-and-white awning.

"Livingston Bank?" asked Ava.

"Yes, what do you see?" Carol came to a stop in front of the glass entranceway of the bank.

"I see my reflection…. Oh my God, look at my hair! It looks like I got in a fight with a wind tunnel."

"It's abysmal," laughed Carol. "In the poetic words of the late, great Henry Froodles, it's *hairable*. You have helmet hair," said Carol, running her hand over Ava's head. "It's messy, but it's adorable."

"You just referred to my hair as adorable? Kittens are adorable, puppies are adorable…," Ava shook her head. "This is so humiliating."

"To me, it says, 'Hey, *safety* before *fashion*.' You are a modern-day rebel—embrace it."

Ava wrapped her arms around her shoulders, "I don't feel the love. My seventeen Instagram fans will never forgive me."

"I'm sure they'll get over it. Now, on to more important things."

"Yes, if you would, please explain to me why we are standing in front of the bank."

"So glad you asked. Ava, what is directly across the street from the bank?" inquired Carol.

Ava tilted her head. "Hmm, could it be the museum?"

"Great job," smiled Carol. "And what part of the museum just happens to be facing the bank?"

"The Egyptian exhibit." Ava turned and looked at Carol, amazement filled her face. "Do you think they deposited the diamonds into the bank? Seems so risky."

"What?" asked Carol incredulously, smacking Ava on the back of the head. "What do ATM's have?"

"Money, and tiny little envelopes for making deposits."

"A camera! You idiot. A camera. They all have cameras," said Carol, jabbing at the camera.

"I know, I know—I was just messing with you, geez…. I make faces at them all the time, hoping that somewhere, some bank manager will be watching the replay and submit my video to an agent in Hollywood."

"At the museum, you were like a bright shooting star," sighed Carol. "And now you implode like a black hole, sucking the very life from my veins." she cocked an eyebrow and looked at Ava. "Too much?"

"Yeah, you lost me at the *sucking the very life from my veins part.*"

Ava turned and looked at the museum, then turned back to the ATM. "Alright, moving past this awkward moment. We need to see the bank's video from the night of the robbery."

"Bingo," nodded Carol. "You suspect they used the window. Now we just need to see *how…* and if we're lucky, *who.*"

"Um, one small hiccup. From what I know about banks, and it's not much, we can't just march into a bank and ask them to show us their security footage. Plus… I'm sure the police have already done that."

"Lucky for us," Carol grabbed the worn brass door handle, "my dad is a good friend of Mr. Talbot, the bank manager."

A small bell jingled as the girls entered the bank. To their right, a row of tellers were busy helping customers. Two small sofas and a couple chairs rested against the opposite wall, and at the far end of the bank were a series of offices. However, the most alluring piece of furniture was a small pedestal that stood like a gallant knight wedged between the two sofas. Atop the pedestal rested a small ceramic bowl, filled with miniature candy bars and suckers.

Unfortunately, the candy would have to wait. Mr. Talbot was just finishing up with a customer. He made eye contact with Carol and gave her a wink as he said his goodbyes to his customer. Ava cast one quick, mournful look toward the colorful candy treasure that lay just out of reach.

Mr. Talbot was the epitome of dapper. He looked like an older Clark Kent. He wore his hair in a hard part, just above his temple. Eloquent wisps of silver hair—strokes from a master's paintbrush—lay just under the arms of dark-framed, 1960s-style glasses. He wore a perfectly tailored gray suit with a red tie that acted like a punctuation mark to an exquisite outfit.

"Wow," said Ava, looking at Mr. Talbot. "Retro meets modern. I approve."

"Thank you, young lady, and good morning, Carol. To what do I owe this pleasure?" Mr. Talbot asked, smiling down at them.

"Hi, Mr. Talbot. This is my friend, Ava Clarke," she said, gesturing toward Ava.

"Nice to meet you, Ava," he said as he shook her hand. It felt like how a banker's hand should feel. Warm and reassuring.

"Nice to meet you," Ava smiled.

"How are your parents?" he beamed down at Carol. "I haven't seen your dad since we lost the bowling tournament." He paused, balled up his fist, and bit into his knuckles, his manicured nails glistening in the fluorescent lighting. "The Concord Cruisers were exceptional athletes. They tormented us. I was hoping your dad had recovered from the loss…."

Carol patted his arm and nodded her head appreciatively. "He took it rather hard, Mr. Talbot. He locked himself in his office and threatened to set fire to his favorite bowling shoes—the orange-and-white Dexters…," she bowed her head for dramatic effect.

"Not his Dexters," whispered Mr. Talbot, barely audible. "That's horrible. I'll give him a call this evening. The best thing to do after falling off a horse is to get right back on."

"Unless… you have a concussion," said Carol. "Then it's actually best to wait a while, and perhaps seek medical attention."

"Yes," he nodded. "Unless you have a concussion." His eyebrows knotted together, as if they were about to duel. "I apologize, girls. What was it you said you needed?" he asked, looking slightly confused.

"Yes, sorry about that, I'll get right to the point. You of course know about the museum robbery."

"Oh, yes, indeed. Nasty business. I'm just glad no one was hurt."

"Well, we're conducting a little investigation of our own, and I'm writing an article for the school paper, the *Cherrywood Chatter*, about the robbery."

"Oh," said Mr. Talbot, sucking in sharply, his excitement palpable. He leaned in and rested a hand on each girl's shoulder, creating a small huddle of exclusivity. "I used to write for the *Cherrywood Chatter* when I was in school. I was their financial advisor in charge of bake sales, car washes…

basically all aspects of fundraising. My articles were as sharp as a tack. My information, though verbose, was filled with financial wisdom. I truly think I made an impact on quite a few of my classmates' lives."

Or helped cure insomnia, thought Ava. Yet, due to her exceptional upbringing, she found herself saying, "Sounds absolutely fascinating."

"Oh, *indeed* it was. Those were the days when writers wrote *real* stories, girls," explained Mr. Talbot, reflecting on the past. "If I hadn't become a banker, I'm sure I would have been a financial reporter, instead of that Elvin Morris on the local news." He gave an exasperated sigh, then looked back at the girls. "I'm sorry, girls. I went off on a tangent. You were asking about the robbery?"

"Don't apologize! I dig your passion, Mr. Talbot. It's inspiring." Ava had the rare ability to make just about everyone feel good about themselves. "We just wondered if the bank's ATM camera records 24/7."

"Oh yes, it certainly does. It's constantly recording, and then that video data is saved to the cloud. I'm not really sure what the cloud is. I always imagine a bunch of computers in a big cloud...," he paused for a second. Ava could tell he was envisioning computers floating on a big, fluffy cumulus cloud. "The video is archived in weekly records... I can retrieve the videos from any computer anywhere in the world, as long as I have an internet connection," he smiled proudly.

"Oh cool," said Carol. "So, it basically works like my iPhone. When I save my pics and videos to the cloud, then I can access them later."

"Exactly," smiled Mr. Talbot. "It's not like the old days where everything was stored on tape."

"Do you ever submit any of the ATM videos to the news, or Hollywood agents?" asked Ava. "For example," she explained, "if you were to see, you know, raw talent?" Ava brushed her purple bangs from her forehead and gave him a quick profile.

Mr. Talbot stared at Ava out of the corner of his eye, his forehead wrinkled just slightly. "Um, no… but I'll keep that in mind next time I binge-watch my surveillance videos."

Ava nodded and smiled an upside-down smile. Upside-down smiles were not natural for her. In fact, it was quite difficult, but she had been secretly practicing in her room for such an occasion. She pulled the corners of her mouth downward, flexing her cheek muscles until they ached. She'd seen her mom do it when she talked with other journalists about important stuff, so she had decided to practice the move on Mr. Talbot.

He looked at Ava confused and squinted his eyes just a little. "So…," he continued, "you want to look at the video because you think it shows the robbery?"

"Yes," Carol nodded excitedly.

"I certainly don't mind you looking, but you do realize the ATM camera is facing the side of the museum, not the front."

"Which is perfect," explained Carol. "We think the thieves accessed the Egyptian exhibit via the windows facing the bank."

"Interesting," said Mr. Talbot. "Well, let's get to it. My office is this way and you girls have a robbery to solve."

The girls followed Mr. Talbot through a set of glass doors, down a short hallway and came to a stop in front of a wooden door with a large golden placard that read "Todd Talbot, Bank President." He unlocked the door and ushered the girls inside.

Natural sunlight filled what would have been a very gloomy office. Mr. Talbot had the typical banker's office. A bookcase lined with business books. A wall filled with various diplomas with golden seals. However, there was one standout feature that was unique to his office, there were bowling trophies EVERYWHERE.

If the bank ever went bankrupt, thought Ava, *this guy could make a fortune selling bowling trophies on eBay.*

His ornate desk was incredibly organized— everything was arranged in perfect, straight rows. On the center of his desk sat two very large monitors. The screen on the left was broken up into six little squares that displayed video of the tellers, front door, ATM, and vault in real time. The second monitor displayed a screensaver of his wife and daughter at the beach.

"That's really cool," said Carol as she pointed to the screen with the security videos. "You can see everything that's going on in the bank at once."

Mr. Talbot smiled. "Gotta keep them honest. Come have a look." He motioned to the girls toward the computer screen.

"Okay, let's see here," Mr. Talbot murmured as he entered his computer's password.

A program popped up on the computer screen. Mr. Talbot clicked on a few things and pulled up a separate window. Then a few clicks later, a sharp gray image appeared… the museum!

Ava gasped in delight. She smiled widely at Carol, who looked equally excited.

"Well, it was definitely windy," said Ava, pointing at a piece of string that hung from the ATM's awning—it was whipping back and forth.

"All right, let's see what the camera caught," said Mr. Talbot excitedly. "I believe the news mentioned that the heist happened sometime between 2 a.m. and 5 a.m. So, let's go to two o'clock and fast-forward until we see something. Stop me if I miss anything!"

Ava and Carol nodded—their eyes glued to the screen. Mr. Talbot jumped ahead until the time at the top of the screen read 2:00 in bold white letters. He then began to fast-forward. Everything was calm and quiet…until 3:32 a.m.

"There! There!" said Carol excitedly, pointing at the screen. "It's a delivery truck."

They watched as the truck came to a stop directly in front of the camera, its red taillights illuminating the side of the museum in a transparent sheet of red light. A thick canvas tarp was draped and tied down over the body of the truck.

"Why would they have a tarp over the truck, unless…," said Carol, answering her own question, "…it's hiding something."

Ava nodded in agreement without taking her eyes off the screen.

The driver's side door opened. Ava and Carol expected to see a person climb out of the truck, but instead all they could see was a squat bright fuzzy glowing ball with arms and legs. Seconds later, another glowing ball emerged from the other side of the truck, however it was much taller.

"I'm not really understanding what I'm seeing," said Mr. Talbot.

"Maybe our geography teacher was right. The diamonds were stolen by aliens or Ramesses's spirit," said Ava.

"No," smiled Carol. "It's ingenious. They knew the camera was here. They're wearing some type of reflective material that's making the camera go wonkers."

The two glowing balls paused for a moment at the back of the truck.

"What are they doing?" asked Carol, noticing a bright rectangular light emanating from the shorter blob. "Oh, never mind, I got it. He's talking on the phone."

The phone disappeared back into the glowing blob. The two glowing orbs moved from the back of the truck, and close to the museum. The angle of the ATM camera didn't allow them to see what the two suspects were looking at, but the girls could guess.

"They're looking at the window," whispered Ava.

Suddenly, a ladder dropped into view, stopping about a foot above the ground.

"That's a rope ladder," said Carol, watching as the wind beat it against the building.

"A super-sturdy rope ladder," added Ava.

Mr. Talbot stared intently at the screen. "Girls, you know what this means? This means someone inside the museum is helping them!"

"I kind of figured as much," said Ava.

Everyone was surprised by the two glowing men's agility. They climbed up the precarious ladder with confidence and speed. Ten seconds later, both men completely disappeared from view.

"Obviously someone passed the presidential fitness test. Did you see them climb that ladder?" asked Ava.

"When we catch them," smiled Carol, "the only thing they'll be climbing is the walls of their prison cell."

"Woah," laughed Ava. "That was dark, but much respect for the realism."

"My parents were *way* into *Scared Straight*. I guess it rubbed off on me," said Carol matter-of-factly.

Nothing was happening on the screen, so Mr. Talbot fast-forwarded a few minutes, until the glowing men reappeared.

"They're climbing down!" Mr. Talbot said excitedly.

As soon as they were on the ground, the two glowing bad guys ran to the back of the truck while the ladder slowly ascended out of sight.

"It's kind of sad," said Ava, crossing her arms. "It only took them like ten minutes to steal millions of dollars in diamonds. I can't even brush my hair in ten minutes."

The thieves dashed to the front of the truck and flung open the doors. The digital clock read 3:45 a.m. The taillights flashed on, a puff of smoke erupted from the exhaust pipe and the truck lurched forward. They left in such a hurry, they failed to notice that the bottom corner of the tarp had come loose. As they pulled away, the wind blew, catching it like a sail, causing it to billow up from the side of the truck. It was just a second, but the three observers caught a glimpse of the clue that was about to turn this case around.

"Did you see that?!" said Carol excitedly. "There was writing or some kind of marking on the side of the truck!"

Ava could barely contain herself. They were about to take down a ring of diamond thieves, single-handedly. She thought about the term *single-handed*, but every scenario showed her using both hands to bring down the thieves. *Double-handedly?*

Mr. Talbot clicked a button with his mouse, it allowed him to toggle the video back to the point before the truck sped off. He slowly proceeded frame by frame until they reached the moment where the side of the delivery truck was visible.

"What's it say?" Carol asked, moving around the desk so she could get a better look.

Mr. Talbot froze on frame 10,210. The image was slightly blurred from the exhaust and movement of the truck. There appeared to be letters or numbers and then some sort of squiggly design. Ava edged closer, squinting at the screen, trying to make sense of what she was seeing.

"We need to enchant the picture and make it larger. I can't make out what it says," said Ava, disappointed.

"You mean *enhance* the picture?" said Mr. Talbot, looking up from the image frozen on his screen.

"No. Enchant it, so we could see it better."

Carol's eyes opened wide. "Ava, you're a genius! You mean the Photo Magic Software, right?"

"That's it," Ava snapped. "I just couldn't remember the name of the software."

"Mr. Talbot, is it OK if I commandeer your computer for two minutes? Ava and I use an online software called Hugo's Photo Magic Software in art class. It's an online photo editing software and it should allow me to zoom in and enchant...," she winked at Ava, "...the image. They call editing the image *enchanting*, to go along with the theme of their software."

"Oh," smiled Mr. Talbot. "That makes more sense. But how are you going to get the image from the video?" He pushed himself back from the desk.

"A little something we like to call screen capture," said Ava, smiling and wiggling her eyebrows.

"If you hold down the *Alt* button on your keyboard and then press the *PrtSc* button, it will take a picture of whatever window is selected on your screen," said Carol. "Then all I do is upload that picture right into Hugo's Photo Magic Software."

Mr. Talbot stared at the girls as if they were aliens. "I'm impressed. This isn't hacking, right?" he asked, slightly concerned.

"No!" laughed Carol. "Ava and I only use hacking when we break through the school's firewalls and change our grades."

"Straight A's for life," laughed Ava, high-fiving her friend. Mr. Talbot looked mortified.

"We're just kidding," smiled Carol, seeing Mr. Talbot's expression.

"We get our A's the old-fashioned way. We bribe our teachers," said Ava, playfully nodding.

"Oh, I'm not hearing this," he said, putting his hands to his ears. "Not hearing this."

"We're just playing, Mr. Talbot," said Carol reassuringly. Her fingers then flew across the keyboard. First, she opened the web browser and loaded Hugo's Photo Magic Software. Next, she took a screenshot of the video and saved it to his desktop. She clicked a square that said *Upload*, navigated to the image and uploaded it. Seconds later, it popped into Hugo's Photo Magic Edit screen.

"Okay," Carol said, feeling *in the zone*. "Now I'm going to do what's called sharpening. This will help us see the image more clearly." Carol clicked a menu that read *filters* and selected *sharpen* from the drop-down menu. Not satisfied with the results, she repeated the *sharpen* command once again.

"Whoa," said Mr. Talbot. "Incredible!"

"I'm not done yet," said Carol as she cropped the picture. She then pressed *Zoom*. The result was perfect. They were staring at the number 346, and what appeared to be the bottom edge of a painting… and perhaps a statue.

"Ohhh, 346," whispered everyone together.

"It's either an address or a telephone number," deduced Carol.

"My money is on a telephone number, and the thing above it kind of looks like the bottom of a picture or painting and some sort of sculpture," said Ava.

"It does," nodded Carol in agreement. "What do you think, Mr. Talbot?"

"I wonder if it's part of their logo… but whose?" he said, racking his brain. "It looks very familiar."

A sharp rap on Mr. Talbot's door made everyone jump. He glanced at his watch and shook his head. "I'm sorry, girls. My 1:30 appointment is here," he said, looking disappointed.

"Not a problem at all," said Carol, smiling. "You wouldn't mind if I copied the image of the truck, would you? It won't take but a second."

"Certainly, go right ahead."

"Great!" Carol unsnapped a wristband that doubled as a USB drive. She plugged it into his computer and dragged the image to her drive.

"Gifts from the computer club," said Ava, noticing the concerned look on Mr. Talbot's face. "You realize that you have literally helped us blow this case wide open."

Mr. Talbot's face lit up. "You really think so? It was a lot of fun," he said, smiling broadly. "Promise me you'll let me know how the case is progressing."

"You got it!" smiled Carol as she hopped up from his computer. "Be sure to give my dad a call. Like you said, he needs to get back up on that horse."

"I sure will," Mr. Talbot smiled kindly. He opened his office door. A sharply dressed woman in an immaculate blue business suit stood waiting patiently for him. She smiled and gave a polite wave to Ava and Carol.

She quickly turned her attention back to Mr. Talbot. "Your 1:30 appointment, Mrs. McKinney, is here."

"Thank you, Linda," said Mr. Talbot with a smile. "Please let Mrs. McKinney know I'll be with her in just a moment."

He turned toward the girls as Linda disappeared down the hall. "Ava," he said, reaching out and shaking her hand, "it was a pleasure meeting you, and I'll be sure to watch the ATM video footage for future Hollywood stars like yourself."

He gave Carol a friendly squeeze on her shoulder. "Good luck and be careful!"

"Thank you, Mr. Talbot. I will."

He held the door for the girls as they quickly made their way into the bank lobby.

"Before we leave, I feel like we should pay our respects," Ava gestured to the candy bowl.

"I agree," said Carol. "We'll need energy for the ride home."

Hands filled with candy, and their spirits high, the girls hurried to their bikes. This was the big break they needed!

6
SECRET NINJA CROUCH SLIDE (DON'T TRY THIS AT HOME)

Sock-footed, Ava slid across her bedroom floor and swiped her laptop off her chest of drawers in one fell swoop. She had once attempted to slide with her no-slip-grip socks and the result had been tragic.

Meanwhile down in the kitchen, Carol was struggling with the sucker wrapper. She eventually gave up, impaled the plastic wrapper with a steak knife and ripped it off. She returned to the table taunting her sucker—*hello, my purple friend, be prepared to meet your demise.*

She was just about to enjoy the fruity flavor when Ava slid across the kitchen, through the door, into the living room. A second later, Ava reappeared, walking nonchalantly with her laptop.

"Nice slide," said Carol approvingly. "Your technique was flawless."

"Thank you," smiled Ava as she placed the laptop on the kitchen table. "They say it's the socks that make the slide. Rubbish! It's pure athleticism and skill." She opened her laptop and typed in her password. An alert popped up reminding her of her piano recital the following Thursday. "Boring…."

"You're so lucky," Carol said. "You get to play the piano—I have to play the bassoon."

"You were the one who raised your hand to play the bassoon in the band. The only one," laughed Ava.

"No," said Carol, sadly shaking her head. "I was raising my hand to go to the restroom. It just happened to be at the same time Mr. Ownby said, 'Bassoon. Any takers?'"

"Ah, I remember the moment. He was so proud of you. And think about it, you're the lead bassoonist!"

"I'm the *only* bassoonist," groaned Carol.

"That makes you the best," said Ava, punching her friend's shoulder.

"Awesome… all my dreams have been fulfilled. I can stop playing the lottery."

"Perfect. That means you are ready to focus on the case."

"If it means you'll stop talking, then yes."

Ava opened her laptop and slid it over to Carol, who navigated to Google Chrome and clicked on Hugo's Photo Magic Software from Ava's favorites. She slipped off her USB bracelet and stuck it into the laptop. Once the program loaded, Carol opened the folder and uploaded the image. The newly enchanted image filled the screen.

"Your talents are limitless," Ava praised. "You never cease to amaze me."

"Flattery will get you nowhere," Carol sighed. "So, looking at the image, there are three components revealed. You may want to get your tiny notebook out for this."

"You're so funny, *not.*"

"Ignoring that comment and moving on. The first clue is the number 346, which we've pretty much established is part of a phone number. The next," Carol zoomed in, "is the lower half of a face."

Ava nodded. "It's a woman's mouth and chin. There is something so familiar about that smile… I know I've seen it before."

"It does look familiar," Carol agreed. "The third clue is the statue. It looks like it's part of a bust of someone's head. Perhaps a famous historical figure like Caesar or David."

"David," Ava rolled her eyes. "I hate that statue. He needs a fig leaf or some board shorts," said Ava emphatically.

"Businesses like to use famous icons as their logos or trademarks. Let's see if we can find any telephone numbers that end in 346 and have something in common with the artwork."

Ava tapped her incredibly small pencil against her forehead. "I know that mouth. Don't worry it'll come to me."

"Ah, the infamous forehead tapping. I've done that a few times," smiled Ava's mom as she sauntered into the kitchen. She had her hair pulled back in a loose ponytail and wore midnight blue glasses atop her head. She was holding a bright orange coffee mug that read "Ain't No Hood Like Parenthood."

"Afternoon, Mom," said Ava, deep in thought.

"Good afternoon, Mrs. Clarke," smiled Carol, beaming up at Ava's mom. "I love the glasses!"

"Good afternoon, and thank you, Carol. How's the investigation coming along?" she asked in the middle of a stretch yawn.

"How did you even know we were investigating something?"

"Mom's intuition. My journalistic power of observation. My ability to spot a story from a mile away."

"That's incredible," said Carol.

"Actually, I used these," she said, pointing to her ears. "You two aren't exactly quiet, you know?"

"Ah yes, the formidable parental listening device," whispered Ava. "They've been my nemesis since I was a child."

Mrs. Clarke placed a hand on the table and took a sip of coffee. "Care to share, or is this top secret?"

Carol looked at Ava, afraid to speak first, fearing that she may break some type of friendship trust rule by divulging information. Ava gave her the smallest of nods.

"So," Carol squinched up her face, afraid to continue. "Ava and I have been collecting clues, trying to solve the museum robbery...."

"Before you say anything, Mom, we're just doing our own safe investigation. We're not talking to anyone, we're just looking at clues—call it, *solving-from-afar*."

"Oh," said Ava's mom as she put down her coffee cup. She crossed her arms and turned her attention back to Carol.

Carol wasn't sure if it was an *Oh* as in *Interesting* or an *Oh* as in *You did what? You're grounded for life.* She eyed Ava's mom, trying to sort out her expression as she talked. "And we've made a major breakthrough." Carol looked at Ava, who waved her hand for her to continue. "In a nutshell, we visited the museum and learned that the thieves broke in through the second-story window, and that they had inside help. We also learned that some of the security video had simply vanished."

Ava nodded and took up the story. "Then Carol had the brilliant idea of going to the bank across the street because the ATM camera faces the side of the museum and the window they used to get in."

"That's good detective work," smiled Ava's mom.

"Mr. Talbot let us watch the bank's ATM video. And this is where it gets really interesting," said Ava.

"Gets? This is already fascinating," said Mrs. Clarke, transforming from mom to journalist. "What did the video show?"

"A delivery truck pulled up to the museum in the middle of the night," answered Ava. "The bad guys wore some kind of reflective clothing that made them look like aliens."

"Interesting," said Mrs. Clarke. "Thieves are using modified glasses that reflect light. It pretty much blinds the camera."

"They tried to be sneaky by covering the side of the truck with a tarp, but the wind was blowing like crazy. It lifted the tarp and we saw the number 346 and we're guessing this is some type of logo." Ava pointed to the picture on the screen. "There's the bottom half of a woman's face and a statue."

Mrs. Clarke leaned in and stared at the screen. "Ah, I see you only have the bottom of the nose and the lips of the woman." Ava's mom began to smile, just like the woman in the painting. "You know who that smile belongs to, right? It's a very famous painting…. May I?" she asked, pointing to the laptop.

"Sure, Mom, go for it."

Mrs. Clarke opened a new tab in the browser. Her fingers quickly raced across the keyboard. She smiled and turned the laptop around to show the girls.

"Ugh!" said Carol, smacking her forehead. "Of course! *Mona Lisa*, painted by Leonardo da Vinci!"

"Mom, you're a genius. Thank you!" said Ava proudly.

"You girls would have figured it out. May I see the image of the van one more time?"

"It's still open," said Ava as she turned the laptop back toward her mom. "Carol thinks that the statue or sculpture is Caesar."

Ava's mom stared at the image and nodded. "That's a great guess. You can see the chin and the neck… and the armor with the fringes on the shoulders. Again, this is a very famous sculpture. I think Carol's right."

"Now we just need to figure out who has a logo with Mona Lisa and Caesar, and 346 as the last three digits of their phone number!" said Carol excitedly.

"Oh, I forgot to ask. How did you know the thieves robbed the museum through a window?"

"We watched them," said Carol. "Someone from inside the museum threw a rope ladder down and they climbed up it. So we know that at least three people are involved."

The thought of the criminals seemed to jar something loose in Ava's mom. "Girls," she said softly, in a tone that every child recognizes as *I'm proud of you, but now it's time to back off*. "I don't mind if you work on clues here or someplace safe, like the library… but these thieves can be dangerous, and I don't want anything to happen to you."

Ava felt like her mother had put training wheels on her ten-speed. *This is our first real case and Mom is already putting on the brakes*. "Mom, we're so close. We'll be super careful," said Ava, her voice filled with disappointment. "You always said I had great instincts—that I was just like you when you were a kid. I *know* how to keep myself out of danger. And…," Ava said, gesturing toward Carol, "…she plays the *bassoon*! Tell me, in all your life as an investigative journalist, have you *ever* heard of a bassoonist getting in trouble *or* putting their life in danger?" Ava gave her mother an *I rest my case* look.

"And again… she casts shade on me…," whispered Carol. She made a mental note to adorn Ava's locker, her notebooks, her bike, her forehead with stickers that read, "Bassoon Life."

Ava's mom stared at her daughter for what felt like an eternity. "I will let you continue your investigation—"

"Thank you! Thank you!" Ava interrupted, jumping up to hug her mom.

"Wait," she said, putting a hand on each of Ava's shoulders, staring into her eyes. "If I even get a *hint* that you girls are doing anything even *remotely* dangerous, your investigation stops." She looked from Ava to Carol and back to Ava. "Is that understood?" she asked seriously.

"Yes, ma'am," they answered quietly.

"Okay," smiled Mrs. Clarke. "Get to work—you've got a case to solve. And I've got an article to write about an eccentric rich man in Ireland. Ironically, they think that this guy may be connected to the millions of dollars' worth of paintings stolen from the Isabella Stewart Gardner Museum."

"That's incredible, Mom. So, they've tracked the paintings to Ireland?"

"How did the pictures get all the way to Ireland?" asked Carol.

"They have secret crime rings that are experts at moving stolen goods out of the country. Private dealers pay thieves millions of dollars to steal and sneak them out of the U.S."

"So, someone like the rich guy in Ireland could do the same thing with the diamonds that were stolen from the museum, right?"

"Yes. Matter of fact, the same mysterious millionaire in Ireland just put a pre-bid on Chopin's piano and the original hand-scored version of *Prelude No. 4* at a private auction. Together, they are worth well over $15 million. I wasn't supposed to know this," she said, giving a mischievous smile, "but I do have a secret, inside source."

"Secret? By secret source you mean Detective Edwards," said Ava matter-of-factly.

Her mother blushed for just a moment, then she quickly regained her composure. "Yes, Blake does help me on occasion."

Carol looked from Ava to Mrs. Clarke, confused.

"My mom and her *secret source* went to middle school and high school together," Ava explained. "They were king and queen of the senior prom. Dad was the kid who presented their crowns. He said tears were streaming down Mom's face when their eyes met."

"Wow, so romantic!" exclaimed Carol.

"I was in pain…," explained Mrs. Clarke. "He poked me in the eye when he put the crown on my head."

"Hey, he said he stole your heart like a thief in the night," said Ava, "and I believe him."

"The only thing he stole like a thief in the night was that powder blue tux and white loafers," Mrs. Clarke said. "Somewhere, there's a naked 1980s mannequin missing a leisure suit."

"Oh my God," Carol snorted, picturing Ava's dad in a powder blue tuxedo.

"Mom, if prom king knows who this guy is, why doesn't he work with the police in Ireland? Can't they just search his house for the missing paintings? He probably has tons of famous stolen stuff!"

"It would be great if it were that easy," her mom replied. "No one is quite sure who he is. Everything is purchased through a series of brokers—and he pays them very well. Supposedly, one broker threatened to reveal his identity… he was never seen again."

"Whoa," whistled Ava, "these guys are serious. I wouldn't want to be called a broker if I worked with priceless art. I think I would rather be called a fixer."

Ava's mother shook her head. "A broker is a person that's like a professional shopper. Rich people use experts like these to make purchases for them so they can buy things anonymously. The broker is usually paid a percentage of the sale."

"They don't only work with shady deals though. My dad uses a stockbroker and real estate brokers."

"Correct," said Mrs. Clarke. "There are good and bad brokers, just like there are good and bad businesspeople. As you learn more about the criminal world, you'll learn that there are very sophisticated crime rings that run just like a business. It's why it's called organized crime."

"Wait. Mrs. Clarke, is your article going to discuss this mysterious guy's identity? I'm only asking because that sounds very dangerous. Like you said, the last guy disappeared."

Ava's smile literally melted from her face. "Mom, you're not really gonna try to find out who this guy is, are you?"

"Yes, I am going to try to find out who he is. But no, I'm not going to try to expose him," Mrs. Clarke smiled reassuringly. "We'd have to go into witness protection, and I kind of like our neighborhood and friends."

Ava didn't look one hundred percent convinced. She didn't like the thought of anything bad happening to her mom. She got up and gave her a big hug. "Be careful, please. You're the only mom I've got."

Mrs. Clarke hugged Ava tightly. "Don't you worry. I'll be careful." She grabbed her coffee from the table, and walked across the kitchen, stopping in the doorway. "Let me know if you need me."

"We will, Mom, thanks again." Ava turned back to Carol as her mom left the kitchen, a determined look on her face. "If this guy is the same guy behind this robbery, he is going to rue the day he was born."

"*Rue*," Carol said, smiling at her friend. "Ingenious."

7
HOW DO YOU SOLVE
A PROBLEM LIKE A LOGO?

Master bassoonist Klaus Thunemann's greatest hits belted from the tiny speaker in Carol's phone. He was just into the kicker of the woeful "JC Bach Concerto" when Ava screamed, "Uncle!"

"What? I particularly enjoy this piece. It's devilishly difficult, don't you think?" smirked Carol innocently. "Imagine the finger placement, so complex!"

"I'm imagining some finger placement right now, and they're around your neck."

"You're missing the point. Classical music is supposed to be calming. Relax your shoulders and let it fill your soul."

"You're about to feel the sole of my foot! Seriously, enough with the woodwinds."

"Fine," sighed Carol, "but I was making tremendous progress."

"Really?" said Ava skeptically.

"Yes, I've made a list of the businesses that would most likely have a logo composed of those historical elements. Would you like to hear my list?"

"Of course. Amaze me."

"Art stores, schools, home and business decorating stores and museums."

"Eh, that's pretty good. I would think our best bet would be an art store. The only trucks I've ever seen at our school were mail trucks, FedEx—"

"Or those food trucks for the cafeteria," added Carol.

"Or... some type of business that caters to museums, maybe some type of renovation business?"

Ava nodded. "I'm going to guess that the business would have to be somewhat local. I can't imagine them driving a truck around in the middle of the night with a tarp on it. Nothing says suspicious like driving your truck around wrapped up like a burrito."

"Oh my God," laughed Carol. "Actually, I could go for a burrito right now. I'm starving."

"Me too," said Ava.

"Me three," came a voice from the living room.

"That woman's hearing scares me.... I truly believe she was a bat in her previous life."

"I heard that!" yelled Ava's mother.

"See?" said Ava, making an *I told you so* face. "Alrighty," she said, turning her attention back to her laptop. "If I draw a twenty-mile circle with the museum being in the center, it includes Livingston, Lexington, Concord and Middleville."

"I guess we should start with Livingston. I can't imagine there will be many art stores," said Carol.

"Yep," said Ava, "I'm on it."

Luckily, Livingston was a small town of twelve thousand people. Ava's search brought up two art stores and an outdoor faux statue garden center. Nothing says *sophisticated* like poorly made Romanesque statues with an accompanying spotlight for your front yard.

Livingston was a complete bust (no pun intended). The number 346 didn't show up in any of the stores' telephone numbers or street addresses. Thirty minutes later, the girls had exhausted all their searches. Not being easily defeated, they expanded their search out another twenty miles, but after another exhaustive search, nothing matched the elusive number.

"I don't get it," said Carol disappointedly. "We searched for phone numbers, for addresses. Who else would have a logo with the painting of Mona Lisa or a Caesar on their truck?"

"A pizza delivery truck?" offered Ava.

Carol brought the picture back up on the computer. "I don't feel like Mona's hungry. I think she's laughing at us. Look at that pretentious smile."

"Oh, you two are on a first-name basis? Suddenly, I feel like the awkward third wheel."

"Me and Mona are besties," laughed Carol. "You know, I'm surprised no one ever stole the *Mona Lisa*. The painting is actually super small, less than two feet wide."

"Really? I always thought the painting was giant. Smuggling a famous painting out of the country seems so simple. You could put it in a FedEx tube and ship it to your buyer. It's not likely they examine every one of those tubes."

"Ava…," whispered Carol, her eyes growing wide. "You're a genius."

"Of course I am," said Ava, her face filling with pride. "Now tell me why."

"Remember when your mom was talking about the private auction, and smuggling stuff out of the country?"

"Yes...."

"Do a search on private auction companies?" asked Carol excitedly.

"Sure." She typed in the words *private auction company* and pressed *Enter*.

Carol scooched her chair against Ava's so she could see the search results. Livingston returned zero results. However, Google revealed a rectangular map, showing two auction companies in the surrounding towns—one in Concord, the other in Middleville.

Only two of the companies listed a website, but the thing that caught their eyes was the Middleville listing. It just happened to have a telephone number ending in 346.

Ava's heart leapt in her chest. "Bingo—346," she whispered.

"That's got to be it!" exclaimed Carol excitedly.

Ava clicked on the link, and seconds later, they were staring at the ornately written words "Prestige Fine Arts Auction Company," and beneath the company name was a very familiar logo of the Mona Lisa and Julius Caesar.

"We found it!" whispered Ava.

"Ava, if my hunch is right, and my hunchiness meter is feeling extremely hunchy, we've just found out who stole the diamonds."

"Your hunchiness is strong, my friend," Ava said. "So you think they're gonna try to sell the diamonds at a private auction? Seems gutsy... and dumb."

"I don't think they would be dumb enough to risk auctioning them. Especially since they were just stolen. I think they have something more creative in mind."

"Similar to my FedEx idea?"

"Very similar," nodded Carol, "but it's not so simple. FedEx takes x-rays of all their packages, so it's too big a risk. Plus, what if the diamonds got lost or stolen by an unscrupulous employee?"

"And we already said that you can't hide them on your person or in your luggage."

"Right," agreed Carol, "because you have to go through Customs. The x-ray machine would definitely spot those. But, and this is a big but—"

Ava snorted. "Sorry, you have to admit that's funny."

Carol sighed and continued, "What if the theft is tied to the billionaire your mom is researching? I mean, think about it. It's the perfect plan. Steal the diamonds, hide them in a priceless antique and then ship them out of the country, hidden inside."

"It's an amazing theory," said Ava. "How do we find out which auction he is bidding on? If you look, they have half a dozen auctions, and then two private auctions."

"Right there," said Carol, jabbing her index finger at the screen. "Click the *Scheduled Auctions* link." The girls waited for the page to load. "Scroll down a little. Stop!" Carol exclaimed. "No! They only list the dates for the public auctions."

"Oh yeah, it says private auctions by invitation only."

"It makes sense. Private auctions wouldn't be very private if the public could see all the details. My guess is they have a select group of people that they work with to ensure secrecy."

"What about this?" asked Ava. "It says auction manifest."

"Manifest? That's usually a list of items. You know, like a ship would have a manifest of what's onboard."

Ava tapped the touchpad on her laptop. A PDF began to open, but then a password window appeared over it. "Never mind, it's password protected," moaned Ava.

"Let me see that," said Carol. She spun the laptop around. "Sorry for commandeering your laptop. Wow," she said staring at the screen, "that's some pretty weak protection."

"Maybe, we could call them and get some information about the auctions," offered Ava.

"Probably not. I mean, they would probably tell you about the public auctions but… I have a better idea," said Carol, a gleam in her eyes.

"You're not going to—"

"Hack them? No. No. No," Carol chuckled. "I'm just going to test how secure their webpage is. Later, if they're not involved in criminal activity, we'll let them know how they can improve their web security. I'm actually doing them a favor."

"And my mom thinks *I'm* the one she has to keep an eye on."

"It's always the quiet ones," snickered Carol. She quickly connected to her home computer and shared the screen. She opened a terminal window and began typing. "I have a text document that has millions of words on it, starting with the letter A. I'll run a program that will test every word on my list to see if it's the same as their password."

"What if it's not on your list?" asked Ava.

"Then we'll try something else." Carol pressed the start button. Instantly, the screen filled with the auction company's URL address and words from Carol's text list. "This could take a couple hours. They most likely have an alphanumeric password."

"I'm guessing that means a combination of letters and numbers."

"You got it. Those are the hardest to—never mind," Carol shook her head in disbelief. "We're in. Their password is literally P@55w0rd."

Carol clicked *OK*, and the password window disappeared. A second later, an official-looking PDF document opened. The header read "Prestige Fine Arts Auction Company." Beneath the header was "Lot 1422."

"Ava," said Carol, stunned. "We've got him!"

"What do you mean we've got him?" asked Ava, confused.

"Look at what the first item on the manifest is: Chopin's Camille Pleyel piano!" Carol's eyes dropped down to the next item on the auction list:

autographed *Prelude Number Four*. "That's the same piano your mom was telling us about!"

"Yeah, that's *way* too much of a coincidence. Does it say when the auction is going to take place?"

"No, it says they will receive an email with a link to the private bidding portal twenty-four hours before the auction."

"Are you able to get into their emails?" asked Ava.

"No, that requires access to their server. All I did was access their website. Accessing their email client is a whole different ballgame."

"So what do we do? The auction could be tomorrow and then we'll be too late." Carol fell back into her seat and closed her eyes, deep in thought. "We've got to find out where they're going to hide the diamonds and stop them!"

"Everything okay in here?" asked Ava's mom, poking her head through the doorway, a twinge of concern on her face.

Carol jumped at Mrs. Clarke's voice, almost flipping the chair over backward.

"I'm sorry, Carol. I didn't mean to startle you," laughed Ava's mom.

"It's okay," said Carol, recovering. "I was just deep in thought."

"You guys have been at this for quite some time. How about some dinner? Perhaps Burrito Gordito?"

"*Burrito Gordito es mi favorito!*" exclaimed Ava. "I've been sitting so long I can no longer feel my legs. My buttocks are tingling."

Ava's mom shook her head and sighed. "Carol, would you like to come to dinner with us? Or perhaps you'd rather escape while you still can?"

"That sounds great, Mrs. Clarke. Thank you."

"So, you're picking the *escape while you can* choice?" laughed Ava's mom.

"Yep!" smiled Carol.

Ava placed her hand dramatically over her heart. "It's shattered. Broken into tiny, tiny pieces," she whispered. She closed her eyes and then opened one, just a smidge, so she could see Carol's reaction.

"Fine," said Carol, shaking her head. "I'll come to dinner with you."

"Really? I could have cared less," said Ava with a shrug. "Youth today, so easily manipulated."

8
OPERATION ANACONDA

Location: Burrito Gordito, Mexican restaurant, 5:45 p.m.

"There I was, in the belly of a giant metal anaconda, surrounded by microscopic bacterial organisms!" Ava's dad paused to take a bite of his beef burrito.

"Dad, weren't you in the ventilation system at an aquarium?"

"Don't knock my dramatic flair," smiled her dad. "Look, you don't make it on the Discovery Channel by being boring. You could help, you know, by adding some dramatic music."

"That would be Carol. She could mesmerize any audience with her haunting woodwind overtures," said Ava, pointing her burrito at her friend.

"Oh my God, Ava, let your dad finish! I for one am on the edge of my seat, Mr. Clarke."

"More like the edge of insanity…," muttered Ava, she turned to her dad. "You're a marine biologist…. Aren't you supposed to be researching things involving um, I don't know, water?"

"If you'd let me finish my story, everything will make sense!" exclaimed Mr. Clarke.

"Let your father have his moment," said Ava's mother, patting her hand.

"He's gonna get exasperated, isn't he? I hate it when he gets exasperated. Last Christmas, it was that cheerful story he told about Legionnaires disease that made the holiday so much lovelier."

"I know," her mother smiled. "I'm sure this one ends on a much happier note… right, Charles?" She gave him that special look that meant *happy ending or we're having meatloaf the rest of the week.*

"Yes, of course, dear. I do hope you know that you've completely destroyed the momentum of my story…. Now, where was I?"

"In the belly of the avocado…," muttered Ava.

"Anaconda! Ah, yes! My headlamp began to flicker, sweat poured down my face, and then I realized my egregious mistake. I had left the Q-tip swabs in my pocket. Not to be deterred, and thanks to my years of yoga—using the *soaring eagle tilts its wings* technique, I maneuvered in such a way that I was able to retrieve the swabs from my pocket!"

"Way to go, Mr. Clarke!" beamed Carol.

"Thank you, Carol," he nodded appreciatively. "I reached out slowly, my hands shaking. What crazed organism inhabited this metallic serpent?"

"It's a question we are all asking ourselves," winked Ava.

"With expert precision, I collected the deadly samples and began crawling backward! Just in time too, because the huge exhaust fan at the end of the ventilation system kicked in. A quick side note, I was having a brilliant hair day until then…."

"So, I'm glad you survived, Dad. Your story is truly epic. I believe the table next to us was enthralled too."

Ava's dad looked at the table beside them. An Indian family rewarded him with a smattering of applause. "Thank you," he said graciously, acknowledging their gratitude. "So, I know you are all wondering what evil pathogen I discovered."

"Yes," whispered Carol.

"Yes," chorused the Indian family, leaning forward in their seats.

"It turned out to be…," he paused dramatically, "the nefariously evil, Stachybotrys!"

"Ohhh," exclaimed the Indian woman in a high-pitched voice. She dropped her fork to her plate with a clatter as her husband patted her hand.

"Horrible," the man whispered.

Ava's father nodded. "Yes, indeed."

"I'm sorry, stackybots what?" asked Ava.

"Black mold. The staff at the aquarium kept getting sick with crazy respiratory problems, and no one could figure out why. I had a hunch that it could be the air they were breathing in. Sure enough, their ventilation system was filled with it. I don't like to brag—modesty and my doctoral ethics prevents me from doing so—but I'm pretty sure I saved their lives."

Another smattering of applause erupted from the Indian family.

Mr. Clarke accepted their platitudes graciously by nodding and mouthing *thank you*.

"Great job, Dad," said Ava, beaming proudly. "A real-world example of biology in action!"

"Great story, Mr. Clarke," smiled Carol. "Excuse me, I'll be right back." She pushed her chair from the table and headed toward the restroom.

"Great. See, Dad? Your story gave her indigestion."

"That's ludicrous," said Mr. Clarke, brushing away Ava's comment. "Carol's very astute and simply appreciates *quality* storytelling."

Ava's mind drifted away from the dinner table as her parents settled into a conversation about work and current events. She felt guilty not sharing everything that she and Carol had discovered with her parents, but they were so close to solving the mystery. Ava jumped as her phone vibrated against her leg.

Her eyes flew up to her parents, expecting them to ask her why she jumped, but they were deep into their conversation and hadn't noticed.

Ava needed to get her phone out without being seen. There was one rule that her parents enforced, NO PHONES AT THE TABLE!

She tried covering her phone with the black cloth napkin, but she couldn't see the message. She looked around, and then her eyes narrowed. "Ma'am," she called out to the waitress who was wiping down a table across from her. "May I have a dessert menu?"

The waitress smiled. "Just one?"

Her parents looked up, trying to catch up to Ava's conversation. "Good point. You may want to bring three. My parents love coffee with their ice cream."

"Thank you, Ava, that was really thoughtful," smiled her mom.

"You're welcome," Ava returned the smile.

The waitress returned with the menus. Ava's mom thanked her, and soon, everyone's attention was turned to perusing the delicious desserts. As her parents focused on a sugary delicacy, Ava stealthily slid her phone out of her pocket. She clicked on the text message. Carol had sent a picture of the top of a large industrial building, and under it were the words "Prestige Fine Arts Auction Company."

Ava stared at the picture of the top of the building and texted back, "How far away is that bathroom?"

A moment later, Ava's phone buzzed again. "Your dad gave me the idea. It's our way into the building. Their ventilation system."

"Are you sending me all of this from a bathroom stall?"

"Yes. I was sitting here, thinking."

"You want us to break into the prestige auction house? And my mom thinks you are the responsible one."

"Do you want to stop the thieves?"

"Of course, but can we just talk about this when we get back to my house…"

"It's the only way, Aves. We'll call it, *Operation Anaconda!*" Carol texted back.

Ava could hear Carol's voice in her head, bubbling over with excitement. "Are you returning to the table anytime soon, or should I have a care package sent to the restroom?"

"Care package sounds great, stall number three."

9
CAROL GETS A CHANCE TO VENT

Carol stared out the car window, willing Ava's dad to drive more quickly. *I should have insisted on him getting the double espresso.* It was already 7:15 p.m. and getting dark outside. In order for her master plan to succeed, they needed to get to the auction house fast, without Ava's parents finding out.

"You girls are mighty quiet. Everything okay back there?" Ava's mom turned toward the girls, leaning between the front seats.

"Yes. I'm in the midst of a food coma," Ava moaned. "I think the double-layer chocolate fudge cake with two scoops of vanilla ice cream did me in. I may find the closest lake and beach myself on the shore."

"You should have split it with Carol like your dad and I did. The cinnamon apple pie was perfect for two people."

"I believe that splitting a dessert in Massachusetts is breaking some sort of town ordinance," Ava replied.

"Definitely against the law," Carol agreed. "It's under the Dessert Sharing Act of 1812. I believe it reads, 'Desserts are not to be shared, anyway, anyhow.'"

"I believe it was amended in 1813 by the Romantic Couples Act," laughed Mrs. Clarke. "I believe it now reads, 'Sharing is caring.'"

"Good one, Mrs. Clarke," Carol grinned.

"Ugh," Ava leaned her forehead against the cool glass of the car window.

"Tonight's a great telescope night," said Ava's dad as they pulled into their driveway. Carol looked up through the moonroof. Even with the front porch light and spotlights illuminating the entire front of the house, they could clearly see the stars.

Ava smiled. "Dad, you're right." She turned to Carol. "We could set up the tent and the telescope. We could tell ghost stories."

Carol caught on to Ava's ruse immediately. "I love that idea. We haven't moon and planet watched in forever!"

"Is it okay if we set up the tent tonight in the backyard?" Ava asked. "We haven't camped out for like months, and it's gonna be cold soon."

"Fine with me," said her dad. "You know me, I never get in the way of you exploring nature... unless you were climbing into an active volcano. That's where I draw the line."

"I lava you, Dad," smiled Ava.

"I lava you, too," he said, erupting with laughter.

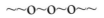

Ava and Carol made a big show of being excited about setting up the tent. They brought out a star guide and a notebook so they could do some sketching. Ava's mom made delicious popcorn cooked in olive oil and sea salt, making the entire house smell edible.

Ava put the popcorn in a freezer bag to keep it fresh and grabbed four juice boxes. Her parents had retired to the living room to watch *You've Got Mail* for the fiftieth time.

"Good night, Mom. Good night, Dad." Ava leaned over and gave each of her parents a hug. "I have my phone, so I'll text you around 3 a.m. if I get lonely."

"Oh wait," said her father as he jumped up from the sofa. He opened the closet and pulled out the largest flashlight Ava had ever seen. "This is the Thor 2000." He cradled it in his arms. "Their motto is 'Put the Hammer Down on Darkness.' I'm not really sure what that means, but this flashlight packs twelve thousand lumens. It will literally turn night to day."

"Thank you, Dad," said Ava as she looked at the huge, clunky flashlight.

"Wield her with care," her father warned. He dropped the flashlight with a *thunk* into Ava's arms.

"Okay, Dad, thank you. I may need Carol to help me carry it back to the tent."

"It's got some weight to it," Mr. Clarke agreed.

"Oh, look, here on the side, says it may be used as a boat anchor."

"Really? Oh, funny, you're messing with me." He leaned in and gave Ava a hug. "Have fun tonight. We'll leave one of the windows unlocked for you," he teased.

"Make sure it's on the second floor. I love a good challenge."

"Will do," laughed Mr. Clarke as he turned back toward the living room. "Love you," he called over his shoulder.

"Love you too, Dad."

Ava hurried over to help Carol who was busy setting up the telescope. "Smart plan, smuggling out the laptop with the sleeping bag," she said.

"Thanks," said Ava. "My parents are busy watching a romantic movie. They'll most likely fall asleep right after that. What's the plan?"

Carol motioned for Ava to follow her into the tent. "Can I use your laptop?" she asked.

"Sure. My laptop, your laptop."

"Thanks," said Carol, flipping open the lid and firing up Google. "Your dad's story about the ventilation system made me realize we could do the same thing to get into the auction house. But I need to check a few things to make sure it will work." Carol logged into Middleville's Building Department system.

"Let me guess, you're searching to see if a teenager can fit into a ventilation shaft," said Ava.

"Close," nodded Carol.

"Really? Because I was just—" Carol turned the laptop so Ava could see the screen. "Contractors have to file their blueprints with the Building Department, and once they do, they become public record," she explained. "This will tell me everything I need to know about the building."

"How the heck do you know that?" inquired Ava, impressed.

"What does my dad do?" Carol typed in the address of Prestige Fine Arts Auction Company.

"He designs houses and buildings… your dad's an architect."

"So, I am logging in as my dad into the Building Department to find the blueprints for the auction company."

"You're so smart. How does your brain even fit inside that misshapen head?"

"I'll explain density and mass to you later," winked Carol. "I found the blueprint. There are three different entries from the roof." Carol traced her finger along the drawing of the rooftop. "One leads to what looks like a series of offices, the second to restrooms, and the third," she paused to take a closer look, "leads to a small, reinforced room with a massive cement slab. And that only means one thing."

"They have a tiger?" inquired Ava.

"No, you nut, it means they have a safe. They put huge cement slabs down and then attach the safe to them. I betcha a gazillion dollars that's where they are hiding the diamonds."

"You think that they would actually keep the diamonds there?"

"Where else would they hide them?"

"I don't know, a super-secret warehouse somewhere."

"Look, we're dealing with corrupt businessmen. We've already made several important connections. The truck at the scene of the crime. The man your mother is doing the story on and the fact that he is involved in an auction."

"Okay, let's say they have the diamonds. Why not call the police and tell them, we think the diamonds are in that safe?"

"Do you honestly think the police are going to listen to us? Plus, they'll have to get a search warrant. There're just too many ways things could go wrong."

"I always thought I was the one that would get us grounded for life."

"We're not going to get caught. I simply need to get into the ventilation system, get into a computer, grab the information that I need, and then we're out of there."

"That easy, huh?" Ava said, looking doubtful.

"I've been crawling around construction sites my entire life. I've got this!"

Ava was quiet for a moment. She looked at the blueprint again. "You said that narrow rectangular thing is the ventilation system?"

Carol nodded. "Mm-hmm."

"How big is it?"

Carol scanned the blueprint. "Twenty-eight inches by twenty-two inches and it slants on about a forty-five-degree angle. So," she said, standing and creating a box with her arms and hands, "about this big."

"Keep holding that imaginary box. I want to see something," said Ava. She ducked under Carol's arms, then stood up inside the virtual rectangle. "That's a tight fit," said Ava, worriedly.

"Look, it's not going to be a problem," said Carol. "I've helped my dad on tons of projects. Leave the ventilation exploration to me."

Ava wasn't about to put up an argument on that one. "The building is two stories. How do you propose we get to the roof?" Ava asked.

"I haven't figured that one out yet. They have a fire escape on the second floor on each side of the building. We just need to be able to get to it, and it's about twelve feet off the ground."

"We also have to get there," said Ava, "and it's like six miles away."

Carol sat and thought. "Rope?" she suddenly blurted out. "We throw it up to the fire escape and climb up it."

"Perfect," said Ava, "I'll just run inside and get my grappling hook. Oh, wait a minute, my grandmother borrowed it."

"What about a ladder?" suggested Carol.

"Could work but would be really suspicious-looking and incredibly hard to carry on two bikes."

"Wait a second," said Carol. "You're going to hate the idea, but it will work."

"Well then, by all means, please share," laughed Ava.

"My dad showed me how to make a makeshift ladder. The only drawback is you and I are going to have to ride six miles with a board that is ten feet long and weighs about thirty pounds."

"Enlighten me about this board you speak of," Ava said, narrowing her eyes.

"I'll do better than that, I'll show you," Carol smiled.

"Sounds like an adventure," smiled Ava excitedly. "I have a great idea—be right back." She snuck quietly into her house, being careful not to make a sound. While tiptoeing upstairs, she grabbed her backpack, her GoPro and head-strap. She paused as she left her room while whispering, "I love you, Mom. I love you, Dad." She silently crept down the stairs and out the door.

"My great idea," said Ava as she pulled the GoPro from her backpack.

"Oh, that is an awesome idea! Okay, we need to get a few things from my dad's workshop. Come on."

They then ran through the darkness down the street to Carol's house. All the lights were off except for the front porch and two large spotlights that illuminated the front of her dad's giant two-car garage. From somewhere down the street, a deep, throaty *woof, woof* echoed through the night.

The girls crept cautiously down the sidewalk. Carol motioned Ava to follow her as she opened the side door to the building. Carol flicked on her flashlight app, illuminating the interior of her father's workshop. The back of the building was filled with power tools, a giant drill press, a table saw, and lots of lumber. Carol searched through the stacks until she found the board she was looking for.

"Here," she said, lifting the ten-foot-long board. "This will be the base of our ladder."

They laid the board out in the yard beside the garage. Carol looked in her dad's scrap pile filled with small pieces of cut wood. She packed her backpack with half a dozen pieces. Then, she grabbed two rolls of duct tape, a pair of pliers, an adjustable wrench, a flathead screwdriver, a Phillips-head screwdriver, and a coil of rope.

"Geez," whispered Ava, "are you starting your own Home Depot?"

"Trust me," said Carol thoughtfully. "We'll need this stuff."

Ava watched as Carol took the blocks of wood that she had gathered from the scrap pile and duct-taped them one by one onto the ten-foot board. When she was done, she had five pieces of board placed about a foot apart down the length of the board.

At the top, she attached a board horizontally, making the final addition look like a very tall T. She stepped back and admired her work. "This is how we're going to get to the top of the auction building."

"Okay," said Ava. "Care to explain?"

"Yep, it's a makeshift ladder. You lean this against the building, and the T at the top keeps it from wiggling back and forth. The small boards I taped on act as steps."

"Big brain, you're brilliant," said Ava. "I'm impressed!"

"Thanks," laughed Carol. "The other tools are just in case I need them in the ventilation system. All right," said Carol as she checked her phone. "It's 10:07 p.m., and we have an appointment with a ventilation shaft!"

Ava and Carol quickly checked to make sure they had everything they needed, grabbed the makeshift ladder, and silently raced back to Ava's house to grab their bikes. Operation Anaconda was officially launched!

10
CHOPIN'S LAST CONCERTO

Carrying a ten-foot ladder by bike for six miles was no easy task, but the girls made good time. Middleville was slightly larger than Livingston, but thankfully, not many people were out during this time of night.

A cool evening breeze was blowing as the girls pulled up to a small park, directly across the street from Prestige Fine Arts Auction Company.

"We made it," Ava kept her voice low.

They quickly checked their surroundings and then hid their bikes, laying them down in a small clump of trees. They broke off some low-hanging branches to cover their bikes as an extra precaution. The last thing they needed was to have their bikes stolen in the middle of their mission.

Prestige Fine Arts Auction Company seemed out of place in Middleville—a small, historic town founded in 1786. Amongst houses of stone and red brick stood a modern geometric spectacle. The walls were made of perfectly polished gray stone, with long, narrow, rectangular windows across the top. The roof jutted out like slices of bread in all different angles. Bright orange light emanated from within, illuminating the building like a huge candle. Outside, the parking lot looked like a virtual forest of perfectly pruned ficus trees bathed in a white glow, illuminated by dozens of security spotlights.

"Okay," said Carol as she looked at the auction building. "According to the blueprints, there is a fire escape on each side of the building."

"That building is huge. And it's super well lit… and we didn't have time to do reconnaissance, so we have no idea what type of security they have."

"Well," said Carol, watching as two cars drove past, "let's get the ladder across the street and hide by those trees." She pointed to the edge of the auction house's parking lot. "It's the darkest area, and we can watch for a few minutes and see if we see anyone."

"Okay," Ava nodded and checked out the road that separated them from the parking lot. "All clear." They grabbed the ladder, bolted across the road, and dropped down behind a cluster of bushes and trees, deep in the shadows.

"Okay," said Carol. "We'll watch for ten minutes. Hopefully, they're—"

"In a golf cart, heading this way," whispered Ava urgently.

The girls dropped flat to the ground as two men in black shirts with black hats that read "Security" passed within ten feet of them. A spotlight, mounted to the top of the golf cart, swept back and forth, creating a wide swath of light in front of them.

Luckily, the men were more interested in their conversation than what was going on around them. Ava and Carol slowly raised their heads above the bushes and watched the golf cart move away from them to the side of the building. One of the guards got out and shone his light behind a huge dumpster, and then up the fire escape. Satisfied, he got back on the cart with his partner. They drove the length of the building—red brake lights flashing—and then disappeared around the back.

"Okay," said Ava quietly. "That answers the security question."

"I wonder how long it takes them to make their loop."

"Good question. We better time them, just to make sure. I'd hate to say that I got chased down by security guards in a golf cart."

"True," said Carol. "Almost as bad as a Segway cop at the mall." She looked down at her watch. "They've been gone one minute so far."

"Get down!" whispered Ava urgently, yanking Carol's shoulder. They just missed being lit up like Christmas trees as a black Mercedes pulled into the parking lot. They watched as the car made its way to the main entrance of the building.

The front door of the building swung open, and a man briskly walked out to the car. Two men in dark suits emerged from the vehicle. The man shook the driver's hand and then shook the other man's hand as they came together in a small huddle. The man from the auction house gestured to the entranceway and escorted them inside.

"Geez, that was close. That's another thing we'll have to be aware of," whispered Carol. "Surprise guests!"

Three minutes later, the girls could see the lights coming from the golf cart. The security guards weren't as unobservant as the girls had thought. They made a beeline across the parking lot to inspect the new vehicle. They parked their golf cart behind the Mercedes so it couldn't back away. One of the guards touched his ear and spoke.

"I bet he's checking on the car," whispered Carol.

Ava nodded. "They don't mess around."

"Especially when you're protecting millions of dollars of inventory."

The security guard nodded, said something to his partner, then resumed their loop. Once again, the girls dropped silently to the ground. The golf cart came within twenty feet of the girls. It was so close, they could hear the guards talking about the upcoming Patriots game.

"All right, Aves," said Carol nervously. "As soon as those taillights disappear around the corner, we run to that stairwell. We'll have about three and a half minutes—that's it."

Just as before, the golf cart came to a stop in front of the fire escape. This time the other guard jumped out, first shining his light behind the dumpster and then checking out the fire escape. Seconds later, the taillights flickered, disappearing around the corner of the building.

"Okay." Electricity pumped through Carol's body. "We're gonna have to be fast and furious. Let's go!"

The girls stood and quickly checked their surroundings. "Go!" exhaled Ava.

Crouched low, they ran to the side of the building.

"We're down thirty seconds," said Carol, ticking off the time in her head.

Ava's heart beat like the drum of a heavy metal band. Even though she knew they had about three more minutes, she couldn't help looking over her shoulders every two seconds.

Carol lifted the board vertically and leaned it against the wall. "Hold the bottom secure!" she said firmly.

"Got it." Ava crouched down and gripped the makeshift ladder.

Carol didn't hesitate. She carefully stepped onto the first wooden board and slowly made her way to the top. Once her shoulders were level with the bottom of the fire escape, she grabbed the support bars. Then, while moving her feet to the top of the ladder, she pulled herself to safety. She looked at her watch. "Two minutes, Ava," she called out. "Hurry!"

Carol lay flush on the cold metal floor of the fire escape. She grabbed the top of the ladder as Ava began climbing. "You got this," Ava whispered as she fought to stop her hands and feet from shaking her right off the ladder. Her brain ping-ponged between *you're gonna make it* and *you're gonna fall and break every bone in your body.*

"Come on!" Carol encouraged her. "You've got this. Come on!" The board wobbled and bowed as Ava climbed, but finally, she arrived at the top. She grabbed the fire escape, and with Carol's help, she pulled herself to safety.

They grabbed the ladder and pulled it onto the platform with them. "One minute left," Carol whispered. In the distance, they could see the golf cart's light making its orbit of the parking lot.

Carol placed the ladder against the building and began climbing to the rooftop. A few seconds later, she was on the roof looking down at Ava.

Ava glanced over her shoulder. It was too late—the golf cart was heading their way! "They're here!" whispered Ava, panicking.

"Ava, get on that board and climb NOW!" hissed Carol through clenched teeth.

Ava grasped the bottom of the ladder. She looked over her shoulder—the cart was about fifty feet away and rapidly closing in. Ava concentrated—one hand at a time, one foot at a time. She looked up when she felt Carol's hand around her wrist.

"Come on!" whispered Carol urgently.

The guard was out of the cart. He shone his flashlight at the dumpster, then turned the beam toward the fire escape. "The ladder!" whispered Carol, her eyes wide with panic.

Ava grabbed the ladder and jerked it upward. The bottom banged the metal railing of the fire escape. Both guards were out of the cart now, shining their lights upward. Ava and Carol lay perfectly still, not daring to look over the ledge. Their makeshift ladder lay beside them.

They could hear them talking and see the guards' flashlights probing the fire escape and the side of the building. It seemed like an eternity, but finally the guards seemed satisfied that nothing was amiss… and drove off.

Ava crept slowly to the edge of the building and looked down. "They're gone," she whispered. A look of relief washed over Carol's face.

"That was close!" Carol said.

"Too close," Ava breathed. Her entire body was trembling. She stared at the sky—a narrow strand of clouds stretched like taffy across the moon. She took a moment to control her breathing. Carol was motioning her to follow her. Ava uttered up a small prayer of thanks and then took off across the rooftop.

Carol stopped and knelt in front of a shiny metallic structure that looked like a small house. "According to the blueprints, this is the ventilation system that will lead me to the room with the safe," said Carol matter-of-factly.

"Be careful…," said Ava quietly, her face filled with concern. "Just like at the museum… I'll stay in touch with you by phone."

"I will," said Carol. Ava helped her fasten the GoPro on her head, and then clipped a small penlight to the side of the head strap.

"Oh my God, Carol, you look just like a spy!"

"I feel like a spy, or a spelunker. I'm going to go with spy." She unscrewed the eight screws that secured the aluminum housing to the rooftop. The vent was pitch black, but plenty wide for Carol's tall, narrow frame.

Ava helped Carol scoot into the opening to the ventilation system. "Good luck," said Ava. She tried to hide the worry in her voice.

Carol looked up, smiled, and gave Ava a thumbs-up. "They'll never know I was here!" She spread her legs to brace herself, wedged her feet against the aluminum walls of the duct system, and began slowly lowering herself downward.

A million thoughts ran through Carol's mind as she descended. She knew that the ventilation system was only about forty feet long, but it seemed like it was a mile. The duct system ran downward at a manageable angle, and then for the last eight feet, dropped nearly straight down.

Carol wedged her arms and her feet against the walls of the duct and slowly maneuvered herself down to where the ventilation system made the eight-foot vertical drop. Wedging her sneakers against the sides of the shaft, she slowly shifted her bodyweight from side to side, inching down until she finally reached the bottom.

She sat quietly, listening. She had done her best to be silent on her descent, but it wasn't easy, especially when you combine rubber-soled sneakers and aluminum. But all was quiet. She gently pulled out her phone and whispered, "I made it. Everything is okay!"

Ava let out a sigh of relief when she heard Carol's voice. She had been crawling along the rooftop, keeping track of the security detail and watching to see if any other visitors arrived. So far, except for the very predictable orbit of the security guards, all else was quiet.

Carol crouched down in front of the air-conditioning vent and listened. The secure room was silent and dark, except for a bright red light that stared at her like a cyclops. Using her penlight, she counted six screws. "Okay," she whispered as she wiped her hands off on her pants. She slowly unscrewed the first screw. *That was easy.* She held the screw in her left hand and was starting on the second when she heard footsteps approaching. She flicked off her penlight and closed her eyes as the room was flooded with powerful, bright fluorescent lights.

She listened intently, willing her heart to slow down. The door to the room whooshed open and men's voices filled the air. She heard a heavy thud followed by the sound of a metallic locking device.

"The Captain will be proud," laughed a deep voice. "A priceless piano, Chopin's last handwritten concerto, and the coup de grâce, the Ramesses diamonds." Carol silently pressed the *Record* button on the GoPro.

"The piano is absolutely gorgeous, a spectacular piece," said a high, nasally voice.

Carol scrunched down as much as humanly possible and peaked through the vent. She could see four men in the room. A tall, wispy man in a dark suit, with black hair streaked with silver, was rubbing his hand across the piano. She guessed the high-pitched voice belonged to him.

Another man, whom Carol guessed was the second man from the Mercedes, was grinning from ear to ear. His bald head glistened like a light bulb in the brightly lit room.

Carol silently removed the GoPro from her head and aligned it with an opening in the vent. She could have kicked herself—she missed the part where they had talked about Ramesses's diamonds.

"The piano itself is worth close to ten million dollars," said the deep-voiced man, "and the concerto should easily fetch close to a million."

"All incredibly amazing and appreciated," said the nasally man. "I was told you have an ingenious plan for delivering the diamonds?"

"Ah, yes," laughed the deep-voiced man. He smiled mischievously. "You see, this piano comes with a secret."

Carol could see the man with the deep voice clearly now. He wore a charcoal gray suit that matched his salt-and-pepper, closely shaved hair.

"You see," he laughed, "Chopin's last concerto will actually deliver the diamonds to your client."

Carol watched the thin man's face fill with confusion. "I'm not sure what you mean."

"George, show Mr. Snow our little secret."

Carol gasped as a man sat at the piano. She recognized him from the museum. It was George, the security guard!

"Yes, Mr. Roach."

George sat at the piano and played a series of notes: *da, da, da, da, dah, dah, dah, duh, da, da, da, da duh.* Suddenly, a tiny drawer about the size of a cell phone slid open.

"Just let the Captain know that he merely needs to play the first thirteen notes of the concerto, and his diamonds will appear," smiled Mr. Roach. George gently tapped the front of the drawer, and it slid back into place.

"That's brilliant," gasped Mr. Snow.

"The hidden mechanism is so perfectly designed that it will not show up on any x-ray. It'll merely look like the innerworkings of the piano."

"This is perfect," gasped the nasally guest, clasping his hand in delight. "And the diamonds… they are safe?"

"Yes, the diamonds will be inside a foam pouch made of high-Z foam, which actually blocks and scatters x-rays. We are taking every precaution necessary to protect them."

"So, the diamonds will be hidden in the piano when you transport it to the auction tomorrow?" asked the bald man, needing reassurance.

"When we deliver the piano and the other items to the private auction tomorrow, everything will be in place for immediate shipment. We'll place the diamonds in the piano before everything is moved to the armored car tomorrow. Tell the Captain that we have arranged for a direct flight of a cargo jet from Hanscom Airport to a private airstrip in Ireland."

"I will let the Captain know. He will be most pleased," said the nasally man, his voice quivering with excitement.

"I'm sure he will," said the deep-voiced man. "Shall we?" he said, motioning toward the door.

The group of men walked toward the door. There was a loud metallic click and then a whoosh as the door swung open. "When can we expect delivery?" Carol wasn't sure who the voice belonged to. She thought it sounded like the bald man.

Just before the door slammed shut, she heard someone say, "We're leaving at noon." Carol sat motionless, waiting another few seconds, and then turned on her penlight. She had everything she needed.

Ava jumped when she heard Carol's voice. "I'm on my way," she whispered breathily.

Ava closed her eyes. Those were the best four words she'd ever heard! "Awesome. Climb carefully!" she whispered, her voice filled with excitement. The electronic *chirp, chirp* of a car unlocking made Ava jump. She quickly traversed the rooftop in a semi-crouch position, not because she had to, but because she thought it looked cool.

Cautiously, she peered over the edge. The super-sleek security golf cart had pulled to a halt in the parking lot. The two guards watched as the Mercedes backed up and pulled away. The guard at the wheel touched his ear. Ava was close enough to hear, "They've left. All's clear." Then, with a high-pitched whine, the golf cart pulled away from the curb to begin another orbit around the auction house.

"Ava," a voice whispered.

Ava jumped back from the edge of the building. She clutched her heart. She was pretty sure it had leapt out of her body and was sprinting away to safety without her. She whirled around to find Carol crouched down behind her. "Geesh, what are you, part cat? I didn't even hear you."

Carol put her hand on her friend's shoulder. "Ava," she whispered breathlessly, "they have the diamonds."

"What? Wait, you saw them? Did you get the diamonds?!" she asked, grabbing her friend's shoulders excitedly.

"No, listen! They're going to hide them in a secret compartment in Chopin's piano."

"That's crazy," Ava whispered. "Then it *is* the dude from Ireland. So, he'll buy the piano at auction, the diamonds will be inside, then it's shipped to him in Ireland?"

"Yes, and since he knows that there are millions of dollars in the piano, he'll feel comfortable outbidding everyone else."

"You've got to admit, it's a pretty good way to smuggle goods out of the U.S."

"Oh, I almost forgot, they refer to the billionaire in Ireland as the Captain."

"Captain?" snorted Ava, rolling her eyes. "For real?"

"It's horrible, I know," Carol smiled.

"We've solved the case, Big Brain. I think we should call the police?"

"Eh… We will…," Carol paused.

"I know that pause," said Ava, giving her an apprehensive look.

"Hear me out. I have a good reason to wait. They're going to hide the diamonds in the piano, right?"

Ava nodded, "According to what you heard."

"Then, they're putting the piano in an armored car. I think that when the piano is safe in the armored car, that's when we bring the cavalry in."

Ava thought for a moment. "I see what you're saying," she agreed. "It's easy for the bad guys to hide something small in a building this big."

Carol nodded in agreement. "Right. If it's safe and secure in the armored truck, there's less chance of them vanishing again."

"So, what's our next move?"

"I'm working on that, but right now we have a bigger problem." Carol looked over the edge of the building. "How are you at climbing down?"

Ava took in a deep breath and glanced back at their makeshift ladder. "Honestly, I'd rather gargle canned tuna fish water."

The girls crept silently to the ledge just above the fire escape and waited for their favorite two guards. They lay on their stomachs, chins resting on their palms, peering over the edge of the building.

"They have the most boring job ever," whispered Carol as they watched them check behind the dumpster and the fire escape.

"They live their lives in three-minute increments. That means they circle this building twenty times an hour. One hundred sixty times in an eight-hour shift."

"They're gone. Come on! You can be scared later." And just like that, the game of cat and mouse began.

Carol held the ladder in place as Ava shakily descended to the safety of the fire escape. She returned the favor for Carol, who called down, "Two minutes!" over her shoulder as she descended.

Ava edged the ladder against the building... then watched horrified as it wobbled and fell with a loud *thud* sound to the ground. "Oh my God!" she whispered.

Carol looked at Ava, her eyes opened wide. "Our ladder! What happened?"

"It must have been on a rock or hole or something.... I couldn't see anything—it just fell."

Carol looked at her watch. "One and a half minutes!"

"Carol," said Ava, "how far is it down?"

"At least twelve feet!"

"I'm five feet. Can you drop from seven feet?"

"All day every day. Why?"

Ava climbed over the railing of the fire escape. She maneuvered until she was hanging from the bottom. "Ava, you're crazy!" shrieked Carol.

"It's seven feet from my feet to the ground. You said seven feet all day every day. Now come on!"

Ava took in a deep breath and dropped. The impact was harsh, but she relaxed her knees, fell forward and rolled. Her palms stung as they hit the pavement, but her arms were saved by the sleeves of her hoodie.

"Come on, Carol. I'll help spot you. Hurry, they are going to be here any second!" Carol climbed over the railing. This time it was *her* turn to be shaky.

Ava saw the lights from the golf cart as it started its first turn at the end of the parking lot. In a matter of seconds, it would make a beeline toward them.

"Carol, NOW!" shouted Ava through clenched teeth.

Carol dropped as Ava threw her arms around her, hoping to help slow her descent. Instead, it felt like Carol had just torn her arms out of their sockets as they both sprawled forward onto the ground.

"Ow!" moaned Carol. "I could have done without the spot."

"You're welcome," said Ava. "I'm putting you in remedial jumping classes if we ever get out of here alive!"

Carol and Ava's heads swiveled simultaneously— the golf cart was making its final turn. "We're trapped," said Carol, panicking.

"No!" shouted Ava. "Grab the ladder—you and I are about to make our cross-country coach proud!"

Carol grabbed the ladder and took off after Ava. The golf cart was getting closer. They raced along the side of the building, barely staying ahead of the headlights. They slid around the corner behind the building just as the cart came to a stop.

"They're going to check the dumpster and the fire escape," gasped Carol. "We've just got to make it back to our hiding place."

Ava grabbed the ladder from Carol. "Let's do this."

The girls clung to the shadows of the building, running as quietly as possible while carrying a ten-foot ladder.

They paused at the front of the building, gasping for air, their lungs burning. The parking lot was so bright it looked like daytime. Carol reached over and grabbed the ladder from Ava.

"My turn!" panted Carol. Ava gladly relinquished the ladder.

They raced across the parking lot to their hiding spot just as the cart came around the far corner of the building. Breathless, the girls sat and watched the golf cart complete another loop. A thought hit Ava as the guard checked behind the dumpster and then checked the fire escape. "We should have just thrown the ladder—"

"In the dumpster," interrupted Carol with a laugh. "I thought of that too."

Ava picked up her favorite ladder, and the girls quickly crossed the street. "If you don't mind," smiled Ava, "I'm going to leave your creation here until tomorrow."

"Please," said Carol. "Good riddance!"

Ava checked her phone for texts from her parents—there were none. She let out a sigh of relief. Her eyes moved to the top of the screen. It was 11:30 p.m.

"Let's get back to the tent just in case my parents check on us," said Ava. "Then, we can work on our plan of attack."

"We should also try to get a little sleep or else we'll be dead tomorrow," Carol said, "and we'll need our wits about us."

"I need all the wits I can get," smiled Ava as she climbed onto her bike. "Let's go!"

11
FINESSE, NOT FITNESS

"Down, down," whispered Ava as the shadow slowly approached their tent.

The girls quickly sprawled on top of their sleeping bags, pretending to sleep. They had made it back just in time. Five minutes earlier, Ava's father would have found an empty tent.

He pulled the mosquito netting down over the front of the tent, and as quietly as possible, zipped it closed. The girls looked tuckered out. He smiled to himself, remembering when he was young. He paused and looked at a couple of the moon sketches they had laid out for Ava's parents (a ruse just in case they got curious). He took one more look at the girls, and then disappeared back inside the house. Ava and Carol lay quietly for a few moments, listening.

Ava sat up and looked at the house. All the lights were off. "Okay," she whispered, sitting up. "What's the plan, Super Brain?"

Carol raised her hand to her mouth as she yawned. "I can tell you what we *need* to make happen. However, making it happen may take a little finesse."

"I think I've had all the finesse I can take, between biking a gazillion miles, climbing, not to mention sprinting with a huge wooden contraption."

"Finesse, Ava, not fitness. It means tweaking."

"Why didn't you just say tweaking?"

"Because it's more like careful tweaking, like skillfully changing something. Why does it matter?

What matters is the thieves are moving the piano with the diamonds to a secret location at noon tomorrow."

Ava nodded, covering her mouth with her hand as she yawned, making a *go on* gesture with the other.

"So, my plan is to get some sleep. Then call the police at the perfect time to stop the armored truck. Otherwise, we may spook the bad guys. Everything is going to require impeccable timing."

"You have proof on the GoPro, so I guess convincing them shouldn't be too difficult."

"I have compelling evidence... unfortunately, it was illegally obtained. I was thinking that I could send it to the police anonymously, but the problem is, everything has to be timed perfectly. We need the police to be at the auction house just as the bad guys are about to pull out."

Ava nodded. "If the police get there too early, the bad guys will be able to hide the diamonds. If they get there too late, the thieves will vanish to some unknown location."

"Exactly," nodded Carol. Ava felt her eyes closing. She shook her head, trying to stay awake. "I'm setting the alarm for eight-thirty," Carol opened the clock app on her phone. "That'll give us about six hours of sleep."

Ava muttered something unintelligible, her face already buried in her pillow. Carol laid back on her sleeping bag and closed her eyes. A cyclone of thoughts whipped around her brain. *There's no way I'm falling asleep tonight...* and then she did.

12
THE CAPTAIN'S CHOPIN FOR A PIANO

Ava jerked awake to Carol's phone, belting out master bassoonist Klaus Thunemann's version of "Flight of the Bumblebee." "Make it stop. Please…," whimpered Ava as she folded her pillow around her head.

"Ahh," sighed Carol. "The bassoon sounds so playful and frolicsome, don't you think? *Frisky* comes to mind. I think he captures the spirit of the bumblebee in flight, don't you?"

"I think he has captured the sound of every hope and every dream I've ever had leaving my body." Ava rolled over and glared at Carol, "Why are you so perky this morning? Be angry, like me."

"It just so happens that while you were enjoying your beauty sleep, I came up with a plan."

"Does the plan involve a brush? I've got a seriously bad combo of helmet hair and bed head, with a touch of crazy."

"We're going to need to do some reconnaissance this morning. We'll need eyes on the auction house." Ava moaned and sat up. "Oh my," Carol grabbed her phone and excitedly jabbed at the screen.

"What is it?" asked Ava, fully awake now.

"Animal Planet. They can stop searching—I've found Bigfoot!"

"You are so funny," Ava laughed, smacking Carol with her pillow.

"Okay, we've got three hours to pull all this together."

"All right," said Ava as she ripped a phone through her tangles. "What did you come up with?"

"Well, we know we can't call the police too early or too late. That means we have to be there. We need to see them put the piano in the truck."

"I kind of expected that," said Ava. "I figured we would have to be on site to let the police know when to leap into action."

"The problem is," said Carol, "the loading docks are in the back of the building."

"We're a couple of kids—no one is going to be paying any attention to us. We could just be hanging out."

"No, George might spot us," said Carol.

"George? The security guard from the museum?" Ava asked, thoroughly confused.

"That's right, I forgot to tell you!" said Carol excitedly. "George was there last night. He played the piano to open the hidden compartment."

"Hmm, makes sense now. I thought that his hands were extremely soft for a hardened criminal."

Carol grabbed Ava's laptop and flipped it open. She typed in the address for the auction company and clicked the map icon. "Bingo! There's a Starbucks directly behind it!" she exclaimed.

"Perfect," said Ava with a nod. "We can get breakfast, decaf mochas, and surveil the building at the same time."

"We'll wait until they begin loading the truck and then call the police. Middleville only has a population of about ten thousand people. It can't take the police more than five minutes to get anywhere in that town."

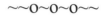

It was 10 a.m. by the time the girls had jumped on their bikes and raced toward Starbucks to set up their secret observation post. They both turned and stared at the Prestige Auction building as they pedaled by. Who would have guessed that one of the largest heists in history had occurred right here in this quiet little town?

The Starbucks parking lot was packed. For a moment, the girls panicked, wondering if they would find a seat. Luckily, it was a nice day, so they were able to find a table at the outdoor patio. A giant metal fence was all that separated them from Prestige's parking lot.

"It's weird," said Carol as she stared at the fence and beyond.

"What's weird?" asked Ava. "My natural beauty? My charisma?"

"Sure," Carol smiled, "that was exactly what I was thinking."

"I thought so," Ava laughed.

"I just think it's interesting that while everyone is sitting around enjoying their café lattes—with their faces buried in their phones—not more than one hundred feet away, stolen diamonds are about to—" Carol stopped talking.

Ava stopped drinking her mocha—a large, armored truck had just pulled up to the gate. "George," whispered Ava as she watched the tall, lanky driver jump out of the truck and jab at a security keypad on the gate.

Moments later, the armored truck rumbled to the back of the building. Ava and Carol recognized the logo: Mona Lisa mocked them with a smug, self-confident grin.

The truck beeped as it backed up to the loading dock. The brakes sighed squeakily, and the truck shuddered, coming to a stop in front of a large outcrop of cement, covered by rubber that looked like a giant car bumper. A large, metallic door at the back of the building began to noisily clank upward.

"I can't see anything!" said Carol anxiously. "The truck's blocking our view."

"Come on!" said Ava as she grabbed Carol's arm and dragged her from her seat.

The girls ran through the parking lot and then up the sidewalk that ran parallel to the Prestige auction building. They stopped alongside the fence when they were directly across from the loading dock.

"Get down, there's George," said Carol quietly as the tall security guard appeared at the back of the truck. The girls crouched behind a trashcan. "If we can see him, he can see us," Carol warned.

"Yeah, I understand how eyes work," Ava replied.

Carol dropped to her knees and peaked around the edge of the trashcan. "We're way too obvious. If anyone pulls up, they're going to know we're up to something. Plus, I can barely see anything from here."

"I have an idea. Grab your phone." Ava pulled her phone out of her pocket, and then motioned Carol to lean in closer. "Thank you," said Ava, pulling the drawstring out of Carol's hoodie.

"Why would you do that?"

"I needed it."

"You have a hoodie too, you know?"

"Use my own? Do you know how hard it is to restring these things? Can I see your phone?"

"Absolutely not," Carol gripped it tightly against her.

"Fine." Ava casually walked over to the "No Parking" sign that was located next to the fence surrounding the Prestige Auction building. Using the string from Carol's hoodie, she tied it in place, then called Carol on FaceTime. She waited until Carol answered, then smiled into the camera. "Now you can see the docking bay."

"Look," Carol said when Ava returned.

Three men dressed in blue overalls stood beside George on the delivery dock. George unlocked the back of the truck and raised the door.

"Looks like they're about to load the piano. Carol, you gotta call the police."

"I know." Carol's heart was pounding. "But if they show up too soon, the diamonds could be gone forever. We have to time this just right."

George leaned lazily against the back of the truck playing with the ends of his mustache. The three men were no longer on the dock.

"Look at him, not a care in the world. I wonder what it's like to not have a conscience."

"Once he's arrested, perhaps you can ask him," suggested Carol.

"I wonder if they'll put his massive mustache in handcuffs too."

"There's the piano," whispered Carol. The piano was completely covered in thick moving blankets. Foam padding covered the edges. The team of men in their blue uniforms were carefully maneuvering it on several dollies to the back of the truck. Carol's heart was pounding. Ava gave her a *what are you waiting for* look.

George and one of the workmen jumped onto the back of the truck while the other men cautiously moved the piano inch by inch into the bed of the truck.

"Alright," said Carol, "it's showtime." Her hands shook as she Googled Middleville Police and hit the call button.

The call was answered immediately by an extremely bored-sounding man. "Middleville Police Dispatch. How may I help you?"

"Hi, I'm calling about the diamonds that were stolen from the Hancock Museum. We know where they are." Carol felt like she was gasping for breath.

"Who am I speaking with?"

"Carol Miller. Sir, we don't have much time. They're being shipped out of the Prestige Auction Company. Please hurry."

The dispatcher's voice rapidly turned from bored to agitated. "Young lady. You do know that filing a false police report—"

"Look, I'm telling you that they have the diamonds and if you don't hurry and send.... Hello? Hello?" Carol turned to Ava completely dismayed. "He hung up on me."

Ava kept her mouth shut—she knew this was no time for an *I told you so*. She needed to figure out what to do, and fast. Then it hit her, Detective Edwards. "Carol, give me your phone. I have an idea—I'm most likely going to be grounded until I'm married, but it's gotta be done." Without a question, Carol handed her phone over. Ava jabbed in the number that her mother had made her memorize in case there was ever an emergency. She hoped for her and Carol's sake, this constituted as one of those times.

The phone rang three times before a gruff voice answered the phone. Detective Edwards.

"Mr. Edwards? It's me, Ava!" Her heart was beating so hard, she was sure he could hear it through the phone.

"Ava, are you okay?" Concern immediately filled his voice.

"Yes and no. Please listen and please believe me. I know where the diamonds are that were stolen from the museum!"

"Ava." His voice was tinged with anger. "You know that this number is *only* for emergencies...."

"Mr. Edwards, I'm not playing. You can be angry at me later, but if you don't hurry, the diamonds are going to be gone forever. We have video, we can prove it, you *have* to believe me." Ava felt dizzy as the words tumbled out of her mouth.

"Ava, where are you?" he demanded.

"We're hiding at the side of the Prestige Auction building. They've hidden the diamonds in a piano and they're about to leave."

Ava could hear the *ding, ding* of the detective's car door.

"How do you know the diamonds are in the piano? Did you see them? Ava, *did* you see them put them in there?" His voice was a mixture of frustration and concern.

"Please, Blake." Ava could feel tears of frustration coming to her eyes. "Trust me. I would never lie to you—please hurry."

"I trust you, Ava. You're just like your mother," he sighed. "Get away from the building and get to a safe place. I'm on my way."

"He's on his way," said Ava. She hurried over to the "No Parking" sign and retrieved her phone.

"They're closing the back of the truck," said Carol in a panic. "If he doesn't hurry, they're gonna get away!"

George climbed into the truck and started the engine. A huge plume of gray-white smoke billowed from the exhaust pipe. He stuck his hand out the window and gave the workmen a thumbs-up.

"This is a nightmare," declared Carol. "What do we do?"

"We could stand in front of the gate—they'd never run over us," said Ava, who was running out of ideas.

"Are you kidding? They have millions of dollars in diamonds in that truck. I don't know what they would do."

"You got a better plan?" She looked at Carol and didn't wait for an answer. She took off for the gate as the truck pulled away from the loading dock. "Come on!" she yelled.

The girls sprinted down the sidewalk as the huge white truck drove along the building, parallel to them. George turned the wheel and headed straight toward the gate.

"Make yourself look huge and menacing!" Ava cried out.

"It's a huge truck—I doubt we'd even dent his grill."

George pulled up to the gate and screeched to a stop. He jumped from the driver's side, said something to his companion and calmly walked up to the keypad to open the gate.

"Hi George, long time no see," said Ava. "How's the museum?"

George's jaw dropped. He scowled at them, quickly regaining his composure. "You two. What are you doing here?"

"I wanted to let you know we found a mate for your mustache. A friendly sea lion named Sualia."

"George, what's going on?" shouted a squat man from the passenger seat. George held up his hand signaling *just a second.* "I should have done away with you two when I had the chance." He pulled his phone out of his pocket. "Now scram before I call the police."

"No need to do that," said Carol, crossing her arms. "We've already called them. They should be here in minute now."

George eyed them suspiciously and then sneered. "Liars." He flung the door open, jumped into the truck and gunned the engine. The truck lurched toward the girls.

Ava and Carol clenched their jaws and held their ground. George's companion punched the dash and jumped out of the truck. Ava's eyes widened. The man looked like a human bowling ball—he was as wide as he was tall.

"Either you move," he said with a thick New England accent, "or I'm gonna permanently move you." He smiled, showing a mouth filled with broken, decayed teeth. Carol wished he'd saved his smile for someone else… like the dentist.

"Suit yourself!" he said angrily.

He grabbed Carol by the arm. She spun toward him, kicking him as hard as she could in the shins. Ava charged him, swinging her backpack like a ball and chain at his head.

He grabbed her backpack and hauled her in. The girls began screaming "Help!" at the top of their lungs. Carol flung her head backward as hard as she could, catching the man square in the nose. There was a loud *crack*!

"Argh!" screamed the man, who fell back while grabbing his face. Suddenly they were free!

Ava spun around and kicked the man in the unmentionables. His eyes rolled up in his head. He made a high-pitched whistling sound like a tea kettle going off as he crumpled to the ground.

"Way to go, foot!" whispered Ava.

A black police SUV came flying over the hill, blue lights flashing in the grill. George no longer seemed to care if he ran over the girls or not. He put the truck in gear and began to pull forward.

"No you don't!" yelled Ava. She flung off her backpack, dragged out the Thor 2000 and pointed it directly at George. The high-powered light struck him in the face like a laser beam. He threw up his forearm to protect his eyes, but it was too late. The truck accelerated forward just missing the girls as they dove out of the way. It flew across the street, hopped the curb, and crashed into a cluster of trees and bushes.

George kicked the door open and leapt from the truck. He tried to get away, but the Thor 2000 had done its job. Still blinded, he ran straight into a tree, and then another tree. He teetered awkwardly and then fell to the ground, clutching his forehead. He moaned as another police cruiser came flying over the hill.

A dark-haired man in a grey suit with the build of a football player ran toward them. He grabbed the girls by the shoulders. "Are you okay?" He quickly eyed them from head to toe.

"Yes. Yes, thank you, Mr. Edwards." She pointed to George, "He's the security guard from the Hancock Museum. And the human bowling ball," Detective Edwards looked in the direction Ava was pointing, "is one of his accomplices."

Detective Edwards gestured toward the rotund man, who was running down the sidewalk toward Starbucks. Two officers took off in pursuit after him.

"The diamonds are in the back of the truck," said Ava. "We couldn't call you until we knew they were there—because if we waited for you to get a warrant...."

"And the building is so big," added Carol. "We were worried they would hide or move the diamonds—and then they would be gone forever."

"It's okay, it's okay," said Detective Edwards, holding up his hand. "You two, over by my car—and..." he held up a warning finger, "do not move."

Two more police cruisers arrived on the scene. Across the Prestige Auction parking lot, a silver-haired man in a three-piece suit was making his way toward them in a golfcart.

"What do you think you're doing?" he cried, shaking his fist in the air. "This is private property. I'll have your badge."

"And you are?" asked Detective Edwards calmly.

"Renaldo White III. Owner of Prestige Auctions, taxpayer and friend of the mayor."

"Delightful. I'm Detective Edwards and I have a few questions for you. Is that your truck?" He pointed to the large, armored vehicle across the street.

Renaldo's jaw dropped. "What have you done? Do you realize that there is a piano worth millions of dollars inside?"

"I'm less concerned about the piano and more concerned that your driver attempted to run over these two girls. And his crony physically accosted them." Renaldo looked at George and the short squat man with disgust.

"Have you heard of attempted vehicular homicide, Mr. White?"

"I have," he gave Detective Edwards a surly smile. "Girls, I apologize." He turned his attention back to Detective Edwards. "These men are simply hired help. They broke the law—do what you need to do," he waved dismissively.

"Mr. White," stammered George in disbelief, "Do something!"

"I'm sorry, George," Renaldo brushed his hands together as if dusting them off. "It's out of my hands. However, I do have very good lawyers," he gave George a knowing look.

"Mr. White," Detective Edwards snapped his fingers to get his attention. "Since your truck was involved in a crime, and a crash, we're going to need to take a look at the vehicle."

"I think not. The two men were clearly in the wrong. However, the contents of the truck are not to be involved in the investigation. We're talking about historical artifacts worth millions."

"Then perhaps you should make wiser hiring decisions. Especially in this case, since the vehicle was used as a weapon. So yes, we will be examining the *contents* of the truck." Mr. White turned red with anger. "You," said Detective Edwards to George. "Where are the keys?"

"Don't answer him, George," snarled Mr. White.

"You are interfering with a police investigation," said Detective Edwards hotly. He pointed to a tall officer with fiery red hair. "Handcuff Mr. White."

"Th-they're in the truck," stammered George.

"Thank you, George." Detective Edwards trudged over to the cab of the truck, climbed inside, and retrieved the keys. He searched through the keyring and found the correct key to unlock the back of the truck. Chopin's piano sat entombed in blue moving cloths. "Ava," he called over his shoulder, "you said the diamonds were hidden in the piano?"

"Diamonds? This is preposterous!" screamed Mr. White, his face as pale as his name.

"Yes," said Carol, answering for Ava. "She has to play the first thirteen notes of Chopin's last piano concerto—then a secret drawer will open."

"Don't touch that piano! It's worth millions!" screamed Mr. White.

"We know," said Detective Edwards. "I believe you've told us a million times."

Ava climbed up into the truck and delicately removed the packing materials protecting the piano. Carol handed Ava her phone—she had loaded the first two measures of Chopin's concerto.

"See?" smiled Carol. "All those years of piano practice are about to come in handy."

"Maybe someday someone will hide something in a bassoon, and you can blow it out," smiled Ava wryly.

"You have such a way with words."

"Okay, here we go." Ava's hands trembled as she touched the piano, Chopin's piano. She took in a deep breath and exhaled in an attempt to calm her nerves. All was quiet as Ava gently tapped out the thirteen notes, just as Chopin had done on this very piano two hundred years ago.

When she hit the thirteenth note, everyone gasped as a small drawer slid open. Ava reached in and removed a small cloth pouch. Every mouth dropped as she carefully poured the contents onto her palm. She and Carol had saved Ramesses's royal diamonds.

13
DO THEY HAVE KNOCK-KNOCK JOKES IN IRELAND?

The FBI stepped in and took over the investigation. Two undercover agents disguised as Prestige Auction drivers delivered the piano and other auction goods to the private auction, then left, according to plan.

Mr. White was told he would get a much lighter sentence if he called and told the people at the private auction everything was okay and right on schedule. He knew he had lost and was cooperating fully with the FBI.

He also sent the Captain a special email with an attachment called "The Last Concerto." Mr. White told the Captain that the first thirteen notes of the concerto would be of great benefit to all who listened.

What the Captain didn't know was that the FBI had embedded an untraceable virus into the PDF attachment. Once the attachment was opened, the virus would allow the FBI to hack into his private network. This would be the beginning of the end for the Captain.

That evening, the auction went off without a hitch. The private broker made the purchases for the Captain. Chopin's piano and the handwritten concerto were loaded onto a plane to leave for a private airstrip owned by the Captain in Ireland. The broker contacted the Captain and told him he would have a *sparkling* morning.

Ava and Carol asked for one *small* favor from the FBI. "I mean," said Ava to the lead investigator, "We did crack the case for you and made you aware of a hidden network of investors."

The FBI agreed of course. Ava and Carol were allowed to send a little present to the Captain.

~~o~o~o~~

Waterford, Ireland – Dragon's Point Airstrip

The Captain sat in his private library filled with famous paintings, sculptures, rare books, and an incredibly ornate stand carved out of pure ivory upon which sat a glass box with a plush velvet cushion. It was created for something very special.

Tonight, he wore his black linen pants, a cardigan sweater, and a blood-red smoking jacket. He picked up his cigar and drew in a long drag. Smoke billowed from his nostrils like a dragon.

His leathery tan face broke into a narrow slit of a smile as six men arrived, carefully carrying Chopin's piano into his library. He leapt to his feet with surprising agility and pointed to an empty corner. The men cautiously carried the piano to the designated area, then bowed to the Captain, who shooed them away with his cigar. They quickly and quietly left the room, closing the door behind them.

The Captain stared at the piano and ran his hand across the wood. He breathed in deeply, his nostrils filled with the scent of history. Reverently, he sat at the piano and closed his eyes. He had printed the music that Mr. White had emailed him, and being an accomplished musician, he only glanced at the sheet of music before setting it aside. Now, sitting at the piano, he needed only to touch the keys. The melody flowed from his fingertips.

As the notes rang out, filling the room, a hidden drawer slid open. He looked down at the satin bag and then at his beautiful ornate display case. *Yes*, he thought, *my collection will be complete.*

With a quivering hand, he reached down and grasped the bag. He carefully opened it and poured the contents into his palm. He stared and shook his head. His brain couldn't catch up with what his eyes were seeing. In his hand lay five children's marbles… and a handwritten note.

Vitriol filled his veins as he read.

Knock-knock.

Who's there?

Jewel.

Jewel who?

Jewel never get Ramesses's diamonds.

"You'll pay!" the Captain screamed, leaping from the piano. "You'll pay!"

14
A MIGHTY HUGE CHECK

Ava and Carol stood on the stone steps of the Hancock Museum and waved to a crowd of journalists and photographers. Overnight, the girls had turned into local celebrities.

"I could live like this," Ava sighed. "All of this adoration and adulation."

"It is surreal," acknowledged Carol. She spotted Gladys in the crowd and bumped Ava's shoulder. "There's Gladys!" They both waved excitedly at their new friend, who was beaming up at them. Feedback from a microphone grabbed everyone's attention.

"Sorry about that, folks," said a thin man in an impeccable gray suit. "Thank you everyone for coming out today. On behalf of the Hancock Museum, it is my esteemed honor to present Ava Clarke and Carol Miller this check for $10,000. Thanks to your investigative genius and courage, you have solved one of the largest jewel heists in American history!" Ava and Carol waved to the crowd and graciously accepted the check. Ava wondered how they were possibly going to fit it in the ATM.

~~o~o~o~~

The next morning, Ava and Carol stopped by the museum. Gladys looked up from the reception desk, her eyes filled with joy. "My two investigators!" she exclaimed. She rushed from behind the counter and gave them both a hug.

"We couldn't have done it without you, Gladys!" said Carol.

"We wanted to stop by and thank you for saving us, and for believing in us," smiled Ava.

"We're also sorry it wasn't under other circumstances," Carol gave an embarrassed smile.

"What in the world are you talking about?" Gladys clucked her tongue. "You two have single-handedly made the Hancock Museum more popular than ever. The phone hasn't stopped ringing." Ava looked at the phone, which wasn't ringing and arched an eyebrow. "Well, that figures," laughed Gladys.

"I guess we better get going," Ava sighed, glancing out the museum doors. "My parents are outside waiting for us. Just so you know, it may be years before you see us again."

"Your parents are that angry?" asked Gladys.

"My mom said that I couldn't leave my room until I was old enough to go to college."

"She did, did she?" Gladys crossed her arms, a mischievous look in her eyes. "Did your mother ever tell you about the Larson train robbery or the famous Middleton pickpocket?"

"No...," Ava eyed Glady's curiously. "Was she somehow involved?"

"Involved? Your mother was knee-deep investigating the crimes. Her shenanigans nearly drove your grandfather crazy. But...," she looked at Ava and Carol kindly, "I know that he was proud of her."

"Did Mrs. Clarke solve the crimes?" asked Carol.

"She did, and many others. So, don't let your mom be too hard on you, and maybe ask her to tell you about Larson's or the Middleton pickpocket."

"I will," smiled Ava. A feeling of pride swept over her. "My mom must have been one cool kid."

"She sure was," Gladys agreed. The phone rang, making them jump.

"I guess that's our cue," said Carol. They waved goodbye and headed for the door, ready for their next adventure.

AVA & CAROL
DETECTIVE AGENCY

BOOK 2
THE MYSTERY OF
SOLOMON'S RING

THOMAS LOCKHAVEN

1
CARB-LOVER'S PARADISE

"I have one question, and one question only," Ava said carefully.

She and her best friend, Carol, sat on the hotel bed with their hands behind their backs, fingers crossed for luck. Out of the corner of her eye, Ava could see Carol biting her lip.

"All right, I'm listening." Beth Clarke, Ava's mom, raised an eyebrow at her daughter.

"Can we…," Ava took a dramatic breath, "order room service?"

Mrs. Clarke leaned back, narrowing her eyes, a smirk pulling at the corner of her mouth. "We have plenty of cereal bars, you know."

Carol elbowed her. "I *told* you!" she whispered. Just moments before, Carol had suggested that they just eat the cereal bars—but Ava had hissed, "*Real food.*"

Ava groaned, rolling her eyes back like she was dying. "But *Mom*, we're in Italy! All we've had is airplane food, and we've been at this hotel for at least three hours! Legally, I believe we are bound by European laws to dine on spaghetti or some other tomato noodle-based cuisine."

"Where does it say that?" Ava's mom teased.

"Right here, in Dad's guidebook!" Ava got up to grab the guidebook her dad had packed for them, a thick, clunky book entitled *Pasta Paradise: A Carb-Lover's Guide to the Italian Homeland*. "Don't be fooled by the cover. There is a whole section on eating mandates established by the highest branches of the Italian government."

"Sounds official, and we don't want to break any laws."

"Hey, at least I didn't ask for a pony."

"Or a unicorn," mumbled Carol.

Ava's mom chuckled and threw up her arms. "Okay! Your dad is currently trekking his way through the Amazon jungle, most likely eating insects… and he did go to the trouble of getting *that* book for you—so, I guess you've gotta order room service."

The girls whooped triumphantly and gave each other a high-five. "European law always works," Ava winked.

"Only one meal each—no appetizers—and a dessert to split. Understood?"

"You got it, Mrs. Clarke," Carol said, crossing her heart. "I'll make sure of it."

"I bet you will," she said back, smiling. "Now, when I'm at my meetings, I need you guys to behave! Ava, don't drive the hotel staff crazy. No crazy adventures. No experiments with the microwave…."

"I just wanted to see if it was a quicker way to cook an egg," offered Ava apologetically. "I had no idea they would explode."

"It was epic," smiled Carol, "but, uhm, more of a learning moment," she murmured when she saw Ava's mother arch her eyebrow.

"Lastly," continued Ava's mom, "movies cost money. We don't want a repeat of our stay in New

York when you binge-watched every Star Wars movie ever made."

Ava smiled. "I gotcha. Mom… your memory is truly impressive."

"Carol," Beth continued, "you're in charge of making sure the room service doesn't get out of control."

"Okay, Mrs. Clarke, I promise," Carol said as she bounced over to the menu on the desk with Ava right behind her.

"Can Dad get my texts in the Amazon?" Ava called out. "I want to send him a picture of our first authentic Italian dining experience."

"Yes, when he's back at base camp with the other scientists, he can download your texts. The SIM card that I put in your phone works in over thirty different European countries."

"Impressive," said Ava. "Thank you, Mom. You rock!"

Ava's mom, a journalist, had invited her daughter and Carol to join her on her trip to Italy for a journalism conference. When Ava's mom suggested it, Carol's parents thought it was a great idea to "teach the kids more about the world." Plus, Ava knew Carol's parents were going to be out of town, and Carol would rather hang out with her best friend than stay with her Great-Aunt Marge, who smelled like old cheese and turnips.

So, Mr. and Mrs. Miller bought Carol a ticket, and the three of them flew way across the Atlantic Ocean to Italy to stay in the fanciest and most beautiful hotel

Ava had ever seen, the St. Regis in Florence. Ava wasn't sure why, but every time she said the name *St. Regis* she heard a heavenly choir belt out "Ahhhh" and then a little bell chime. She was pretty sure Carol heard it too, but she was too cool to mention it.

Their hotel room was huge, with two gargantuan beds, one for Ava's mom and one for Ava and Carol, with a view of the Arno River right outside their window.

"I'll be back in a couple of hours," Ava's mom said, dropping a kiss on each of the girls' heads. "Remember, no *big adventures*—and I'm looking at you, Ava." Mrs. Clarke pointed two fingers at her eyes and then one back at Ava.

"Bye, Mom!" Ava said, waving her away. "Love you more than chocolate!"

Carol looked at Ava, shocked. "Really?"

"Okay," laughed Ava, "she's a close second."

As the hotel room door clicked behind Mrs. Clarke, Ava and Carol tackled the menu again.

"Oh my gosh, we should order the pasta primavera, the cheese ravioli, get a marj-hair-ita pizza, and this… whatever this thing is," said Ava, pointing at the dessert page to something that looked layered with cream and chocolate.

"Okay, first off, the word you just destroyed is a margherita pizza, and second off, your mom just said we can't go overboard with the food," Carol explained. "I'm not going to take the fall for your—"

"Orrrr," Ava drew out, interrupting Carol, "we could order everything on the menu and make a castle out of all of the food and live there forever. Maybe that's what a 'carb-lover's paradise' is, like in the guidebook," she snorted. *Adults are so weird.*

"C'mon, let's just pick something and call room service to bring it up. Dibs on *not* having to call them," Carol rushed to say.

"Ugh," Ava sighed. She thought about arguing about it, but she knew she'd been beaten. "Rats. Fine," she said, sticking out her tongue to Carol's *Hah!*. "Do you know what you want?" she asked, grabbing the receiver off the phone.

They decided on spaghetti with extra meatballs for Ava. Carol wanted something called lasagna casareccia, so Ava had to hand the phone over anyway so Carol could properly pronounce it.

"Did you hear how I rolled my r's?"

"Did you see how I rolled my eyes?" Ava retorted.

"I'm just saying, if you would practice your Spanish more, you'll pretty much be able to understand all the romantic languages."

"Do I look like I'm interested in romantic languages?"

"Spanish, French and Italian are all romantic languages, and are all based on Latin."

"So if you can speak Spanish, you can understand Italian?"

"Eh, many of the words are very close, so you can kind of get a gist of what the person is talking about," explained Carol.

"Good to know. However, I'm only interested in one language," Ava said, wiggling her eyebrows.

"Oh," Carol sighed, "I'm afraid to—"

"The language of… loooooove," said Ava, scrunching her lips into a tiny O.

"I used to think there was hope for you, but I think all is lost," said Carol, hopping onto the bed.

"Speaking of lost," said Ava seriously. "Do you have a map? Because I just got lost in your eyes." Ava was pretty sure Carol's groan could be heard across the Arno River.

A knock came on the door a half hour later. Carol thanked the room service waiter with an emphatic "*Grazi*!" Ava dug in her pocket and fished out a beautiful shiny quarter. She placed it in the gloved palm of the waiter and winked. He looked from his hand, back to Ava, and then back at his hand—a confused look on his face.

"Oh yeah, sorry! *Grazi*!" smiled Ava as she waved goodbye and shut the door in his face.

The warm smell of marinara sauce filled the room, and Ava breathed it in like she hadn't eaten all day. Carol set the tray down on the floor, where they had laid out towels to make a picnic.

"This looks awesome," Ava said, picking up a shiny silver fork and digging in.

"I was so ready," Carol agreed.

With her mouth full of noodles, Ava picked up the remote. "Let's watch something! I bet you there's a Disney movie or something on here."

"Listening to 'A Whole New World' in Italian would be pretty mind-blowing," her friend said, as Ava flicked through the channels.

But everything was either a boring adult news channel or a ridiculous little kid show. Nothing was in English, anyway. Finally, they settled on dubbed reruns of *Mr. Bean*, and set to work on their dinners. Little by little the food disappeared, the tiramisu, the dessert Ava had decided on—which had coffee in it of all things—was devoured, and the girls ended up in a food coma, staring blankly at the screen.

"Hey, Carol," said Ava after ten minutes of sprawling on the floor feeling like a zombie. "I'm making an executive decision as the appointed leader of adventurous exploration and declaring that casual exercise is necessary."

"What?" Carol asked, stretching and yawning.

"Oh, come on, it took me, like, five minutes to come up with that," Ava protested.

"To come up with that entire thing?" Carol sounded incredulous. "Really?"

"Do not sass your appointed leader of adventurous exploration!" Ava said, mock-insulted. She nodded to the yellow light coming from their window. "The Arno River is right outside! Let us go walk alongside it and bask in its glory."

"You know we can't go anywhere," Carol said, raising an eyebrow. "Your mom's rule. And," said Carol, looking out the window, "it's starting to get dark outside."

"To clarify, she said that we're not allowed to go crazy with the *adventures*. She never *actually* said that we couldn't leave the hotel. It's a perfectly legitimate loophole."

Carol crossed her arms. "I don't know, Ava. Your mom's been super nice about this trip. I don't really want to make her mad."

"Here, look." Ava reached onto the bed and grabbed a map from her mom's pile of important stuff. She pointed to a red dot. "This is the St. Regis. Over here…," she dragged her finger an inch to the right, "…is the Arno River. It's right there, next to our hotel. All we have to do is cross the street and we'll be there."

"That's the Lungarno Amerigo Vespucci highway. America was named after him in 1507 by the way." Carol added. "And for your information," she cocked her head, her long ponytail swaying to the side. "It's a highway, not a road."

"Meh, semantics," Ava declared, waving her friend's comment aside. "Carol, you can see it from here!" Ava stood up, dragging Carol to the window. Outside, the city sparkled in the evening, the rooftops of the old buildings pointed to the sky, making their window look more like a painting than a pane of glass. "See it? It's just a small road, with lanes going each direction. It's totally close, and Mom would never get mad. Besides, we'll be back before you can say *ciao*."

"It does look pretty cool," agreed Carol, thinking out loud. Finally, she flashed Ava a brilliant smile. "All right. I'm down. Let's go."

Ava let out a cheer. "Yes! Grab the room key, Watson, and we'll be on our way."

"How come I'm Watson and you're Sherlock in this scenario?" Carol asked.

"Because I'm the one who makes the dumb suggestions and you're the one who makes sure we don't end up getting killed," Ava said, shrugging.

Carol paused before nodding. "Yeah, that sounds about right."

The two excitedly shoved on their sneakers over their socks, racing each other in tying them. Carol grabbed her dark purple coat with a flower design on the collar and tossed Ava her jean jacket with rhinestones on the front pockets.

"Don't forget your phone!" she called.

"Got it," Ava said back as she quickly slipped her iPhone into her jacket. "Do you have the room key?"

"Yep!" shouted Carol. "We're all set. Let's go!"

Ava shut the hotel room door and the girls headed down the hallway. They were excited to be on an adventure and explore Florence, Italy! As Ava pressed the button for the elevator, she looked up at their reflections on the gleaming ceiling. She imagined them walking out of the St. Regis into the great unknown, crossing the perilous two-lane highway, and hiking across the treacherous sidewalk path to finally arrive at the oceanwide Arno River. What obstacles would they meet on the way? A grumpy doorman who refused to let the two girls out of the hotel, or even her mother marching right through the door, upset that Ava had been a bad influence on Carol? Who knew what lay ahead?

Ava smiled to herself. *This is going to be so cool.*

2
CAPTURED

"Wow!" exclaimed Carol as they left the hotel, the huge crystal-clear glass doors swooshed closed behind them. "It looks even prettier at night!"

"You're right," Ava agreed. It was quiet outside, but the lights from across the river shone brightly, the water acting as a mirror against the city and the night sky. The streetlights were tall and ornate, looking like what Carol thought old-fashioned oil lanterns would look like. Carol inhaled sharply—the fresh air totally different than the hotel's air. It carried the scent of the city: traces of spiced cologne, cigarettes, and freshly made Italian food.

"See?" said Ava, completely obliterating the magical moment. "The river's right there. We'll be totally fine."

"All right, all right," Carol said, groaning good-naturedly.

Ava offered her arm. "M'lady, would you care to join me on a stroll to the other side of the street? A mini-tour of what I like to call the sparkling jewel of Italy—Florence."

Carol giggled and wrinkled her nose. "Why are you talking in a British accent? We're in Italy, you nut."

"I'll catch onto the Italian accent later," Ava said, knocking her shoulder against her friend. Carol took her arm, knocking her back.

"At least the road's deserted," Carol surmised as they looked both ways before they crossed. They strode to the river, breaking away from each other at the last second to rush to the cement wall and peer over it. The cool air hit their faces as they gazed out at the river, its dark waters rippling lightly in the breeze. It stretched beyond what they could see, and they drank in the sight of it.

"Beautiful," whispered Carol, eyes wide. "This is so cool."

Ava nodded in agreement, looking down into the inky black water of the Arno River. "I wonder if it's filled with sharks... Italian sharks maybe?"

"I'm sure, and probably mermaids—this is the perfect time of the year for mermaid sightings."

Ava laughed with her friend. "What do you think is going on with that guy?" asked Ava, pointing toward a man who was leaning over the railing of a bridge that spanned the Arno River.

"Don't know," shrugged Carol. "Maybe he's looking for a mermaid. Or... maybe, he's a mer*man*!"

Ava squinted her eyes. A pale-yellow light washed over the man, making his bald head glow eerily, like a miniature moon. Tiny wisps of white hair danced on his head in the cool breeze.

There was something peculiar about the old man. As he stretched his hand out over the water, a quick succession of light flashed from his outstretched hand. The man hesitated for a few moments and then the series of flashes began again. The man's head swiveled left and right as he took in his surroundings. The girls quickly crouched below the wall.

"Why are we ducking?" whispered Carol.

"I don't know," said Ava, shaking her head. "Maybe because he's acting weird and if he sees us… he might stop whatever he's up to?"

Carol nodded, agreeing. The girls slowly slid upward, their eyes just above the top of the stone wall.

"Ava, look at that!" Carol whispered, pointing at the water.

Ava followed Carol's finger and saw a sleek black vessel approaching in the water, headed toward the bridge. It almost blended in, like it was a part of the Arno River. Small bursts of light, mimicking the same flashes the old man had made, came from the front of the speedboat. Someone was responding to the old man with the same pattern of flashes. He glanced around anxiously. The girls dropped again behind the stone wall to avoid being seen.

"What the heck is going on?" whispered Ava.

A large, ominous shadow passed over the girls. Ava was about to peek over the wall when Carol grabbed her shoulder, pulling her down beside her, putting a finger to her lips. The girls watched as a sleek black car, headlights off, quietly hissed by.

"Electric," whispered Carol, seeing the confused look in Ava's eyes.

The girls watched as the car stealthily passed by as quiet as a ghost. The old man seemed completely oblivious to the impending doom until its shadow consumed him. The girls gasped as two men leapt from the car.

In a flash, two men leapt from the car and grabbed the old man. One of the men pulled a black hood over the man's head. Carol grabbed Ava's hand and squeezed it, digging her nails into her palm. The old man screamed angrily, lashing out with his fists and feet with the ferocity of a tiger. But he was no match for the attackers, and they pushed and shoved him into the rear of the car.

Ava and Carol stood, paralyzed. Everything seemed to be going in slow motion.

With expert precision, the driver reversed the car, right back onto the Lungarno Amerigo Vespucci highway, heading the opposite way from where it had come. Away from Ava and Carol. Carol couldn't decide if she was more terrified for the old man or relieved that they were going away.

Before she could decide, though, a small pastry truck darted out from a small alley just a little way down the road. The men's sleek car careened to the right to avoid the truck and launched over the curb, slamming the driver's side of the car into a streetlight.

Carol and Ava could see some sort of struggle happening inside the car, and they both let out huffs of relief when the old man kicked the rear door open. Without a moment to spare, he threw himself from the car and rolled out onto the street and got to his feet. The girls could see the driver furiously throwing his shoulder against the car door trying to get out, but the crash had wedged his door shut.

The old man turned to run, then quickly changed his mind.

"Why isn't he running?" whispered Carol anxiously as the girls began scrambling closer, hidden by the shadows in the courtyard.

Ava didn't answer—she was completely focused on the events unfolding in front of them.

The girls watched horrified as the other bad guy began clambering out of the side of the car after the old man. Just as the man gripped the outside of the car's doorframe to crawl out, the old man viciously kicked the door closed. The man howled in pain as the door slammed shut on his hand and the window smashed into his face.

Lost in the heat of the moment, Ava froze. Carol reached up, grabbing Ava's elbow. "Get down—they'll see us!"

The old man's eyes locked with Ava's for a moment, and then he turned and raced away.

"Come on," whispered Ava urgently. "Come on!"

Clinging to the shadows, the girls silently followed the old man across the piazza right next to the St. Regis. They watched as he passed by the famous statue of Hercules strangling the Nemean Lion, and then disappeared into the shadows down a small alley. The girls stole a last look at the kidnappers' car, and then raced off into the darkness after the old man.

A car door slammed behind them as they followed the old man. Carol stole a quick look over her shoulder. She could see one of the men clutching his nose, which seemed to be broken.

Carol grabbed Ava's shoulder. "Uhm, we need to hurry! We've got company!"

The girls sprinted down the narrow alley, passing banks and touristy shops long since closed for the evening. Ava and Carol dropped behind a row of mailboxes—they could hear the clattering of the pursuers' shoes clapping against the stone walkway. They would be here in a matter of seconds.

The old man skidded to a stop in front of a shop with the sign "Libreria Aurora" in large blue letters hanging above it.

"Bookstore," Carol said under her breath.

Using his elbow, the old man smashed the glass pane in the door. Ava silently noted to look into the power of the human elbow. They watched as the broken pieces of glass fell to the man's feet. He reached through the opening and twisted his arm to unlock the door. They heard a small tearing sound. He grunted; his jacket had caught on a piece of glass still on the doorframe. He made a quiet grunt of victory and it swung open, as his jacket dislodged. He glanced in the direction of the girls as if he knew they were there, and then he hurried inside the bookstore.

Ava was just about to move closer to the store when Carol grabbed her sleeve. "They're here," she whispered. Carol pulled Ava back into the shadows and they flattened their backs against a darkened doorway. Within seconds, the two men rounded the corner and ran down the alleyway, shouting to each other as they looked around. Ava could see streaks of blood on the man's cheeks and chin.

The tallest man, who had been driving the car, pointed to the bookstore's door and the smashed glass that reflected in the moonlight on the ground. He said something in gruff Italian, and the other responded in a deep voice, nodding. The tall man held a small black device in his hand. A bright blue electrical charge flashed, making a crackling noise.

"A taser," gulped Ava.

Carol nodded nervously.

The girls watched as the men rushed into the bookstore. They heard more yelling, but it was hard to distinguish between the voices. Suddenly, dozens of crashing sounds came from inside the store.

With her heart in her throat, Carol winced as she heard a loud *boom*, and then another *CRASH*. There was more yelling and then another crash, this one setting Ava's teeth on edge. A blue light flashed—a short scream followed, and finally silence. The silence was somehow scarier than the noises.

One of the men stepped out of the store straightening his suit jacket, his shiny leather shoes too close to the girls for comfort. Carol stared up into his face. His nose, twisted to the side… his eyes dark and evil. The man looked up and down the alley. With his face twisted in pain, he took a phone out of his jacket pocket. The old man's kick had done some damage; his fingers were swollen like sausages, and Carol wondered if they were broken. Using his good hand, he quickly swiped a finger across the screen, dialed a number, brought the phone to his ear, and began to speak in rapid Italian.

Carol strained to catch some words, but he was speaking too quickly and softly. Seconds after her hung up, a black car appear at the mouth of the alley. A loud grunt came from inside the shop. The second man, wearing a suit, backed out of the doorway, dragging the old man whose arms hung limp by his side.

"Aiutami," the man in the suit said to his counterpart, who went to him and took the old man's other arm. His head lolled forward like his bones were made of jelly. *He must be unconscious,* Ava noticed with worry. They dragged him back to the car and flung open the back door. Ava lifted her head out of the shadows, trying to see more. Eyes filled with concern, she searched for a sign that he was still alive. *Please let him be okay.*

The man's eyes opened a fraction, and an ember of hope flamed in Ava's chest as his eyes met her. He glanced down to his side, and she followed his gaze. With his hand hidden from his captors, she saw his fingers moving. They were tiny movements, but Ava knew enough sign language to understand what he was trying to sign to her. She spread her fingers apart, then brought her hands together, interlocking her fingers with her thumbs sticking out. The sign for American.

She watched as he quickly moved his fingers. She mouthed the letters as he formed them, committing them to memory.

F-I-N-D L-U-C-A.

With a new sense of urgency, Ava nodded once to the man, his eyes closed as she ducked her head back into the shadows. "Carol," she whispered. "Make sure you get the license plate number of the car!"

The girls remained crouched in the doorway until the car sped off into the night. When they were sure the car was gone, they stood, breathing huge sighs of relief.

"That was so, so, so crazy," Ava breathed.

"You got that right," Carol said, shivering.

They stood in the shadows together, waiting to feel normal again.

3
LUCA

"Okay, I have no idea what just happened, but we need to get back to your mom," Carol said, her voice sounding strained. "We've got to call the police."

"Wait! No! We need to make sure that no one else was in the bookstore. He told me to find Luca," said Ava urgently.

Carol paused. "What do you mean he said find Luca? He never said a word to us."

"Three years of taking sign language classes in summer camp—that's how he told me. He told me to find Luca."

"Are you sure?"

Ava nodded. "I'm sure."

"Okay," Carol reluctantly agreed. "We'll see if anyone else is in there. If not, we go straight to the police."

Ava nodded in agreement and Carol took a big breath, looking down each end of the alley before they walked toward the door. The girls pulled out their phones and flipped on their flashlights.

"Oh, no," Ava said aloud.

The girls slowly stepped through the doorway. The store was a disaster. Tables of books had been flipped over. Bookshelves toppled. The cash register lay on the floor atop a stack of papers. The room looked like it had been hit by a hurricane.

"The old man said to look for Luca. Maybe they're in here and they need help!" said Ava.

Carol nodded, "Split up!"

Suddenly the lights flashed on, and Carol blinked and staggered backward, momentarily blinded.

"Cosa fai?" came a woman's voice, screaming. Carol hurriedly translated it in her head. *What are you doing? "Che cosa hai fatto al mio negozio?"* *What have you done to my store?*

Carol's hands went up and her eyes widened as she tried to find her voice amidst the panic. *"Mi dispiace! Non parlo italiano."* Carol whipped her head around, suddenly realizing she was alone. "Ava?!" she called out desperately. "Where are you?"

Suddenly, a crowd of Italian police officers appeared in the doorway. Two of them were tall enough to dwarf the girls. Ava raced from between two bookshelves to Carol's side. They stood facing two officers and a large, squat Italian woman who looked like she could rip a phonebook in half.

Carol grabbed Ava, pulling her in close, happy to have her friend by her side once again.

"Vandals! Did you do this?" one of the officers asked roughly in English, his accent thick.

"No!" answered Ava. "No!"

"What did you do to my store?!" bellowed the woman as she surveyed the damage, her arms gesturing to the destruction around them. "What did you do to my store?!"

Ava looked around, thinking fast. She knew she had to tell the truth, but she didn't know how much of the truth to tell. *All of it,* came the answer in her mind, but Carol had taken the lead already.

"Ma'am, please believe us. We did not do this to your store. We're tourists visiting Italy with her mom, Mrs. Clarke, who's here for a journalist convention," she said, gesturing to Ava. "We were walking by the Arno River when we saw two men in a black car grab an old man off the bridge."

She told how they had struck a streetlight and how the man had attempted to escape and had broken into the bookstore to try to hide from the bad guys. The bookshop owner and the police listened intently, nodding during different parts of the story.

When Carol got to the part about how they'd heard crashing inside the bookstore after the men had followed their target, the bookshop owner's face twisted up like she had sucked on a lemon. She didn't say anything, though, until Carol finished recounting what had happened.

"We were going to run to the hotel to call the police… but we were afraid they may have hurt someone in here," Carol said, gesturing around. "We knew we weren't supposed to… but the way they treated the old man…," Carol's eyes dropped to the floor.

"Bene allora," said the bookshop owner, studying the girls with quizzical eyes. "It is obvious they are just young girls, and not a part of the damage. Look at their clothes—they did not do this."

The girls felt the policemen's eyes scrutinizing them. Slowly, the expression of the officer in charge softened and he nodded, letting out a sigh. "Girls, walk me through the story once again."

"Wait, wait!" insisted the robust storekeeper. "The girl's mother is probably worried to death. Should we not contact her?"

The officer in charge hesitated, then nodded. "Yes, let's do that before their mother calls and reports the girls missing."

The woman grabbed Ava by the hand. "Where are you staying?"

"The Regis," replied Ava.

"And what is your name?"

"Ava. Ava Clarke"

"And your mother's name?"

"Beth… Beth Clarke."

The woman nodded and marched forward through the clutter, finally finding the phone buried underneath an upended table. Ava tensed as she heard the woman's voice speak rapidly in Italian.

Thirty minutes later, the girls sat in the back seat of the police cruiser. They rode in silence back to the hotel, both girls staring out opposite windows. Ava couldn't bring herself to feel bad. She felt like she had done what was right. She replayed the events of the night over and over in her mind: seeing the old man's hand, shakily signing the words… *Find Luca.*

Who was Luca? Was the shop bookstore owner Luca? Did she know Luca? Ava wanted to go back to the bookstore right then and there and look around to see what she could find—she had so many questions.

She slowly turned toward Carol. Ava could tell by the way her head hung that her friend was upset. Mrs. Clarke was like Carol's second mom… and she knew her mom was going to go ballistic when the girls pulled up in a police cruiser.

Ugh, Ava thought, *not just a police cruiser… but a police cruiser on their first night in Italy.*

As they neared the hotel, the girls could see Ava's mom standing outside of the entrance, talking with a security guard. Ava immediately felt a stab of guilt. She didn't want to make her mom worry. Carol felt her throat shrink the moment she saw Mrs. Clarke. It was obvious: the woman was furious.

"Ava! Carol!" Mrs. Clarke shouted when she saw the two approach with the policemen on either side of them. They went to her and she hugged them, a glint of relief amidst the anger still clear in her eyes. She looked between the men and the girls. "What in the world happened?"

"Ma'am, could we have a word with you?" the lead officer asked politely.

"Yes, of course. Girls, I want you to go straight into the lobby, find a couch, and do not move from that spot. I'll be in there in just a minute to talk to you about the meaning of *not going too far.*"

"Okay, Mom," Ava said quietly, shame weighing her down. Carol nodded and they went through the doors. Carol glanced back once, feeling powerless. This was the absolute worst. Not only did they fail to help the mysterious old man, but now Mrs. Clarke was upset too.

Together, they sat on the first couch they found, a gold velvet one with cushions that sunk luxuriously beneath their weight, but not too much. Normally, they'd be talking about how it was, without a doubt, the prettiest couch they'd ever sat on that also happened to be comfortable. But they didn't say a word to each other. Despite the excitement of what had happened, the gravity of the situation had settled onto their shoulders and the events of the night had left them gravely quiet.

Five minutes later, Ava's mom walked in without the policemen. She spotted the girls and went over to them.

"Alrighty then," she said without a smile. "Let's go back to the room."

It was a painfully quiet elevator ride. Not even the pretty reflective ceiling of the elevator distracted them. Carol stood in misery. She hated it when adults were upset with her, and Mrs. Clarke was one of her favorite grown-ups. Ava felt it too, chewing on the inside of her cheek. The food and tiramisu they'd devoured sat like a rock in her stomach.

Finally, they arrived. No sooner did they walk into the hotel room, with the door shutting behind them, did Ava's mom whip around with her hands on her hips, her jaw clenched in anger.

"What in the *world* were you thinking?" she demanded. "Do you have any idea how dangerous a situation you put yourselves into? And did I not *explicitly* say that I didn't want you to go far?"

"I don't know what *explicitly* means," Ava said quietly, her eyes downcast.

"It means 'out loud,' Ava," Mrs. Clarke replied, still fuming. "It means, I definitely told you to do the exact opposite of what you did. Do you know how scared I was to come back to the room to find your jackets gone, with you nowhere in sight? We're in a different country! I know you're both big on adventures, but this is the kind of adventure that you can't have while it's just me looking out for you. Do I make myself clear, girls?"

"But the old man was in trouble!" blurted Ava. Carol looked at her, eyes saying *what are you doing?!*, but Ava ignored her. "Mom, you have to hear what happened."

Mrs. Clarke settled back, crossing her arms. "Telling me excuses won't make you any less grounded when we get home, young lady."

"*Mom*, this is important!" she implored her. Without waiting another moment, Ava began to describe what had happened. After a while, Carol jumped in too, feeling braver.

"We really just wanted to make sure that the old man was okay," Carol insisted at the end of Ava's retelling, her ponytail bobbing up and down as she nodded vehemently. "We stayed hidden until the bad guys were gone… we just wanted to make sure no one was hurt, and then we were going to go straight to the hotel to call the police."

Mrs. Clarke's eyes flicked back and forth between the girls. Finally, she sighed and hugged them both again, squeezing them tightly. "I'm glad you both are okay." Ava sighed. There was no bigger relief than knowing your parents weren't disappointed in you anymore. "And I'm glad you both have such courageous, big hearts. But you have to promise me not to do anything like that again, okay? Call the police. Don't try to fix stuff on your own."

"Okay, Mrs. C."

"Okay, Mom...." Ava's voice lowered. "We really were just worried about that old man...."

Mrs. Clarke drew back, looking tired but no longer angry. "I'm going to take a shower and wash off the worry." She glanced at her watch. "I think it's past time that you guys got ready for bed. When I come out, I want to see you in bed."

Agreeing, the girls went to their suitcases as Ava's mom walked into the bathroom, shutting the door behind her. Ava waited until she heard the shower running before she motioned Carol over.

"What is it?" asked Carol excitedly.

"Remember how we split up when we went in the bookstore?"

"Yeah," nodded Carol. "Of course."

Ava reached into her pocket... and pulled out a tattered envelope.

"Is that... blood?" asked Carol.

"Yeah. He must have cut the heck out of himself because he used a jagged piece of glass from the window like a knife blade."

"What do you mean?" asked Carol, confused.

"When I shut the door, I found the envelope on the back of it, with the glass stabbed through it."

Carol's jaw dropped, and she looked at Ava. "Ouch!"

"Double ouch," said Ava. "Our friend had a really bad evening."

"Well," said Carol hurriedly, "what are you waiting for? Open the envelope!"

Ava carefully opened the envelope, dumping the contents onto the bed. A strangely shaped metal ring and a small piece of paper fell onto the comforter. Carol lifted the ring; the metal was smooth, with deep grooves on each side. The decorative face of the ring looked like it had been sliced in half. The body of the ring had strange symbols etched into it... it looked like Egyptian hieroglyphics. The way the ring was made, Carol guessed there was another matching piece that completed or interlocked with the piece she was holding.

Carol turned the ring over in her hand....

"Okay," smiled Ava. "I can see your brain whirring. What are you thinking?"

"I'm thinking you are missing the second part of this ring. Do you think maybe a piece fell out? Maybe he dropped it in the bookstore?"

"What do you mean?" asked Ava as she took the ring from Carol.

"You see these grooves and the decorative face? It's made to interlock with another ring. You know, like those best friend necklaces that are like half a heart, and when you put them together, they make a whole heart."

"Yeah… I know exactly what you mean… and notice I don't have one," smiled Ava.

"That's because I only give them to my best friends."

"Oh," said Ava. "Funny. Hurtful, but funny."

"Well," said Carol continuing, "I think this ring is like that. I think it locks together with another piece."

"Okay, cool… but honestly, it looks like a cheap piece of jewelry, not worth risking your life for."

"True," nodded Carol. "Maybe this will answer our question." She unfolded the piece of paper, and her eyes narrowed. Someone had drawn a strange symbol made up of four lines with a small circle balancing on the left side.

"What does it mean?" Ava whispered to Carol.

"I have no idea," Carol studied the symbol. "Any ideas?"

"An ostrich? A stork standing on one leg?"

"It looks more like a constellation or zodiac symbol," said Carol thoughtfully.

Ava whipped out her phone and began typing. "Maybe that's what he meant by 'find Luca,'" she said excitedly. However, after a couple minutes of searching the internet, Ava couldn't find a constellation or a zodiac symbol named Luca.

Carol stared at the symbol, her brain spinning as she tried to make a connection… but she had to admit, she was stumped. She looked at Ava and shook her head. "I have no idea what it means."

"It means," said Ava, smiling, "that we need to pay our favorite Italian bookstore another visit."

"And you think your mom is going to let you simply waltz over there after her lecture tonight?"

"Oh yes, after I convince her how old and delicate the store owner is, and that she has a sick husband, and the store is her livelihood… and that these bad, bad men did so much damage… that without our help…." Ava paused, offering a devious smile.

"That little, old, fragile woman needs us," nodded Carol in agreement. "So… back to the bookstore?"

"Back to the bookstore," winked Ava.

4
PANTSING: IT'S A THING!

"Oh, man, Ava," murmured Carol. "I don't know about this."

"Why are you worried? Look at those biceps," said Ava as she poked her friend's arms. "The bad guys would take one look at those bad boys and bolt."

"My biceps look like very tiny, sad, deflated balloons," said Carol, flexing as she walked by a pastry window.

"You need to be more positive," implored Ava. "Is the balloon half full or half empty?"

"I think your brain is half empty."

The girls had spent a wonderful morning with Mrs. Clarke, sitting out on the balcony, eating breakfast—watching Florence come to life. Carol thought it was amazing, like a Broadway production. The trio took turns guessing the occupations of different people as they passed beneath their balcony at the St. Regis. The morning brought tranquility—and renewed hope. To Carol, it seemed as if the events of the night before had been a dream....

A beautiful gondola, shaped like an elf's shoe, passed by. A man dressed in black pants with a blue-and-white-striped shirt expertly navigated the river, using a long paddle. Everything seemed so peaceful—just how she had imagined Italy.

Ava had convinced their mother that the owner of the bookstore could barely walk, much less move... and that there was no one to help her since her husband was sick and frail. She insisted that they help the poor old woman, who was probably at this very moment sitting on the floor, surrounded by piles of books, sobbing.

It took some incredible acting, but Ava was able to convince her mother that only they could help the poor bookstore owner. Mrs. Clarke finally agreed, but she insisted that the girls had to go straight to the store, and then text her immediately when they arrived safely.

They, of course, did not mention their true intentions: find the other half of the ring, and find out if the lady had any connections to anyone named Luca… or if she had any idea how they could find Luca.

As if on cue, Ava and Carol stopped just around the corner of the bookstore, far enough away that they could just peek at the entrance. There were still a few fragments of glass, trapped within the coarse stonework, glimmering in the afternoon sun. From their angle, they couldn't see much else. A kind of nervous air hung between the two friends as they peered into the bookstore. Ava quickly texted her mom, letting her know that they had arrived safely at the bookstore, and that she was the best mom who had ever lived.

Ava glanced over at Carol, who was feverishly biting her lip. "Someday you are going to chew your lip off, and they are going to have to make you a new lip… and just so you know, I am not donating part of my lip for your lip replacement. It would be too weird."

Carol turned to face Ava. "Really, that's where you draw the friendship line? We are risking going back to the store and having the owner call the police on us."

"We have to check it out," Ava insisted. "It's the only way to figure out if she knows anything about Luca, and if the second part of the ring is there. As far as your lip is concerned... I have no comment."

Ava slipped her hand into her jacket, feeling the envelope against her fingertips. She was all too aware that such a wild part of this crazy adventure was sitting just in her pocket.

"Why do I always let you talk me into crazy things? Let's go for a walk, at night, in a foreign city... let's chase after crazy kidnappers...," Carol muttered beneath her breath.

"Now is not the time for self-reflection and reasoning!" Ava tsked, swatting her best friend.

A clatter came from inside the bookstore, and a woman's voice speaking angrily in Italian quickly followed. Ava's eyes widened. They noticed the shattered pane in the door had been replaced with cardboard, with the word *Aperto* handwritten on it.

"Ahem," said Carol, grabbing Ava's shoulder. "You know, we could come back later... she seems really focused and...."

Ava rolled her eyes and shrugged her shoulder free. She slowly pushed the door open and stepped inside.

"Che cosa? Chi c'è?" What? Who is there?

They stopped just inside the doorway, looking at each other. Neither said a word until Ava's shoulder bumped Carol's. She shot her friend a look: *Say something.*

"*Buongiorno*, ma'am. It's us, the two girls from your shop last night," Carol said loudly, but she didn't walk closer for fear that the woman would chuck a book at them. Ava didn't blame her. Strange, angry Italian women were at the top of her list as the scariest people ever, followed by angry Italian kidnappers, then clowns—what magical powers do they possess that so many can fit into a car?

"Ahh, the little girls who were in trouble, hmm?" she said. "Come in. Do not be ghosts in the doorway."

Ava wanted to volunteer that she was not a "little girl," that she was twelve and basically a normal human being at that point, but it was obvious that the bookstore owner had been through a lot and didn't need to be argued with. Ava took a step forward, and without missing a beat, Carol walked with her.

As they came into fuller view of the room, Ava looked around and recognized the bookstore's interior. It looked so different in the daylight. Dusty yellow sunlight lit up the books that still lay strewn across the floor, along with the upturned tables and chairs, broken glass, and spilled objects. Dust that hadn't quite settled floated in the air, particles catching the light. In the center of all of it was the woman, her graying hair tied up in a bun with a red bandana to keep the flyaways back. She had a dirty apron tied around her waist, her floral skirt swaying past her calves.

Obviously, one book this woman was missing from her collection was one on fashion, thought Ava. *Bandanas are so 1980s.*

Carol, however, could clearly see the lines on her face, and she felt another pang of sadness. The woman had made some progress, but for the most part, the place was still a mess.

"Whoa," Carol breathed as she looked around. Ava nodded. It looked worse, actually, since they could see all the damage this time.

"Why you just stand there?" the woman demanded. "I do not have time for visitors who want to watch as I work."

"Mi-mi dispiace," Carol said, stammering. She cleared her throat. "May we help you?"

"Why? You make this mess?" the woman barked. The girls jumped. She looked the pair up and down for a moment. With a dry laugh, she swept an arm across the room. "Terrible. They destroy my shop and do not even have the decency to leave… hmm… what you Americans say? A vacuum?"

Ava giggled. "Because that's the right way to leave a place like this, right? So long as they hand you a dustpan at the end."

She snorted. "If only. Well, I needed some new displays," she said, looking at two smashed tables laying at her feet. "Now these ruffians have given me the opportunity. But if you want to help, start by shelving the books… they're everywhere."

The girls nodded, jumping into action. Carol crouched down, picking up an armful of biographies.

"What are your names again?" asked the woman as she righted a table.

"I'm Ava, and this is Carol," said Ava, gesturing to each of them. "She's the one with the large biceps.... I'm better known for my incredibly high IQ and—"

"Ability to annoy everyone," Carol laughed, interrupting her.

The woman chuckled. "You may call me *Signora* Coppola."

"Buon giorno," offered Ava, curtsying.

"Dear Lord," whispered Carol, shaking her head at Ava. "She's not the queen."

"It's *buongiorno*," corrected *Signora* Coppola. "Treat like one word. And now, books." She fluttered a hand toward the ground.

"Libros," answered Ava proudly, gesturing at the books.

"No," said Carol, smacking the back of Ava's head. "She wants you to *pick up* the books."

"I knew that," Ava curtsied again.

Carol looked at Ava, who shrugged and bent down to start gathering books. Every once in a while, Ava would pick up a book to show Carol, who would ooh and try to translate the title. *Signora* Coppola would roll her eyes when they did this, but not in a bad way, Ava thought. She looked like she found the girls funny, which relieved both of them. The last thing they wanted was to upset her further.

"I guess this one would stay the same," Carol chuckled as she held up the binding of a *Harry Potter* book.

"Only if you say it right," Ava replied. "Ma'am, how do you pronounce 'Harry Potter' with an Italian accent?"

"Better than if you say it with an American one," answered the woman, and the three of them laughed.

Carol smiled. She liked *Signora* Coppola. Her store had been ransacked, furniture broken, and yet she was humming what Carol imagined was a popular Italian tune. She was happy they were helping her.

Ava returned to the front of the store near the doorway, where she had found the envelope that contained the ring and the symbol. Pretending to be placing books on a lower shelf, she crouched down and began searching the floor for the other half of the ring. The door to the bookstore opened, nearly smacking her in the forehead. A tall man walked into the store and stood quietly. Carol and *Signora* Coppola didn't appear to notice as they righted a table.

"*Signora* Coppola... may I ask you a question?" asked Carol.

Signora Coppola answered her, but Ava didn't hear. Her eyes were on the newcomer, and she was frozen to the spot. *Oh my God*, she thought. *Oh my God, oh my God, oh my God.*

Carol knew she was putting a lot on the line, but she felt like she could trust *Signora* Coppola. "The man... the old man that was taken from your store last night... he said 'find Luca' as he was being dragged away. Do you know what…?" Carol stopped midsentence and followed *Signora* Coppola's stare. She felt her throat constrict, her heart threatening to beat right out of her chest.

The man made his way across the room, casually picking up a fallen book and examining it and then placing it on a table.

"Mi scusi, signore, come posso aiutarla?" *Signora* Coppola said to the man. *How can I help you?* Carol quickly translated in her head. She looked at the man, her lips squeezed shut to keep her jaw from dropping. She could see Ava by the door; her face wore an expression of frantic disbelief.

Why was he here? Did he have any idea who they were? Slightly, ever so slightly, Carol shook her head once. Ava nodded once in return. Her expression molded, to the best of her ability, into one of normalcy. The two continued to pick up books, though much more stiffly than before. Neither of them could say it out loud, but they both knew it.

The man was one of the kidnappers from the night before!

"Buon pomeriggio," he said, nodding to the woman, an empty smile filling his face. He took out a badge and showed it to the woman, who walked forward to look closer. "My name is Inspector Rossi," he said in Italian. "I am looking into the intrusion and attack that occurred here last night. I was wondering if you found anything that may be of interest, say a wallet… keys… anything…."

As she responded, Carol did everything she could to avoid looking at him. The girls cringed when they heard *Signora* Coppola motion toward the girls and mention their names. Ava looked up sneakily, her eyes hidden by her side bangs. The man was studying the two of them, a suspicious look appearing on his face. Ava looked away, heart thrumming in her chest. She was shaking, and she could only hope it wasn't too noticeable.

"Grazi, signora," he said to the woman. He turned to the girls, dipping his chin and flashing a smile, along with his badge. "How nice *Signora* Coppola has some helpers. She informs me you two girls were here last night during this… mmm, tragic event." He shook his head, glancing around and making a *tsk-tsk* sound with his tongue. "Truly terrible."

Now that he came closer, Carol could see that his eyebrows were thick and hung over his eyes like drapes, shading them. He had a long, thin nose and a bottom lip that dwarfed his upper lip. He smiled easily but there was something off about the way he did, like he had a hundred secrets and it was so funny that the world didn't know a single one. Carol decided that even if he wasn't a kidnapper, which he totally was, she'd dislike him anyway.

Similarly, next to her, Ava was looking at the man coolly. Carol recognized that expression. If he tried to grab them, punch him in the nose.

His grin widened, and Ava was sure it wasn't just her imagination that it turned eviler the farther it stretched—he resembled a real-life Grinch. He reached into his jacket pocket and pulled out a notebook.

"Hmmm… ah yes, here we are. I simply need to review my fellow officer's notes with you…. So, you two girls were witnesses to the crime?" he asked, his lips formed into a smile but his eyes filled with pure evil. His hand carefully brushed open his jacket so only Ava could see the taser hooked to his belt.

Ava looked at Carol, not sure how to respond. If they didn't play along, he may hurt them or, worse, *Signora* Coppola.

Signora Coppola looked at them quizzically. "He is an inspector, girls." She nodded at them briskly. "Go on, answer him."

"Perhaps the girls would feel more comfortable at the *stazione di polizia*. We could stop and pick up your parents, of course," he said, nodding toward *Signora* Coppola. "Perhaps this would be more agreeable?"

Ava tried to convey the fact that something was wrong to *Signora* Coppola through her eyes, but she simply seemed to think the girls were being disrespectful.

"My parents don't like police stations, or post offices, or anything to do with bureaucracy really," Carol shrugged. "Nothing personal."

He inched closer, and instinctively the two inched away. "This is a very serious crime. I'm quite sure you would like to help us solve it, not only for the poor man who was kidnapped but also for your friend, *Signora* Coppola."

Signora Coppola looked from the girls back to the man… confusion filling her face.

"Look," Rossi said, spreading out his hands. "My partner is outside. Let's say we take a nice ride to the police station." He leaned in uncomfortably close, close enough that they could smell the sourness of old coffee on his breath. Ava wrinkled her nose. Ick. "Perhaps a nice ride will jar your memory."

Ava slowly shook her head at Carol. "I think Ava should call her mom and meet us here. Then we can follow you to the police station. Besides, you need *our* help. We are not the ones that committed the crime. So, we are doing you a favor."

Rossi's smile twisted and became a tight thin line on his face. His eyes narrowed. He was just about to speak when Ava started.

"Besides," said Ava, looking between the "inspector" and her best friend. "I just remembered we haven't had lunch. You may not have *hangry* here in Italy, but back in the States, believe me… it's a real thing."

"What?!" Rossi spun around, facing Ava. "This is maddening," he yelled, jabbing his finger forcefully into her sternum. "You will come with me and you will come with me now!"

"Now wait a minute!" cried out *Signora* Coppola. "They are children! What are you doing?!"

Ava stepped backwards, but her foot caught on a small tower of books. With a cry, she tripped and fell, falling on her butt. She blinked and saw a tattered white envelope on the floor next to her. She gasped.

It'd fallen out of her pocket. Right in front of her eyes, almost in slow motion, the ring slipped out of the envelope, rolling on the floor before it stopped. Ava quickly grabbed the ring and paper and shoved them into her pocket. Haphazardly, with electricity pumping through her fingertips, she looked up.

The man's eyes were glued on Ava's pocket. He was basically salivating. Ava blinked and realized with horror he had seen the ring. The way he looked at it was like a shark and a small, defenseless fish. The ring had to have something to do with the kidnappers!

"What have we here?" he inquired, his voice awkwardly high. Completely absorbed, he took a step closer to Ava, his attention riveted. Ava looked beyond his looming figure for a second to see Carol carefully sneaking behind Rossi. "Are you hiding evidence from the crime scene?"

Carol had a plan. It was a daring plan, but since it had worked in last year's sixth grade class where Joey Templeton got three detentions in a row for *pantsing* people, it'd probably work here too, right? Praying to whatever saint was in charge of gravity or fashion, Carol yanked down on Rossi's pants with all her might.

"PANTS!" she shrilled at the top of her lungs, the man's pants pooling at his ankles—with small, cute pigs and strips of bacon dotted all over his boxers.

"Ava, RUN!" shouted Carol. She was right, it was time to go. Stumbling over the books, Ava got to her feet.

"Sorry, *Signora* Coppola!" Carol yelled, racing toward the door. She glanced behind them to see the man struggling to pull up his pants.

Ava slammed both palms into the door, with Carol piling in behind her. The door swung open, crashing into a man with a large bandage on his nose. The impact of the door crushed the cigarette in his mouth and sent him reeling backwards onto the sidewalk. The man grabbed his nose, howling in pain.

The girls leapt over him. Looking back over their shoulders, they could see Rossi fighting to regain control of his pants while *Signora* Coppola beat him with a large book and pushed him out the door.

"Get them, you idiot!" Ava heard Rossi's high-pitched voice shout, even though they were already half a block away. "*Get them*!" he screamed.

5
EXTINGUISHED

"That's Nose Guy," yelled Ava, suddenly realizing whose face she had just slammed the door into.

"Who?" yelled Carol as they raced down the alley, the faces of curious shop owners and tourists were a blur as they passed by.

"The guy last night with the hurt nose. Nose Guy."

"Oh!" Carol's eyes flicked to her peripheral. Behind them she could see the foreboding shadow of the tall man racing like a stick figure behind them, a strange whistling sound coming from him. "He's gaining on us!"

Ava quickly stole a glance over her shoulder. She was surprised sparks weren't flying from his Italian loafers as he chased them down. The man was clearly gaining on them with each stride, his nose whistling like a squeaky toy with each breath.

"Hang in there, we're almost to the hotel," puffed Ava, recognizing the start of the Piazza Ognissanti. Just beyond them was the Arno River, and she could see the back of the St. Regis from where they were. They were so, *so* close.

"We're going to make it," she breathed out sharply. They turned the corner to the front entrance of the St. Regis, bolting as nimbly as they could after making a hairpin turn. The doors swooshed open. Ava and Carol jumped inside, just in time to see Nose Guy attempt to put on the brakes, only to be betrayed by his Italian loafers. He floundered, his arms waving wildly, as he skated right past the doorway, sliding another six feet before coming to an awkward stop.

Had they not been *that* close to being caught by legit kidnappers, Ava would have thrust a huge white card in the air with "9/10" on it for the man's near-perfect execution of the Italian slide. *Whoosh*....

The girls gracelessly ran-walked to the elevators, trying to get as far as they could away from the man without causing a disturbance.

They need not have worried. Visitors lined the check-in area. The two bellhops were busy struggling across the lobby with two massive luggage carts overfilled with expensive luggage, followed by an impeccably dressed man and woman who were mercilessly berating the bellhops.

The girls reached the elevator, and Ava hit the open button about a million times. Carol looked nervously behind them. Thankfully with a *ding*, the door slid open, and the two practically jumped in. Carol hit the ninth-floor button just as the evil, loafer-wearing villain walked through the hotel doors. He immediately spotted the girls.

"Uh, Ava," said Carol.

"On it." Ava punched the door-close button over and over again as the man speed-walked toward the elevator. He reached out with his good hand, and Ava realized with dread that they were about to be caught.

"Ava...," cried Carol, her voice strained with panic. "Either the ninth-floor button isn't working or this door won't close."

Ava looked around frantically and saw the fire extinguisher on the wall. Without a second thought, she yanked it from where it was attached and pointed the nozzle toward the kidnapper.

His eyes went crossed as he stared down the hose of the extinguisher. She couldn't believe it. He didn't stop. "You have no idea what you are doing!" he shouted, less than two yards away, teeth bared.

"I do," she replied, and winced. "I'm getting grounded for a month." Her thumb pressed down, and the nozzle went off, spraying puffy white extinguisher spray all over his face, just as he was about to reach them. Ava shouted "Here!" and chucked the fire extinguisher at the man, who shockingly caught it against his chest. The doors closed and Ava fell back against the rear wall of the elevator, releasing a blast of air from her lungs as the elevator shot upward.

Carol stared at Ava, and for a good five seconds, neither of them said a word. "Nice shot," she finally smiled. "He has officially been extinguished."

"Nice one!" laughed Ava. "So, why did you hit the ninth floor? We're on the fifth floor."

"Because," said Carol, jabbing the five button, stopping the elevator as they approached the fifth floor. The elevator *dinged* again and the door slid open, absurdly sooner than it did in the lobby. "I wanted him to enjoy his nine flights of steps. He'll think we are on the ninth floor. Come on!"

The girls sprinted down the hallway to their room, skidding to a stop in front of their door. Ava fumbled for her key card, then she paused.

"A-*vah*," said Carol exasperatedly. "What are you doing? He could be here any second."

"My mom might be in there," she replied pointedly. "Unless you want to explain why we're breathing like a pack of rabid wolves were chasing us, we have to fix ourselves up. Aren't you the one who usually reminds us?"

"Yeah, okay." Taking a quick second to calm their breathing and fix their clothes—just in case Ava's mom was already back from the morning meetings—they exhaled together, grinned, and opened the door. "Oh, and by the way, lions are scary enough without them having to be rabid."

"Point taken," acknowledged Ava. "Now move—you're blocking my lighting…. Mom? You here?" Ava paused, listening.

No answer. They pushed the door open wider and walked in. No sign of her at all.

"Ah," breathed Ava. "That's kind of a relief. I know we'll see her later, and I've had my fill of adults for the moment."

"Fair enough." Carol turned and locked their door.

Ava shed her jacket and launched herself onto their bed, bouncing on the springs. "Ughhhh… Italy is exhausting."

Carol turned and looked at the back of Ava's head buried among the pillows. She remembered that when they were little, and whenever they'd watch a movie with a scary or super-awkward part, Ava would bury her head between couch pillows like an ostrich who was afraid. "Hey. You all right?"

"We were just chased from a wrecked bookstore by a creepy Italian villain, right after we stood up against *another* creepy Italian villain," she said, voice muffled by pillows. "I'm fine. I do my best thinking this way—the less oxygen to the brain the better."

"Yeah," sighed Carol. "It's also your best angle…."

Ava peaked up from her pillow and grinned. "Thank you for the compliment. I bet it's moments like these that you wish you could soothe yourself by playing your bassoon."

"It's true, if nothing more than to annoy you," smiled Carol as she wiggled her eyebrows.

"I just feel sorry for *Signora* Coppola. It's bad enough that they destroyed her bookstore, and then to have the nerve to walk in like they owned the place?"

"I like her—she's got sass. She deserved a lot better than that," Carol scoffed.

"And the old man… the ring, Luca, that weird symbol… Nothing seems to fit together."

"Oh, I was just asking *Signora* Coppola if she knew Luca… but that's when Rossi ruined things."

"Yeah, it's crazy," Ava pushed herself up from the blankets. "Did you see Rossi's face when he saw the ring?"

Carol shook her head. "I was too busy depantsing him."

"That was epic," said Ava, a smile growing on her face. "Absolutely brilliant. I wish you'd seen his boxers."

Carol laughed. "I more wished I'd seen the look on his face when it happened."

"Sheer, obliterated freaking-outness," stated Ava. If anyone back at school had known what Carol had done, she'd be a legend.

"Honestly, I'm just glad he was wearing boxers!" laughed Carol.

"Yeah, me too."

"Can I see the ring?" asked Carol, plopping on the bed in front of Ava and crossing her legs into a pretzel. She settled her hands in her lap, waiting.

Ava scrambled off the bed to snag her jacket off the floor, then jumped back on the bed. As she sat up, the envelope slipped out of her jacket pocket a second time, falling onto the comforter. When Carol gave her a look, Ava sighed, exasperated. "Okay, so my jacket pocket is obviously not the ideal place to keep this thing. From here on out, you are the official ring bearer."

"Excuse me. Why do you think I'm capable of holding onto this crazy super-secret thing?" Carol replied.

"Because I'm sure as heck not, and I trust you more than myself!"

"The Sherlock and Watson duo strikes again," muttered Carol, casting a sidelong glance. Their eyes met, and they burst into giggles.

"Okay, okay," Ava said, though it felt good to laugh after the whole ordeal, "we're a no-nonsense pair right now." She opened the envelope and handed Carol the ring.

"It is definitely half a ring. It looks like it's bronze," said Carol, turning it over in her fingers. Her eyes squinted and she scooted over to hold it under the bedside lamp. The light glinted off the metal, catching Ava's eye. "But check it out—this is kind of weird. It has a very peculiar pattern on its face. It sort of looks like a—"

"Pentagon?" offered Ava.

"No," said Carol slowly. "A pentagon has five sides." That wasn't quite it. She searched her mind to come up with the right word, and when she found it, she almost wished she hadn't. "A *hexagram*."

"A hexagram?" asked Ava as chills raced up her spine, making the tiny hairs at the back of her neck stand up in attention. "Uhm, big brain, isn't the hexagram the...," she gulped, "devil's symbol? That can't be it."

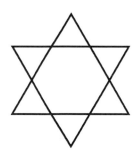

"Hmm...," was Carol's only response as she twisted the ring under the desk lamp.

"Oh, man," Ava groaned. "No way. Please, please tell me that we don't have a cursed ring. If I start saying *my precious* or become extremely fond of burlap cloaks and bad hair.... Carol, are we going to have to hunt down a pit of lava to destroy this thing? I didn't even watch all *The Lord of the Rings* movies! We don't even know how this thing ends!"

Ava continued to rant about the bathtub being the safest place during tornadoes and the apocalypse was supposed to happen ages ago until Carol, rolling her eyes, got up and plucked a grape from the tray on the desk. Without wasting another moment, she threw it at Ava with perfect aim, thwacking her in the head.

"Hey!" Ava narrowed her eyes. "You heard my mom earlier: No food fights in the hotel room."

"Ava, quit it!" she said. "Think for a second. Why would they kidnap an old man? Why would bad guys be so desperate to get whatever he had?"

"He had the ring," said Ava matter-of-factly, looking at her friend. "The old man had the ring. And he hid it. They were obviously after the ring."

Carol nodded. "I bet my Klaus Thunemann T-shirt we're supposed to find Luca, and he'll know what to do with the ring, and how to help the old man."

"I'm not going to even ask… because I feel like the truth is sadder than anything I could ever imagine. However, I would like to remind you that bassoon rhymes with buffoon."

"He is a world-famous bassoonist," sniffed Carol as she crossed her arms.

"I rest my case," said Ava, ducking as Carol whipped another grape at her.

6
MICHAEL THE ARCHANGEL

Carol grabbed her tablet from her backpack and web searched "hexagram ring."

Carol sighed. There were hundreds of results, mostly dealing with the occult. "Ava, I don't know how much we're going to find using the power of Google."

Ava crouched to peak over her shoulder. "I'll help. Sometimes four eyes are better than two." After about five pages of scanning results, something caught Ava's eye. "Wait. Click that."

"I don't know if that has anything to do with what we're looking for, Ava," Carol said doubtfully.

"I'm not talking about the kitten playing with yarn on a hexagram," she said. Her index finger pointed at the tablet screen. "That one."

Carol clicked it, and a new page came up. She raised an eyebrow. "*Solomon's ring*. Sounds biblical."

"Maybe Luca is actually Harrison Ford…. Does it say directed by Steven Spielberg?"

Carol shook her head and began to read aloud. "No, listen. God gave King Solomon a ring that had magical powers to control and entrap demons. The ring was made of brass and iron. There were two pieces, and when they were placed together, the wearer would have incredible power over the spirit world. The four jewels gave Solomon power over spirits, animals, wind, and water. The four red jewels signify the power over these four realms.

"The ring is said to be part of Solomon's secret treasure, which many believe today has been moved from hiding place to hiding place across the globe, hidden and protected by an ancient secret society of warrior priests—bound to protect the ring and powerful artifacts from falling into the wrong hands. Many men have died in their attempts to find or steal the treasure."

Ava stared wide-eyed at Carol. "Wait a second. That sounds like our old man. He definitely wouldn't go down without a fight... and he risked his life for that ring." She leaned back and crossed her arms, exhaling slowly. "Do... do you think that the old man was a warrior priest?"

"It's possible, isn't it?" she responded. "Something made him trust you in an instant... so we know he wasn't making rational decisions," smiled Carol. "Think about it.... I mean, I don't believe in all of the magical, fantasy stuff. But, what if it is real? Like in that *Raiders of the Lost Ark* movie? What if this ring actually gave the wearer magical powers?

"I mean, those are grown men... and they are willing to beat and kidnap an old man for something that looks like an old piece of junk jewelry."

"I think we have our answer then," Ava said.

Carol nodded solemnly and met her friend's eyes. "For now, we've got to protect this ring, until we find out what's really going on!"

Mrs. Clarke texted the girls that she would not be back for lunch. Ava desperately wanted to go outside and breathe some fresh air, and go to an outside café, but Carol insisted that it would be much too dangerous… and Ava had to agree this time that Carol was right.

As Carol continued to comb through the internet, looking for information to tie the ring, Luca, and the strange symbol together, Ava ordered a large spaghetti and meatball entrée and a half loaf of bread.

"We need a murder board," said Carol decidedly.

"A what?"

"A murder board. You know, like on the detective shows where they put all of their clues on a board on the wall and then figure out how they all tie together."

"Oh, that would be awesome, but—"

Ava's thought was cut off by a knock at the door. "Wow, that's some really fast room service!"

"Wait," whispered Carol. "Look through the peephole to see who it is."

"Good idea," whispered Ava as she tiptoed to the door. She peered through the small peephole. She could see the top half of a twenty-something-year-old woman with a cute little hat. "It's okay; it's a hotel woman."

Ava opened the door slowly, leaving the chain hooked. "Hello," smiled Ava, looking around the woman for a cart or steaming hot tray of food.

"Madam, a gift has arrived. The woman left it at the front desk and asked that I deliver it personally—uhm, a Miss Ava Clarke."

"Oh." Ava cleared her throat and stared suspiciously at the small gift bag in the woman's hand. "I wasn't expecting anything. Who is it from?"

The young woman glanced down at the bag. "I'm not sure, madam; she said it was important."

Ava paused a moment and unclasped the chain. "Okay, thank you very much," said Ava, accepting the bag from the woman.

"Oh, how thoughtless of me! One moment please," Ava raced across the hotel room and grabbed her purse, retrieving a shiny quarter. "Here you go," she said, smiling broadly as she placed the quarter into the palm of the woman's hand. "Have a wonderful day." Ava abruptly shut the door and turned her attention back to Carol.

"Wow," said Carol, shaking her head. "You truly are out of touch with reality."

Ava ignored her comment, too eager to explore the contents of the mysterious bag. Reaching in, she pulled out a small paper book, held together with a stapled binding. A handwritten note was attached to the cover.

"Who's it from?" Carol asked.

Ava studied the note while shaking her head. "It's from *Signora* Coppola, from the bookstore—and whoa, is her spelling horrible! I can barely read this." She handed the note to Carol. "See what I mean?"

"Oh, she's thanking us for our help," she said, a small smile starting in the corner of her mouth. "She's Italian, Ava. She did her best to write this in English so we can understand it."

"So…," prompted Ava.

"She said she found the book on the night of the robbery and thought that we might have dropped it because it is an old tourist guidebook from a place called La Villa De Cathedral. She also wishes us well… and of course to be careful."

Ava and Carol turned their attention to the book. On the cover was a picture of a beautiful statue of Saint Michael the Archangel, wings arched with robes cascading down from where he stood. His face was solemn, but his eyes drew Ava in, making her study his face. Hmm-ing to herself, she turned the book over. The binding around the spine was falling apart just a bit, as old books do, and based on how soft and yellow with age the pages were, Ava was sure it was a pretty old book.

She was about to dive into the book with Carol when a sharp *knock knock* on their door made the girls jump.

"Room service," a man's voice sang out, trilling the *R*s. The girls had been so excited about getting the package, they'd forgotten about lunch.

Ava walked quietly to the door, leaned forward, and looked through the peephole. The man's face looked long and distorted through the lens. Ava could see the corner of a cart draped in a white cloth as well as a collection of silver serving dishes.

She turned to Carol and gave her the thumbs-up. The man smiled at the girls and quickly backed into the room, pulling his cart with him. Carol thought it was ironic that the man who served the food was exceptionally thin. Ava liked him because of his rebellious tie clip (a monkey with green eyes) and pants that were at least two inches short, showing off mismatched zebra striped and leopard spotted socks.

Asking for permission, the man swiftly cleared the small table in their room, placing the newspaper and Carol's tablet onto the couch like they were priceless jewels worth millions of dollars.

Ava and Carol oohed and ahhed as he stepped back from the table. Each girl had a heaping plate of spaghetti, with two meatballs and freshly ground parmesan cheese in a small glass bowl. With the waiter in attendance throughout their meal, they each had a salad, a bowl with olive oil and herbs, two pieces of Italian bread, and a glass of Pellegrino sparkling water. In the center of the table, he had placed a small white vase, filled with a bouquet of colorful flowers.

Ava clapped... completely overwhelmed by the artistry, and for the first time in her life, she reached into her purse and gave the man *two* shiny quarters.

The man left, wondering if it had been his presentation or the socks that resulted in the tiny tip.

Ava closed her eyes, breathing in the delectable cacophony of flavors. She looked up at Carol, who was busy doing something on her tablet. "How can you possibly be on your tablet at a time like this?"

Suddenly, Ava felt her phone buzz in her back pocket. She grabbed her phone, thinking it would most likely be her mother. Instead, it was a text from Carol: *You have been gifted "Tipping for Dummies" from Carol Miller.*

"Funny. Quarters are not a joke! People appreciate the weighty feeling of a nice shiny coin in their pocket."

"Mm-hmm…," said Carol as she grabbed the book and began casually flipping through the pages, not really expecting to find anything. "This book is really old," she said, dipping her bread into an olive oil and fresh herb mix.

She checked inside the cover to see if anyone had written their name or any notes, but she didn't find anything. The book was text-heavy with some photos, but something made Carol suddenly inhale sharply.

"Ava, look." Her finger traced across the soft, worn paper until it reached a small symbol printed at the middle of the page. Under it was a small block of text. Carol couldn't make out all of the words, but she could understand *simbolo di San Michele.* "Symbol of Saint Michael," she whispered.

She pointed excitedly to the picture on the next page of the sculpture.

"Ava," she started. "Ava, oh my gosh. I think we may have just found Luca."

"Wait, what?" exclaimed Ava. "What do you mean?!"

"Look," said Carol, tapping a small block of text. Ava leaned in closer. Beneath the sculpture were the words "Villa De Cathedral, Michele Arcangelo, 1465. By Luca Delia Robbia."

"The sculptor's name is Luca!" said Carol excitedly.

"Only one problem," said Ava, shaking her head. "He's probably dead by now."

Carol closed her eyes for a moment and exhaled. "Of course he's dead—he would be like six hundred years old. When the old man said 'find Luca,' maybe this is what he meant. The symbol that we found is for Michael the Archangel, the artist Luca…," she paused while she read his name, "Robbia created the sculpture… all of these things can't be coincidental."

Ava flattened out the book on the table. "There is something written in the margin." She pulled the page out flat. Scrawled into the margin of the page were the words "*sblocca lo scroll*."

"Okay," said Ava, tilting her head. "Any idea what *sblocca lo scroll* means?"

"Well, obviously it has something to do with a scroll. Give me a second." Carol grabbed her tablet and searched the word *sblocca*. "Ah," she said, nodding. "It comes from *sbloccare*, and it means to unlock!"

"So, unlock," whispered Ava enthusiastically. "Unlock the scroll! Uhm, Carol… which scroll are they talking about?"

Carol held the book close, squinting one eye. The book was old and the pictures gray and faded, but she could just make out what looked like a scroll in Saint Michael's left hand. "It looks like Saint Michael is either holding a scroll or a paper towel holder."

Ava grabbed the book from Carol and examined the picture. "Or one of those big pepper shakers that they have at fancy restaurants. I'm going with scroll, though. One problem: How do we find this statue? We're in Italy; everywhere you look there's a statue. They even have statues of statues," moaned Ava.

"The Villa de Cathedral. The statue is located at the Villa de Cathedral."

"We—" Ava's phone jumped to life, gyrating across the table. "One sec," said Ava, holding up a finger to Carol. "It's my mom." Carol busied herself on her tablet looking for the best route to take from the hotel to the Villa de Cathedral. Thankfully, the cathedral was only a few blocks from the hotel, and the street was lined with dozens of small stores, which meant lots of people and hopefully safety.

"Mom's on her way," said Ava, placing her phone on the table. "She warned us to stay in the room. She said that a conference attendee said that there had been a crazy man in the hotel lobby earlier, wielding a fire extinguisher."

Carol snorted. "He sounds dangerous. I think your mom's right... we'd better stay put."

"I'm sure everything will be okay," winked Ava. "I hear Inspector Rossi is on the case!"

"Oh," laughed Carol. "In that case, I just have one thing to say. Pants!!!"

7
VILLA DE CATHEDRAL

Smack! Ava awoke the next morning to a kiss on the forehead from her mom. "You're leaving already?" said Ava, stretching and yawning simultaneously. "We've hardly spent any time together."

Ava's mom smiled at Ava as she brushed her hair gently from her face. "I promise to make it an early day today. We'll go sightseeing and have a fancy dinner together this evening, I promise."

"And... Mom?"

"Yes," said Beth, looking into Ava's eyes lovingly. Was her daughter about to say something endearing?!

"I would like to report a robbery... and I know who the thief is."

"What?" asked her mom, worry now filling her face.

"I want to report the theft of that dress you are wearing, because I'm stealing it when we get back to the States. Mom, you look beautiful."

"Ava, Ava, Ava," laughed her mom, relief filling her face. "I'll see you this afternoon."

"Okay," smiled Ava. "Love you, Mom."

"Love you too," said Mrs. Clarke softly.

The door clicked behind her, and Ava stared up at the ceiling, a smile plastered across her face. She had the coolest mom ever.

~~o~o~o~~

The girls hesitated as they exited through the hotel's sliding glass doors. Their heads swiveled back and forth, searching for anyone suspicious. Florence had come to life. The tourists were easy to spot with their maps and phones out, looking confused. Locals worked their way around them, muttering their annoyance in Italian. Bicycles, cars, and colorful Vespa scooters zoomed by on the Lungarno Amerigo Vespucci highway. The sunlight, sparkling like a thousand diamonds, danced across the Arno River, creating a perfect backdrop.

Ava closed her eyes and smiled. Carol laughed to herself: The controlled chaos probably matched what went on in Ava's brain, every second of every day.

After what seemed like an entire two minutes of searching for bad guys, the girls decided that the coast was clear. Carol had mapped out a simple route to get to the Villa de Cathedral on her phone. As they threaded their way through numerous small shops, Ava used the reflections of the glass storefronts to make sure they weren't being followed. Having skipped breakfast, the duo darted into Luigi's Bakery and purchased freshly baked cinnamon raisin bagels coated with to-die-for cream cheese.

Ava thought the bagel was the most delicious thing she had ever tasted in her life. Carol thought the cream cheese must have been made in heaven and sent to Luigi's by angels each morning.

"There's the Villa de Cathedral," said Carol excitedly—gesturing toward a colossal stone building that looked more like a castle.

The Villa de Cathedral was a beautiful piece of architecture with nine majestic towers reaching toward the heavens. Ominous windows reached upward through pointed architecture. *Flying buttresses*, recalled Carol from their art class. At the top of the largest tower, a winged angel stood, raising a sword skyward. Above the archway was a massive balcony containing dozens of sculptures of saintly men. Carol stared at the arched ceiling as they stepped through the doorway. It seemed to pierce the sky.

Ava started walking first, heading to the heavy-looking doors. They were heavy, sure enough, and Ava had to really use her strength to pull open one of the doors, gripping onto the iron and heaving. They walked into the spacious opening, every wall holding an ornate sculpture built into the architecture. The cathedral was filled with golden light that glinted off the polished pews and marble statues, and it smelled of incense, smoky spice, and old wood.

"These cathedrals are more like works of art than buildings," said Carol to Ava.

She nodded. "It's incredible," said Ava, taking in the view.

It looked like something out of a fairytale, where the hero stumbles upon an abandoned castle hidden in the mountains, ancient and beautiful.

"Oh, man," Ava murmured. "This is beautiful. But it's going to be super hard to find that sculpture."

Carol shook her head. "It's Michael. He's important, so they'd probably put him in a place of importance. Like…," she pointed to a statue behind the sanctuary, "there."

Ava looked at Carol, eyebrows raised. "Remind me never to challenge you in a game of I Spy."

"You wouldn't stand a chance," laughed Carol as she bumped Ava's shoulder.

The girls walked through the cathedral up to the statue, which towered over them. Carol couldn't believe it was just a statue. The waves in the Archangel's robes looked so real, and he was every bit as beautiful and intimidating as she imagined an angel would be in person. In one hand he held a spear and in the other hand a scroll. The girls surreptitiously examined the statue, each walking around, looking at the Latin script written below him to the top of his sculpted head.

"Carol," said Ava. "What exactly did that writing say in the margin of the book?"

"Unlock the scroll," she replied quietly.

Ava glanced around, trying not to look suspicious while scrutinizing the statue. "How exactly do you unlock a scroll?"

"I have no idea," said Carol. "It looks like it's a solid piece of marble." She looked around wearily. "There are security cameras everywhere, Aves… we don't want to draw a lot of attention."

"Right, we need to act like tourists," nodded Ava. "I'll stand in front of the statue. Act like you're taking pics of me from different angles, but focus on the scroll."

"Perfect!" agreed Carol as she reached for her phone.

Ava stood in front of the statue, striking touristy poses, while Carol zoomed in on the scroll.

"I got some great pictures, Aves. Your parents are going to love these," smiled Carol.

"Oh, I bet they will. Mind if I scroll through them?" smiled Ava, playing along. "Get it, *scroll* through them?"

"Next time you are alone with your thoughts," said Carol through gritted teeth, "please take a moment and Google the word *subtle*."

The girls huddled around Carol's phone, but, try as they might, they didn't see anything that looked like an opening for a key.

"Maybe there's a button, or you have to twist it?" suggested Ava.

Carol magnified the picture even more. A series of symbols encircled the top and bottom of the scroll, but other than that, there were no other markings on the scroll.

"I wish I read old symbols…."

"Yeah, I don't recognize…," Carol stopped. "Okay, I do recognize one symbol, except it's upside down."

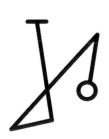

Carol dragged her finger across the screen, centering the image.

"That's the symbol for Michael!" Ava whispered excitedly. "The same one on the paper! Except... it's upside down."

Carol nodded and continued to stare at the image.

"Why would it be upside down?" inquired Ava. "I mean, certainly if Luca sculpted Michael he would...," Ava watched in horror as Carol suddenly climbed up on the base of the statue. "Carol! You can't touch a crazy old statue!"

Using her fingernail, Carol placed it on the edge of the upside-down symbol... and pulled. The marble symbol snapped off into Carol's hand. A small hole appeared. Carol's heart was pounding, adrenaline rushing through her body.

"Carol! Get down—people are looking!" Ava's head spun from side to side. "We are *so* going to jail! Get down!"

"Ava, chill! I found something!" The hole was tiny, the size of a matchhead. And from the hole, a tiny piece of knotted thread protruded.

Ava heard the squawk of a walkie-talkie in the distance. A security guard appeared from a hidden door across the sanctuary. *"Carol...* we have company!" hissed Ava.

Carol set her jaw and gave the string a gentle tug. There was a soft mechanical click, and then, from out of the base of the statue, a thin, small, copper cylinder rolled out onto the floor.

"What in the absolute heck…," whispered Ava, as she quickly reached down and snatched the copper tube off the floor.

Carol jumped down from the statue. The security guard was running toward them.

"Carol!"

"I know!" she cried out. "Run!"

"Stop!" yelled the guard.

Ava and Carol weren't about to stop. They raced through the cathedral, pushing their way through stunned tourists. They burst through the sanctuary into the cathedral's rotunda. They could see the massive doors that would lead to freedom. But just as they put on a burst of speed, a huge guard stepped in front of the door, his legs spread wide, his huge, beefy arms crossed defiantly across his chest. A grin crossed his face as if to say, *Come on, try me!*

Carol was about to shout to Ava that they needed to find another way out when the door opened behind the guard. Ava saw their chance! "High-low!" she screamed. Ava dove headfirst, sliding along the slick marble floor through the beefy guard's legs. Simultaneously, Carol ran at the man at breakneck speed. At the last moment, Ava kicked out at the back of the man's knees, sending him sprawling onto the floor as Carol hurdled him and continued through the doorway.

The girls ran down the steps and down the street, looking back only when the cathedral was a tiny dot behind them. Winded, the girls sat down on the grass, under a small grove of trees, fighting to catch their breath.

"High-five for the high-low!" wheezed Carol.

"That was crazy," gasped Ava. "I cannot believe you climbed up on that statue."

"It's the quiet ones you always have to be afraid of," smiled Carol creepily.

"Well, it was brilliant," praised Ava. She was about to pull out the small copper tube when Carol put her hand on her arm.

"Probably not the best idea to do that here."

Ava looked around. "Yeah, you're right. Let's get back to the hotel."

8
DON'T MESS WITH NUNS

The girls began their journey back to the hotel, both glancing around every now and then to make sure they weren't being followed.

"Ava, stop and tie your shoe," whispered Carol suddenly.

"What?"

"Stop and tie your shoe. I need to see something."

Ava immediately understood; she knelt down and began retying her shoe. "What is it?" she asked as she double knotted the laces.

"They're getting smarter…."

"Who is getting smarter?" said Ava, standing.

"The bad guys. Don't turn around, but there is a man in a suit, wearing sneakers—he's been following us since we passed the bus stop."

"Oh, great… and he's wearing sneakers? With a suit? I hope they're at least stylish."

The girls picked up their pace, maneuvering through the crowds of tourists and locals—catching sight of him on the huge glass windows as they passed each store.

"In here!"

Carol grabbed Ava's arm and they ducked into a busy ice cream parlor. They weaved and dodged through a crowd of patrons enjoying their ice cream and gelato. "*Scusami*," said Carol over and over again. She heard Ava saying it too, but they didn't stop for a second. They continued to work their way to the back of the store, as far away from the entrance as possible.

They reached the back of the ice cream store and turned toward the rear door. The hairs on Ava's neck stood straight up as the man in the suit calmly maneuvered through the parlor with the grace of a shark. Ava could see a swirl of tattoos starting from his jaw and disappearing into the collar of his shirt. His hair was buzzed short, revealing a nasty purple scar that ran the entire width of his forehead.

If he had two bolts on each side of his head, he would look like Frankenstein, thought Ava.

Ava poked Carol, who looked at her friend with a panicked expression. She nodded to the counter, where a girl with a freckly, bored face and hair twisted in a bun, took a couple's money and handed them change.

"Come on," said Carol urgently. "Follow me!"

Ava followed Carol as she crawled through a sea of legs and feet toward the counter, their sneakers skimming the ground quickly. Shouting "*scusa*" to the girl behind the counter, Ava and Carol leapt over the counter and burst through a door into a kitchen, where young men and women were busy scooping ice cream and making homemade cones. The girls raced through the kitchen shouting apologies and pushed through a screen door. Looking left and right, Carol chose left and the two began running as fast as they could.

Moments later, Ava heard the door slam behind them. She risked a glance over her shoulder. The man was already racing toward them.

"Here he comes!" yelled Ava.

The girls had almost made it to the end of the alley, where they heard the hissing of brakes as a bus pulled into a bus stop.

"The bus!" shouted Carol.

Just a few more steps! The girls glanced back over their shoulders, which was a horrible mistake. Ava felt a jolting impact against her chest. Carol's legs smashed into something, sending her airborne. There was a flurry of black robes and a sickening clatter.

For a split second, Carol thought they'd run right into a second bad guy. That was... until she saw a black and white habit fly into the air. Ava and Carol had slammed into a nun riding a shiny red bicycle, knocking her off her bike.

"*Mamma mia!*" exclaimed the woman, haphazardly brushing off her robe and regaining her habit and straightening the large cross that hung around her neck. She glowered at the girls with all the wrath of God.

"*Scusa,*" said Carol desperately. She then pointed at the man in the close distance, running after them. She searched for the words in her head, wishing she'd had a dictionary on her. "Uhm, *male*! *Aiuto*. Uhm... hm." She stumbled over her words. "*P-per favore, signora. Aiuto.*"

The nun looked at the man and then back at the girls. She nodded, understanding dawning on her face. *This man is chasing two children! How dare he?!* She lifted her shiny red bike, blocking the alley.

"*Correre!*" she yelled at the girls. *Run!* The girls didn't hesitate—they took off to the right down another alleyway, throwing "thank yous" back to the nun as they sprinted away.

Neither could help but look back. They saw the nun whip back her robe, a picture of absurd drama, and from her belt hung a huge wooden paddle. Something visceral happened to the man, a change crossing over his face. He skidded on his heels, eyes dropping to the paddle like it was made of barbed wire. The nun smoothly and swiftly drew it from her belt like St. Michael slaying his dragon and raised it above her head, the glare she'd given the girls earlier now intensified. As the man attempted to stop his momentum—shouting challengingly, "No! *No!*"—the nun swung the paddle, thwacking the man's head.

THWACK.

Both of the girls winced. *Oooh, that had to hurt.* It worked, though, and he turned and began racing back up the alleyway, the nun coming after him, a flurry of black robes whipping around her, her tongue spitting fire. The girls grinned at each other.

"*Mamma Mia!*" laughed Carol.

"I think that nun's my new role model," said Ava.

"Next stop, the hotel?" Carol puffed as they ran.

Ava nodded. "So long as we make it there alive."

9
NEVER UNDERESTIMATE A QUARTER

The girls raced up the Piazza Ognissanti, the gray stones beneath them practically rumbling as they left small earthquakes in their wake. The wind picked up, and Ava's hair whipped around her face, twisting the strands and making them rough. She had a strange feeling of déjà vu and realized, around twenty-four hours beforehand, they were being chased through the same piazza, by the same kind of people. *Oh, man!*

"Remind me," puffed Ava, "to tell you about a training idea for our track team. It involves dangerous and angry criminals."

"I think I already know what you have in mind," laughed Carol.

"Do you think they were in the cathedral? Or do you think they just spotted us leaving?"

"I think they were watching us," said Carol as the girls slowed to a walk as they approached their hotel. "I think they followed us to the cathedral, but they didn't approach us because they wanted to see what we were up to."

"Oh," nodded Ava, "like they thought that we might know something... and when they saw us with the statue...."

"And the copper tube... they came after us."

As the girls turned the corner toward the hotel's entrance, Carol grabbed Ava's arm.

"Not again...," moaned Ava.

Sitting on a bench was a man smoking, dressed in a perfectly tailored suit. He had a hat on top of his shiny, greased hair, and a cigarette that dangled from his lips like a bird with a worm. They watched him touch his ear and then nod to no one they could see.

"He's here for us," muttered Ava. "He has to be watching to see if we come back to the hotel. And he looks like the others." She rolled her eyes. "It's like those first two kidnappers just kept giving birth to more and more bad guys."

"We have to find another way inside, and I don't think we can use any fire extinguisher tricks this time around."

"I could use it to put out his cigarette," winked Ava. "Don't these guys know it's bad for their health?"

"Come on," nudged Carol. "There's gotta be an entrance in the back."

As they circled around, Ava could see a large truck parked at the delivery bay. The smell of bread wafted their way, and the two inhaled together, breathing in deep. It smelled delicious.

"Okay, I think we could get into the hotel if we use their help," Ava said, pointing at the truck.

The girls crept closer to the truck, watching as two workers transferred bread into the hotel via a huge metal ramp. Each box of freshly baked bread was heaved up and placed on a hand pallet truck, which a worker then rolled up the ramp through a doorway.

Carol caught on and quickly stepped onto the ramp after the last worker headed through the doorway. Ava followed her, looking warily behind them as she went.

The room was filled with barrels of olive oil stacked against the right wall, linens on a set of shelves, and other hotel supplies organized around the room.

"If we weren't being chased, I could literally eat this room," Carol whispered.

Ava watched as the deliverymen ducked through a makeshift door that looked a lot like a heavy leather drape with a plastic rectangular window. The girls crouched next to each other behind several barrels of olive oil, waiting for the delivery drivers to leave. A couple of minutes later, they heard voices, and then one by one, the drivers pushed their hand trucks through the door and down the ramps.

Carol peered through the window and gave Ava a thumbs-up.

"One more second," Carol whispered. Ava nodded.

From where she could peek over the barrel, she saw one of the men walk to the delivery truck, waving at another worker and shouting something friendly in Italian. The man shouted back, laughing with ease. The third waved goodbye as the remaining workers went down the ramp. The girls could see him push a button on the wall. A metal door, which looked a lot like Carol's parents' garage door, began sliding down on the back of the truck, closing off its opening. The last man, satisfied, walked through the room and then exited through the hanging leather door, the sound of his heavy boots disappearing with him.

"That took forever," said Ava, peeking her head farther up. "Think it's clear?"

"I think so," said Carol, standing up. "Whatever's through that door will probably get us into the hotel."

The girls moved cautiously through the door. To their right was a hallway, with a dark blue arrow painted on the wall that said *Cucina*.

"Kitchen," said Carol aloud.

"Sounds like the best way to sneak back into the hotel," whispered Ava.

The girls walked down the hall until they reached the double doors marked *Cucina*. Ava pushed through and was instantly affronted with a mixture of people yelling and scurrying about. People dressed in chef uniforms with tall mushroom-shaped hats on their heads handed each other pots and pans, and orders were shouted left and right. It was an organized mess of chaos, with full meals appearing on plates like magic as they were passed to the back of the busy room.

A woman who looked to be in her mid-thirties with pale blond hair and light green eyes was brusquely walking to her station when she spotted the girls. She stopped, her hawk gaze studying the two, flicking between one and the other.

"American?" she put her hands on her hips.

"How did you know?" asked Ava.

"Because you are staring at my staff like they are aliens, and you are not supposed to be in here. What are you doing?" she asked, severe annoyance clear in her eyes.

"We're lost," volunteered Carol.

Ava nodded. "We don't know how we got here. Could you tell us how we could get back to the lobby?"

The woman sputtered, "*Ragazze sciocche*!" She pointed a finger to a bright red exit sign on the other side of the kitchen. "Get out of here, immediately! We do not have time for your little games."

In a flash, Ava recalled how terrifying Mrs. Coppola had been the night they first met her. This woman reminded her of Mrs. Coppola too well. *Maybe her daughter?*

Without a second to lose, the girls scrambled through the kitchen, rushing around the chefs and different stations to get to the exit sign. As they pushed through the door, they immediately faced another pair of double doors; these appeared more ornate with a small window built into the door. Carol went on her tiptoes to look through.

"These go to the lobby," Carol stated. She looked back at Ava. "Take a look."

Ava got on her tiptoes. Within seconds, though, she groaned. "We're still in trouble. Rossi's sitting on the middle couch, pretending to read a newspaper! See him...? What's with these guys and newspapers? Haven't they heard of the internet?"

Carol shrugged and gave an *I have no idea* expression. "So, what do we do? We can't go back through the kitchen."

Ava smudged her face against the window, looking left and right across the hotel lobby. "We have to get to the stairs."

"How are we supposed to get to the stairs with that guy sitting there?"

Ava pointed. "There! We could use that."

Carol squeezed in beside Ava and looked through the window. Her eyes followed the direction of Ava's finger. There was a huge cart half-filled with luggage parked about ten feet away. Carol glanced at Ava. "The luggage cart?"

Ava nodded. "Yes, single-file, and our first stop is that giant fake plant. We can hide behind that and then when we're sure the coast is clear, jet over to the cart." Ava paused momentarily. "Want to go first or should I?"

"Are you sure this is a good idea? I mean…."

"You climbed on top of an ancient statue in a cathedral…."

"Point taken," agreed Carol, "but you go first."

Ava pushed the door open slightly, just enough for the two to slip through. She immediately dropped to the floor and began army crawling to the plant.

"Why not just leap out the door and do a cartwheel and a bunch of ninja rolls?!" hissed Carol when they were safely behind the plant.

"What do you mean?" asked Ava, mystified by Carol's remark.

"Don't you think if anyone had seen us, it would have been much more suspicious to see two kids laying on their bellies, slithering across the floor like human snakes and hiding behind a plant?"

"Ah, but that's why you're Watson and I'm Sherlock. You think with intellect and reasoning; I think with my gut. Plus, you proved my point; no one saw us. So my plan worked."

Carol shook her head and moaned. "We'll have a conversation about reality later."

Ava ignored Carol's last comment. She carefully poked a finger through the leaves of the plant, slowly parting them so she could see Rossi. "I have a plan to distract him," she whispered. She reached in her jeans pocket and pulled out a quarter. *If I could just hurl this far enough for it to make a loud noise, we could take off in the other direction while he's distracted.*

"If you're going to distract him, try to aim for the wall closest to his head," volunteered Carol.

Ava nodded. "Good idea." She breathed in and out, focusing her concentration. When she was sure Rossi was looking away, she stood and whipped the quarter toward him. She watched as the quarter flew through the air… and with a *thwack*, smacked him on the side of the head. *Oh God, oh God, oh God!* Ava dropped quickly to the ground behind the plant.

"Hey!" yelled Rossi sharply, jumping to his feet, looking around the lobby.

Carol looked at Ava in disbelief. "I thought you were going to distract him, not hit him in the head!" she yelled-whispered.

The man circled around the couch before looking up at the ceiling and rubbing his head. He looked back down and paused. Bending, he picked up the quarter and held it in front of his face, turning it over carefully. An American quarter—Montana on one side, an eagle on the other.

He touched his ear, and the man outside stood up and walked into the lobby.

"Perfect," sighed Carol. "Now we're really dead—there's two of them."

"Nope," Ava clenched her jaw. "I have an idea."

"No, no, no, your ideas are going to land us in Italian prison!" Carol exclaimed quietly.

"Trust me," whispered Ava. "I was just a little off."

Before Carol could say anything, Ava quickly stood and whipped out another quarter. They said nothing as it sailed through the air—this time missing the men, but striking a large blue vase filled with flowers on a pedestal. The quarter struck the thin glass, shattering it, and both men dove to the floor.

Ava nodded proudly. "Bull's-eye." She had created the illusion of a gunshot.

Carol's eyes flew open! Ava grabbed her wrist, pulling her up as they bolted to the luggage cart.

"Okay, not exactly as I planned... but effective, right?" asked Ava once they were hidden again.

"Ask me again if we make it out alive." Carol watched in horror as a hotel staffer scurried over to the two men and they all began looking around. The bellhop was speaking into a walkie-talkie; the girls were sure he was calling Security.

"Follow me," whispered Ava urgently. Ever so slowly, she started pushing the luggage cart to the doorway on the other side of the room, aiming for the sign that read "Stairs."

The girls weren't sure if it was the slow *squeak, squeak* as the wheels turned or the cart that magically began moving by itself, but the bellhop and the two men suddenly froze and turned toward the luggage cart.

"Ava…," said Carol slowly, getting more and more anxious as the men turned and began quickly walking toward them.

"*Now.*" Ava yanked open the door and began sprinting up the steps.

Scrambling to keep up, Carol leapt up the steps two at a time. As they ran, she looked at her best friend. "You may want to actually *tell* me your plans if you want them to work!"

"Sorry! But look, first floor!" They didn't pause for a millisecond, hurrying up the stairs.

The girls raced up the steps, using the handrails to whip them around each corner. "Fifth floor, we're almost there!" Ava cried out. She could hear the footsteps of the chasing men, pounding on the staircase below them.

In full sprint, Ava burst through the doors and whipped out the room key. They flew through the hall, passing a table with a huge bowl filled with beautifully colored glass marbles, all blue and pink. On a whim Carol smacked her hand against the bowl, flipping it over. The hallway filled with hundreds of shiny glass marbles, rolling on the carpet with dull *pings*.

Just as they rounded the corner, the girls heard a series of loud *oooph, oooph*s. The bad guys landed heavily on the balls, falling over themselves.

"Nice going!" Ava said to Carol. With another burst of speed, the girls made it to their door, swiped the card, and jumped inside the room.

"Shhhh, wait," Carol whispered as she held the door shut. Sure enough, they heard the men pound past, shouting angrily in Italian to each other. Ava quietly locked the door and fastened the chain. Carol let out a long breath. Ava leaned her shoulder against the wall, running her fingers through her hair. They stared at each other, panting.

"I think the bad guys are falling for us!" laughed Ava.

"What?" asked Carol, bewildered. "Oh… the balls. Funny," she snorted.

The girls fist-bumped—they had made it.

10
SANTA FLORIAN DEL FUOCO

After catching their breath in their hotel room, the girls hurried over to the desk. Carol stood beside Ava as she grabbed the desk chair and knelt on top of it.

"Okay," said Ava excitedly, "let's see what all of this craziness is about."

Anticipation raced through Carol, making her hands fidget with excitement. Ava pulled the copper cylinder from her pocket. It was the length and diameter of an ink pen. The ends were sealed with what looked like red wax. Ava gently shook the tube while holding it up to her ear. *Nothing.*

"It looks like the ends are sealed with wax," offered Carol.

Ava nodded. She grabbed a paperclip from a stack of her mom's papers on the desk and straightened it. Carefully, she worked the wax out of the tube. Ava turned the cylinder over, holding her hand out beneath it in case something came out. The two held their breath. They knew, without speaking, that whatever the cylinder held, it was their best chance of finding out what to do next.

Ava tapped the open end of the cylinder on her palm. There was the slightest rattle, and then a small, brittle scroll slid into her hand.

Ava offered it to Carol, who picked it up gingerly. She spread it out between her fingers before flattening it against the desk. It was hard to read, the words scrawled in slanted cursive with blotted ink. It was also hard to read them because they were written in what looked to Carol like Latin.

"What's it say, big brain?" inquired Ava.

"I'm not sure…. I think it's written in Latin."

"There's also a map," pointed out Ava. A very roughly hand-drawn map lay below the mysterious writing.

"One second," said Carol as she retrieved her tablet from beside her bed. She opened Google Translate and typed the words *posizionare il rotolo sull'altare della luce.*

Carol's eyes narrowed. "Place… the scroll upon the Altar of Light."

"Okay… this gets weirder and weirder," moaned Ava. "Let me guess, the map is supposed to lead us to the Altar of Light?"

"I think so," said Carol, studying the map.

"I wish some divine bearded guy would just come out from the clouds, point a finger, and say, 'Hey you, go there.'"

Carol nodded. "There is a shortage of divine bearded guys, that's for sure, but… we do have the next best thing."

"A map that looks like it was drawn on an Etch A Sketch?" laughed Ava.

"Whoa, that was retro. I'm pretty sure that this is the Villa de Cathedral where we found the scroll, and if we follow this line through the city, it leads to… hmmm…."

"It leads to *hmmm*? Is that Italian?"

"Well," said Carol, thinking. "According to the map, it leads to something called the Santa Florian Del Fuoco."

"Santa Florian? Is that Santa's cousin?"

"I think Santa means saint. Give me a second," said Carol as her fingers tapped away on her tablet. "This doesn't make sense. It says Saint Florian is the patron saint of chimney sweeps and firefighters. He died in 304 AD."

"You're kidding, right? Chimney sweepers get their own saint?"

"Apparently, *del fuoco* means 'of fire.' So this is a church named after a saint, who guards chimney sweeps and firefighters."

"Maybe it's some kind of clue and we're just missing it," said Ava. "It says to place the scroll on the Altar of Light... maybe it really means Altar of Fire? I don't know.... Where is the church exactly?"

"I'll need to consult *Signore* Google Map," Carol said. After searching online, she looked at Ava with a confused expression. "I can't find anything on Google for a church or building named Santa Florian Del Fuoco."

"Okay," said Ava, pointing at the map. "What is *that* thing? It could be another landmark. It looks like a bird... or an airplane."

"Wait, maybe it's an airport," said Carol. "It has three words in Italian beneath it. Aquila di Dio."

"*Aquila*? Something to do with water... and God?" guessed Ava. "A water god? Noah? The clue is in the Ark!"

"Slow down," laughed Carol. "Okay, first of all, *aquila* has nothing to do with water; it means eagle. But, if we put it all together, the phrase translates to Eagle of God." On a whim, Carol searched "Eagle of God Florence."

"I never knew God had an eagle…," mused Ava as Carol typed. "I thought that was just an American bird."

"I found it! It's a statue. And according to our lovely hand-drawn map, the statue is directly across from the Santa Florian Del Fuoco. We just need to find that statue."

"Awesome, big brain—you're brilliant!" Ava's phone buzzed, startling her. "My mom…," blurted Ava, nodding at the phone. "She says that she's looking forward to spending the afternoon with us."

Ava quickly texted her back, letting her know that everything was awesome and that she and Carol were excited about spending the afternoon with her. She finished off with "I love you" and added half a dozen heart emojis to her text.

"So, if my mom's going to be here soon, we've gotta get moving."

"Unfortunately, we can't just leave."

"Rossi and his mutants…?"

"Rossi and his mutants," confirmed Carol, nodding. "Plus, I don't think we've endeared ourselves to the hotel staff. The fire extinguisher, the kitchen, the vase in the lobby, the decorative bowl filled with marbles in the hallway…."

"Okay, okay. I get your point. We're probably not their favorite guests."

"That's the understatement of the year," muttered Carol.

"What about one of the fire escape doors? There's one at the end of our hall."

"And, what if we open it and it sets off the alarm? They're gonna kick us out of the hotel for sure."

"Well, if we can't take the stairs and we can't take the elevator… how do you suggest we get downstairs? Teleport?"

"You actually had a brilliant plan. Two words," smiled Carol. "Fire. Escape."

"You just said that the doors for the fire escape probably have alarms."

"They probably do," laughed Carol as she grabbed her jacket. "Follow me. I've got a trick up my sleeve you're gonna love."

Carol slid the paper scroll into the tube and put it in her pocket. She turned to Ava and smiled. "Alrighty, let's wrap this mystery up—I'm starving."

11
FIRE

"I hate heights! You know I hate heights!"

"Just don't look down," warned Carol moments after climbing out of the window at the end of their hotel hallway. She stood on a narrow, metal, grated platform that jutted out from the side of the hotel. Despite the handrails, Ava was petrified.

Ava slowly crawled out the window and stood shaking beside her friend. She closed her eyes as a wave of vertigo washed over her. She gripped the side of the hotel as her knees buckled.

"Breathe," Carol advised in a soothing voice. "Breathe through your nose."

"I'm gonna *punch* you in the nose," hissed Ava.

Ava looked at the platform of twisted black metal. She could see the ground some sixty feet below through the grated floor. "Right now," gasped Ava, "the angry hotel staff seems like a much better option."

"Look, there is a platform between each set of stairs." Carol counted ten stairs between each platform. "Just take it one section at a time."

Ava nodded. *One set of stairs at a time.*

Carol descended slowly, watching as Ava turned and climbed down the stairs on her hands and knees like a child. She felt horrible for Ava; she could see her entire body trembling as she slowly made it down each platform.

"Okay," Carol said softly. "This is our last stop. I just need to lower this ladder down and it will take us down to the ground." Ava barely nodded. Carol lowered the huge metal ladder. It was connected to a pulley system that made a screeching noise like fingernails on a chalkboard as it lowered. The ladder clunked noisily to a stop about a foot from the ground.

Carol grimaced. "Okay, Aves, we gotta hurry."

Ava carefully followed Carol down the ladder, her sneakers making a *thump* as she landed. Carol bumped her shoulder gently and smiled. "You made it!"

"I did," smiled Ava proudly, feeling the color return to her face. "But I think I may need a new pair of underwear."

"Too much information," laughed Carol. "Now seriously, we have to go!"

The girls ran along the side of the hotel, careful to take in their surroundings and make sure they weren't being followed. The map took them on a journey, through alleys and narrow roadways, twisting and turning like a serpent. Perhaps it was the triumph of getting away from the bad guys and finding the scroll, but there was a zing in the air between the two girls.

Or maybe the *zing* in the air was real! Ava suddenly screeched to a halt. "Do you smell that?"

"What is it?" asked Carol, confused.

She followed Ava's trembling finger. A street vendor was tossing a disc of dough high into the air. He was making fresh pizza. Carol felt her stomach grumble; it had been hours since their last meal.

"Pizza!" whispered Ava. "Italian pizza right in the middle of the street!"

"It's a sign," whispered Carol.

The girls ordered two pieces of sizzling hot pepperoni pizza and then found a small wooden bench under the shade of a beautiful oak tree. The girls moaned with each delicious bite of pizza.

"Okay, change to our plans," said Ava as she wiped her mouth with the back of her hand. "You continue on to the... burning altar thing. I'll stay here and keep the pizza guy company and an eye out for the bad guys. I'll text you if I see anything suspicious."

"You're such a good friend," smiled Carol as she wiped the grease off her fingers. She studied the map and then stood up to get her bearings.

"So, how much further, fearless leader?" Ava asked.

"It actually looks like we're almost there."

"Okay," Ava wiped the rest of the grease off her fingers. "Let's get going. We've gotta beat my mom back to the hotel. We're already in enough trouble."

The girls continued their trek through the city, snaking down a long, winding alley. This part of the city didn't look as friendly as the touristy area surrounding the girl's hotel. Trash littered the alley, and graffiti was splashed across rows of buildings as if they were brick canvases.

Carol held up her hand and stopped. She looked up from the map. "Here...?" she exclaimed—her voice filled with confusion.

Neither spoke for a second. Ava felt the wind rush out of her. A massive wave of disappointment enveloped Carol, and she felt herself sag. "Oh, man…." She looked at the map and pointed. "This has to be right! See, the statue of the giant eagle… it's over three hundred years old. It was supposed to be right beside the statue."

Carol jabbed her finger at the map. "See?!"

Ava looked, and sure enough, directly across the square named Santa Florian Del Fuoco was a poorly drawn eagle, but an eagle nonetheless. But what lay in front of them was a huge expanse of land, filled with rubble. No kidnapped old man, no magical protectors, and definitely *no* Altar of Light.

"One sec!" Frustrated, Ava marched up to the first person she saw, a mustachioed man tending to the tires of his bike.

"Sir, *parli inglese*?" Ava asked, doing her best not to butcher the Italian language.

He nodded, stood up, and dusted his hands off on his jeans.

"My friend and I are trying to find the Santa Florian Del Fuoco. Do you know where it's located?"

The man pulled at the end of his mustache, chuckling. Ava stared at him, confused. Maybe she'd said it wrong? She tried again. "Maybe I misspoke. I'm looking for the *Santa Florian Del Fuoco*." She over-enunciated each word, hoping that would help.

"Ah, little girl," he said in a thick Italian accent. "I think…."

"Wait," said Carol, interrupting him. She held out the scroll to him. "It's a map," she said. "We found it in a library book," she fibbed, not wanting to give him too much information. He took it from her, then narrowed his eyes at the drawing.

"Ahh, *povere ragazze*." He tried to contain his chuckles. "I don't know who wrote this for you, but someone has played a joke on you girls. There is no Santa Florian Del Fuoco. Saint Florian of Fire?" he laughed. "This building does not exist."

"Saint Florian did exist!" Ava insisted. "He was the patron saint of firefighters and chimney sweeps!"

"That may be," smiled the man gently, seeing the girls were truly upset. "But," he continued, "the rubble you see behind you, this was the old firehouse…. It was nearly two hundred years old, but an earthquake damaged it so badly that the city was forced to tear it down."

Ava looked at Carol incredulously. "This was a firehouse, not a church? This was all some kind of crazy joke? Are we being punked?"

Carol shook her head. "Saint of firefighters… I can't believe it."

"Well," said Ava, turning and motioning at the rubble behind her. "From the looks of the building behind us, it looks like Saint Florian called in sick…. Thank you, sir."

The man nodded and waved as he wheeled his bike away. "Good luck on your adventure."

Carol and Ava sat down on the curb of the street. The same thoughts swirled around their heads. There was no way this was all a joke. A man had been brutally kidnapped, a woman's store destroyed, men had chased them through their hotel. There was just *no way* this was an elaborate joke.

"We're missing something," Carol sighed. She looked at the map. Why would it lead them to a place that didn't actually exist?

Aggravated, Carol rolled up the map, but as she went to insert it into the cylinder, she dropped it onto the dusty road. "Great," she said, picking it up and blowing the dust off the container. She froze. The dust revealed a tiny inscription at the top!

Ava stood up and brushed off the seat of her pants. "What is it?"

"I don't know—there's something written on it." Carol turned the tube. The writing was so tiny she could barely read it.

"Let me guess," said Ava. "This end up?"

"No," said Carol, squinting. "It looks like I Corinthians 313."

"Isn't that a book from the Bible?" Ava asked.

"I think so...."

Ava was already swiping away at her phone. "Yep. First and Second Corinthians were written by someone named Paul and are in the New Testament. What did the inscription say again?"

"There is an *I* in front of Corinthians and then 313."

"Okay...," acknowledged Ava.

"Wait, you said there was a Corinthians one and two, right?"

Ava nodded. "Yes...."

"Okay, so the *I* could be the Roman numeral for one. So it would be first Corinthians 313. The numbers after Corinthians would be the chapter and the verse. How many chapters are in First Corinthians?"

Ava's fingers quickly tapped on her phone. "Sixteen."

"So, it has to be chapter three, and the second two numbers would be verse thirteen."

"Already on it," said Ava excitedly. She looked at her phone and then looked back at Carol. She cleared her throat. "'Every man's work shall be made manifest: it shall be revealed by fire...'" Ava looked up at her best friend. "What does *manifest* mean?"

Ava could tell that Carol's big brain wheels were turning as she began chewing on her lower lip. "*Manifest*," Carol smiled, "means to display or show something."

Carol's mind was going a mile a minute. *Every man's work shall be made manifest—because it shall be revealed by fire....*

Carol's eyes flew open. "We gotta get back to our room! We need to start a fire. Stat!"

12
KIDNAPPED

"Mom," Ava called out breathlessly as she locked their hotel room door behind them.

There was no reply. Ava turned to face the room, and she gasped. Carol's jaw dropped. The hotel room had been destroyed. Their suitcases had been emptied on the floor—clothes were strewn everywhere. The pillowcases had been pulled off and thrown—mattresses askew—chairs on the ground. The contents of her mom's purse were poured onto the desk, and her mom's wallet and planner were on the floor.

"Mom?" Ava called again, but this time her voice came out as more of a whimper, and her chin trembled. Carol reached out and found her hand. Ava squeezed it tightly. "She's not here," Ava murmured, choking up. Her breath started coming out in short, panicked bursts. "Carol, they took her."

Ava let go of her friend's hand to walk through the room, looking at the mess. One of her mother's lipsticks, a pretty berry color, had been uncapped and smashed onto the floor. Ava remembered that it was her mother's favorite. She bent down to pick it up, rolling it around her fingers. That feeling of cold helplessness drained from her face, and instead, she saw red.

"Carol, they *took my mom.*"

"Ava…," Carol started but had no idea what to say. She walked over to comfort her friend, but as she came closer, she could see Ava's eyes were filled with rage.

"I swear, if they *hurt* my mom…," she bit out.

"Ava, don't think like that," pleaded Carol, looking around. This was so, so awful. "We're going to figure this out."

"We can't call the police," Ava said. "If we call them, we have no idea if it will actually be the police. For all we know, Rossi has men on the inside."

"I know," said Carol gently. "We'll…," she stopped midsentence. Ava's phone was vibrating.

"It's Mom!" As Ava pressed the phone to her ear, a heavily accented voice began to speak. "Listen and listen well," it said. Ava's blood chilled, and she looked at Carol. It wasn't her mom; it was Rossi.

"Return what is rightfully ours and we'll let your mother go."

13
THE MAP'S SECRET

"Where is my mom?!" shrieked Ava. She felt Carol grab her arm, but Ava couldn't be stopped. She was on a full-blown, ticked-off rampage. "You guys have been chasing us all over Italy and now you've kidnapped my mother. Are you insane?"

"*Little girl—*"

"Do you not *have* mothers?!" screamed Ava.

"You will calm yourself!" commanded Rossi. "Or else—"

"Ava, we don't know what they're going to do," Carol insisted quietly, eyes huge.

Ava stared at Carol for a second. Finally, she blew out a breath and closed her eyes. Carol was right. It didn't matter how upset she was. They had to focus on getting Ava's mom back safely.

"How do I even know she's okay?" Ava asked into the phone, her voice cracking at the end. She breathed in slowly, suppressing a sob.

Ava heard a rustling noise and then her mother's voice came on. "Honey, it's me."

"Mom!" her voice broke. "Mom, are you all right? Where are you?"

"Honey, I'm okay, I promise." She sounded tired, but Ava could hear the relief in her voice. She felt it too. "We're going to get through this. Just listen to the men, and… give them what they *think* they want. Listen to them."

Rossi's voice came on the phone again. "Ava, was it?" He chuckled. Ava had never heard someone so evil. "Meet us at the Piazza Carlo Goldoni in one hour. You and your little friend will come alone. And if there are any police… well, let's just say it won't be good for your mother. No tricks, no games. Bring the scroll and the ring."

"You hurt my mom…," started Ava, white-hot tears making their way down her cheeks. Her hands shook with rage, and she swallowed hard. "You hurt her, and you'll wish you were never born."

Ava heard an annoyed sigh. "Piazza Carlo Goldoni, in one hour. No games, little girl." The call went dead, leaving Ava with nothing more than silence. She held her phone away from her face, hands still trembling. Carol gently took it from her and set it down. She put a hand on Ava's shoulder.

"Ava, I'm sorry," Carol said, her face white. She couldn't even begin to imagine how scary this was for her friend. It was scary enough *not* being Ava's mom's daughter right now. She pulled her into a hug. "I am so sorry." Carol felt a shudder make its way through Ava, and she hugged her tighter. "We're going to find a way to get her back."

"I think my mom was trying to give me a clue…," she said, pulling away, wiping her eyes with her sleeve. "She said, 'Give them what they *think* they want.' We can't just give them the map and the ring! All of this will have been for nothing!"

"We do have to give them the map and the ring," said Carol. Her eyes sparkled a little. "But, your mom may be right. Give me one second…. It's about the clue that we found on the copper tube," Carol called from the bathroom. She returned holding an iron and a miniature ironing board, meant to be placed on a tabletop. She grabbed a cup off the table, filled it with water, and then poured it into the front of the iron.

"What in the world are you doing?" asked Ava, thoroughly confused.

As she plugged in the iron and changed the temperature setting to steam, she started explaining. "At first, it didn't hit me. But think about it: Everything involving that darn tube and scroll has had to do with fire. The name of the saint, the name of the altar—and then the biblical clue from Corinthians that it will be revealed by fire. So, I kept asking myself, *what will be revealed*? Then I kept thinking of the word *manifest*—like something was hidden…."

"And then no longer hidden," whispered Ava, hope filling her face.

"Exactly," nodded Carol. "And since we can't really create a fire in our room, I thought the closest thing would be an iron."

Ava watched as Carol gently pulled the map out of the tube. She opened the map and spread it across the ironing board, and then while ever so carefully pressing the steam button, she lightly ran the iron over the entire map.

"Whoa!" shouted Ava. "It's working! It's working!"

Before they knew it, their simple map that looked like a child's drawing had turned into something that even Blackbeard and his pirate fleet would approve of.

"Of course, the heat activates a chemical in the paper, making the actual map appear," Carol said.

"All of my dad's dreams of me becoming a world-class biologist… wasted," Ava shook her head.

Carol unplugged the iron and pulled out her phone, and while Ava held the map spread open, she snapped a couple of quick photos. Smiling, she slipped the phone back into her pocket. "Now, we have the real map."

Ava pressed her shoulder against her friend's shoulder. "Carol, I don't think 'big brain' does you justice."

Carol waved her away. "You have a lot on your shoulders; otherwise, you would have been all over the heat thing."

"Now, for the real Altar of Light," Carol continued. The map was quickly fading as the paper cooled. "Okay," said Carol, holding the map up to the light. Her eyes quickly searched until she came upon the words *Altar of Light* written in Italian. "Oh man!"

"You found it?!" asked Ava excitedly.

"According to this map, the altar is at a temple next to the Rennes-le-Château."

"Okay, not a problem," said Ava. "We give them the scroll, get my mom back, and we go to the right altar. They'll never know!"

"Not so easy," said Carol, shaking her head. "The Rennes-le-Château is in France, plus they asked for the ring *and* the scroll."

"Oh yeah...." The information hit Ava like a ton of bricks. Any newfound hope she had went right out the St. Regis window. Disappointed, Carol looked at the map, the paper rapidly cooling. The details disappeared little by little, just like their options. She was just about to roll up the map when Ava stopped her.

"Carol, hold the map steady for a second." Ava was holding her phone. She quickly snapped a few pictures. "Just in case."

Carol nodded. "Good idea. Sadly, none of this matters without the ring," said Carol, half to herself, "even if we find the altar."

"I know, but I have to get my mom back.... I feel horrible about the old man, I really do... but it's my mom. I... I just don't see what's so special about the darn ring. I mean if I saw it on a sidewalk somewhere, I wouldn't even bother to pick it up."

"Yeah," whispered Carol, absorbed in thought. She paced back and forth across the room. She looked back at Ava. "You're a genius!" Carol quickly unzipped her pocket, grabbing the ring. She took it over to the bed and laid it down onto the silk sheet. She took out her phone and snapped several photos of the ring from both sides before picking it back up. Carol nodded at Ava, a big grin filling her face. "What exactly did your mom tell you?"

"She said she was okay, and to give the men what they *think* they want."

"Your mom is brilliant… now I know why she's an investigative journalist. The key is *think* they want… and I think I have the answer."

"Okay… I'm all ears," said Ava excitedly.

"Do you think your mom would be extraordinarily angry if we made a small purchase from a local jeweler?"

"You're not really asking that question, are you? What do you have in mind?"

"A credit card, and your amazing skills of persuasion."

14
BAMBOOZLED

Ava followed Carol across the piazza to a jeweler's shop she had noticed near *Signora* Coppola's bookstore. Carol had filled her in on the plan during their quick journey. They paused briefly, collecting their thoughts.

They were on a mission, and there was no time to waste. Ava pushed the door open, which signaled a tinkle of a bell. As they walked in, they could see glass displays covering the walls, filled with beautiful rings, necklaces, earrings, and bracelets. There was a bench in the center of the room, and a counter. The whole place sparkled, and to top it off, it smelled lightly of lemons.

"Wow," breathed Ava. "I could live here."

"*Posso aiutarla?*" asked the man behind the counter. He leaned over it, studying the girls. Gray hair surrounded his bald scalp like a halo. Scruff covered his slightly sagging cheeks, and while they made it look like he was frowning, Carol could see laugh lines on the corners of his eyes. He wore a button-up white shirt and a black vest that hung over his belly.

"*Parli inglese?*" Carol inquired.

"*Sì,*" he said. "How can I help you girls?"

"I was wondering, are you the owner of the store?"

"Yes. I'm Nico Gabriella, and my daughter Mary runs it. Now, how can I be of service?"

"Sir... Mr. Gabriella... we really need your help," blurted Ava, who marched up to the counter. "We have a huge school project that's due the moment we get back to the United States, and we're taking off on a plane tonight. We're trying to find King Solomon's ring. You know the famous ring?"

"Oh yes... I've heard the story. It gives the one who possesses the ring magical powers."

"Yes... something like that," acknowledged Ava. "Well, I sorta fibbed. I told my teacher I knew where to find it...."

Carol interrupted: "We found a man online who was selling a map that was supposed to lead us to the ring... and well, the map turned out to be fake...."

"Imagine that," he smiled politely.

"And now, I'll be returning back to school, without the ring," Ava said. "I can't fail this class, sir. I figured if I showed up with a ring that resembled Solomon's ring... then my teacher would at least understand how hard I tried."

"If you could help us, you might literally be saving our lives," said Carol, pleading.

And my mom's, Ava added silently.

"A school project, hmm?"

"Yes, sir," Carol unzipped her pocket and showed him the map to help bolster their story. "And here are some pictures we found on the internet. It was the closest we could find as a historical reference to the ring."

Carol handed Mr. Gabriella her phone. "Do you think you could help us?"

He looked at the photos for a moment before shaking his head. "*Mi dispiace*, girls. I have much to do today—I'm sorry." As he turned away, Ava leaned over the counter, putting her hands on the glass.

"Sir. Please." She looked at him, eyes growing huge. "We're desperate. I can't repeat the seventh grade; I really need your help."

He hesitated, looking at her.

"Please, sir." She pulled the American Express card out of her pocket and put it on the counter. "If this isn't enough, sir, I will get more... please."

Something in Ava's voice caused Mr. Gabriella to pause. "Are you sure this is just for a school project?" he asked not suspiciously, but more fatherly.

Ava fought back the tears, desperation filling her heart. "Yes, sir," she whispered.

He tilted his head and sighed. "Okay." He gently pushed the card back to Ava. "Put your money away. I do not want you to be sad. Please," he smiled, "put your money away, *piccolo angelo*." *Little angel.*

"Oh, thank you, Mr. Gabriella," cried Ava. "Thank you."

"*Prego*," he replied. He nodded to a leather-cushioned bench. "Now, go sit, and I will be done as quickly as I can." He took Carol's phone with him, looking at the photo. He shook his head and grumbled a little as he disappeared into the back room behind the counter.

With huffs of relief, the two sat down on the bench and waited. And waited. And waited. First, fifteen minutes passed, then twenty, then twenty-five. They began shifting uncomfortably, too aware of the time. They only had twenty minutes left to get to the Piazza Carlo Goldoni.

Finally, after thirty minutes, Mr. Gabriella reappeared, holding a polished ring and smiling. Ava jolted up and hurried over to him.

"Here, *piccolo angelo*," he said, placing the ring in her palm.

Ava's mouth fell open in amazement; the ring was a perfect replica.

Mr. Gabriella chuckled at her reaction. "There you go, eh?" he said, a grin in the corner of his mouth. "And if your teacher don't like it, tell them that they can take their complaints to Nico Gabriella."

"Thank you so much!" Ava exclaimed, throwing her arms around him.

"Thank you, Mr. Gabriella!" smiled Carol.

He grinned and patted Ava's back, and then with an "ehh," he waved them out of the store. Ava glanced back to smile one more time at Mr. Gabriella before they shut the door and were off again.

"We have to hurry," Carol said, panic clear in her voice. She handed the real ring to Ava, who shoved it into her sock. The fake ring went into Carol's pocket. "We don't have much time, and we've never been there before."

"Let's go," agreed Ava, and they were off, dashing to get to the Piazza Carlo Goldoni. Ava felt like she was running faster than she ever had before as they raced to their secret meeting place. Everything could be lost if they didn't get there in time.

The girls arrived at the Piazza Carlo Goldoni, stumbling onto the stone area surrounded by larger buildings. Carol bent over, placing her hands on her hips gasping for air. She couldn't help but feel a little trapped. She looked around wildly until she spotted it: a black SUV with tinted windows was parked at the curb. The streetlight above it was conveniently broken. She bumped Ava's shoulder and nodded at the SUV. That had to be them.

Just like clockwork, Rossi climbed out of the passenger side of the vehicle, shiny Italian shoes glinting in the light. The driver, a tall, thin man, still wearing a bandage on his nose, got out and leaned against the car, watching the girls. Ava recognized him as Rossi's partner who had chased them. She glowered at the man. He should've stayed extinguished.

Rossi strode over to the pair. Ava and Carol could practically hear the other's heart pounding. He approached them and smiled, his bottom lip stretching until it was thin. He stopped when he was a few feet away.

"I trust that you have brought what I requested?" he asked.

Ava nodded. "We did," she answered bitterly. "Now, where's my mom?"

The man turned and snapped his fingers The back window of the car lowered. Ava's mom sat in the back seat. She stared at her daughter, a piece of duct tape over her mouth. Even from where they stood, Ava could see that she looked frazzled and anxious.

Ava's breath caught in her throat. "If you do anything to my mom, Rossi, you are going to be in a world of hurt."

Somehow, that grin stretched further. He looked eviler than any Disney villain she'd grown up with. A chill ran down her spine. Ava pulled out the map, keeping the copper tube hidden, and Carol pulled out the ring.

"I kept my part of the deal," hissed Ava. "Now you keep up yours."

His eyes stared at the ring. A greedy look appeared in his eyes. He began salivating again, just like he did in the bookstore the day before.

"Rossi!" shouted Ava. His head snapped up. "I'm not waiting anymore. You have what you want, now give me my mom!" Her anger sparked, and she wanted to charge at the man.

"Not so fast," snapped Rossi. "We need to make sure that the scroll and ring are real."

"Look," said Carol furiously, stepping forward. "We don't care about any stupid scroll and some cheap ring. We're sorry we ever got caught up in all of this craziness. Look at us! We're twelve years old! We don't want the scroll or the ring; we just want her mom back!"

The man hesitated, thinking to himself. Ava could practically hear his thoughts from where she stood. *Maybe the girls really don't have any idea what they have.* He flicked his fingers, motioning for his partner to open the door to the vehicle. Ava's mom stumbled out and stood by the car. Another man slid out the back behind her, his hand inside his jacket.

"Mom," cried out Ava.

"Say another word, and she disappears," promised Rossi. "Now, let me take the ring and the scroll. If they are both authentic… then I'll keep my deal."

The man let Ava's mom take one step toward the girls. "Mom," whispered Ava, her eyes pleading with her to tell her what to do.

Rossi stepped forward, his hand outstretched in front of him. "Now… or I'll have my men *take* them from you. Your choice," he hissed, brushing his jacket aside to reveal the taser.

Ava stared him in the eyes, anger coursing like venom through her veins. He took the map from Ava and put it into his suit jacket. He then reached out his hand and closed it over the ring like a trap, snatching it from Carol's trembling hand. He let loose a chuckle and held the ring up to the light. "Marvelous," he whispered.

He glanced at the girls. "Oh, you have no idea what you've done." Rossi snapped his fingers. Ava's mom was shoved back into the car.

"Wait," started Ava, taking a step forward. He spun on his heel quickly and began to stride away.

"Wait, no! We had a deal!" She dashed after Rossi and grabbed him by the arm. With amazing strength, he flicked her off like she was a bug. She crashed to the ground, bouncing off the gray stones of the piazza, banging her knee and elbow. She gritted her teeth and struggled to stand.

"*Mom!*" yelled Ava, jumping to her feet and running toward the SUV.

Rossi calmly climbed into the passenger side and drove away, taking her mother with him.

Ava watched as Carol chased the SUV, tugging off her shoe as she ran. With an audible shout, Carol hurled her shoe at the car. It roared off, unbothered by her futile attempts, into the night.

"Why did they take my mom?" whispered Ava, coming to a stop. "We gave them what they wanted."

"They kept her as insurance… they want to make sure the scroll and the ring are real."

"What happens when they find out it's not?" asked Ava.

"I'm guessing," paused Carol, "they are going to be very angry… and demand the real ring, or there will be consequences."

Ava's knee and elbow stung as she moved. There was a kind of uncontrollable ache in her stomach. It made her feel like the wind had been knocked out of her. She wrapped her arms around her stomach, feeling like she was about to throw up.

"What do we do?" Carol wondered aloud, hands on her hips. "It's only a matter of time before they figure out that the ring is fake. How long do you think it will take them to figure out the map?"

"They don't have the copper tube with the main clue… so chances are they won't figure out the map."

"Unless the old man that they kidnapped knows the secret of the map…. I'm sure they have ways to make him talk." Carol shuddered at the thought.

"There's only one thing we can do," said Ava. She sniffed and lifted her chin. "They are desperate to get the ring. They will do anything for the ring. They're not going to do anything to my mom as long as we have this ring."

"So… what are you thinking?"

Ava's eyes flicked to Carol's. "How well do you speak French?"

Carol's jaw dropped. "Are you serious?"

Her eyes turned steely. "Dead serious. And this time, the trade is going to be on *our* terms."

Carol smiled. "I like your moxie. Those guys are going to regret the day they met us."

15
FIRST CLASS

"Ava, the taxi's here!"

Ava appeared from the bathroom with her backpack slung over her shoulder. "Just grabbed our toothbrushes. Do we need anything else?"

"I think we're good. I have the tablet and a ton of cereal bars. We both have a change of clothes, and our phones and chargers, right?" Ava nodded. Carol slung her backpack over her shoulder too. "Good. Let's hurry. We still need to check in and I don't know if it's different in first class."

Ava let out a laugh. "Do you think they'll put down the red carpet for us?"

Carol shrugged. "If they do, I'm calling Leonardo DiCaprio as my date."

"That's fine. He's kind of looking like an owl these days."

Carol scoffed. "Ugh, does not!"

"Does too."

"Seriously, he doesn't."

"Who?" replied Ava.

"Leonardo," replied Carol, confused.

"Who? Who?"

"Oh, I get it, funny… an owl joke," moaned Carol. "Come on."

Soon, they settled into a cab. "All right," said Carol. "We have to travel to Rennes-le-Château, which is only a thirty-minute taxi ride from the airport to *Abbeye Mont Saint-Baptiste*."

"Right. And that's where you think the Altar of Light is located?" Ava asked.

She nodded. "According to the *actual* map, it's the only place there would be an altar in the area."

Ava noticed the driver looking at them strangely in the rearview mirror, his finger thumping nervously on the steering wheel. Something about him didn't seem right… but Ava couldn't get Carol to stop talking. She was in nonstop jabber mode.

"So," Carol droned on, "it's actually a very short flight from our airport in Florence to Perpignan, France."

"Okay," smiled Ava to Carol. "Great to know. What I'm wondering is how much further to the Florence airport."

"We're about five minutes away," the driver responded. "There's very little traffic tonight. I couldn't help but hear you were flying to France. Where is it you said you were flying into? I know France very well. I could perhaps suggest some places you would like to visit."

Carol noticed Ava's tiny headshake. "Oh no," smiled Carol. "Thank you so much. We're meeting my parents there at the airport—they've been to France many times."

"Of course, of course," smiled the driver. The next few minutes were filled with uncomfortable silence. It felt like they would never reach the airport. Finally, the cab pulled into a circular drive, filled with cabs, vans, and people walking toward the terminal. The girls quickly clambered out of the cab, grabbing their backpacks. Ava waited, tapping her foot, as Carol paid the driver. The man thanked Carol and then drove off, his cab mixing with the traffic leaving the airport.

"Okay, so did you think the driver was acting a little suspicious?" Ava queried. "I mean, he was staring at us strangely in the mirror… and then those questions."

"I guess," mused Carol. "But truthfully… right now I find everyone suspicious."

Ava nodded. "It's like we can't trust anyone."

The fluorescent lighting in the airport made everyone look pale and sickly. *You could make a killing opening a tanning salon in here*, thought Ava. Carol glanced at her phone. They had a good hour to kill before their flight, so they decided to grab some food from a small deli named Firenze's.

While Carol checked them in for their flight, Ava grabbed a couple of sandwiches and two bottles of water. When she rejoined her friend, she noticed Carol had a huge smile on her face.

"Thanks to all of the traveling your mom has done with her Amex card, you are now looking at two first-class passengers." She showed Ava her phone listing them as seated in Row 3, seats A and B.

"You are a genius. I've never flown first class!"

Carol laughed and shut down her tablet. "It wasn't me, but I'll take the compliment."

The girls gulped down their sandwiches as they watched the crowds pass through the airport. The airport was small but incredibly busy.

"Now I know why there wasn't any traffic tonight," Carol motioned to the crowd. "They're all here."

"I know, right? I guess we should find our gate," said Ava as she stuffed the last bite of her sandwich in her mouth.

"Yeah," said Carol, looking around. "There should be a directory or something…."

"Right there." Ava pointed to an electronic board divided into departures and arrivals. The girls scanned the board, double checking their tickets and flight numbers.

"Gate 7," smiled Ava. "It's our lucky number."

The girls walked toward their gate, mixing into a cluster of people that scurried about in all directions. Two armed security guards passed them, staring, their faces unsmiling. Ava could see Carol tense as they passed. The two men stopped and conversed with one another, looking toward the girls.

"Don't turn around," Ava whispered. "Just keep walking." The girls made it to Gate 7 and quickly sat in an empty row of chairs. Carol believed that at any second, she was going to feel a hand on her shoulder… but the security guards never reappeared.

"I don't know," said Carol with a worried look on her face. "We are just two kids… and we're trying to board an international flight."

Ava nodded. "Haven't you seen on the news where kids do this? Just last week a fourteen-year-old flew to Australia using his grandmother's credit card. Plus, I have a plan."

"Oh no," whispered Carol. "It doesn't include whipping a quarter at the gate attendant to distract her, does it?"

"No," laughed Ava, "but it will involve something I'm amazing at."

"You're going to annoy them into letting you on the plane?" asked Carol as she crossed her arms.

"No, I'm going to use my charm and my incredible acting skills."

"That's two things," clarified Carol.

"Carol, I'm about to adopt a family."

"What does that even mean?" asked Carol, bewildered.

"Watch and learn," said Ava confidently. "Watch...."

"I know," finished Carol, sighing, *"and learn."*

A throng of people began gathering around the boarding area as the airport staff started calling out zone numbers. Ava and Carol stood, grabbing their backpacks.

"Hang back for just a second," said Ava, watching the crowd.

"No problem!" said Carol, relieved. "On second thought...," she grabbed Ava by the shoulder, "if you get me arrested, Ava Clarke...."

"Shhh!" Ava whispered. "Just play along, and give me your backpack."

Ava found her target. An American couple looking to be in their late thirties had gathered at Zone 1, assigned to first class customers. Ava turned on her charm by complimenting the woman on her jacket and incredible taste in fashion.

"Are you involved in the fashion expo in Paris? Perhaps a model?" Ava gushed.

"Who me?" smiled the woman, putting her hand to her chest, obviously flattered.

Ava expertly eased the woman into a conversation as Carol stood by, silently watching the exchange. Slowly, craftily, Ava maneuvered the conversation. She told the couple that she and Carol were flying to meet her mother, who was an international journalist, and how Carol had slipped in the shower and broken a rib. It was a tragedy, but Ava, being an amazing friend, had become her caretaker and luggage hauler. The woman patted Carol on the shoulder gently. "You poor darling," she purred.

Carol smiled, then fake-winced from the make-believe rib pain.

"If you wouldn't mind," said Ava, "we're flying first class too. Would it be too much trouble to help me with her backpack? I need to help her into her seat, and I don't want to cause a huge commotion."

"Oh, of course not!" The woman turned to her husband. "George, help that young lady."

Carol turned on the drama, bending over slightly, stepping forward gingerly.

"George, don't just stand there. Help that poor girl!"

George shot his wife a *you gotta be kidding me* look, but then awkwardly put his arm under Carol's arm, helping her forward.

Again Ava gushed her thanks, telling them how thoughtful they were. The gate attendant called for first class to board. The woman greeted the girls' new adopted parents, and then scanned Ava and Carol's tickets, smiling and waving them through.

"Oh my gosh, that was close," Carol whispered.

Aboard the plane, George helped Ava and Carol with their luggage, looking just like a doting parent. Ava awkwardly hugged him and then snuggled into her massive, comfy-looking recliner.

They looked at each other and smiled widely. Ava let out a sigh of relief and giggled as she fastened her seatbelt. They had done it. Their plan had worked.

Carol looked over at her friend and smiled. She was glad that for the moment, Ava had something fun to distract her.

"I feel like a movie star," sighed Carol. "This is the best."

Ava suddenly sat back upright, a new kind of excitement coming over her. "I just realized what we can do with first class seats," she said.

"What?"

"Hold on, I'll show you." She turned to a flight attendant. "Sir, could we please order two Shirley Temples with lots of cherries?"

"Certainly," the man replied, dipping his head and smiling to himself, bemused.

"Might as well make it a cup on the side filled with cherries," she added. "It's for medicinal reasons. I was diagnosed with scurvy."

The man arched his eyebrow, looked at Ava quizzically, then walked off to the front of the plane.

Carol laughed and bumped Ava with her shoulder. "I can't believe you asked for a cupful!"

"He'll be well rewarded," smiled Ava as she reached into her pocket and pulled out a shiny quarter.

16
THE ALTAR OF LIGHT

A sudden jolt awakened Ava as the plane touched down at the Perpignan airport. She sat up in the seat and shook her head, clearing the cobwebs. "Did I fall asleep?"

"You did. You were exhausted... and it was really the only way I could watch my movie without you interrupting me." Carol smiled at her friend and nudged her shoulder.

"Geez, thanks...."

Exiting the plane and airport, Ava and Carol accepted help from the kind couple, not wanting to appear as if they had deceived them. The woman hesitated; she seemed torn about leaving two kids on the sidewalk outside the airport. But Ava told her that her mom was just running a little late—that they would be fine.

As the woman looked back once more, a sharp pain stabbed Ava's heart. She knew that look; it was the worried, concerned look of a mother whose gut tells her that something isn't right. Ava dug deep, waving and smiling to the woman, assuring her that they were fine. Reluctantly, the woman acquiesced and climbed into a waiting taxi with her husband. Ava watched the red headlights disappear in the darkness as she sped off into the night.

"Ava!"

Ava breathed in the night....

"Aves! Come on!"

Ava snapped her head around to see Carol motioning her over to a taxi. A small yellow VW bug with a black stripe around the middle was nuzzled up to the curve, its electric engine purring like a kitten.

"*Parlez-vous anglais?* Do you speak English?" asked Carol as they climbed into the cab.

"Wow, you've really been expanding the languages you're learning," whispered Ava, impressed.

"*Oui.* Where do you want to go?" the driver asked in a thick French accent.

"Abbeye Mont Saint-Baptiste, in the Rennes-le-Château area," Carol replied.

"Oh," laughed the driver.

"We have a lot of repenting to do," smiled Carol.

"I see," said the driver, still chuckling. "Sit back and relax, and I'll have you there in no time."

The girls stayed silent during the drive, each staring out the window, watching the blur of landscape pass by. Ava's mind was spinning, trying to put the pieces together. It felt strange putting their hopes in a mysterious map... and an ancient legend.

Outside the girls' window, the scenic view quickly turned mountainous, grass coating huge plains with gnarled and twisted trees hunched over like old men. Carol wished they could pull over and explore. There was so much to see here, but they needed to keep going. They had people to help.

The car finally arrived at an open area surrounded by trees. The driver stopped, motioning to a building.

"Abbeye Mont Saint-Baptiste," he declared.

"This is it?" asked Ava, staring at the church.

"In all its glory," smiled the taxi driver, sweeping his hand in front of him in a flourish.

"Thank you for driving us," Carol said to the driver as they got out. She leaned in his window as he swiped Ava's mom's Amex through a portable card reader attached to his phone.

Ava pulled out a quarter and handed it to him. "Thank you for the ride, sir. *Adios!*"

"That's Spanish," said Carol, shaking her head.

"*Merci, et bonne chance,*" said the driver distractedly, looking at the quarter in the palm of his hand.

Carol leaned in toward the driver. "I added the tip when I swiped the card," she said softly to the driver.

"Ah!" He winked knowingly at Carol and then pulled the car in reverse. Within seconds he was gone. Carol turned around to look at the abbey. Ava was already marching toward it.

This place is beyond creepy, Carol said to herself.

The stone was gray and streaked with age, strips of moss growing here and there. The gothic arches weren't as magnificent as the cathedral's, but, somehow, the abbeys were more foreboding. There was a kind of air that emanated from the abbey, one that settled on Ava's skin and gave her goosebumps. It put her teeth on edge.

"This place feels off, doesn't it?" she said to Carol, who pursed her lips in agreement.

"Kind of looks like it could collapse at any moment," acknowledged Carol.

"I guess that's part of the mystical charm."

Carol paused. Pulling out her phone, she brought up the image of the map. "This is it—the Altar of Light is supposed to be in there," she nodded toward the crumbling temple.

"Okay," whispered Ava. She walked forward and opened one of the doors, waiting for the roof to come crashing down on them. When all appeared safe, she stepped cautiously through the doorway into the church. She could feel Carol right behind her. Inside wasn't much better than the outside. It seemed airier, but that feeling of strangeness was more potent inside. She just couldn't put her finger on why.

The ceiling loomed over them like an angel of lethargy, swooping and dark with arches that dissolved against the walls into darkened stained glass. The tiles on the ground were arranged in a mosaic that branched out into spirals. They were so weathered and old, though, that it was hard to tell they were a design at all. No one was inside the church but an elderly, hunched-over man who slowly swept the floor. He had a crown of white hair around his bald head, soft-looking like the tufts of feathers on a duckling. His back was hunched, with a brown cloak draped over his shoulders. He reminded the girls of the old man who'd been kidnapped.

"Think it's okay if we go up to the altar?" Carol whispered.

"I don't know," said Ava hesitantly. She looked at the old man, his back bent with age—seemingly hypnotized by the back-and-forth rhythm of his broom whisking across the floor like a pendulum. Ava looked at Carol. "I don't think he's gonna mind… not sure if he even knows we're here."

Carol nodded. "We didn't travel this far to stop now."

"Exactly," whispered Ava, tightening her jaw.

The girls slowly walked to the front of the church and paused before the altar. Ava stared at the simple piece of architecture. At the base, two large slabs of gray stone stood about three feet tall. A thick, rectangular stone slab lay across them. Etched into the top of the stone was the symbol for Michael the Archangel!

Ava felt her breath catch in her chest… this had to be the Altar of Light. But how was something so simple supposed to help her find her mother?

She sat on the cool stone floor in front of the altar and began removing her sneaker and sock, where she had hidden the ring.

Sweep. Sweep. Sweep. Sweep. The sound was crisp and dry as the bristles of the broom scraped across the stone floor. Ava looked up at Carol as she removed the ring and held it in her hand. It looked so tiny… so inconsequential. Carol smiled at her friend and held out her hand. It wasn't that Ava needed help standing up… it was simply the fact that Carol wanted her to know that she was there for her. That no matter what happened, she would be there for her friend.

Ava turned and faced the altar. "Please… help me find my mother," her voice barely audible.

Ava slowly stretched out her hand above the altar. She hesitated. Everything had become eerily silent. She placed the ring onto the altar and waited. Nothing happened. No bolts of lightning piercing the night sky, no magical beings… only silence.

Ava closed her eyes, battling the tears that fought to be released. Her hands clenched into fists, her body trembling, disappointment threatening to suffocate her. Carol placed her hand on her friend's shoulder, resting her head against hers.

A voice gentle yet filled with authority startled the girls. It was the old man who had been sweeping the church. "My child, what is it that you've placed upon the altar?"

Ava looked at the man, feeling foolish, feeling overwhelmed…. "It's a ring," she whispered. "I'm sorry if I offended you or the altar."

"Why would you place a ring on the most sacred of altars, my child? This altar is for spiritual gifts."

"Because the scroll told us to find the Altar of Light. I thought that maybe if I put the ring on the altar… it would help me find my mother." Ava's face sank. She closed her eyes, hot tears spilled down her cheek.

"So, you are the ones who found the Archangel's scroll," he said kindly.

Carol nodded. "We figured out that the map had a hidden secret."

"And once you figured it out, the map led you here, to my sanctuary," smiled the old man.

Carol nodded again. "That's right. Wait, you said *your* sanctuary? Are you a priest?"

He took a step closer to the girls. "Yes, yes I am, and this... beautiful, archaic pile of rubble is my home," he laughed.

"But the bad guys... they have the map. If they figure it out, then they'll come here. I know you are a priest and all... but these guys are evil, and they have tasers."

The priest turned and looked into Ava's eyes. "My child, evil will always try to take, to destroy...." He gently touched her chin, raising her face to his eyes. "I promise you—we are here to put a stop to their madness. And don't be so hard on yourself by giving them the map. They will have to follow it, like a moth to a flame...," a soft smile broke across his face. "And unfortunately for them, their greed will be their doom."

Ava's bottom lip quivered. This was all too intense. "The men told me if I gave them the ring and the scroll that they would return my mother," said Ava, her voice breaking. "But they lied."

"But... you still have the ring?" asked the man, looking confused.

"It's a long, long story," replied Carol, "but yes, we still have the ring."

A look of relief passed over the old man's face. He reached into his robe and removed a small black cloth satchel. His fingers disappeared into the pouch for a moment and then reappeared. "Does your ring look like this?" he held out a small ring, revealing what appeared to be the other half of Ava's ring.

Ava nodded, her eyes growing wide. "You have the other half of the ring," she whispered.

"Yes." The old man approached the altar. He made a few hand motions over his forehead and chest. Then after whispering a few words, he placed the ring onto the altar, on top of Ava's ring. As if by magic the two rings interlocked, and the hexagram symbol on the front glowed a golden red. Carol scrambled backward, Ava following her.

"No way!" gasped Ava.

"Ava!" Carol breathed, looking behind them.

Ava whirled around, her mouth falling open. A dozen men and women dressed in black had positioned themselves in a semicircle behind them. Their eyes were laser focused, their mouths pulled taut. But as the priest turned, holding out the ring for everyone to see, their serious faces transformed into astonishment.

"These two brave young ladies are the reason you have been summoned here tonight," said the old man as he moved beside the children. "For they have returned to us King Solomon's ring. However, their bravery has come at a cost." He gently rested his hand on Ava's shoulder. "This child's mother has been kidnapped, and as you know, they have also taken one of our own." Ava's face burned as she felt the attention of the group on her.

"Andrew," he said, turning to face a huge, hulking man with fiery red hair and green eyes. "Secure the abbey and then meet us below…. I'm quite sure we are already being watched. We will need to proceed with caution."

As Andrew rushed off, the priest motioned for Ava and Carol to follow him. He led them to a solid wall of stone. One by one he pushed a series of stones, and a hidden doorway appeared.

Ava looked at Carol. "It's like the bat cave! A real hidden passage!"

The girls followed the old man through a narrow stone passage, huge wooden beams arched overhead. The air smelled musty and damp, reminding Carol of her parents' basement. Rows of lights, anchored to the walls, illuminated the narrow hallway. The group came to a stop at a huge wooden door, reinforced with strips of iron. The priest fished out a set of keys from beneath his robe, and moments later the door swung open.

They followed the priest as he descended down a section of stone stairs that connected to another hallway and then to another large wooden door.

"You would need a map just to figure your way through this thing," whispered Ava.

Carol nodded. "It's amazing."

The old man paused in front of another door. "Here we are."

He unlocked the door and ushered the girls forward. Ava and Carol shook their heads… this was not what they had expected at all. The room was filled with computers, massive flat screens that took up the entire wall, and technology the girls had only seen in movies.

The priest, seeing their confused expression, laughed out loud. "What were you expecting, a bunch of Knights of the Round Table?"

"We just thought… well actually, I'm not sure what we thought, but it wasn't this," said Carol, her eyes orbiting around the room.

"I'm just so confused," whispered Ava.

"This is one of our mission control rooms. We have several like this all across the globe," explained the priest. "We are tasked with protecting and moving priceless religious artifacts all over the world."

"You do a great job of hiding this place! Not trying to be rude, but the church upstairs looks like it could collapse at any second."

"Ah, yes. Perception is everything. You perceive that this place is just another old church, one of thousands in Europe about to crumble to the ground… but this façade allows us to do the Lord's work secretly and mostly uninhibited."

"Mostly?" inquired Carol, suddenly a part of the conversation.

"Ah, clever girl. Yes." He leaned in, whispering. "There is a powerful group that would like nothing more than to use treasures like Solomon's ring for nefarious reasons."

"Evil reasons," said Carol, seeing the confused look on Ava's face.

The priest quickly walked to the front of the room. Every head turned toward him. The girls listened as he laid out a three-part plan: safely hide the ring, rescue Ava's mom, and free Nicholas, the old man whom Ava and Carol had witnessed being kidnapped.

There were very few questions. This was an elite team with centuries of experience bestowed upon them by the protectors who had come before them.

When he was finished, the priest removed his robe. Underneath, he too wore a black suit, with a black turtleneck. The girls noticed that he now moved with a commanding authority. The hunch was gone, and there was a powerful light burning in his eyes. He no longer resembled the old, hunched man, sweeping the abbey. He exuded power in every movement. His eyes alighted on the girls. "Okay," he smiled, gesturing to the girls to follow him. "It's time to set a trap."

17
THE GUARDIANS OF THE RING

Ava and Carol quickly followed the priest through another set of winding passageways, finally coming to a stop in front of another stone wall. The girls waited for the priest to push the stones again. Instead, he paused while a razor-thin red light passed across his eyes. Moments later, the stone wall slid open. In the moonlight was a row of four black SUVs.

"Oh, no, no, no. What is it with these people and black SUVs?" protested Ava, stopping in her tracks.

"It's okay, Aves, I think they're the good guys." Carol linked arms with her. "I mean, c'mon. He made the ring whole again. And he took us into his way cool command room… I think we can trust them."

Ava sighed. "But just to let you know, I've seen enough black SUVs to last me a lifetime."

She continued forward and the priest quickly escorted the girls to one of the SUVs. He opened the back door and Ava and Carol slid into the car. The priest walked around the back of the car and then climbed into the back seat with them.

"Sir. What did Ava and I get mixed up in? Why are so many people after the scroll and the ring?" asked Carol.

"Why not keep it in a safe deposit box? I hear they are extremely affordable," added Ava.

"Those are great questions. Since we have a bit of a drive, I'll fill you in on a little history. For thousands of years, we have protected King Solomon's ring, and for that matter, many famous ancient relics. Not only are many of the treasures priceless, but many have magical powers that we can't even begin to understand. But one thing we do know: this power would be devastating in the hands of evildoers.

"Just like with the knights before us, Solomon's ring will be divided into two halves again, and then each half of the ring will be whisked away to a safe hiding place, to opposite sides of the globe."

Ava turned to Carol. "Did he just say we are going to opposite sides of the world?"

"I'm pretty sure he said the *ring* would be taken to opposite ends of the world." Carol hesitated. "Won't the bad guys just follow you? I mean, they've been one step ahead of us, no matter how careful we've been."

The priest smiled. "Oh, they will try. But when you've been guarding a secret for centuries, you pick up a few tricks here and there."

"And airline miles…," offered Ava.

"And airline miles," he laughed.

"Oh, and I also learned that blasting a fire extinguisher at someone full force in the face is a wonderful deterrent! And a great way to quit smoking."

"Sounds like the voice of experience," said the old man, looking admiringly at Ava.

"Let's just say that ever since we witnessed Nicholas get attacked by Rossi and friends, they have been chasing us across Italy. So, we've had to be extremely creative," smiled Carol.

"Ah yes, Rossi... he is a bit of a nasty fellow. However, it seems to me that you two have executed your evasive strategy flawlessly."

"Not really flawlessly," said Ava. "If Carol and I had done a better job, Rossi wouldn't have my mom."

"Ava," said the priest gently. "Rossi wants one thing, and that's the ring. Right now, you have something in your possession that he desperately wants. You wield all of the power right now, and he knows it."

Ava shook her head and tried to smile. She hoped that the priest was right. She hoped with all her heart.

"Carol, tell me, how did you wind up with the scroll and the ring? I was confused in the church because you said that you traded the ring and the scroll for Ava's mother... yet you still had half of the ring."

"Well, I knew that if we gave the ring to Rossi he would win. I was afraid if I gave Rossi the ring he wouldn't keep his word, and then he would have Ava's mom and Nicholas. We also knew that we couldn't trust the local police... another long story. So, I took pictures of the ring, and then Ava convinced a local jeweler to make an exact replica of the ring... that's what we gave Rossi."

"Ah, brilliant!" The old man's face filled with admiration. "And then you solved the clue, to find the map that led you here?"

Carol nodded. "We figured out the map first. Once we knew where the Altar of Light was located, we no longer needed it... so we gave that to Rossi. We followed the map to the abbey, and well, you know the rest."

A glorious smile grew on the old man's face, making the white stubble on his chin and cheeks stretch. He closed his eyes and nodded to himself. After a moment, he opened them to look at the girls, his expression filled with light. "Girls, I cannot begin to tell you the debt of gratitude we owe you."

"So you're actually them?" Ava spoke up. "The warrior priests defending Solomon's ring like in the movies?"

"There's no denying it now," the old man replied, smiling and unfolding his hands. "Though I wouldn't necessarily say 'warrior.' We are peaceful men of God carrying on a legacy in order to ensure peace in this world."

"So, who are the men who are trying to take the ring?" asked Carol.

"We believe they're a part of a covert sect of radicals, attempting to steal and use the power of Solomon's ring for evil. The ring is very powerful, but there are also many other treasures that are equally, if not more, powerful than the ring. Our task as Templars is to make sure these artifacts stay hidden, no matter what the cost."

Carol leaned forward in her seat—her eyes wide. "When you say other powerful artifacts, do you mean like the Ark of the Covenant?"

The priest smiled. "Like the Ark of the Covenant. The man you call Rossi used to be in the Italian Mafia, but now he is a part of a new, dangerous group called the New Prophets, and they will stop at nothing. Rossi is merely a marionette being controlled by his master's strings. Frighteningly, we know that we now have spies deeply entrenched in our group and... we have no idea who they are."

"Well, that's terrifying," muttered Carol, shifting in her seat. "How could spies get into a secret society like yours?"

"Our lives are simple lives... we take a small pittance for pay. Our lives are devoted to keeping these ancient treasures safe. However, groups like the New Prophets try to lure us to the dark side, promising us riches beyond belief.... I fear that greed has taken over the heart of some of those among us. That is why many times we hide pieces of religious artifacts in multiple places."

"Geez, whatever happened to normal bad guys? Like *Scooby-Doo* villains."

Carol nodded. "No kidding." She looked back at the priest, narrowing her eyes. "So, you *are* a Templar?"

"Yes, we are called the Templars," the priest said, a glint of pride in his eyes. "Perhaps I can tell you more later. But...," he looked out the tinted window of the SUV, "I'm afraid we're almost to the Porte De Brasilia."

"Whoa, whoa, wait a second—we're driving to Brazil?" asked Ava, sitting up straight in her seat. "No way would my mom be okay with *that*. Have you seen the bikinis they wear?"

"No, no, no," laughed the old man. "We are going to the coast. The Porte De Brasilia is right here in France, about… ten minutes away."

"Oh, thank goodness," Ava sighed as she leaned back in her seat. "I know that you guys have been hiding things for hundreds of years, but do you really think a caravan of black SUVs is discreet?"

The priest smiled. "Point well taken. However, soon enough, you'll realize there is a *very* good reason why we are all driving the same vehicle and why we are all dressed the same."

"I'm still confused. Rossi has my mom, and he wants the ring. How is sending it off to opposite ends of the globe going to help me get my mother back?"

"I know it seems confusing, but we have set up an elaborate trap for Rossi and his men." He motioned for the girls to lean in, then whispered so no one, not even the driver, could hear him. "Remember how I told you that there are spies amongst us?"

The girls nodded silently.

"You are going to have to trust me, okay?"

Again, the girls nodded silently.

"Also," said the priest, speaking out loud again. "I know for a fact that your mother is here."

Ava felt her heart leap. She narrowed her eyes. "How do you know that?"

"Because shortly after your plane arrived, a private jet arrived from Italy. I know that the jet was met on the runway by… it sounds ridiculous now… a black SUV."

"They have their own jet?" asked Carol.

"Yes," smiled the old man. "They have a great deal of resources at their disposal. My contact at the airport informed me of their arrival. He also just sent me a photo from a surveillance camera from the airport." He handed his phone to Ava. "This is your mother, no?"

Ava's heartbeat quickened as she stared at the grainy photo. It was her mother! She was here, in France! "Yes!" she exclaimed. "That's my mom."

The priest leaned forward, speaking rapidly in French to the driver. The driver nodded and flicked off his headlights. He whipped the wheel to the right, tearing off the main road onto a small gravel road. Up ahead was a taxi, hidden in the shadows.

"Wait, what's going on?!" asked Carol.

The old man leaned forward in his seat. "Girls, listen! We have but seconds! There has been a change in plans."

Carol and Ava looked at each other wildly. What was happening?

"Listen," said the old man, his voice filled with urgency, "to rescue your mom and ensure her safety, we must work quickly! Here's what we have to do. Listen carefully—it's our only chance!"

Seconds later, the girls bolted from the car, racing to the taxi, hoping they had made the right decision to trust the old man.

18
THE CHASE

Ava and Carol jumped into the back of the taxi, which instantly lurched forward, slamming them hard against the back seat.

"Buckle up, girls, it's going to be a bumpy ride." Carol tried to figure out his accent, but it was one she had never heard before.

Ava pulled out her phone. Pulling up her calls, she zeroed in on her mom's phone number. The phone rang three times, and then the voice she instantly recognized and despised answered.

"*Pronto*!"

"Listen," said Ava, her voice shaking with emotion. "I have what you want," she said lying, "and you have my mom. The stupid map sent me to some crazy priest, who only wants the ring for himself."

"Where are you?" asked Rossi suspiciously.

"We are in a cab heading for Porte De Brasilia to go back to Italy. The priest and his clone army were trying to follow us, but our taxi driver lost them."

"Do you have the ring? The *real* ring?" he hissed—his voice full of venom.

"Yes, I have my half. The old priest and his men have the other half. He tried to trick us into giving him the ring, but I'm done playing games. You two can fight it out. I'm done with your ridiculous hocus-pocus battle. I just want my mom," said Ava firmly.

"You know all about playing games. I have your mother—this is your *last chance*."

"Aves, please be careful. You don't…."

Ava's breath rushed out of her when she heard her mom's voice.

"Mom, it's okay!" cried out Ava. "I'm giving them the ring. This will all be over!"

Ava could hear Rossi's breath on the phone; she could tell his wheels were turning. Right now, she would do whatever she could do to get her mom back.

"Do we have a deal?!" Ava asked while gritting her teeth. "If so, meet us at the Porte De Brasilia boathouse. We're four minutes away."

Ava didn't wait for an answer. Her hands were shaking so much, the phone fell from her fingers to the floorboard. Carol pulled Ava against her. "You did great," she said, hugging her friend. "You did great."

"Thanks," whispered Ava, trembling, her voice barely audible.

The girls looked through the taxi's windows into the night. The Templars' black SUVs had vanished as if it were a dream. From the back seat they could see the driver's flat gray hat perched on top of a mass of curly hair. The driver's reflection in the windshield showed bushy eyebrows and a mustache…. Was he a Templar too?

The tiny car bounced and rocked as the driver took curves on the narrow road at breakneck speed. Carol and Ava found themselves smacked together and then suddenly slammed against the opposite side of the car.

"Precious cargo back here!" shouted Carol

"Sorry!" shouted the man back to them. "We must hurry!"

"It won't matter if we all die," yelled Carol, as the car narrowly avoided a large outcrop of rock. Suddenly, the car roared onto a paved road. Before them, they could see the ocean. Above them, the sky glittered. The taxi slowed; they were approaching the Porte De Brasilia boathouse. A black SUV was parked along the side of the road.

Ava looked at Carol. "Here we go," she whispered.

The taxi cautiously pulled alongside the black SUV, its engine still running. With a hiss, the SUV's window lowered. Rossi peered out at the girls, smiling evilly. He turned his head and spoke to the driver, who lowered the rear window.

Inside, Ava could see her mom. Their eyes met and a surge of anger flushed through Ava's body. Her mom smiled at her... the kind of smile that says, *I'm okay. Be careful. I love you!*

The taxi backed away to the front of the SUV and stopped. "Okay," said the driver, nodding to the girls. "Good luck!"

Ava opened the door and both girls slid out. The wind whipped off the ocean. Ava sucked in the salty air, trying to clear her mind. Carol moved close to Ava, her shoulder pressed against her, silently letting her friend know she was there for her.

Rossi, along with his partner whom the girls had nicknamed "The Nose," climbed out of the car.

Ava reached into her pocket and pulled out a small black box. Rossi's eyes greedily followed her hands, his mouth stretched into a wide grin.

Rossi took a step toward the girls. "I only have one thing to say to you…."

"Whatever," said Ava. stealing away his moment of power. "I get my mom, and you get the ring. Then you *leave us alone*!"

Like déjà vu, Rossi snapped his fingers and his cohort opened the side door. The Nose forcefully pulled Ava's mom from the vehicle. He stood grinning like a Cheshire cat, holding her arm tightly.

Ava's heart leapt to her throat. She needed to focus and keep her wits about her. Now was *not* the time to get sloppy.

Rossi, apparently happy with how things were going, turned back and sneered at the girls. "Satisfied with the merchandise?" he hissed, laughing at his own joke.

"Mom!" Ava cried out, her voice breaking. "Are you okay?"

"Yes, yes—Ava, be careful!"

Ava nodded and took a step toward Rossi. Something was wrong. The priest had promised he would be here, with the Templars!

"The ring," demanded Rossi, walking toward Ava.

Then Ava saw it. Behind Rossi, two quick flashes of light burst through the darkness. They were here! The Templars were here!

"Here!" she growled. "Now give me my mom."

Ava opened the box containing another fake ring, drawing Rossi closer, and just as he reached for the box, she threw it to the ground. *Whoosh!* A thick cloud of smoke erupted, engulfing Rossi and the bad guys.

"What?!" he screamed, stumbling backward and coughing, clawing at his eyes.

Suddenly a throng of people dressed in black outfits, covered from head to toe, surrounded Rossi's SUV. He spun around, confusion filling his face. "What? What is this?!" he screamed.

In the confusion, Ava's mom saw her chance to escape, throwing an elbow into The Nose's face. "My nose!" he screamed as she slammed the heel of her shoe into the instep of his foot. He fell against the SUV, screaming, his hands covering his battered nose.

She bolted toward Ava but was grabbed by one of the Templars. "This way!" he yelled. "This way!"

"Ava be careful!" yelled Ava's mom.

Ava watched as the two Templars quickly led her to an SUV guarded by another Templar. "We'll get the girls—you'll be safe here!" said one of the men as he slammed the car door behind her.

The Templars closed in, forming a tight circle around Rossi and his men. Rossi looked at Ava and Carol, hatred filling his eyes. "Clever girls!" he spat. "You'll regret this!"

One of the figures dressed in black stepped forward, shouting out orders. The girls recognized his voice as the priest's! The priest turned to Rossi. "You should know by now that evil will never triumph over good."

He snapped his fingers and three Templars rushed forward, grabbing Rossi and his minions. "Secure them!" the priest ordered.

Rossi's head hung as two men grabbed him and began marching him to another black SUV. The Nose surrendered immediately, allowing himself to be escorted to the waiting SUV; he wasn't about to put up a fight.

The remaining Templars circled around the priest. He gave each of them an identical black box. No one knew if the box they held actually contained a real half of King Solomon's ring or a fake. Only the priest knew the contents of each of the boxes. Once the boxes had been handed out, he spoke only one word. "Go!"

The priest's plan was working perfectly! The Templars raced toward the dock, where a series of black Jet Skis, moored along the dock, waited for them. Each Templar would ride a Jet Ski out to a separate seaplane, deliver their black box, and then the seaplane would take off toward opposite ends of the globe. The ring would once again vanish into the unknown.

Ava began sprinting to the SUV to see her mom. They had done it! They had captured Rossi and freed her mom, and the ring was about to be hidden away for good!

But then… a scream tore through the night, causing Ava's feet to skid to a stop. She whirled around. *What?!* She couldn't believe it. Somehow Rossi had broken free!

"No!" screamed Ava as Rossi savagely kicked a man laying at his feet. Ava watched confused as another Templar turned and attacked another Templar... literally hoisting him up onto his shoulders and then slamming him against the car. The man crumbled to the ground in a tangle of arms and legs.

"No!" yelled Carol. "Ava, he's the spy the priest was talking about!"

The girls stared in disbelief as Rossi and the spy chased down the real Templars. The girls heard an electrical hiss. Rossi fired his taser, striking a Templar in the back as he raced to the ocean. The man collapsed and lay motionless on the ground. Rossi leaned down and snatched the black box from the man.

The girls watched in horror as Rossi's cohort tackled another Templar just as he was about to reach the dock. The man crashed heavily to the ground. Rossi's man leaped to his feet and kicked the man savagely in the ribs. He ripped the black box from the man's hand, laughing.

The old man's plan was falling to pieces in front of them. The other Templars continued their mission, refusing to turn back, undeterred by the chaos behind them.

Carol couldn't take it. She wasn't about to let Rossi get the ring! Setting her jaw, she raced off toward the bad guys.

"Carol!" screamed Ava, but it was too late. "I'm sorry, Mom!" she yelled, and then she bolted after her friend. Rossi and his men had messed with the wrong girls.

The remaining four Templars raced down the dock, their feet pounding on the wooden planks. One by one they climbed down onto black Jet Skis bobbing in the water. Seconds later, the Jet Skis roared to life, racing out into the ocean to the waiting seaplanes.

Rossi and the spy raced ahead as the girls gave chase. Rossi slid on the dock, his head twisting left and right. He was losing precious time looking for a Jet Ski. Carol sprinted down the dock only a couple seconds behind him. Her mind was reeling. What the heck was she going to do once she caught up to Rossi? She knew she had to do something fast—Rossi was getting away!

She heard the roar of the Jet Ski come to life. She reached the edge of the dock just in time to see Rossi untie the mooring rope. Rossi looked up at her and laughed. "You're too late, as usual." He pulled back on the throttle. *"Arrivederci!"* he cried, Italian for bye-bye.

"Arrivederci to you too, pizza face!" Carol replied. With a powerful backhand swing that would have made Serena Williams proud, she nailed him square in the chest with a boat oar she found on the dock. The impact flung him backwards into the water.

Carol clambered down the ladder, oar in hand, and jumped onto the Jet Ski. She hoped it was like her moped. She pulled back on the throttle and it roared to life, shooting her forward along the dock.

Ava raced down the dock in chase of Rossi's minion, who had commandeered another Jet Ski. In the distance, she could hear powerful engines coming to life. The seaplanes! Some of the Templars had made it!

Ava looked around desperately for a way to stop the spy before he disappeared out to sea with one of the black boxes. She spotted a large fishing net wrapped around one of the dock's huge support poles. She struggled to free the net, which seemed to catch on every splinter and chunk of wood. Finally pulling it free, she ran to the edge of the dock and threw it on top of the man.

Disappointingly it seemed to have little effect… the man, covered in the net, gunned his engine and took off from the dock, looking like a bug trying to escape a spider web. Ava watched helplessly as the man had just about freed himself from the net. He was getting away!

She looked around frantically for a way to help. Suddenly, Carol whipped around the other end of the dock. A wall of foamy water sprayed on either side of the Jet Ski. She leaned forward, holding the oar like a lance, as she raced toward the man.

The bad guy, suddenly seeing Carol bearing down on him, quickly tried an evasive maneuver. But like a trained knight, she nailed him in the chest with her makeshift lance. The man flew backwards off his Jet Ski, splashing into the water, still entangled in the net.

Ava didn't hesitate. She jumped into the water, swimming with strong, powerful strokes to the man's Jet Ski. "Awesome!!!" screamed Ava to Carol.

Ava jumped on the Jet Ski. Then, spinning it around, she and Carol grabbed the net, hauling their catch to the shore… and into the arms of the French police.

"Where did you guys come from?" yelled Carol.

"We'll take it from here," said the officers. They laughed at the man, who was still trying to fight his way out of the net, his face covered in muck and seaweed.

"There's another man up… never mind," laughed Carol, as she saw Rossi being escorted up the dock by two more police officers, looking like a wet cat.

"My mom!" shouted Ava. Ava raced up the shore to a small throng of people. From out of the group emerged a smiling face. "Mom!" yelled Ava, emotion filling her heart, tears pouring down her face. She ran to Ava, grabbing her, pulling her into her arms, burying her face in Ava's hair, kissing her forehead.

She reached out and pulled Carol into the hug, thanking her for taking care of Ava. Carol closed her eyes, feeling as much a part of the Clarke family as her own.

As the small trio pulled apart, Ava's mom stared deep into her daughter's eyes. She wiped a tear from her cheek with the back of her hand. "Ava Clarke," she whispered, "you are grounded until you are thirty."

"I know," smiled Ava, not caring. "I know."

As Ava and Carol walked arm and arm with Mrs. Clarke, wide smiles appeared on their faces. Tears streaked down the priest's cheeks as he helped pull a tired and disheveled old man from the back of Rossi's SUV. It was Nicholas!

The two men embraced, and as they pulled apart, the old man turned, catching Ava's eyes. A smile formed across his wrinkled face as he raised his hand and signed the words *T-H-A-N-K Y-O-U*.

It was too much for Ava to handle. Breaking free from her mom's arm, she ran over to Nicholas and threw her arms around him.

19
THE TEMPLAR'S CROSS

The girls stood in a small room in the abbey with the old priest. It was a simple room with a world map, an old desk, and a few chairs. He was once again wearing his worn brown robe and sash.

"We're so sorry we failed you," said Ava. "We had no idea Rossi and his partner would throw their boxes into the ocean if they got captured."

"I want to be happy," said Carol. "Ava's mom is safe, and Nicholas is safe, but like Ava said… in the end, we failed."

The old man smiled, a smile of warmth and pride at Ava and Carol. "Things aren't always what they seem to be. Not only did you rescue your mom and my dear friend Nicholas, but you also helped me find and catch Timothy."

"Timothy?" asked Ava.

"Yes," he sighed, "Timothy. His family has been in the Templars for over four centuries. But sadly, the lure of riches blackened his heart, and he turned against us."

"I'm sorry," said Carol. "I know how it feels to be betrayed by someone you love."

"It's a common theme in Disney movies," explained Ava.

"Thank you," he said kindly. "Now, do you girls remember what I taught you about perception?"

"Yes," said Carol. "People believe what they perceive to be true."

The old man nodded. "Exactly… even if it's not true." The girls watched confused as he pulled back his robe, removing a cloth satchel. He gently dumped out the contents into his palm, revealing Solomon's ring.

"Wait…," said Ava. "How? Okay… I am so confused right now."

The priest smiled. "I'm sure you are, what, with all of the dramatics, the Templars racing off in a huge fanfare to take the ring to the opposite ends of the earth…. It was just that. Nothing more than a huge fanfare, a production, a diversion to fool the bad guys. The New Prophets, and other nefarious groups like them, will try to track those seaplanes, and if we're lucky, it will take them a decade before they realize they've been duped."

Carol and Ava's mouths dropped open.

"You are good!" laughed Ava. "Better than the Avengers!"

The old man looked at the girls and laughed. "Ah, the Avengers, but who needs them when we have you two?"

The girls laughed. It was good to see the old man smiling, his eyes filled with light.

"This is incredibly awkward," said Carol, "but in all of the chaos and confusion, we never asked you your name."

"Ah," the old man smiled mysteriously. "I was wondering when you were going to get around to that. My name is Michael."

"Just like the Archangel," whispered Ava.

"Just like the Archangel," winked the old man affectionately.

"Seems fitting," smiled Carol.

The old man glanced at his watch and then looked down at the girls. "I have something for each of you. The Templars will forever be indebted to you, and your bravery." He reached into his cloak and removed a necklace with a solid gold medallion of the Templar's cross.

"Ava," he said, smiling affectionately, "this is for you, for your bravery and your tenacity." He gently placed the necklace around her neck. He then kissed her forehead. Ava felt her cheeks go red, a sense of pride filling her heart. "Thank you," she whispered.

"Carol." He looked into her eyes; she could feel the gratitude radiating from him. "I have something for you as well." He pulled out an identical necklace and placed it around her neck. "I give you this necklace, only worn by the Knights Templar. This is for you, for your bravery, your wisdom, and your devotion to your friends." He gently kissed her forehead.

Speechless, Carol raised her hand to her chest, feeling the golden cross.

"These necklaces will be a signal to other Templars around the world that whenever you are in need, we will be there for you."

"It's better than a car insurance commercial!"

Carol smacked Ava on the back of the head. "Respect, honor, humility... anything," said Carol, rolling her eyes.

The old man laughed, shaking his head. "Ava, I will always remember your wonderful sense of humor." Ava hugged him.

Michael led the two girls back into the sanctuary, where Ava's mother sat quietly. He spoke briefly to her while the two girls made their way to the Altar of Light. It had been a crazy journey, but they hadn't given up.

They jumped as Ava's mom's voice gently called out to them. "Girls, it's time to go." Ava and Carol each locked an arm into Mrs. Clarke's arms and slowly walked through the church. The trio turned and waved in unison to Michael as they walked out the door and into the night.

Michael laughed a wonderful laugh from within the church when he heard Ava's voice cry out, "No, not another black SUV!"

Ava & Carol Detective Agency

BOOK 3
THE HAUNTED MANSION

THOMAS LOCKHAVEN
WITH EMILY CHASE

1
LIVINGSTON FESTIVITIES ARE HORRIFYING

"Do you want to hear a *real* ghost story?" Ethan Palmer leaned forward, leering at the children who sat huddled in a half-moon around a roaring campfire. The fire cracked and hissed, rebelling against the cold December night.

It was four days before Christmas, and as was Livingston tradition, the kids had spent the afternoon engaged in snowball fights, sledding, and ice skating on Lake Crystal. But now… Ethan Eugene Palmer had decided that the evening of festivities should take on a more sinister tone.

Ethan's face was thin and pale. His green eyes sparkled mischievously in the firelight. He was a few years older than the rest of the kids, and he seemed to take great pleasure in scaring the life out of them.

His unusually red lips curled into an evil grin as he began to spin the tale.

"Everyone here knows the old Butcher house, right?" he asked, jabbing a stick into the fire, sending a fiery cloud of embers skyward. "Well, I found out why it's been empty all these years. You want to know why?" He paused, looking at each of the children as if daring them to speak.

Finally, a very small voice whispered, "Because it's haunted?"

"No, Riley," smiled Ethan. He shook his head at the group. "At least someone has the courage to speak up.

It's something much more evil than your ordinary ghost. Much more evil."

"They're politicians," offered Ava.

"Nice one," whispered Carol.

Ethan glared at the two girls. The usually animated group of children fell silent… as silent as a graveyard.

He rubbed his hands together as if he were about to enjoy an exquisite feast. Then Ethan lowered his voice, and began to speak slowly, mysteriously.

"Most of you have never heard of Jack and Ruby Butcher. But as children, they used to play in their grandparent's house. They had the run of the house, except for their grandmother's room. That room was strictly off limits.

"Their grandma had died, two years earlier… and they say George Butcher, the grandfather, never got over her death." He paused, letting the story settle in.

"One rainy afternoon, while their grandfather was sleeping, Jack and Ruby got bored, and decided to play hide and seek.

"You've all played hide and seek right?" Ethan smiled as the children nodded silently. "Just like you and me… Jack probably placed his hands over his eyes, and softly counted one, two, three, while his sister ran to hide.

"No one knows why… but Ruby decided to sneak up the stairs to her grandmother's bedroom. She didn't want to wake her grandfather, so she took off her shoes, and slowly crept up the stairs.

"She had just reached the top step, when she heard her brother creeping around looking for her.

"Her heart was pounding, she knew that she wasn't supposed to go in her grandma's room... but when she reached for the doorknob, the door swung open, all by itself.

"She didn't know what to do, she didn't want to get caught by her grandfather or her brother. So she rushed into her grandmother's room.

"Ruby crept over to the closet and paused. Should she open it? Jack would never look for her there! She pushed her finger down on the latch, and with a metallic click, the door creaked open."

Ethan reached out his hand, pretending to be Ruby reaching for the door.

"When she opened the closet door, the smell of moth balls and stale air hit her like a ton of bricks.

"She was scared," Ethan whispered, "but Jack had just reached the top of the stairs. The closet was tiny and filled with her grandmother's shoes and clothes... Ruby decided that she would *just* fit.

"She reached in and began to slowly push her grandmother's clothes apart. Suddenly, a bony hand circled around her wrist, squeezing, crushing! Ruby tried to scream, but her throat closed."

Ethan's eyes narrowed evilly. "The skeleton hand began pulling Ruby into the closet!

"'Come, come my sweetie,' a cackling squeaky voice laughed. Ruby's eyes dropped to her wrist... her grandmother's charm bracelet dangled, from the bones.

"Ruby gripped the doorframe with her other hand, but she wasn't strong enough," Ethan said whispering.

"Ruby could feel her fingers slipping. Her socked feet slid into the closet. The skeletal arm yanked hard, and Ruby's fingers slipped from the door, clawing at the air… she closed her eyes and fell."

Ethan paused. The children were silent, pressed up against one another, barely breathing. Hanging onto his every word.

"Ruby looked up from the floor. Her brother stood over her, a broken lamp in his hand. A bony finger and their grandmother's charm bracelet lay on the floor at Jack's feet.

"Suddenly, the children's grandfather and father rushed into the room. They looked from Jack to Ruby. A purplish black bruise in the shape of a human hand began forming on Ruby's wrist. Jack tried to speak, but the words wouldn't come.

"And then…," said Ethan slowly, "the grandfather turned to the father and smiled… 'you said you liked the little boy the least.' The father nodded… and without speaking, shoved Jack backward into the closet. Before Ruby could do anything, a skeletal hand wrapped around Jack's waist and pulled him into the closet.

"The very next day, the family disappeared and were never seen again… but they say, Jack's ghost still haunts the Butcher house. That's why it's still empty. "Ah perfect timing," he smiled at the frightened children as he climbed to his feet. "Your parents are here. Make sure you ask them to drive by the old Butcher house on the way home." He grinned excitedly, waving to the parents as they approached.

Shaken, the children scrambled to their feet and scurried off to the safety of their parents' arms.

"Sleep well!" Ethan called out, obviously pleased with himself. The holidays had officially started.

"That was terrifyingly creepy," whispered Ava as she stood, wiping the snow from the seat of her pants.

"I thought we were gonna sing and roast marshmallows," said Carol, "not give the kids nightmares."

"Your singing gives me nightmares... so I kind of preferred the ghost story," winked Ava.

"You know," smiled Carol, "if we take Whitmore Street, we can walk past the Butcher house on the way home."

Ava made a face, "Really?"

"Ava Clarke," smirked Carol, "what happened to your sense of adventure?"

"It takes a pass when it comes to evil spirits, zombies, me dying in a closet...."

"Come on," said Carol grabbing Ava's hoodie by the sleeve, "it's just an empty old house... what's the worst that could happen?"

2
THE WORST THING HAPPENS

Moonlight fought its way through thick billowy clouds. Streetlights decorated with giant wreaths hung their heads, bathing the snow-covered streets in a pale white light. The girls' snow boots crunched loudly as they traversed Whitmore Street, the home of the Butcher house.

A cold December breeze awakened the trees from their slumber, making a clickity clackety sound that gave Ava the heebie jeebies. She pulled the collar of her puffy purple ski vest up around her neck and grabbed her Santa hat from her vest pocket.

"Woah," said Carol, "Whitmore Street doesn't play around when it comes to decorating."

"It's incredible," agreed Ava, "puts Whoville to shame."

"I can see the Grinch now," laughed Carol, "...forget Whoville, tonight it's Whitmore!"

"Hey, you're stealing my mojo," laughed Ava, "I'm supposed to be the funny one."

"You are the funny one, funny looking," Carol snickered.

The residents of Whitmore Street either forgot that there was a dilapidated old spooky house in the middle of their neighborhood, or they went overboard with Christmas cheer, trying to draw attention away from the house. Everywhere Ava and Carol looked, houses were blanketed in rows of multicolored lights. Golden light shone from windows decorated with electric candles. There were manger scenes, giant candy cane fences, inflatable snowmen and wooden deer made from logs.

Sandwiched in between the holiday cheer... sat an old, abandoned house... surrounded by an old, broken-down wooden fence.

The girls came to a stop. Somewhere in the distance they could hear a dog barking, otherwise, the night was silent.

"Okay," whispered Ava, "we did it, there it is, the Butcher house. Can we go now?"

Carol stood staring at the house. Years of neglect had taken its toll. The wooden shutters that remained, hung precariously from their hinges. The huge steps leading to the front door were broken and sagging. Jagged glass like broken teeth jutted upward from window frames. But it was the darkness, darker than night, darker than shadow, that seemed to ooze from every window and every door of the Butcher house.

"Yeah...," she paused thinking, "I bet this used to be a beautiful house."

"Okay... I think the cold has frozen your brain, let's go. After seeing this neighborhood, I have to reprimand my parents for their lackluster dedication to holiday decoration."

Ava trudged away, already planning additions to their house when Carol whispered excitedly. "A light! I saw a light!"

"What?"

"I saw a light turn on in the house," whispered Carol, "in the basement!"

"You're seeing things. There's no way that house has electricity."

"I know what I saw!" Carol crept closer to the house, crouching behind a small stone column.

The girls stared at the house, waiting, but the house remained dark.

"Maybe it was just a reflection… I mean this neighborhood is lit up like a—"

"It was a light, I saw a light in the basement."

"Okay," said Ava holding out her hands, "I believe you!"

Ava's phone buzzed. "Great, it's gonna be my parents wondering where we are."

"Okay," acknowledged Carol disappointedly. "I guess we better get going."

The light from Ava's phone illuminated her face while she texted her parents. Carol's eyes scoured every inch of the basement one last time, looking for any hint of light.

"Okay," smiled Ava, patting her friend on the back, "my mom's making hot cocoa."

"I love your mom's cocoa," Carol smiled.

The girls walked up the small incline back to Whitmore Street, leaving the Butcher house like a creepy dream behind them.

Ting, Ting…

Crunch. Crunch.

Ting. Ting.

Crunch. Crunch.

Ava paused, "Did you hear a bell?"

Carol stood, breathing quietly, tiny puffs of white smoke escaping her lips. She listened intently.

It was the faintest of sounds. *Ting. Ting.* Like the ringing of a tiny bell. The sound seemed to come from behind them.

Ava couldn't stop herself. It was as if her eyes had a mind of their own. Against her will, she turned and looked at the Butcher house. Carol was right, she could now see a tiny sliver of light in the basement window!

"Carol, I see it," whispered Ava excitedly.

Carol began quickly walking back to the house. "Come on, we've got to get closer."

"Who do you think it is?" whispered Ava. Her eyes scanned the moonlit blanket of snow that surrounded the Butcher house. "There are no footprints."

Carol's eyes quickly scanned the front of the house. "I know," she whispered as she crouched by a crooked pole, supporting what was left of the fence.

Ava hurried over to Carol....

"Shhh," whispered Carol, holding a finger to her lips.

"Sorry, the snow is really crunchy."

The light grew brighter for a second, and then only a sliver remained. Something or someone was definitely there.

Ava's heart quickened. Inside her head, curiosity battled common sense. "We should crawl to the window," suggested Ava, "that way we won't make as much noise."

"Good idea," Carol paused....

Ava felt a chill along the back of her neck.

A shadow had fallen over them…. They could see two furry arms, and a body… with no head.

The girls turned their heads in unison, standing over them, was a headless creature! It had an elongated fury torso, and thin sinewy arms that ended in enormous clawed fingers. Where the head was supposed to be, there was only a thick stump of a neck.

The girls screamed in terror, as the creature swiped at Ava, its claws just missing her face! She fell backward, hard onto the snow. She backpedaled on the slippery crusty ice like a crab. The creature lunged at Carol as she dove headfirst into an icy snow bank.

The creature reached down grabbing Carol's candy cane striped hoodie, lifting her off the ground! Ava grabbed a board from the fence, and struck the creature hard on the back. The creature stumbled, dropping Carol, whirling on Ava!

"Run!" screamed Carol.

Ava didn't need to be told twice, the girls ran slipping and sliding toward the street, the monster right on their heels!

3
TRAPPED

Ava and Carol raced down Whitmore Street. Carol motioned to her right, and Ava followed her through a yard decorated like Santa's workshop. Inside the house, a dog began jumping up and down at the front window, barking ferociously.

Ava looked over her shoulder, the headless creature was closing in! The girls scrambled through the backyard, into a small cluster of woods. They each stood silently behind trees, trying to calm their breathing.

They could hear its footsteps, the slow crunch, crunch in the snow, getting closer. Carol swallowed hard. What was going on?!

Ava was staring at her wide-eyed… trembling.

The woods had gone silent. The girls strained their ears listening. Nothing.

Carol ever so slowly peeked around the tree. There was nothing but shadows. She slowly exhaled. Then suddenly, she was yanked against the tree, the bark digging into her cheek as stars exploded in her head! Snow showered down on her and the creature. She wrenched her hand backward, twisting and turning, until her mitten came off, freeing her hand. The monster threw it to the ground, and the girls were off, running for their lives!

"Follow me!" yelled Ava.

Carol and Ava sprinted through the woods, and down a narrow path. They hurdled a small chain hanging between two wooden posts. Less than thirty minutes had passed since the girls had sat here at Lake Crystal, listening to Ethan Palmer's horror story… and now the girls were living it!

The girls breathed heavily, the cold air burning their lungs, smoke pouring from their mouths like steam engines. They crossed the shore, and then Ava leapt onto the icy lake and slid expertly. Carol did the same, leaping onto the ice she crouched and slid like a snowboarder. The monster hesitated for a moment, and then dashed onto the ice, only to come crashing down on its back.

The girls didn't waste a second, they pushed off with their heels, using their boots like ice skates. Within moments, they had crossed the frozen lake and jumped down, into a cluster of icy boulders that covered a steep slope.

The girls huddled behind a huge rock, hoping the monster would give up. Looking around, Ava realized they had made a mistake. They had trapped themselves between two huge boulders, with only one way out.

Carol looked at Ava, her crystal blue eyes filled with fear.

"Don't worry," whispered Ava, "we got this!"

She stared at the opening between the two rocks— a miniature avalanche of smaller rocks, slid down the hill directly behind them. Ava's fingers clawed at the snow-covered ground, looking for anything she could use as a weapon. Her fingers circled around a cold stone, the size of a golf ball. *Perfect!*

Crunch. Crunch. The footsteps grew closer. Carol was sure the monster could hear her heart pounding against her chest. A dark shadow slowly slid over the rock where the girls hid. Carol pressed back hard against Ava... they were trapped! Ava squeezed the rock hard, it was going to be her only chance.

"Boo!!!!!"

Ava jumped up screaming "*Yaaaaaaa!*" like a wild woman and hurled the rock at the beast....

Except, it wasn't the beast, it was Kevin Chen... one of the older neighborhood kids.

Ava watched horrified as the rock flew like a missile and hit Kevin in the chest with a loud thwack!

"Owwwww!" he said placing his hand on his chest.

"I'm so sorry Kevin! I thought you were...."

Carol slammed her hand over Ava's mouth. "She thought you were a bear. You know, lots of bears this time of year. Can never be too careful."

Kevin arched an eyebrow, then nodded, "Yeah... my bad, sorry I scared you guys."

"Sorry I almost shattered your sternum," said Ava.

"Oh that," laughed Kevin, "it was nothing, don't worry, I barely felt it."

"What?!" asked Ava insulted. "I mean yeah, my foot slipped on some ice when I went to throw it. Normally I can pretty much hurl a rock over a mile."

Carol raised her eyebrows and smiled at Kevin. "She's been known to exaggerate just a little."

"Hey, George Washington threw a rock across the Rappahannock River... and no one doubted him... so show a little respect."

"Okay," laughed Kevin holding up his hands in surrender. "We believe you!"

"What's that?" asked Carol pointing to a small rectangular object in Kevin's hand.

"It's a motion capture camera. I was grabbing it when I saw you guys run behind the boulder."

Carol's eyes flickered over to the boulder where they had been hiding just moments ago, and then up the small hill to the edge of the lake. *Kevin must have scared the creature off.*

"Why do you have a motion capture camera in the woods?" asked Carol.

"I actually have several set up. There's all kinds of wildlife out there."

You're telling me, thought Carol.

"Oh cool, my dad has one of those," replied Ava, "have you seen anything interesting?"

"Sure," said Kevin, "coyotes, fox, wild turkey and a beaver family. You'll have to come over and check out the pictures some time!"

"Oh wow, thanks," said Carol, "that would be awesome."

Ava's phone vibrated. She reached into her pocket and stared at the screen, her head dropped. "Oh boy," she moaned, "I'm in so much trouble."

"Don't worry," said Carol putting her arm around Ava's shoulders. "I'll be your backup."

Ava smiled. "Come on Kevin, walk with us. You can tell us more about the wild beasts that lurk in our forest."

"You would be surprised!"

Ava and Carol looked at each other and smiled…. *You wanna bet?* thought Carol, *you wanna bet?*

The trio climbed up the hill to the lake, slipping and sliding their way to the other side. No one noticed the headless monster, hidden in the trees, watching them from the shadows.

4
HOODWINKED

"Good morning, and ouch!" said Ava, checking out Carol's scraped and swollen cheek. "That looks like it hurts."

Carol smiled, "It looks worse than it feels."

"In that case, mind if I thump it?" asked Ava a little too eagerly.

"What? What kind of question is that? Of course, I mind. Someone needs to check your Netflix browsing history; I'm worried about you."

"Awe," said Ava, bumping her shoulder into Carol, "someone cares."

"Give me strength," whispered Carol, gazing skyward.

"Did your parents ask about your face?"

"Yeah, I told my parents that my sled and I had a brief collision with some shrubbery."

"Good thinking!"

"I thought so too," replied Carol.

"Too bad it wasn't mistletoe; you could have crashed and gotten a sympathy kiss from Noah Riley, a.k.a secret crush." Ava made the shape of a heart on her chest with her two hands.

"I'd rather kiss a frog," said Carol, shaking her head.

"That can be arranged," laughed Ava.

The girls walked quietly for a moment, taking in the scenery. It felt good to laugh. A blanket of snow covered Livingston. Overnight, the road crew had done their job. The sidewalks had been shoveled and the streets cleared.

Carol loved walking down Main Street at Christmastime. Livingston did Christmas right. Street corners were adorned with beautiful old street lights, wrapped in garland and red ribbons. Storefronts glistened with displays decorated with Christmas trees and wreaths. Classical music played old holiday classics. Everyone seemed happier, kinder.

Ava took in a deep breath; the aroma of pumpkin spice coffee and hot apple cider filled the air. The girls stopped and purchased two cups of hot chocolate and then continued toward the center of town.

"I was thinking about last night," said Carol suddenly. "I think that it was Ethan... or one of his friends. Think about it. He tells a scary story..."

"...and he practically dares us to go by the Butcher house," added Ava, seeing where Carol was going.

"Exactly. And when we do...," nodded Carol, "...a headless monster suddenly appears and chases us. It just seems a little suspicious to me."

Disappointment filled Ava's face; she was hoping they had a new mystery to uncover.

"Plus, there's this," said Carol, handing her phone to Ava.

Ava tilted the phone so she could see it in the bright sunlight. "That jerk! You mean to tell me I was frightened to death by a cheap $49 synthetic-fur costume from Amazon?!"

"We both were.... He's probably got Amazon Prime," winked Carol.

"So witty… but really, it doesn't make sense," said Ava, shaking her head.

"You're right," replied Carol, pointing. "Look!"

Ava turned, following Carol's gesture. Just ahead of them, yellow police tape was stretched across the sidewalk and the entrance to the Charter Bank.

The girls recognized Mr. Charter as he stood and talked with three uniformed police officers and a man dressed in a gray suit and black trench coat. Behind them were two Livingston police cars and a black SUV with the letters "FBI" on the side. A crowd of people had gathered on the sidewalk, talking excitedly.

"Whoa!" exclaimed Ava. "That doesn't look good."

"Not at all," replied Carol. "It must've been a robbery."

The Charter Bank was the oldest bank in Livingston, dating back to 1806. The bank had been passed down through generations of Charters.

Ava stood shaking her head. "Why would anyone rob a bank right before Christmas? Not only is that completely uncool… it's just evil."

Carol was about to reply when she felt a tug on her sleeve. She looked behind her into the eyes of a blond-haired boy wearing a black hoodie and jeans.

"Derik," she whispered.

"Derik?" asked Ava, quickly turning.

He quickly put his finger to his lips and then looked around, making sure no one had noticed him.

"Derik, what's going on? Are you okay?" asked Carol.

"Yes and no," he replied. "Follow me. I can't talk here."

The trio quickly skirted around the crowd and then ducked under the yellow police tape. A uniformed officer who looked like a bulldozer with a buzz cut immediately stopped them, blocking their path with his immense body.

"Holy moly," whispered Ava.

"I'm sorry," he said dryly. "Charter Bank is closed today."

Derik Charter pulled the hood from his head. The officer immediately recognized him, replacing his stern look with a tight smile.

"Morning, Mr. Charter."

"Morning, Officer Tiny," said Derik.

"And these are—" he prompted, motioning to the girls, obviously not happy with them being there.

"*Close* family friends," said Derik.

The officer hesitated, obviously not pleased with the situation, but nevertheless he stepped aside.

"Here," said Ava, handing the officer her hot chocolate. "I just bought it, and I haven't drunk from it. You look like you could use it more than me."

The officer shifted his immense frame and stared at the steaming cup of hot chocolate. A tendril of smoke wafted up to his nose.

"Thank you," he replied gruffly.

"You're welcome," replied Ava, giving him a massive toothy smile.

The first thing that hit the girls was the acrid smell that filled the lobby. It reminded Ava of the time she was seven years old and had jabbed a fork into the electrical outlet—zap, sparks, and smoke—and then the lights went out.

It also reminded her that she had blamed Carol for the fork incident.

"Sorry," whispered Ava.

"What?" asked Carol.

"There's a reason why my parents only allowed you to use plastic forks at my house… until last year. I'll explain later."

Carol gave Ava the all-too-familiar *you're a strange human being* look and then turned her attention to Derik. "What exactly happened?" asked Carol, looking around the bank lobby.

"Someone broke into the bank last night—we're not exactly sure when or how—and stole nearly half a million dollars."

"A half a million dollars?!" gasped Ava.

"I'm terribly sorry, Derik," said Carol, shaking her head. *A half million dollars….* She could barely comprehend that much money. "What will your dad do?"

"He's going to do everything that he can do to catch the thieves."

The girls looked up as Mr. Charter walked into the bank lobby. He was elegantly dressed, his hair combed into a perfect part. You would never have known that he had been up all night.

"Mr. Charter," said Carol, "we're so sorry about the robbery."

"Thank you, girls. I never thought that it would happen. Nearly two hundred years in Livingston… this is the first time Charter Bank has been robbed," he shook his head sadly.

"Dad," began Derik, somewhat unsure how to proceed, "Ava and Carol just got back from Italy— they actually helped recover an extremely valuable artifact that was stolen… and they helped the police right here."

"I know," smiled Mr. Charter politely, holding up his hands. "They solved the museum robbery and helped the police catch a group of smugglers."

"So, I just thought… it wouldn't hurt to have them look around," prodded Derik gently.

"That's up to them," Mr. Charter's eyes narrowed. "Do you want to see if the investigators missed anything?"

Ava set her jaw and placed her hands on her hips. "Count us in."

The girls followed Mr. Charter through a row of offices, down a narrow hallway to the back of the bank. At the end of the hallway there was a huge imposing gate made of titanium bars blocking the entrance to the room that housed the safe. The gate made a huge clunking noise as Mr. Charter unlocked it.

In the center of the room stood an enormous vault. The girls stared unbelieving at the eighteen-inch hole burned through the wall of the safe.

"Carol, look!" gasped Ava, pointing at the hole in the safe.

"The FBI believes they used a tool called a plasma cutter," said Mr. Charter.

"A plasma cutter? Sounds like a sci-fi weapon!" exclaimed Ava.

"Yes, it does," Mr. Charter nodded. "Unfortunately, this sci-fi weapon cut a gaping eighteen-inch hole through six inches of layered steel."

"How did they get all of that equipment in here without anyone noticing?" asked Carol.

"Well… that's the thing. Plasma cutters come in a portable unit that looks like an oversized toolbox. They are quite portable."

"Oh," replied Carol as she walked over to the safe. The door was open, revealing an upended money cart, huge bags of coins, and walls of safety deposit boxes.

"What *exactly* did they take?" asked Carol. "I mean, the safe deposit boxes aren't damaged, and there's still a lot of stuff in here."

"Cash," answered Mr. Charter. "We had a lot of extra cash for Christmas…. They picked the perfect time of year to rob us."

"Smart," whispered Carol. "The coin bags would have been too bulky, and breaking into the safe deposit boxes could take a lot of time."

Ava's eyes roamed around the interior of the room. "How did they get in?"

"We have no idea. The doors and windows were locked from the inside. The titanium door was still locked and armed, and the alarm was never triggered."

"What about the ventilation system?" asked Ava, pointing to the ceiling. Directly above the safe was a small rectangular vent about the size of a shoebox.

Mr. Charter shook his head. "Agents searched the roof; there were no footprints, and the ventilation system hadn't been tampered with. Plus...," he paused, thinking, "...a child couldn't fit through that system."

"What about the security video?" asked Carol, pointing to a camera mounted in the corner.

"Nothing. The thieves stole the hard drive and cut the internet cable, so there was no backup to the online server."

Ava shook her head, "It's like they teleported here."

"It was well planned," acknowledged Mr. Charter.

"Nothing on the traffic cams or store cams?" asked Carol.

"The police are going through store video and street cams, but these guys are professionals. They aren't hopeful."

"Do you mind if we take some pictures?" asked Carol. "We promise to keep them private."

Mr. Charter hesitated, "Go ahead. I have to replace this old safe anyway. It's nearly 160 years old." He placed his hand on the side of the old safe.

Carol looked at him. She was sure his mind was flooded with memories.

Ava and Carol spent about twenty minutes taking pictures of the vault, ceiling, walls, windows, doors, and floor.

Ava asked Mr. Charter, "Did anyone take a picture of the crowd?"

"No… why?" asked Mr. Charter.

"Because many times suspects come back to the scene of the crime as a part of the crowd. That way they can observe the investigation."

"Sounds risky. I mean, coming back to a place you just robbed," said Mr. Charter.

"They are usually in disguise… but you never know."

"I'll ask Lieutenant Norris," Mr. Charter clasped his hand and exhaled.

The girls recognized this all-too-familiar pattern of body language as: *It's time to finish up here*.

"Well, I think that we've got enough to go on for now," said Carol, smiling. "We'll let you know right away if we come up with anything."

"Thank you," smiled Mr. Charter. He led the girls through the hallway back to the lobby. "Thank you again, Ava. Thank you, Carol," he said, smiling at both girls. "Let me know if you find anything."

"We will," the girls chorused.

Derik walked with the girls onto the front steps of the bank. "Thank you for taking the time to look around… it was really cool of you."

"We'll make this case our top priority," said Ava seriously.

"Thank you," Derik smiled. "You guys are awesome. Do you really think you can solve it? I mean… these guys are pros."

"Yeah, but they're human," replied Carol with a smile. "And humans make mistakes…. It's just like my grandma used to say: 'It only takes one lose thread to unravel a blanket.'"

"I like that," said Derik. He stared at Carol for a moment. "Can I add my number to your phone?"

"Sure!" Carol unlocked her phone and handed it to Derik.

"Be sure to share it with Ava," he smiled as he typed in the digits.

The girls said their goodbyes, their minds filled with their new mystery… oblivious to the tiny black drone that hovered high above the bank, watching them.

5
THE LAIR

"We actually have two mysteries," said Ava as she grabbed a piping-hot sausage pizza from the microwave.

The girls had turned Ava's basement into a crime-solving think tank called The Lair. Using some of the award money from the Hancock Museum of Archeology, the girls had created a state-of-the-art crime lab.

A laptop and printer sat perched on a desk at one end of the room, with an old couch in the middle of the room that faced a huge, stand-alone magnetic whiteboard. The far end of the room had a small kitchenette, and behind the whiteboard on the back wall was a table with a microscope and chemistry set—a gift from Ava's dad, a prominent biologist.

Carol was hunched over the laptop. A moment later, the printer began whirring. "Here they come," said Carol. "The pictures we took at the bank. So, what were you saying about two mysteries?"

"Well, before our walk yesterday was rudely interrupted by the bank robbery, you said that you thought the headless monster was Ethan or one of his friends."

"Yes…," recalled Carol.

"Well, we know that Ethan can be immature, but in the end, he would never do anything to actually *hurt* us. Think about it, whoever was dressed up as the headless monster… the way he grabbed at us, the way he yanked your beautiful face into the tree… and then kept chasing us…. Ethan would have never done that."

Carol nodded, "Yeah, you're right." The thought actually made her shudder. "So, who do you think it is?"

"I'm not sure," said Ava. "All of this seems strange. The Butcher house… and then the bank."

"Do you think they are connected?"

"Your guess is as good as mine, but I have an idea that might help us find out."

"I'm all ears," said Carol. "Fire away."

"I'll be right back."

Ava disappeared through the doorway and up the stairs, while Carol attached the pictures from the bank onto the whiteboard. She dated the pictures and then wrote a brief description beneath each one.

On the far right of the board she wrote the word "Suspects" and underlined it twice. She stood staring at the whiteboard. They really didn't have *any* suspects. Ava popped into the room holding a camouflaged, rectangular device with an antenna.

"I'm afraid to ask," said Carol, eyeing the device in Ava's hand.

"This," began Ava proudly, "is a wireless trail camera. Remember Kevin had them to watch woodland creatures? Dad uses his for work."

"Cool… and this is gonna help us *how*?"

"This bad boy has a motion detector and can see in the dark. If there is any type of movement, it will snap a picture. It also has a live video feed. Meaning we can eat pizza and spy on the Butcher house at the same time."

"And you plan on putting this…?"

"We plan on putting this on a tree, facing the Butcher house. If there's anything suspicious going on, we'll see it. Safe in our secret hideout."

"I'm impressed," said Carol, smiling. "You keep coming up with ideas like that, and I may keep you on the payroll."

6
OPERATION NIGHT STALKER

The moon shone so brightly it looked like a train barreling down from the heavens toward the girls. As Ava and Carol walked down the sidewalk, Ava could see the lights from TVs glowing from living rooms and families in kitchens preparing for dinner.

Ava had grabbed her dad's Thor 2000 flashlight in case the headless guy appeared again. The Thor 2000 would temporarily blind anyone who was unfortunate enough to be on its receiving end—which seemed like a brilliant idea at first, but then she remembered he was headless and didn't have eyes.

The girls paused when they reached Whitmore Street. In the distance, they could see the Butcher house. Carol shivered, her finger unconsciously touching the bruise on her cheek.

"Okay," said Ava, "we need to find a tree within one hundred feet of the house that gives us the view we need."

Carol's eyes traveled from the house to a small clump of trees. It was perfect—the trees stood on a small hill that looked directly down toward the house. "Right there, it's our best vantage spot," she pointed.

"All right," said Ava, "let's do this."

The girls ran between two houses, clambered over a fence, and then crouch-ran to the cluster of trees. They sat quietly in the shadows, listening for any movement. Carol unzipped her jacket and pulled out a pair of binoculars.

Carol stared through her binoculars at the house for what seemed like an eternity.

"Well," prompted Ava, "see anything?"

"Nothing. It's completely dark."

"Okay," whispered Ava, "I'm gonna set up the camera."

Carol nodded, "I'll keep an eye out."

Ava crawled on her hands and knees to the front of the cluster of trees. She sat with her back to the tree as she unzipped her backpack and pulled out the camera. The camera had small straps that allowed her to secure it to the tree. Ava switched the camera to the "on" position, waited for the green light to come on, and then crawled back to Carol.

Ava crouched beside Carol and pulled out her phone. She typed in the IP address assigned to the camera into her browser, and instantly the Butcher house came into view.

"Whoa!" whispered Carol. "That is freaking awesome! It's, like, perfectly clear."

"I know," whispered Ava. "I had no idea it would work this well." She was afraid that it would turn out to be a grainy disappointment, but the image was clear and crisp. "Let's get back to The Lair before my parents realize we are missing."

Video surveillance turned out to be incredibly boring. Carol had hooked an HDMI cable from the laptop to their TV so they could watch the house, but aside from the occasional car, or neighbor walking a dog, nothing out of the ordinary happened.

Ava jolted awake. *What was that?* she thought, sitting upright on the couch. She and Carol had fallen asleep on the couch watching the Butcher house. A half-filled bag of microwave popcorn had spilled over them. Ava's reaction startled Carol awake as well, and her eyes froze on the TV.

"Ava, look!" Carol jabbed her finger at the screen.

Ava's eyes grew wide—the headless monster had their camera. The girls watched in horror as the camera rotated, and they saw themselves on the television screen. They jumped from the sofa and looked around the room, confused.

"How are we on the—"

"There!" screamed Carol, pointing to the window at the back of the room.

Ava clawed at the light switch. "Get down!" she whispered.

Ava and Carol crawled to the other side of the couch. They could see the dark shadow of the headless man outside the window. Suddenly a chilling voice came from the TV, filling the room.

"This is your last warning," it growled. "Accidents do happen."

There was a thud as the creature dropped the camera. The girls stared at the TV as the camera slowly sank into the snow. They listened to the crunching of his footsteps as he disappeared into the darkness.

"I really, really do not like that guy," Ava muttered.

Carol shook her head, still trembling. "At least he brought back the camera."

7
DIAMONDS

Ava threw a vicious front kick and then a hook, followed by an uppercut. Her opponent's eyes narrowed, her mouth sneering.

"Oh, you think you can handle this?" Ava growled.

Carol shook her head. "Are you fighting yourself again?"

Ava stared back at herself in the mirror. "Someone's got to protect us." She threw another flurry of punches and kicks.

"I think I'll choose the girl in the mirror," said Carol.

"Me?" asked Ava happily.

"No, not you. Your reflection."

Ava was about to retaliate when Carol's phone chimed. A second later, Ava's phone vibrated too.

"It's Derik," said Carol, looking up from her phone. "Key's Jewelers was robbed last night!"

"Key's Jewelers?!" Ava exclaimed. "What the heck?"

"Texting Derik now," replied Carol.

Ava waited impatiently as Carol's fingers flew across the screen. Moments later, her phone buzzed.

"Oh, cool," said Carol, reading. "His dad is good friends with the manager of Key's Jewelers. He said he's got something important to tell us. Is it okay if Derik comes over?" asked Carol.

"Of course! I'll let my mom know he's coming."

~~o~o~o~~

"Wow," whispered Derik, turning in a circle, taking in the room. "This is where you solve your crimes?"

"It is," smiled Ava. "Its official name is *The Lair*."

"The Lair," he repeated. "I like it." Derik walked over to the whiteboard. "These are the pictures you took from our bank. Have you found any clues yet?"

"Not yet," said Carol. "We've really just started to piece things together."

"I'm sure we will," added Ava quickly, seeing the disappointment on Derik's face.

"Derik, what was it that you wanted to tell us about the jewelry robbery?" asked Carol.

"Oh, yeah. Well, my dad is good friends with Tracy Morris...."

The girls looked at him expectantly. "Sorry, Derik, we have no idea who that is," admitted Carol.

"Tracy is the owner of Key's Jewelers. She stopped by the house this morning to speak to my dad about the robbery. I wasn't really supposed to hear their conversation... but—"

"But you did?" asked Ava excitedly.

"I did," he nodded. "it was like déjà vu. The thieves broke in and cut open their safe... and took all their cash and diamonds."

"Oh," said Ava. "I thought they locked the diamonds in those little display tables."

"They keep some of the less expensive pieces in the displays, but their cash and most valuable pieces are locked in the safe at night."

"Out of sight, out of mind," said Carol.

"Exactly. Tracy said she went in early this morning to get ready for their big Christmas sale when she realized the store had been robbed."

"Let me guess," said Carol, "no alarm, no video, doors and windows still locked."

"Yep… my dad asked her the same questions."

"You don't suppose these are inside jobs, do you?" asked Ava. "I mean, employees would have the alarm codes."

"Their alarm system works pretty much like the one at our bank. To disable the alarm, you have to type in a passcode. Each time the passcode is entered, it records the date and time."

"And I'm guessing that no one entered the code?" asked Carol.

"Nope. When the police checked, the alarm was armed at 7:00 p.m. when she left work. It wasn't accessed again until 7:00 a.m. the next morning."

"How do you get into a locked room without triggering an alarm and then vanish?" wondered Ava out loud.

"Not only get in, but get in and out with a plasma cutter, bags of cash… and diamonds," added Derik.

Carol walked around the room, tapping her head. Something was right there on the edge of her brain, just out of reach.

"Carol," shouted Ava, "look at the video!"

"Is that the Butcher house?" asked Derik.

Carol nodded, eyes glued to the screen. A laser-thin line of light shone through one of the windows.

"Did you see it?!" Ava quickly reset the video from the night before back thirty seconds. Two seconds later, the light appeared.

"Wait, why do you have a video of the Butcher house… and why is there a light inside?"

"Do you remember Ethan's story about the house being haunted?" Carol asked.

"Yeah…," said Derik.

"Well, Ava and I decided to kind of check it out for ourselves."

Derik smiled. "I should have known you two would—"

He froze, staring at the TV. Suddenly, the video camera was ripped from the tree. It arched skyward for a second and then the video went dead. The trio stood silently staring at the screen.

"Well, that was violent," whispered Derik.

Ava and Carol nodded. Suddenly, the video feed began playing again.

The video jostled and jumped—but one thing became clear.

"It's the back of my house," said Ava.

A headless shadow loomed on the outside of the house, and then there they were, Ava and Carol asleep on the couch.

Ava watched herself bolt upright on the couch; she could see her mouth moving, her breath caught in her throat.

Then the creature's voice filled the room. "This is your last warning," it growled. "Accidents do happen."

The monster dropped the camera, and the screen was filled with icy static as the camera sank into the snow.

A chill raced up Carol's spine as she and Ava looked at each other.

"*What* just happened?" asked Derik. "What was that?"

"That headless thing is what chased us a couple nights ago," said Carol. "It wants us to stay away from the Butcher house."

"The video was from a trail camera we set up in the woods near the house. It has a live video feed, so we thought we could safely monitor the house from The Lair. Obviously I didn't do a great job of hiding the camera," added Ava.

"So, you are telling me that a monster chased you from the Butcher house?!" Derik yelled.

"No," said Carol. "I'm telling you that someone *dressed* like a headless monster chased us."

"The fact that he knows where we live makes things a little more… unnerving," added Ava.

"That video was mega creepy," said Derik.

"Oh yeah, my dad's camera." Ava poked her head outside. "It's snowing hard."

Carol grabbed her boots and jacket. "Awesome! I'll go out with you. I want to see if our headless friend left any tracks."

"Like snow boot tracks," laughed Derik, "or big furry ones?"

"I'm betting on size twelve snow boots," replied Carol.

The trio trudged along the back of the house to the window where the headless monster had watched them the night before. There were only slight indentations left in the snow; the heavy snowfall had pretty much covered the monster's footprints.

Carol knelt and ever so gently began to brush away the new fluffy snow that had fallen and covered the tracks. "It's too hard to tell what's what…. And if the snow keeps falling like this, you won't even be able to tell he was even here."

"Yep," replied Ava. She was on her knees digging through the snow, looking for her dad's camera. Derik dropped down to his knees to help.

"If you didn't know your dad's camera was under here, you wouldn't find it until spring," said Derik, scooping through the snow.

Carol froze in place…. Suddenly, everything clicked.

"Guys, I think I know how they broke in! Come on!"

8
CAN YOU DIG IT?

"Where *exactly* are we going?" asked Ava as they trudged through the snow.

"To the one place that can prove my theory right! The Livingston Public Works Department."

"Sounds fascinating," moaned Ava. "How come your clues never take us to say… the mall? Starbucks?"

The Public Works Department was located on Bell Street about a quarter of a mile from the center of town. The streets were filled with laughing and chattering holiday shoppers and tourists, colorful bags swinging from their arms. The trio paused in front of Key's Jewelers. Ava's heart felt a sudden pang of sadness. Inside she could see sparsely filled display cases—and there was Tracy Morris inside, sipping her coffee, looking utterly lost.

Ava turned toward her friends—she could tell by their somber expressions that Derik and Carol saw Tracy too. In a time when Livingston was usually filled with holiday cheer and excitement, an evil menace seemed determined to ruin Christmas for everyone.

"We're gonna catch whoever did this," said Ava. She pulled her hand from her glove and touched the window, feeling the cold glass. In her heart of hearts, she knew that they were going to make this right.

"Okay," said Carol, "we need to get moving. I'm not sure how late Public Works is open today."

Per Derik's suggestion the trio made one more quick stop. They grabbed three steaming hot decaf mochas and then continued their journey.

"This is perfect sledding snow," said Derik as they crossed the railroad tracks.

"Yeah," said Carol, agreeing distractedly. Right now, sledding was the last thing she was interested in.

"Where is this place?" groaned Ava. "I can no longer feel my face."

"Right there," said Derik, pointing. "It's the only brick building... well... besides the post office and the dentist office. Oh, and that new lawyer's office. Never mind. It's that brick building with the dark-green shutters."

A man with a scruffy beard wearing a Livingston Tigers football jersey was shoveling the sidewalk leading up to the public works building. He stepped aside and leaned on his shovel, giving the trio a curious stare as they passed by.

"Cah-ful on those steps," he called out in a thick Bostonian accent. "They're wicked slippery."

"Thank you!" Derik yelled back.

The man wasn't kidding. Even though the steps were covered in rock salt, the steps were still treacherous.

"If I fall to my death," began Ava as they ascended the stairs, "you can have my shoes."

"So gracious," said Carol.

"I wasn't talking to you," smiled Ava.

"I'll treasure them forever," said Derik, laughing.

Stale, warm air greeted the trio as they stepped into the lobby. The walls were painted a pale blue and were covered with paintings and photographs of Livingston and historically notable Livingstonians. Tiny speakers festooned in the corners of the room played an ancient version of "Silent Night."

"Frank Sinatra," whispered Derik.

"Where?" asked Ava.

"The music. The man singing is Frank Sinatra."

"Oh, cool. I like his voice. Is he in a group?"

"Yes," answered Carol. "The Backstreet Boys. Focus, Ava."

"Sorry…."

The trio approached a massive oak desk that stretched across the center of the room. Behind the desk they could see a series of hallways illuminated by flickering fluorescent lights.

"This place is in need of some serious interior decorating," whispered Ava. She looked at Carol and Derik. "I don't see anyone. Should I?" she asked, pointing at a small brass bell that sat on the desk.

"Go for it," said Derik.

Ava smacked the bell twice with the palm of her hand. "Whoa, that was a lot louder than I thought it was going to be."

From somewhere in the back of the building, they heard shuffling, a door slam, and then hurried footsteps.

"Well. Hello, hello, hello." A thin man with a goatee and ponytail appeared behind the desk. Ava cringed as he wiped his nose on his sleeve and then interlaced his fingers, cracking his knuckles.

"Hi, Mr. Cooper," said Carol.

"Good afternoon… and do I know you?" he asked, narrowing his eyes.

"Your nametag," smiled Carol, pointing to a black tag with white lettering that read *H. Cooper*.

"Oh yes, yes," his hand flew up to the tag. "I always forget about that thing. So, how can I help you?"

Derik and Ava turned to Carol. This was her big moment.

"I was visiting the Livingston government website—"

"She doesn't get out much," said Ava.

Carol turned, giving Ava the angry-eyes look.

"Sorry," said Ava, "please continue."

"The site said that you archive all of the maps of the city here. Many dating back to when Livingston was first settled."

"Yes, we do," said Mr. Cooper, his face filling with pride.

"Awesome! Mr. Cooper, we're looking for—"

"Please call me Harvey."

"Okay, um, Harvey… I'm looking for a specific map, one that shows the underground tunnel system below Livingston."

Ava noticed Harvey grip the edge of his desk a little tighter.

Carol pulled her phone from her coat, and after a series of swipes, she turned the screen to Harvey.

"The website said that this map is here. The one that shows the entire tunnel system. Do you have it?"

"Why are you interested in the tunnel system? Most of it collapsed and was filled in nearly one hundred years ago."

Carol was caught off guard by Harvey's reaction.

"We're working on a historical painting of Livingston for our history class," said Derik, jumping in. "We're painting a panoramic of the city from the 1800s, the 1900s, and present time. We just wanted an accurate representation and thought showing the tunnels would be a cool addition."

"Most of my classmates have no idea that they even exist," offered Ava.

"Yes, yes, I suppose most people don't," Harvey replied. "Give me just a second."

"Whoa," said Carol softly as Harvey disappeared down the hallway. "Good job!"

"Captain of the debate team," smiled Derik. "Gotta be quick on my feet."

"I've got really quick feet," said Ava. "They just don't connect to my brain like yours."

"Here we go…," said Harvey as he carefully laid out an aerial picture of the entire city. The picture was about four feet wide and two feet tall. It was composed of what looked like a series of individual photos that had been stitched together.

"I'm confused," said Carol, studying the photo. "Where are the tunnels?"

"Oh, right here," said Harvey, pointing at the map. "These dark gray lines underneath the buildings represent the tunnel system. See, here's the old church, and right here is the town hall. This is Main Street," he said, tracing his finger along the map.

"That's Main Street?" asked Ava.

"Yes, there's the Main Street Diner. See how the tunnel system went right under the Baptist church? They used the tunnel to smuggle food and supplies."

"And you're sure this is accurate?" asked Carol.

"Oh yes, this is the official government map for Livingston… you can see the date and government seal right here."

Carol's shoulders slumped. "Do you mind if I take a picture for us to use… you know… for our project?"

"Oh, certainly," smiled Harvey. "Take as many as you like."

"Thanks," mumbled Carol as she zoomed in on the map and took several photos.

"Well," said Harvey, folding his hands together. "I'm about to close up shop. Anything else I can help you with?"

"No, sir," said Carol.

"Harvey. Just call me Harvey. 'Sir' makes me feel old."

"Thank you, Harvey," said Carol. "You've been a big help."

"You're welcome," he smiled. "Merry Christmas."

"Merry Christmas," said the group as they walked to the door.

"So," said Derik as they paused on the top of the steps. "You thought the bad guys used the tunnel system."

"Yeah," sighed Carol, clearly upset. "I thought I'd figured it out."

"It would have made sense," said Ava.

"But according to that map, from what I could tell, the tunnel never ran beneath your dad's bank or the jewelry store. Sorry, guys."

"It's okay," said Ava, resting her head on Carol's shoulder. "We'll figure it out."

9
DIVE BOMBER

"I'm dead," cried Derik, jumping up from his seat.

"What is it?" asked Carol.

"My parents' Christmas party is tonight!" gasped Derik. "I was supposed to help get the house ready. Ugh!"

He yanked his coat from the back of his chair, knocking it loudly to the floor.

"Derik," said Ava, picking up the chair and helping him with his coat. "Give your dad a call—tell him you're on your way."

He gave Ava an *are you kidding me* look.

She countered with, "Trust me on this one. You have no idea what we've put our parents through."

Derik hesitated. Darkness had snuck up on the trio as they ate grilled cheese sandwiches and discussed the case at the Main Street Diner.

"Geez, I didn't even realize it was dark outside. How long were we here?" asked Ava.

"At least a couple hours," said Carol, hurriedly throwing some money on the table.

Derik reached for his pocket, but Carol shook her head. "Don't worry about it; we gotta get going! You grab lunch next time."

"Wow," smiled Derik. "Thank you. You guys are awesome."

"We know," winked Ava playfully. "Now get going." She shoved Derik toward the door.

The girls stepped a few feet away from Derik, giving him some privacy while he called his dad.

"Okay," said Derik, looking a little less panicked. "He's still angry, but I managed to calm him down some."

"I'm sure he's got a lot on his mind right now," said Carol. "We'll walk with you to your house."

The trio took a shortcut through the center of town to save time. They hopped a fence at the Brown Recreation Center and trudged across the soccer field. The snow glistened and sparkled like tiny silver diamonds on a sea of felt beneath the moonlight.

"Everything looks so beautiful, so pristine," said Carol. "I almost hate to walk across the field, you know, it's completely untouched."

"Like your YouTube channel," snickered Ava.

"Har, har, so funny."

Derik stopped in his tracks. "Did you hear that?"

Ava pulled her earmuffs down from her ears. "What am I supposed to hear?"

"I hear it," said Carol. "It's a *buzzing*."

Suddenly a huge black drone screamed above them, flying only inches from their heads.

"Whoa," yelled Derik, ducking.

"What the—?! Run!" yelled Ava.

The children dove into the snow as the drone arched and dove again, rocketing through the air like a missile.

Carol sat up, looking around, trying to see who was controlling the drone.

"Crawl along the fence," yelled Derik, pointing to the fence that bordered the park. "It can't get us there!"

The trio scrambled toward the fence, fighting their way through the knee-high snow. Wham! The drone struck Carol in the back of the head, knocking her face down into the snow.

"Carol!" screamed Ava. She crawled through the snow to her. "Carol, are you okay?"

"I'm okay," said Carol, grabbing the back of her head, her vision filled with stars.

"It's about to dive again!" yelled Derik. "Come on! We gotta get to the fence."

Ava looked over her shoulder. She could see the drone make a tight circle in the sky. It raced toward them just as they reached the fence.

"Are you hurt, Carol?" asked Derik, concern filling his face.

"Just my pride," said Carol, gently shaking her head, still seeing stars.

The drone hung in the sky, buzzing like a giant mosquito, watching its prey.

"If we jump the fence and stay against it, the drone can't get us," said Ava.

"Great idea," said Derik.

The drone moved closer, hovering almost directly in front of them. A red light pulsed.

"It's recording us," whispered Carol.

Ava grabbed a handful of snow, packing it into a snowball. "Go away!" she yelled, hurling it at the drone. The drone remained motionless, unmoving, mocking her.

"I wish I had my baseball bat," said Derik angrily. "I'd go King Kong on that thing."

"Right now, we just need to get out of here," said Carol.

"Okay," agreed Derik. "On the count of three?"

Ava and Carol nodded.

"Ready...? One, two, three!" yelled Derik.

The trio spun and leapt up, grabbing the fence, pulling themselves up and over. They then fell to the ground on the other side in a tangled mass of arms and legs.

The drone rose high up in the sky, directly overhead, still watching.

"Okay," said Ava as they quickly untangled themselves. "We stick along the fence and then make a run for it between those houses. Then we stay close to the houses and trees until we get to Derik's house."

Derik and Carol nodded.

"All right," said Ava. "Let's go!"

But just as Ava's boot hit Fir Street, an angry roar erupted behind them.

"What?!" yelled Derik as a sleek black car came barreling toward them. They watched in horror as it launched off the street, rocketing up onto the sidewalk.

"Watch out!" screamed Carol, tackling Ava, knocking her out of the path of the car.

The car's engine revved as it slid off the sidewalk, just missing the children, fishtailing wildly as it hit the road.

"Derik, are you okay?" yelled Carol as she sat up.

"Yeah…," he whispered, barely able to speak.

They watched as the car slipped and slid around the corner, speeding away into the night.

"Obviously he failed driving school," said Ava, dropping her head back into the snow.

"They tried to kill us," Derik whispered.

Carol shook her head. *What did we get ourselves into?*

10
NEVER JUDGE A PICTURE BY A PICTURE

Carol stood in front of the crime board. It had been forty-eight hours since the first robbery, and so far, the only suspect was a sketch of a headless monster that Ava had affectionately named Brom Bones—the name of the headless horseman.

"This is driving me nuts. I can't tell what's what," said Carol, her nose literally pressed against the photo of the tunnel system.

"Well, we know this is the old church," said Ava, "and this is Main Street Diner... and this I think is Willerbees Antiques."

"That's weird," said Carol. "I thought that the tunnel system ran under the Hancock Museum...."

"It did. It's part of their tour. Remember, they have a glass enclosure around the entrance."

"Maybe that part of the tunnel was built after the photo?" proposed Carol.

"Or maybe it's a mistake," offered Ava. "We don't have anything to compare it to."

Carol's eyes lit up. "Oh, yes we do! Grab your coat; the museum closes in ten minutes!"

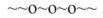

The girls stood at the top of the museum steps, their hands on their waists, their lungs heaving. Ava grabbed the door handle and pulled. It was locked. She smooshed her face against the glass. She could see light inside, but as far as she could tell there was no one inside.

"We're too late," Carol pointed to a small closed sign. "Everyone's closing early for the holidays."

"But they won't open again until after Christmas," groaned Ava. "It'll be too late."

The girls sat down on the steps, watching the endless stream of traffic. Every time they thought they were about to have a huge breakthrough in the case, something stopped them in their tracks.

"We're still no closer to solving this case than we were two days ago," said Carol.

"I know… we've been stumped before. I don't even know what to do next," said Ava.

"I would suggest getting out of the cold," said a singsong voice.

The girls' heads spun around. It was Gladys, the museum's concierge.

"Gladys!" yelled Ava. She jumped up, wrapping her arms around the petite, silver-haired woman.

"Hi, Gladys," beamed Carol, giving her a big hug.

"Come inside, come inside. You'll catch your death out here," she fussed, her brilliant gray-blue eyes sparkling just as brightly as ever. Gladys worked the front desk at the museum. She had helped the girls solve the mysterious theft of the famous Ramesses diamonds and become a great friend. "So," said Gladys, smiling, "what mischief are you two up to?"

"We're trying to solve another mystery," said Ava. "The bank and the jewelry store robberies."

"Oh, yes! I've been following that story in the news. Horrible, and right at the holidays."

"It is terrible," said Carol, nodding in agreement.

"How's your investigation going? Any spicy tidbits?"

"Well… it's kind of hit a roadblock," said Carol. "I thought for sure I was on to something. But, according to a map that we got from the public works building, I was wrong."

Gladys tilted her head. "How so?"

Carol turned back to Ava. "Can you grab the map out of my backpack and show Gladys?"

"Sure." Ava pulled the map out, handing it to Carol.

"Why not spread it out on the desk, dear. That way I can see it a little more clearly."

"Good idea," Carol smoothed it out across the surface of the help desk. Gladys swiveled a desk lamp over the picture. "See what I mean?" asked Carol, pointing to the map. "The tunnel system runs beneath the museum, but on this map it doesn't."

"Hmm…," Gladys studied the map intently. "Well, this isn't right… this isn't right at all. Where did you say you got this?"

"It's the official map from the public works building," said Carol.

Gladys looked at the map and then at Carol. "One second," she held up her finger and fished around in her desk drawer for a moment and then pulled out a gargantuan magnifying glass. "Ah, perfect," said Gladys, holding it up to her eye.

"Whoa," whispered Ava. "Your eye is huge."

"Yes," laughed Gladys. "Wait until you're eighty; there are all kinds of little surprises. Okay," continued Gladys, leaning in. "Yes, the signature beneath the seal... it says Wilbur Jones."

"Is that bad?" asked Ava.

"Not bad—it's just that Wilbur Jones died in 1842, and the map is dated 1846."

"Who was Wilbur Jones?" asked Carol.

"He was the head of the town council. His signature is on many of the maps and prints here."

"That's why we're here... not because of the signature, but we want to compare this map with the one upstairs."

"Let's do it," replied Gladys excitedly. She snatched the photo off the desk and began walking briskly toward the stairs. "Well... don't just stand there like a couple of statues," she said over her shoulder. "Come on!"

The girls followed Gladys up the winding staircase and down the hall to the History of Livingston exhibit. Gladys flicked on the lights. The walls were filled with fascinating black-and-white photos displaying an illustrative timeline of the history of Livingston. It was fascinating to see historical landmarks that were built two hundred years ago still being used today.

However, Carol only had one thing in mind, and that was the massive photo of Livingston taken in the 1860s by an aerial blimp. And that picture just happened to hang at the very back of the exhibit. Beneath it was an amazing illustration of the intricate tunnel system that serpentined beneath the town.

Carol's heart began to race. She spotted it, clear as day. The tunnel system ran directly beneath the bank and the jewelry store! "Look, Ava!" Carol cried out. "The tunnel, it passes directly beneath the bank—"

"And the jewelry store," said Ava excitedly.

Gladys stretched out the map Carol had brought her beneath the picture. The tunnel systems were remarkably different from each other.

"Who gave you this map?" asked Gladys.

"A man who works at the public works building. Hector... Harold..."

"Harvey," interrupted Ava. "Harvey Cooper."

"That's right," nodded Carol.

"Hmm," frowned Gladys. "I don't know anyone named Harvey, but I do know for certain that this is not the original document. It's a fake."

"So, Harvey duped us?" asked Carol angrily.

"Someone did," nodded Gladys. "Not necessarily Harvey. He may have been fooled as well."

"I don't know," said Ava. "He seemed to know a lot about the map, remember? He knew the location of every landmark."

"Why would he go to the trouble of creating a fake map?" mused Carol.

"I think you know the answer to that," said Gladys.

"Gladys," Carol pointed to the photo, "this narrow road is Mall Street, but I don't see Whitmore Street."

"This is Whitmore Street, right here," replied Gladys, tapping the map, "and this is the location of the old Butcher house."

"But... it says morgue," said Carol, confused.

"Well, actually, it was a hospital and a morgue. During the Revolutionary War, Samuel Butcher used the top floor as a makeshift hospital, the first floor to perform his surgeries, and the bottom floor as a morgue."

"Eeesh, no wonder there are so many scary stories about that house," said Ava.

"What's scary is Mr. Butcher never had any type of medical training. Ironically, Samuel Butcher was actually—"

"A butcher," said Carol, finishing her sentence.

"That's right," agreed Gladys. "The stories that I have read would give you nightmares. Many said that Samuel lived up to his last name." She paused, letting this sink in. "When Samuel died, his children renovated the house and tried to put the past behind them, but many people in the town, well… they never forgot about Samuel's atrocities. So, a long time ago, in the middle of the night, the Butchers simply disappeared, leaving everything behind."

"That is officially creepy… and sad," whispered Ava.

"Yes, yes, it is," agreed Gladys.

"Carol… I'm gonna need that night-light back," said Ava.

"Gladys," Carol stared at the tunnel system, "it looks like the tunnel system extended all the way out to the Butcher house."

"Yes, it did. Actually, it was one of the first sections of the tunnel built in 1775. If you follow it with your finger, you can see that it leads to the old church.

Many of the graves that you see behind that church are filled with patients from the Butcher house."

"Last question, I promise," said Carol. "It looks like there's a small section of tunnel that leads from the Butcher house to Crispin Pond?"

"Ah, yes, Crispin Pond. That was a small, man-made reservoir. At one time a huge portion of the Livingston community used it for water. They drained it about fifty years ago. It's conservation land now."

Carol remained silent for a moment, chewing on her bottom lip. "Gladys, I think you may have just blown this case wide open."

Gladys's eyes sparkled, and her face filled with pride. "Us girls gotta do what we gotta do to keep this town safe," she said, laughing.

Carol gave her a conspiratorial smile. "Yes, ma'am, we do."

Gladys led the girls downstairs and back into the lobby.

"Thank you so much," said Carol, giving Gladys a big hug. "We promise to keep you in the loop!"

"You better!" smiled Gladys. "You better!"

It was 8 p.m. when they stepped out of the museum. In the distance, the deep tones of the church bell filled the night.

"Eight o'clock," Carol broke into a run. "Come on!"

11
TUNNEL VISION

Ava and Carol lay flat on their bellies, staring across a shallow, snow-covered ravine, which they had learned from Gladys, used to be Crispin Pond. Now, it resembled a moon crater filled with rocks and scraggly bushes poking through the snow. There was, however, one other thing that brought a smile to Carol's lips: tire tracks. And those tracks disappeared behind a wall of dirt and rocks.

It was pitch-black outside, except for the occasional break in the clouds, revealing a full moon.

"Can your blood freeze?" whispered Ava through chattering teeth.

"Only your brain can freeze; so, in your case, you have nothing to worry about."

"If you're implying that I—"

"Shhh, voices!" whispered Carol excitedly.

Ava nodded. She could hear the voices—and their feet crunching across the snow. Seconds later, car doors slammed shut.

"They're leaving," whispered Carol.

The car engine struggled. Ava could imagine the man turning the key and pressing the gas pedal over and over. Finally, the engine roared to life. Thick smoke billowed upward from behind the rock wall.

"Thank goodness," whispered Ava. "For a moment I thought we were gonna have to push them."

Moments later, the car appeared. It was the perfect car if you wanted to go unnoticed: an older model, dark gray Toyota. The car stopped for a moment as the driver rolled down his window, took one more hard drag of his cigarette, and then flicked it away in a fiery arch. The girls were close enough to hear it sizzle as it hit the snow.

The car slowly crept away as the driver closed his window, snow crunching under its tires. It seemed to take an eternity for the car to cross the ravine and pull onto the main road. Ava and Carol didn't move until the red taillights had completely disappeared into the darkness.

"Okay," said Carol, slowly standing. "Let's go."

"Wait," said Ava, grabbing Carol's arm. "We can't just walk across the ravine; they'll see our footprints."

"What do you suggest—we fly?"

"Yes. I have a pouch of this glittery powder; just sprinkle some on top of your head…."

"Ava! Seriously."

"Fine, follow me," said Ava. "I saw this in a movie."

Ava worked her way down the rocky incline until she reached the edge of the ravine. She then sprawled belly-down onto the snow.

"Well?" she asked, looking over her shoulder.

"I'm coming, I'm coming," said Carol.

Carol joined Ava, and like two water spiders they traveled across the snow to where the car had appeared. There was a massive hill made of dirt and rock that the thieves had used as a natural barrier to hide their car behind.

Unsure what lay on the other side, Carol crept along the bottom of the hill. She grabbed her phone and clicked on the photo app. Slowly she extended her arm, using her phone to see what was around the corner.

"Whoa," whispered Carol.

"What is it?" asked Ava.

"Come here—you've got to see this."

Ava scooched over beside Carol as she adjusted the phone so Ava could see the screen. Just beyond the wall was a huge slab of cement resembling a giant pizza oven, the opening sealed by an enormous iron plate that looked like a manhole cover—only the cover had a gaping two-foot hole cut through the center of it.

Ava let out a low whistle; the entrance to the tunnel was pitch-black. "I hope you're not claustrophobic…."

Carol held up her phone and took a couple pictures. "Just in case," she smiled unconvincingly.

Ava grabbed her Thor 2000 flashlight from her backpack and flicked it on. "All right," she said, shining it into the entrance of the cave. "It's now or never."

The first thing the girls noticed once inside was the dank, earthy smell that permeated the tunnel.

"Ugh," moaned Ava. "It stinks in here."

"Try breathing through your mouth," offered Carol.

Ava played the beam of her flashlight along the ceiling and walls. Jagged chunks of rock and roots erupted from the sides and top of the tunnel. The floor was made of packed earth, and the ceiling was supported by thick beams of wood that looked like railroad ties. The only source of light came from Ava's flashlight, which was powerful enough to let them see well into the distance.

"It must have taken forever to dig this tunnel," said Ava. "And it's still in amazing condition."

"It is," agreed Carol, checking her phone. "They've been gone seven minutes. We gotta move fast. If we get caught, we're goners."

"Okay," said Ava, picking up her pace. "No need to—"

Ava stopped in her tracks. She put her hand on Carol's shoulder as she flicked off the flashlight. The darkness of the cave was suffocating. Carol fought the panic rising up through her body. *Breathe,* Carol told herself. *Breathe.*

"Do you see it?" whispered Ava.

Carol nodded. She could see it. The faintest of light shone up ahead. Using their hands on the walls of the tunnel, they moved forward until they reached the source of the light.

There was a wooden ladder that led to what looked like a trap door. Light in the yellowish-orange range escaped around the edges, and a looped string hung down close to the ladder.

"It's like the access door to my attic," whispered Carol. "You pull the string and it opens."

"Got it," whispered Ava.

"Only problem is we don't know if there's anyone inside."

"I got that covered," whispered Ava. She grabbed her phone and reached in her backpack.

"A selfie stick?" asked Carol.

"Watch and learn." Ava attached her phone to the selfie stick and then opened the FaceTime app. Carol's phone buzzed.

"It's me—answer it," Ava said helpfully.

"Ahh," Carol's face lit up. "I see what you're doing."

"You catch on fast," smiled Ava. "Wish me luck!"

Ava placed a foot on the first rung of the ladder; it felt sturdy. She climbed up to the top of the ladder, and with one hand pulled ever so gently on the string. The access door opened just a smidge, bathing Ava's face in light and making her grimace.

Carefully, she raised her phone through the opening, and then, using her selfie stick, she slowly rotated her phone 360 degrees.

Using FaceTime, Carol was able to see everything in the room. "Ava," she called up in a low voice. "The room's empty!"

"Here goes nothing!" Ava pulled on the string, completely opening the access door. Warm air and light filled the tunnel. Ava paused at the top of the ladder, letting her eyes adjust to the light. Then, she slowly pulled herself up through the opening into the room.

Ava spun around, doing a quick surveil. The room officially gave her the creeps. She crouched over the opening and gave Carol the thumbs-up. Ava trembled as Carol climbed the ladder; she was sure someone was going to sneak up behind her.

She breathed a sigh of relief as Carol's head popped through the opening. Ava grabbed her by the forearm and pulled her onto the floor.

"Holy moly," said Carol, looking around. "This place is disgusting."

Ava nodded her head as she slowly lowered the trap door.

"See what you can find, and fast!" directed Ava.

The room was lit by a single lightbulb and a tall, skinny lamp held together by duct tape. Two makeshift desks made from cardboard boxes sat in the center of the room. Each desk had a laptop and was connected to wireless hotspots. In front of the desk was a standing children's chalkboard, filled with images and maps.

The windows were covered with thick black cardboard. In the far corner of the room, black coveralls hung on a makeshift clothes rack constructed of wooden dowels suspended from the ceiling by fishing wire. Beneath the coveralls were three large backpacks and a machine on wheels that looked like some kind of generator.

Ava pulled at the corner of one of the pieces of cardboard covering the window. She crouched down and squinted through the opening. It took a moment to get her bearings, and then she realized exactly where they were.

"You were right, Carol. We're in the Butcher house. It's the basement."

Carol nodded. She was staring at the chalkboard, her hands on her hips. "Ava, come here quick! Look at this!"

Ava rushed over to Carol's side. "Here's the map of the tunnel system. Look right here," she said, jabbing excitedly. A red circle was drawn around the bank and the jewelry store.

"Carol... there's a—"

"I know," said Carol. She stared at the third circle; it was drawn around Archie's Collectibles.

"Why Archie's Collectibles? Are they gonna get matching lockets?"

"No. Remember, these guys seem to like things quick and easy. My guess is they're after his collection of rare baseball cards. Remember his pride and joy, the Babe Ruth card? That card alone is worth seven hundred thousand dollars."

"Oh yeah," said Ava, "and he has some super valuable comics...."

"Ava, take some pics of the board. I'm gonna see what else I can find, and I'm setting my alarm for five minutes."

"Good idea," agreed Ava as she grabbed her camera and began taking pictures.

While Ava grabbed evidence, Carol began rummaging through the papers on top of the makeshift desks. Not expecting anything to happen, she tapped on the track pad. The laptop jumped to life, displaying a web page that said their travel itinerary had been emailed to them. Carol's heart began pounding... there was a Gmail tab open in the browser. "Please!

Please," she whispered. She clicked the tab, and there it was: an email from JetBlue.

"Yes! Um, Ava," began Carol, "I'm pretty sure they are going to rob Archie's Collectibles tonight."

"Tonight, as in *tonight*?"

"They have a 5:20 a.m. flight out of Rhode Island, and get this: They're going to Mexico City."

"If they get to Mexico," worried Ava, "they'll disappear forever."

"That's why we have to stop them," said Carol, scribbling the flight information on a scrap of paper.

"If we can find where they hid the diamonds and money, they can't leave! They won't leave without that," said Ava.

Carol glanced worriedly at her phone; they had three minutes to find the stolen goods and get out of the house.

"Where do you think they would have hidden it?" asked Ava as she flew around the room, searching under tarps, boxes, and mountains of junk. "There's, like, a million hiding places."

"Could be anywhere," said Carol. "They have this entire house. It could be in the walls, under a loose floorboard.... It could...."

Carol paused; her heart began to beat wildly. She could hear voices coming from the tunnel!

"Ava! Ava! They're coming."

12
A DARING ESCAPE

Ava spun in a circle. "The stairs!" she whispered urgently, pointing to a narrow stairwell that ran against the back wall. The girls raced over to the stairs, cringing as the old staircase creaked and groaned under their weight.

An old wooden door was all that stood in their way of escape! Ava grabbed the doorknob and twisted. It was locked. *Maybe it's just stuck,* she hoped. Ava grasped the handle with both hands and twisted. The doorknob didn't budge!

Ava turned to Carol wild-eyed, her heart pounding. They could hear the sound of footsteps climbing the ladder.

"Hide!" hissed Ava. "Hide!"

The girls stormed down the steps, just as the access door began to rise.

"Back here," whispered Carol. Ava followed Carol through a dark doorway into a small laundry room.

Ava scrambled onto an old washing machine and tore the black cardboard from the window.

"What are you doing?" asked Carol, panicking.

"Escaping. Watch the door!"

Carol crouched in the doorway, staring at the trap door. A gloved hand appeared and then a man's face—short blond hair, jagged bangs, square jaw. Carol shrank back into the shadows.

"Come on, stupid window," growled Ava through clenched teeth.

"Ava, hurry!"

Ava tugged on the window frame with all her might. Suddenly, giant cracks raced across the thin, narrow pane. Shards of glass fell from the window into the snow, leaving a row of jagged pieces, like razor-sharp fangs along the bottom of the frame. *That works,* she thought.

"Almost got it. Just need to pull these pieces out," said Ava, desperation filling her voice.

"It's too late! Get down," pleaded Carol. "They're here!"

"I've almost got it," whispered Ava. "Stall them!"

"How?" asked Carol incredulously.

Carol quickly took in her surroundings. *Washing machine, dryer, metal shelves, hot water heater, and a nasty sink with gross brown stains.* Carol shook her head. This wasn't good. They were trapped!

Cold sweat ran down Ava's neck. Her hands were trembling so badly that she cut herself repeatedly on the razor-sharp glass. It didn't help that less than twenty feet away she could hear the thieves' voices. She could make out a woman's voice and two men. *They must be eating,* she thought, as the smell of Chinese food filled the air. She dared to steal a quick glance over her shoulder.

Carol was lying on the floor, her phone out. She was using it to spy on the bad guys. Ava looked back at the window. It wasn't perfect, but she had removed enough glass for them to make it through. She placed the cardboard back over the window, hiding the missing glass.

Soundlessly, Ava lowered herself from the washing machine onto the cement floor and crawled over to Carol.

"It's ready," whispered Ava.

"Okay," replied Carol softly. "They're eating. It's now or never."

The girls crawled over to the washing machine. They stopped and listened. The conversation had turned to their Archie's Collectibles heist.

Ava climbed up on top of the washing machine. She removed the black cardboard, placing it outside the window, and then carefully pulled herself through the basement window and out into the snow.

Crouching beside the window, Ava turned to help Carol through.

"Careful," Ava whispered, "there's a lot of glass." Ava waited… no response. "Carol?" Ava whispered.

Something must have gone wrong! What if they come in the room and see the cardboard missing and the broken window? Ava grabbed the cardboard and placed it over the window. She shook her head; it felt like she was trapping Carol in the room. *What do I do?*

Carol had just climbed up onto the washing machine when she heard a chair scrape across the floor. Someone was up and moving!

She tried to let Ava know what was happening, but it was too late—footsteps were moving toward the laundry room.

Dropping to the floor, she squeezed between the wall and the washing machine.

A dim overhead bulb flicked on. Glowing spots danced in Carol's eyes as they adjusted to the light. Each footstep sounded like thunder as it came closer to where she was hidden. She willed her body to stop shaking. The footsteps stopped. From around the washer, she could see a huge boot and leg—and then a horrific screeching sound. This was it; it was all over!

Carol mentally kicked herself, *get a grip*, the screeching sound was merely the dryer door being opened. Air rushed out of Carol's lungs like a slowly deflating tire. He was doing laundry. Carol could hear the man breathing as he moved the clothes from the washing machine into the dryer. The man slammed the dryer door shut, and with a press of a button, the dryer whirred to life.

"Please. Please. Please," prayed Carol. "Please leave."

Seconds later, her prayers were answered. The light flicked off, and once again she was bathed in darkness. Slowly, Carol crawled to the doorway. The man from the laundry room had joined a tall man with a blond crew cut and a petite but athletic-looking woman at the chalkboard.

The sound from the dryer was a two-edged sword. It would cover any noise that Carol made, but it also made it almost impossible to hear the bad guys. Carol made a quick calculation in her head. From the chalkboard to the utility room… at least two or three seconds. That was all she needed.

Ava was going crazy. Carol was trapped and she had to get her out. Somehow, she needed to draw the thieves' attention away from the laundry room. *The front door!* Yes, she would bang on the front door, and then....

Ava jumped backward as Carol burst through the window, pushing the cardboard away with her head.

"Carol! Carol!" screamed Ava, grabbing her by the arms and pulling her through the window. "You're okay! That was too close."

"It was nothing," said Carol, replacing the cardboard over the window. She looked at Ava and smiled. "Come on, it's time to take these guys down!"

13
POLICE PAJAMAS... IT'S A THING

Derik was listening to music when he felt his phone vibrate. The text appeared on his screen: *Backyard, hurry!* He ran to his bedroom window and looked out. Below, Ava and Carol were waving frantically.

He threw his headphones on his bed and rushed downstairs. His dad's Christmas party was in full swing. He grabbed a jacket from a hook as he sprinted down the hallway and out the back door.

"Ava! Carol!" he yelled. "What's going on?"

"We found the bad guys," said Ava, her voice filled with excitement.

"You did?! Where?"

"We'll explain everything to you, but right now we really need your help," replied Carol.

"Okay," nodded Derik. "How can I help?"

"Is Archie...?" Carol paused. "I don't even know Archie's last name. The guy that owns Archie's Collectibles, is he here?"

"Yes, his whole family is here... it's a virtual 'who's who' of Livingston inside."

"What about Detective Edwards?" asked Ava.

Derik thought for a moment. "I think so. I know Lieutenant Norris is here."

"I don't know Lieutenant Norris well enough," said Carol.

"Okay, I'll check. If he is, what do I say?"

"We need you to discreetly let Detective Edwards know that we're outside, and we need to talk to him. *Discreet,* being the keyword."

"He's a family friend," said Ava. "He won't ask any questions, just tell him we need his help."

"Got it," said Derik, turning toward the door.

"Wait," called out Carol. "One thing… right now, we don't know who's helping the thieves. We have to be careful—we don't want to tip them off."

"I understand," he said, holding up his hands. "Don't worry," Derik smiled. "I'll just yell for him from across the room the moment I see him."

"Perfect," smiled Ava. "You should turn off the lights when you yell his name. The more pandemonium, the better."

"Got it, discreet pandemonium. I'll be back in a flash," said Derik as he disappeared inside.

He wasn't kidding. Seconds later, Derik appeared, followed by Detective Edwards. As always, the detective was dressed in an impeccably tailored three-piece suit, his hair perfectly combed above eyebrows that accentuated his dark-brown, brooding eyes. A single hand-stitched snowflake adorned his festive, ruby-red silk tie.

Ava imagined that he probably had official police pajamas that he slept in, just in case someone broke the law in his dreams.

"Ava, Carol, everything okay? What's going on?" he asked, a concerned look on his face.

"We're fine, Mr. Edwards. We just needed to talk to you in private," said Ava.

"Okay," he said, clasping his hands. "What's this all about?"

"There's going to be a robbery tonight," started Carol.

"Carol, how do you know…?"

"I'm sorry," said Ava, interrupting him. "We can't really talk here," said Ava eyeing the door.

"We know that there is at least one person on the inside who helped orchestrate the robberies here in Livingston. They may even be here at the party," clarified Carol.

"All right," said Detective Edwards. "I'll get my car. We can go to the police station."

Ava and Carol looked at each other and shook their heads. "So far, the bad guys have been one step ahead of us, and if they see us going to the police station, it might spook them," said Ava.

"We have to proceed carefully; we know that we are being watched," said Carol.

"It's true," nodded Ava, "One of the bad guys tried to decapitate her with a drone. And… they may have at one time… tried to run over us with a car."

"Run over you with a car?! What?!" Detective Edwards exclaimed. "Ava, why didn't you report this?"

"I'm telling you now—it happened this evening. If I had said anything earlier, the bad guys would have gotten away. Plus my parents would have barricaded me in my room until I was thirty-nine. My parents said I could get married when I was thirty-nine," said Ava noticing Derik's strange expression. "Please, Blake—

I mean, Mr. Edwards—Carol has a plan to catch these guys. We just need your help."

Detective Edwards's face grew taut as he exhaled sharply. "Fine! But from now on, no more secrets, understood?!"

"Yes, sir," the trio chorused, doing their best to look remorseful.

"Okay," said Detective Edwards, "where do you suggest we plan our attack, since the police station doesn't seem to be an option?"

Ava and Carol turned to each other, already knowing the answer—"The Lair," answered Ava, smiling. "The Lair."

14
CAROL'S PLAN

The night burst into a flurry of activity. From the safety of The Lair, Carol took Detective Edwards step-by-step through her plan for catching the crooks. Ava could tell from the look on his face that he was amazed at how Carol had connected all of the individual pieces of evidence on the crime board.

While Carol worked her magic, Ava called Gladys, asking for her help. She gave the group a thumbs-up as she hung up the phone.

"She'll meet us at the museum and have everything ready," announced Ava.

Derik was busy on the phone as well, grabbing the last piece of the puzzle that would complete the operation. "I promise, I promise." He nodded his head as he talked. "Yes, sir. Thank you so much."

"We got it," Derik smiled. "Mr. Roberts will drop off the cleaning van at Green Central Parking Deck in thirty minutes."

"Perfect," said Carol, nodding. "My dad is on the way over with his car. Detective Edwards is going to drive us to the parking deck, where we'll meet Lieutenant Norris and his men."

"So, we're all hiding in the cleaning van?" asked Ava.

"Yep, we'll all hide in the van, which will take us to the delivery zone behind the museum. There's a massive canopy over the delivery area. We'll be able to sneak into the museum without being seen," said Carol.

"I must tell you, I'm extremely impressed," said Detective Edwards, smiling. "I may have to replace my team with you guys."

"Don't you guys have to do tons of paperwork?" asked Ava.

"Oh, yeah," nodded Detective Edwards, "we have reports for everything, even reports for reports."

Ava looked over at Carol, whose eyes were glassing over. "*Reports*," Carol whispered dreamily.

"Carol! Snap out of it. Sorry, Blake—I mean, Detective Edwards—we're more like 'bull in a china shop' types of detectives. We wreak mayhem, break a few things, and then quietly walk away."

"So close," sighed Carol, shaking her head at Ava. "So close."

"Oh," added Ava. "I forgot to mention, we always get the bad guy."

"Or girl," added Derik.

"Or girl," smiled Ava. "We have a certain image to uphold."

"Okay," said Detective Edwards, glancing at his watch. "That was a little more than I expected…. Let's get this show on the road."

"This is going to be epic," smiled Ava. "Absolutely epic!"

15
WORTHINGTON TUNNEL EXHIBIT

10:17 P.M. Worthington Tunnel, Hancock Museum

Ava, Carol, Derik—and what appeared to be Livingston's entire police force—stood at the entrance to the Worthington Tunnel Exhibit. A four-inch-thick glass enclosure surrounded the opening to the tunnel. A podium in front of the display contained a detailed map of the tunnel system.

Gladys motioned everyone over to the podium. "This red dot designates the Worthington Tunnel entrance." She traced her finger along the map, "You'll need to follow this passage until you reach the main tunnel."

"Are there any markings? Anything to navigate by?" asked Detective Edwards.

"No need," said Gladys. "This passage will take you to the main tunnel. You'll make a left...," Gladys moved her finger up the map, "...for about...," she paused while she counted the little lines on the map that designated twenty-foot sections, "...about six hundred feet."

"Anyone have a six-hundred-foot ruler?" laughed one of the police officers.

"You don't need one," answered Carol. "The average adult walking step is about 2.1 feet. So, once we reach the main tunnel, it will be about...," she paused, doing the math in her head.

"Two hundred and eighty-five steps," smiled Derik.

"Ohhhhh, you stole Carol's thunder," winked Ava.

"What? My dad's a banker," laughed Derik. "Numbers are in my DNA."

"*Your* number's gonna be up, if you mess with her *moment* again," said Ava, making air quotes.

"So," said Detective Edwards, "we follow the first passage, make a left at the main tunnel, walk 285 steps, and we should be there."

"Exactly," nodded Gladys. "There is a small passage that leads directly under Archie's Collectibles."

"Perfect," smiled Detective Edwards.

"Sir, I have a question," said Officer McCoy, looking pale and worried. "Why are we taking the tunnel? I mean, couldn't we just use the cleaning van?" he shrugged.

Ava looked at the police officer. A thin line of sweat glistened across his forehead, just under his spikey blond buzz cut. *Someone is not a fan of dark and confining spaces*, thought Ava.

"Two reasons. First, we know that they are surveilling their targets via a drone. If they see anything suspicious, they're gonna cut their losses and vanish. Secondly, they're not going to break into a building that is occupied," said Detective Edwards.

"Okay," nodded Officer McCoy, sounding defeated.

"Our biggest hurdle is going to be the grate that is used for drainage in his restoration room. Archie said that there's a massive lock on it, and as far as he knows, it hasn't been opened in over fifty years. We'll have to cut through the lock, breach the grate, replace the lock, and get into position before the suspects arrive."

"Won't they be suspicious if they see a new lock?" asked Officer Louis.

"No, thanks to Gladys," replied Detective Edwards. "She has given us a beautiful lock from the 1950s. Unfortunately," he said, turning to Gladys, "they are probably going to melt it into a pile of glob."

"It's a small sacrifice for the greater good," smiled Gladys.

Derik nudged Ava. "Someone's an Avengers fan."

"Once we're in position," continued Detective Edwards, "we'll wait for the suspects to enter Archie's. Once they're inside, I'll send an alert to Lieutenant Norris and Officer Louis. They'll position themselves below the grate in case the suspects attempt to escape back into the tunnel."

"What about the drone operator?" asked Officer Davis. Ava and Carol both recognized Officer Davis from the bank. She was short, compact, and athletic, with a fiery stare that could melt ice.

"Officer Tiny and Wilks will be stationed half a mile away in separate cruisers. Once the suspects are in the store, we'll alert them to move in. The drone operator should be close by. Any more questions?" asked Detective Edwards, eyeing the group. "Good. Get your gear on, check your radios, and we'll get moving." He turned his attention to Ava and Carol.

"We know," said Ava. "We hide in the reading room until either you, or another officer, comes to get us."

"Exactly," he smiled. "No exceptions."

"Yes, sir," said the trio, nodding in unison.

"All right," barked Detective Edwards as he stepped into the tunnel's entrance. "Let's do this."

Gladys punched a code into the alarm box connected to the enclosure and then unlocked the heavy glass door. She gave Ava and Carol a big hug.

"Be safe," she whispered, her voice filled with worry as they disappeared into the tunnel.

The narrow tunnel was dark and musty. Giant spiderwebs stretched across the group's path, covering them in sticky goo. Spiders' eyes glistened creepily in the light from their headlamps. The air was cool, but it felt thick and smothering, like being wrapped in a wet blanket.

Up ahead, Ava couldn't help but feel sorry for Officer McCoy. His breathing was erratic, and his nose sounded like a cheap whistle. She grabbed the collapsible ladder he was carrying, hoping that would at least help a little. She could see Detective Edwards swatting down spiderwebs. *Where do all the spiders go when he knocks down their webs? Never mind.* She shivered at the thought of it. *I don't want to know.*

Suddenly, the passage opened up into a massive tunnel. A network of large wooden support beams arched upward and spanned across the top of the tunnel, reinforcing the ceiling.

"Amazing," whispered Carol, surprised that the beams looked to be in surprisingly good shape over a century later. She wished she could take a picture for her father, an architect—maybe later.

"Okay, this is the main section of the tunnel," said Detective Edwards, shifting his backpack. "Which means we're about three minutes from Archie's. Keep your eyes and ears open."

"I like this much better," whispered Ava, "way less spiderwebs."

Carol nodded. "It's crazy that this huge tunnel runs below our town and hardly anyone knows about it."

"You could literally drive a car through here," added Derik. "Insane!"

"I hope I'm right about this…. What if the bad guys decide to go somewhere else, or they just disappear? What if the plans we saw were just a decoy?" Carol whispered worriedly.

"Carol, you're overthinking things," said Ava, switching the ladder to her other hand. "They have no idea that *anyone* saw their plans. These guys think they are invincible, and that, my friend, is what's gonna be their downfall!"

"I guess so," whispered Carol.

"I know so," smiled Ava.

Detective Edwards signaled for everyone to stop as he slipped into a narrow passageway. Moments later he reappeared. "This is it!" he whispered excitedly.

Officer Davis took up guard position at the entrance while the rest of the team moved single file into the tunnel. The passage opened up into a rectangular room about the size of a small shed. Officer McCoy placed a flashlight vertically against the dirt wall, illuminating the room. The room had large wooden support beams with huge metal girders that supported a concrete foundation. In the center of the ceiling was a huge metal grate, with a massive padlock that looked to be a hundred years old.

Detective Edwards shrugged off his backpack and removed a crowbar and pair of bolt cutters. Ava opened the ladder directly below the grate.

Carol opened the flashlight app on her phone and aimed the light at the padlock.

"Thanks, Carol," said Detective Edwards as he scrambled up the ladder. He carefully guided the bolt cutters through the shackle of the lock and squeezed with all his might. He twisted and twisted in a sawing motion—Carol winced at the amount of noise he was making. After struggling for a couple minutes, he jumped to the ground and turned to Officer McCoy. "I can't make a dent in this thing—you try."

No matter how much McCoy grunted, twisted, and squeezed, the lock wouldn't budge. He climbed down the ladder, his face red from exertion and frustration. "We should have brought Tiny," he said, wiping the sweat from his hands. "He probably could have broken the lock with his bare hands."

Tiny wouldn't have fit through the first tunnel. Detective Edwards grabbed the bolt cutters and attacked the lock again, twisting and pulling. Sweat poured down his face into his eyes. He stared up at the grate, shaking his head.

"Sir," said Carol, "I have an—"

Officer Davis raced into the room. "I can hear voices! They're coming."

Ava thought Detective Edwards's teeth were going to shatter before the lock. He slammed the handles of the bolt lock together, cutting into the shackle of the lock, making small cuts into the metal, but unable to cut all the way through.

"I have an idea," said Carol more forcefully.

"What?" said Detective Edwards hotly. "I'm—I'm sorry, Carol. What is it?"

"I've seen my dad's workmen do this on the job site. Officer Davis needs to push the crowbar through the shackles—she'll twist while you cut. Since there's only one ladder…," she turned to Officer McCoy, "…she's gonna need to stand on your back."

Carol barely got the words out of her mouth before Officer McCoy was on the ground on his hands and knees and Officer Davis was standing on his back. Carol handed her the crowbar and grabbed her around the hips to hold her steady while Ava held the ladder.

"I'm going to see where they are," said Derik, racing out of the room. Derik's heart beat wildly in his chest. As soon as he stepped into the main tunnel, he could hear voices moving toward him. Voices—and a loud, repetitive squeaking noise. *The plasma cutter,* he thought. *That's what's making the squeaking noise.*

Detective Edwards opened the bolt cutter wide and twisted it into place. "On the count of three," he said. "One! Two! Three!" A loud grating sound filled the room as dirt and debris rained down on top of them. Ava and Carol cringed at the noise.

"What is up with this lock?!" asked Detective Edwards incredulously, wiping the dirt from his face.

The voices were much closer now! Derik could see flickers of light flashing on the walls of the tunnel. He raced into the room. "They're almost here," he said urgently. "I can see their flashlights!"

Detective Edwards nodded at Officer Davis. "Give it everything you got! On the count of three. One!

Two! Three!" Carol could see the tendons in Officer Davis's neck as she twisted with all her might.

There was a loud scraping sound of metal on metal, and then—*POW!* It sounded like a gunshot as the shackle snapped in two. It took a moment for Detective Edwards to realize what had happened before he urgently whispered, "Move! Move!" He pushed up on the heavy grate and slid it aside.

Ava rushed out to grab Derik. She could hear the voices clearly. They had maybe forty-five seconds!

"Carol, you first," said Detective Edwards. "Remember, straight to the reading room and hide."

"Yes, sir," she whispered.

He lifted her up and helped her through the grate. He helped Officer Davis up next and then quickly handed her the backpack and ladder. "Ava, Derik, you're next!"

He quickly helped everyone else through the grate. The squeaking of the wheels stopped; he could hear a male voice say, "This is it." They were at the entrance! He leapt up, grasping the edge of the grate. And with the help of Officers Davis and McCoy, the detective was pulled into the room. Without a second of hesitation, they quietly slid the grate back into place.

Detective Edwards had just enough time to replace the lock with the decoy when one of the thieves shone their flashlight directly at the grate. Suddenly, a whooshing sound filled the room, followed by a bright blue flame that began melting the lock away.

Detective Edwards and his team disappeared into the darkness. They made it, and not a second too soon.

17
ARCHIE'S COLLECTIBLES

Ava, Carol, and Derik scampered behind a cream-colored sofa closest to the front door. Ava peeked over the couch, scanning the reading room. There was a fireplace, two more cream-colored couches, and a half-dozen chairs with long, flat tables in front of them. A variety of potted plants were placed in each corner, and the walls were filled with colorful covers of super-old comic books.

Ava dropped back beside Derik and Carol. "I hate being stuck in the reading room… it's like being banished to a library."

"A library with cool furniture," added Derik.

"Shhh!" whispered Carol, placing a finger to her lips.

The trio listened intently; they could hear the plasma torch fire up, the grate being moved to the side, and then footsteps. Heavy footsteps.

"Here they come," whispered Carol excitedly.

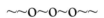

Detective Edwards's fingers swiped across his phone, sending out a text he had already prepared: *Deploy.*

He knew that as soon as Lieutenant Norris got the message, his team would be on the way. He held up four fingers to Officers McCoy and Davis. The thieves would get the surprise of their lives in four minutes.

The thieves were professionals; they worked quickly and efficiently. A tall man in a black hoodie rolled what looked like a cooler on wheels across the floor and down the hallway. He paused at a large wooden door and nodded to a shaggy red-haired man in a green hoodie. The man jammed a crowbar into the doorframe and yanked. The wood cracked and splintered around the lock.

"Good enough," said the man in the black hoodie. He took a step back and kicked the door open.

"Like taking candy from a baby," he laughed evilly.

"A rich baby," replied the other thief.

Seconds later, a familiar whooshing sound filled the office.

"He must have his safe hidden in his office," whispered Derik bitterly.

The girls nodded. Anger surged through Carol's veins. They had destroyed his door, and now they were destroying his safe. *What is taking Detective Edwards so long?*

Detective Edwards looked at his watch and took in a deep breath. In sixty seconds, Lieutenant Norris would be in position. Suddenly, a woman with a shaved head and black combat boots was standing less than five feet from where he was hiding.

He watched as she crouched below a series of glass display cases. *What is she doing?* She flicked a switch, and a little green light went out. *She is turning off the alarms!* The woman removed a pair of bolt cutters from her jacket and began cutting off the locks.

Detective Edwards signaled to his team: It was *go time.*

"Livingston Police!" yelled Officer Davis, rushing toward the thief with the shaved head. The woman whipped around. If she was surprised, it didn't show. She raised her hands in the air, a smirk on her face.

"Well, hello, Officer," she smiled.

"Drop the bolt cutters, now!" said Officer Davis, drawing her taser, inching closer toward her.

"Oh, these?" said the woman coyly.

"Drop them now! I won't ask—"

Officer Davis dove to the side as the bolt cutters whipped past her head, sinking into the wall with a deep thud. She covered her head with her arms as a heavy lamp came crashing down onto her.

The woman hurdled over the display case and raced through Archie's, heading for the front door. She was going to escape!

Detective Edwards and Officer McCoy cautiously approached the hallway, tasers drawn. The man with the shaggy red hair jumped out of a closet, swinging a crowbar. Officer McCoy ducked under the blow and tackled the man to the floor, sending the crowbar flying.

The tall thief in the black hoodie stood defiantly in the hallway. He brandished the wand of the plasma cutter, flames shooting out the end like a six-inch, fiery blue knife. His pale, olive-green eyes stared at Detective Edwards, unblinking, fearless.

"Put the torch down," demanded Detective Edwards. "This isn't going to end well for you."

"What?" the man asked, as if confused. "This thing?"

He raised the flaming wand to the ceiling, triggering the sprinkler system. Instantly, a powerful jet of water sprayed into Detective Edwards's face, momentarily blinding him. The thief rushed forward, dropping his shoulder into the detective's chest, driving him to the ground.

Detective Edwards groaned and rolled to his side as the thief raced back toward the tunnel. "Norris!" he gasped into his radio. "He's coming!"

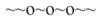

Water poured from the ceiling; emergency strobe lights flashed. The woman with the shaved head burst through the doorway and slid into the reading room. Ava pulled her soaking-wet, matted hair from her face and peered around the edge of the couch. She watched in horror. The woman was going to get away!

"The couch!" whispered Ava to Derik and Carol. "Hit her with the couch!"

The woman crashed into the front door. She gripped the slippery doorknob and then, to her surprise, she was suddenly airborne, as the trio slammed the couch into her like a battering ram. She landed hard, skidding across the floor.

"Got her!" yelled Ava. But her excitement was short-lived. The woman leapt to her feet, glaring at them.

"Out of my way, or I'm going to snap your necks," snarled the woman.

"That's not good," gulped Carol. "She's like a super ninja."

"You don't scare us!" yelled Ava.

"Speak for yourself," said Derik. "I personally find her terrify—"

Derik didn't get to finish his sentence as the woman steamrolled over him. Using his chest as a springboard, she jumped up and over the couch. She slammed the bolt lock open with the palm of her hand and grabbed the doorknob.

"Oh, no, you don't!" screamed Carol like a wild banshee.

She jumped onto the couch and launched herself onto the woman's back.

"I'm coming," yelled Ava, slipping and sliding around the sofa. She closed her eyes and dove at the woman's legs. To her surprise, the woman didn't fall. However, she did find herself wrapped around the woman's leg like a monkey.

"Get off me!" yelled the woman, kicking violently while simultaneously slamming Carol against the wall.

"Not gonna happen!" yelled Ava, imagining herself as a rodeo rider. The woman was incredibly strong. Ava was beginning to wonder how much longer she could hang on, when she heard Derik's beautiful voice cry out, "Face... plant!"

Suddenly, the woman groaned and toppled to the floor. The girls looked up to see Derik smiling, holding a broken flowerpot in his hand.

"Get it?" he smiled. "Face... plant."

The woman moaned as the trio sat on her back. Officer Davis rushed into the room, slipping and sliding.

"Boom! Ride's over, crazy lady," said Ava to the woman, pretending to drop a microphone.

Officer Davis stared in amazement at the woman moaning on the floor, her head covered with mud and flowers. "You guys okay?" she asked, trying not to laugh.

"We're fine," smiled Carol. "The plant," she said, pointing to the broken pot, "not so much."

Detective Edwards turned the corner just in time to see the blond-haired thief lower himself through the grate. Seconds later, he heard a loud electrical zap. He winced, knowing that the man had run right into Lieutenant Norris and his taser.

Wiping the water from his eyes, he made his way back to the hallway. Officer McCoy had just handcuffed the thief with the shaggy hair. He turned and gave Detective Edwards a thumbs-up.

~~0~0~0~~

The sprinkler system and flashing strobes had finally shut off.

"This is horrible," said Carol, looking around at the destruction. *Hopefully, his most valuable items are in the safe or in display cases.*

A blinking red light flashed in the front window of Archie's, catching Ava's attention. She glanced up, just in time to see a black drone fly away. Running to the door, she flung it open and stepped out into the street. A tall thin man jumped into a sleek black car, but not before Ava recognized him: Harvey from the Public Works Department.

"Carol!" yelled Ava. "Wardrobe!"

18
MAY THE FORCE BE WITH YOU

The trio ran through Archie's into a room filled with display cases containing costumes from famous movies.

"Grab a costume and get changed! We've got to hurry," yelled Ava.

Carol flung a vintage Captain America costume to Derik. "Change into this," she said, pushing him out the door.

Ava scanned the display cases. *Wonder Woman… no. Batgirl… no.* She needed something warm and mobile, and that's when she saw it. Gumby!

Carol peeled off her clothes and began pulling herself into a furry Chewbacca costume.

Moments later, Derik rapped on the door dressed as Captain America. He quickly crossed the room and grabbed a red, white, and blue scooter with a large white star.

"You know what to do, right?" asked Carol, narrowing her eyes.

"Trust me, I'm on it!" said Derik, nodding.

"Godspeed, Winter Soldier," said Ava, as Derik ran to the front door and zipped away on the scooter.

"Ava? Carol? What the heck are you doing?" asked Detective Edwards, a confused look on his face.

"We're catching the drone pilot—it's Harvey, from public works," said Ava, putting on a large pair of green foam boots.

"Tell Officer Tiny to meet us at Crispin Pond!" said Carol. "We won't do anything until he gets there!"

"If he sees you, he'll disappear," said Ava. "He's got a tunnel system with tons of secret exits, two cars… please, Blake!"

"We promise we'll hide in the woods until Officer Tiny gets there. I have a plan," said Carol.

"Time is *not* on our side right now," said Ava. "We know what we're doing."

Detective Edwards shook his head and exhaled. "I'm going to regret this, aren't I?"

"If he gets away," said Ava, "then, yes. We're blaming it all on you."

"Okay. Wait for Officer Tiny before you do *anything*!"

"Yes, sir," said Carol, putting on her Chewbacca mask.

"May the force be with you," laughed Officer Davis, shaking her head.

19
DERIK SEES BLUE

Ava and Carol crouched behind a clump of snow-covered evergreen trees, at the edge of what was once Crispin Pond. A chill ran through Ava's body, making her shudder.

"I should have picked a warmer costume," she whispered, wrapping her arms around her body.

"Yeah, mine's quite toasty," replied Carol. "Do you think we made it in time?"

"I don't see any fresh tire tracks," said Ava, pointing at the pristine, freshly fallen snow.

"My question is, where the heck is Derik? He had a huge head start on us," said Ava.

"I know," said Carol, grabbing her phone. "He was supposed to text us when he got here."

"Maybe he's in trouble," said Ava.

"Harvey could have kidnapped him, or worse!" whispered Carol.

Ava looked at Carol. "Are you thinking what I'm thinking?"

"I never thought I would say this," said Carol, dropping her head, "but most likely… yes."

Without another word, the girls crept across the icy ravine, crouching behind the huge rock wall that hid the thieves' car. Ava crawled on her hands and knees and peeked her head around the corner. The thieves' old gray Toyota was still there!

"Derik!" she hissed, holding her foamy green hand to her mouth. "Derik, are you there?" Nothing.

She crawled back to Carol and shook her head. "The thieves' car is still there, but there's no sign of Derik."

"I'll try texting him," whispered Carol, fearing the worst.

Carol had just grabbed her phone when they heard footsteps crunching in the snow. Ava crawled on her belly, peering around the edge of the rock. A tall, thin man with a goatee and ponytail was struggling under the weight of two black duffle bags.

She slid back behind the rock. "It's Harvey," she hissed. "He's got two heavy duffel bags!"

"The money and the jewels," whispered Carol. "Did you see Derik?"

Ava frowned and shook her head. "No," she whispered.

The sound of the trunk slamming made the girls jump.

"We can't wait for Officer Tiny—Harvey's going to get away!" said Carol.

"You're right," replied Ava, leaping to her feet.

"Ava, what are you doing?!" hissed Carol.

"Come on, I've got a plan!"

"Wait," said Carol, grabbing Ava by the elbow. "What's the plan?"

"I'm making it up as I go along!" yelled Ava as she dashed around the rock wall.

Harvey opened the car door and had one leg in the car when Ava shouted, "Harvey! Harvey Cooper!"

Harvey whirled around to face the girls. He shook his head and rubbed his eyes. Was that really Gumby and Chewbacca?

"Who are you?" he yelled. "What do you want?"

"We know what you did, Harvey. We know you stole the money. We know everything about you!"

"Oh, it's you two. I'll send you a postcard from Mexico," he laughed as he climbed in the car and slammed the door.

Carol and Ava jumped aside, expecting him to roar away, but the car didn't move. They could see Harvey beating the steering wheel and screaming. Then, as if it were a dream, Derik appeared from behind a rock. He marched up to the hood of the car, a fistful of wires dangling from his hand.

Carol punched Ava in the shoulder. "Look! He ripped out...." She shook her head, not knowing what to say. "He ripped out a bunch of important-looking wires!"

Enraged, Harvey kicked open his car door. Derik's eyes flew open wide as he ran screaming, hiding behind a pile of rocks. Harvey turned and stared evilly at the girls.

"You're gonna pay for this!" he screamed, racing toward the girls.

"Don't you have a plane to catch?" yelled Ava, trying to run in her Gumby costume.

Harvey grabbed Ava by the back of her foam head, pulling her toward the car, her feet dragging across the snow.

"Unhand her!" yelled Derik from atop a huge boulder, brandishing his Captain America shield.

Ava kicked and twisted, but Harvey held on tight. Just as he reached into his jacket for the car keys,

Derik let out a ferocious scream. "Fly!" he shouted as he hurled the shield at Harvey.

Unfortunately, the shield weighed about twenty pounds. It flew about three feet and then sank into the snow. Even more unfortunate, Derik slipped from the huge boulder, crashing to the ground face first with a loud *oomph*.

He lifted his head and whispered "blue lights," and then collapsed back into the snow.

Harvey, momentarily distracted, screamed as Carol whipped a snowball directly into his face. Ava threw herself backward into him, knocking him onto the car's trunk. Just as he sat up, she hurled another snowball into his face.

A terrifying look filled Harvey's eyes, making Carol gulp.

"No more games," he growled. Keeping an eye on the girls, he opened the trunk of the car and pulled out a tire iron. "You couldn't leave well enough alone, could you?"

Ava looked at Carol; there was no way they were going to outrun Harvey.

"Follow me," whispered Ava. "I got a plan."

Ava bolted toward Derik with Carol right on her heels. Dropping to her knees she slid and grabbed the Captain America shield. Just as she put her arm through the shield's handle, Harvey took a wild swing at her with the tire iron hitting the shield.

The vibration from the blow sent a shockwave from her arm to her feet. Ava shook her head; it felt like her entire body was vibrating. She had just recovered when Harvey swung again—this time at her side. She dropped the shield to her side; the sound was deafening. The force knocked her to her knees.

"I think I broke my face," whispered Derik, "and my ankle."

"It's okay, buddy," said Carol, whipping another snowball into Harvey's face.

Harvey turned toward Carol and raised the tire iron. "You little—"

Bwong! Harvey's eyes rolled back in his head as Ava smashed the metal shield into his shins. He made a weird groaning noise as he fell to the snow, grabbing his lower legs. Carol rushed forward and grabbed the tire iron, while Ava approached from the other side, holding the shield.

"Game's over, Harvey," smiled Ava.

In the distance, the girls could see a mountain of a man rushing toward them, tufts of smoke billowing above his head like a steam engine. It was Officer Tiny.

"Better late than never," winked Carol.

Ava nodded, smiling.

"You girls all right?" he asked, gasping for breath.

"Yes, sir!" smiled Ava. "We present to you: one criminal," she said, pointing her shield at Harvey, "officially gift wrapped."

"The only thing he's missing is the bow," smiled Carol.

Harvey's head hung on his chest. In the distance, a snowmobile appeared over the ridge of the ravine, speeding toward them. A blue light flashing on the front.

"Blue light," whispered Derik, pointing at the snowmobile.

"That's right," smiled Carol as she helped him sit up. "Blue light."

"Is he okay?" asked Officer Tiny as he handcuffed Harvey.

"I think he may have broken his ankle," said Carol.

"And my face," mumbled Derik.

"And his face too," nodded Carol, gently brushing the snow off his Captain America mask.

Detective Edwards and Officer Davis roared up on a red snowmobile, sliding to a stop beside the old Toyota.

"Ava," called out Detective Edwards, leaping from the snowmobile. "You guys okay?"

"Better than him," said Ava, pointing at Harvey. "We seriously messed up his vacation plans."

"Derik may have a broken foot and a horribly bruised ego," Carol added.

"Officer Davis, if you could…," Detective Edwards prompted.

"I'm on it, sir," she called out as she hurried over to Carol to help her with Derik. "We'll get you over to Emerson ASAP, Mr. America."

"Captain," groaned Derik, smiling, "it's Captain."

"Lieutenant Norris is on the way to the Butcher house right now to see if his team can locate the stolen goods," said Detective Edwards.

"Yeah, about that... I'm sorry, but... I'm afraid the stolen goods aren't there anymore," said Ava, putting on her saddest face.

"What?" said Detective Edwards, instantly serious. "Are you sure?"

Ava nodded. "They were sending the stolen goods out of the country. But... if you were to open that trunk...," she smiled, pointing at the Toyota.

A huge smile filled Detective Edwards's face. "Ava Clarke, I don't know what I'm going to do with you."

Officer Tiny tossed Detective Edwards a set of keys. The detective looked at the keys for a second and then handed them to Ava.

"Here, you do the honors."

Ava turned and tossed the keys to Carol. "This was all Carol's plan," smiled Ava. "This is her moment."

"Thanks, Aves!" said Carol, taking the keys.

She unlocked the trunk, and then, struggling, placed the heavy bags on the ground in front of her. Everyone gathered around her as she unzipped the first duffel bag. There was an audible gasp from the group. The first bag was filled to the top with bundles of hundred-dollar bills.

"The bank's money," she whispered giddily.

She pulled the next bag closer and unzipped it. "Whoa," she whispered as hundreds of diamonds sparkled like stars in the moonlight.

Carol looked up and smiled at the group gathered around her. It was going to be a happy Christmas after all.

20
NOT AGAIN

It was the night before Christmas. A giant white moon hung in the sky. Wispy dark clouds, like pulled taffy, raced across the sky. In the darkness of the forest, evil lurked!

Ethan shivered and looked at his phone. *Where is he?* he wondered.

He had received an urgent text from Kevin Chen: *Meet me at the Butcher house! There's something you've got to see!*

Ethan stood at the top of the driveway. There was no way he was going any closer to that creepy old house alone. He pulled off a glove and held it in his teeth while he texted Kevin: *Where are you?!* He whirled around. *What was that?* Did he hear a stick snap? "Kevin, is that you?" he yelled out, his voice shaking more than he would like.

A light flashed on in the Butcher house. Ethan crouched down behind a small brick column at the end of the drive. He dared to sneak a look—it was an old man, standing at the window staring directly at him!

Suddenly, there was a scream and a loud thrashing in the woods. He stood to run, but his feet wouldn't move. There was another scream, and then Carol appeared! Her jacket and pants were ripped; she was trying to run, but it looked like her leg was injured. "Help! Help!" she cried out, falling into the snow.

Then Ethan saw it. His breath caught in his throat. It was a headless monster! A shrill, mind-numbing scream escaped Ethan's mouth. The headless monster turned toward him. Ethan's feet felt like lead, like in a dream when you can't run.

"No! No! No!" shrieked Ethan, backpedaling as the monster drew closer. He closed his eyes and stepped backward, tripping over a tree branch, falling hard onto his back. "No!" he screamed, crossing his arms across his face.

"And… end scene—that's a wrap, guys," called out Ava.

"What… what's going on?" asked Ethan, sitting up, completely confused.

"First," said Ava, moving her phone from person to person, "I'd like to thank Carol for playing the scared kid. You were brilliant," Ava smiled.

"Thank you," said Carol, bowing.

"Kevin… masterful," praised Ava. "That's all I can say."

"I felt like I was one with the monster," he smiled.

"It showed," laughed Carol. "Truly, a moving performance."

Derik hobbled up the driveway toward the group, his foot in a cast. "Derik, you did a phenomenal job as the old man."

"Thank you," smiled Derik, holding up a rubber mask.

"And lastly," said Ava, whirling back to Ethan, "I would like to thank you for your role as the frightened bully. You were flawless. Well, that ends our holiday production—time for the wrap party," laughed Ava.

"What the heck was this all about?" yelled Ethan, angrily jumping to his feet.

"We knew how much you like frightening people. We thought, in the spirit of giving, we'd scare you a little," said Carol.

"I wasn't scared," sneered Ethan, laughing

"Oh, interesting," said Ava, swiping her finger across her phone. The group literally jumped when she hit play—Ethan's scream was so shrill.

"I'm not sure," laughed Carol, "but I believe you shattered a few windows."

"Okay, okay, you got me," he smiled. "Fair's fair."

"Now, we're willing to forget all of this in the spirit of Christmas… if you promise not to scare the life out of the little children next year," said Ava, crossing her arms.

Ethan looked at the group, and then at Ava's phone.

"Not even a little?" he asked.

The group looked at each other and smiled. "Hey, we're not scrooges," smiled Derik. "We're talking about within reason."

"Okay, I promise. I promise only to scare children within reason," said Ethan, holding up his hands in surrender.

"Okay, that's that. Moving on," smiled Ava. "My mom's catering the wrap party at my house. Steaming-hot cocoa, and her famous homemade sugar cookies."

"You had me at sugar," smiled Derik.

Carol turned, looked at the Butcher house, and smiled; they had turned a horrible story into a positive one. They had captured the thieves and found the money and the diamonds. She threw her arms over Ava and Derik's shoulders and began belting out "We Wish You a Merry Christmas."

The group laughed and sang at the top of their lungs. It was a perfect night. As they arrived at Ava's house, Ethan gathered everyone into a close circle.

"Thank you, guys, for being so cool. And one other thing," he leaned in and whispered, "you guys wanna hear a scary story?"

AVA & CAROL DETECTIVE AGENCY

Thank you for reading the first three books in the *Ava & Carol Detective Agency* series! We hope you enjoyed them! Please leave a review on Amazon, Goodreads, or Barnes & Noble, we'd love to hear from you! Sign up for info on upcoming books at our website: avaandcarol.com

Order *Ava & Carol Detective Agency: Books 4-6* and embark on another exciting mystery adventure. The second bundle set includes: *Dognapped*, *The Eye of God*, and *The Crown Jewels Mystery*.

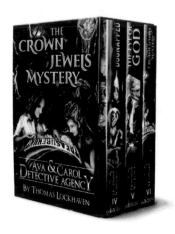

"Encouraging for girls. 11-year-old daughter really took to this series and wasn't a huge reader though always encouraged to be one. She chattered to us about the predicaments of the protagonists and some of the historical aspects of some of the plots."

If you love historical fiction, then you'll enjoy *Calista Chase Time Sleuth: Blackbeard's Treasure*. Great for ages 9-12 who enjoy reading time travel adventures.

"Adventure, drama, family, crime solving and historical fiction, this book has it all! Calista is a strong female character who finds herself in the middle of an adventure she never could have imagined. You'll find yourself pulling for her and on the edge of the page, great read!"

If you're looking for a fantastical adventure, you may enjoy the much-loved series of *Quest Chasers*.

"These two authors can WRITE! It didn't take me long to read but I was definitely spellbound from the first chapter. There was so much fantastic action and terrifying danger in this book that I couldn't put it down! I thought it was fabulous and fun!"

Learn about new book releases by following Thomas Lockhaven on Amazon and Goodreads, or visit our website at twistedkeypublishing.com.

Made in United States
North Haven, CT
20 November 2022

27010673R00238